SUN ALLEY

SUN
ALLEY

Cecilia Ştefănescu

Translated from the original Romanian by
Alexandra Coliban and Andreea Höfer

istrosbooks

English-language edition first published in 2013 by
Istros Books
London, United Kingdom
www.istrosbooks.com

This novel was first published in Romanian as *Intrarea soarelui*
by Editura Polirom, 2008

© Cecilia Ştefănescu, 2013
Translation © Alexandra Coliban and Andreea Höfer, 2013

Edited by Susan Curtis-Kojaković

Artwork & Design@Miloš Miljković, 2013
Graphic Designer/Web Developer miljkovicmisa@gmail.com

The right of Cecilia Ştefănescu to be identified as the author of this work has
been asserted in accordance with the Copyright, Designs and Patents Act, 1988

ISBN 978-1-908236-06-7

Typeset by Octavo Smith Ltd in
Constantia 10/12.75

Printed in England by CMP (UK), Poole, Dorset
www.cmp-uk.com

This edition has been made possible by the financial support granted by
the Romanian Cultural Institute, Bucharest.

I

SAL'S AFTERNOON

If that darkness had suddenly burst like a bubble, it would have spilled its odourless juice and spread all over the walls of the concrete cube, melting the white shadows that constantly circled the bed and furrowed the room. Their terror and dreadfulness would have evaporated in a second, leaving them cast into oblivion forever. But they kept undulating in the air, squirming across the walls and slicing the darkness; swelling and trickling down the fresh duck-egg-blue paint and between the snowy peaks of pargeting. Then they fell still, resuming their places and watching over the boy who slept peacefully, legs wide apart, with one knee bent and one arm dangling.

Above him, a couple of hairy guys clad in studded leather covered in studs, bent slightly forward with their guitars resting on their hips, were gazing into the distance, their eyes shiny embers scanning the rocky horizon. Ten cars stood aligned nearby, ready to shatter the thick air and plunge into a devilish race. A layer of dust had covered their smoky windscreens like a fishnet, and the huge wall of open engines behind them rose menacingly in anticipation of the start of the race. The drivers sat perfectly still, not a fibre on their waxen faces moving: all gazed straight ahead. Only the iris of one of the drivers had been erased, leaving a white, cold globe that seemed to presage death.

A fine and scintillating fog had descended, and from behind it the big, round sun prepared to emerge, like a chocolate coin covered in tinfoil. Right next to the cars, though keeping a certain distance, a wooden knight bent over the body of an unconscious girl. She was frozen still, with her skirt plumped up and her boots hanging in midair, while the knight gripped the sabre at his waist with one hand and with the other helplessly clutched her arm. The girl lay on the green grass, and her ruby lips, her rosy cheeks and her golden hair matched his embroidered uniform, teeming with blazonry and insignia.

Yet in the half-bent body of the helpless and desperate young man, in the way he concealed his face beneath the khaki felt hat and held her lifeless hand, sinking his fingers into the pinkish flesh, a well-kept secret lay hidden. Any minute, tears could start falling from his well-shielded eyes, and you might see him collapse over the girl's stone-still body while, at the same time, you wouldn't have been surprised to see her opening her blue eyes, stirred by the pain of the one who, rather more dead than alive, pressed her now with all his might, with all the years he had gathered in his bones, his flesh, his muscles and his skin.

But the only motion in the room came from the rolled-up bedclothes. It was the chubby toes with close-cut nails that first started to twitch, followed by an arm that fell limp over the margin of the bed. Lastly, the hypnotic head with dishevelled hair emerged, partly from a dream and partly from reality: balancing on a narrow edge, leaning now on this side, now on the other.

Sal half-opened his eyes, staring through his eyelashes at the striped wall in front of him. Then he closed his eyes again and the stripes resumed their rocking against the rattling of a car that had just passed on the street. He rose for a second, staring at the ceiling, and then turned on his side. The darkness in the room was furrowed by the golden ribbons of light flickering through the lowered blinds. Sal sat up, staring sleepily ahead.

It was late afternoon and, by the faint light straining to pass through the wooden slats, he was sure it was long past the time he was supposed to call Emi. He thought of crashing back down and searching for the warm hole the crown of his head had left in the pillow's down, but was deterred by his neck, wet with perspiration, and the sweaty palms that he had been waving in the air for a few moments, cooling him down. He was waiting for the moment in which he would realise that it was terribly late and that Emi, poisoned by the endless minutes passed in relentless countdown, would no longer answer.

He jumped up like a robot and fumbled around the room,

stumbling over a chair and moaning in pain. Finally he managed to spot his trousers, pulled them on quickly and, after a few seconds of lying in wait to make sure there was no one spying on him on the other side of the door, scuttled away. He left behind a big, golden dust cloud, a glittering powder that glazed his footprints, while the pink soles of his feet sparkled, nested in their footwear, releasing pheromones and bright messages.

When finally outside, at an adequate distance a few houses away, he sniffed the air happily. Then, cautious not to bump into one of the boys, he started for Emi's place, balancing on the edge of the pavement.

Emi's mother had called him 'the special boy', accompanying the words with a deprecating grimace and shaking her head in a way that meant that she had seen boys of that kind before. She used 'special' like some people do when trying to be condescendingly polite, referring to some kind of handicap or simply to a death-row convict whose case, in their opinions, is totally hopeless, but to whom they magnanimously lie one last time. But he never answered her spiteful words – on the one hand because she was his friend's mother, and he understood very well that if you had a girl like Emi, you lived with the permanent terror that the world, seized with admiration or possessed by envy, would sooner or later make her disappear; on the other hand because Emi herself was more important than his hurt pride, and last but not least because he had been brought up never to engage in arguments with older people, regardless of what they said. He would flatly say 'Good day' and reply 'Thank you' when he was offered something and even before refusing; he never left the house before saying goodbye to everybody and he usually never phoned between three and half past five in the afternoon, because that was when people took naps.

Emi was the only one with whom he ignored the rule: for three years, excepting the times they were on vacation with their parents, every day at four o'clock Sal would lift the receiver and insert his finger in the rotary dial of the telephone. At the other end of the line, after no more than two rings, he would hear her thin voice: always surprised, as if she had absolutely no clue who could possibly call at that hour, feigning her indifference so poorly and so touchingly when she seemed to recognise him at last. He imagined her rounding her mouth in a prolonged and demure 'Hello', followed by an interval and then by a short 'Ah!' that set everything back in place. So that it would always be clear that *he* had been the one calling and it was also *he* that wished to see her, he invited her out – he lured her out of the house, out of her safe shell, her hospitable cocoon.

She was merciless, especially on herself; she had enforced a draconian schedule that she followed unfalteringly and mysteriously. She would wake up at six every morning, and she never went to bed before midnight. She would constantly complain that the eighteen hours were barely enough for her to do all that she had in mind; she had lists of books to read, diaries to keep, places to go, people to see. Her vacations were similar to her school hours except that, when she became the manager of her own time, she became maniacally rigorous and punished anyone who would upset, even by a minute, the meticulous agenda of the day. He liked her like that, paradoxical and conceited – he took her conscientiousness as a whim – but he had no doubt that behind her struggle against time another secret lay hidden, well guarded and terribly seductive.

He had liked her right from the start, when he had found her on Harry's rug swimming among piles of *Pif, Pionniers de l'Espérance* and *Rahan* magazines. A thick cloud of dust had risen around her, making all the other boys seek refuge in the hall and leaving her to rule over the magazines, the pages of which were covered in a layer of slime mould mixed with dust and the grease left by the tips of fingers that had once turned them over.

Emi had been waving a pair of scissors above her head and looked like an Amazon determined to decimate her subjects, hacking their faces and limbs to pieces and cutting off the roots that kept them alive in their intergalactic environment. Thanga the *R* roller, the fair Maud, Tsin-Lu with her slanting eyes and the handsome Rodion lay at her feet. She had abandoned Mr Wright and Tom, for their lives had been shortened from the beginning

8

anyway. The girls' images, she had cut out carelessly, while she had preserved every millimetre of suit and every hair on the images of boys. Disaster lay all around her, but nobody knew; she had been left alone because she had promised to dust the magazines, to wipe them clean and put them in chronological order – and they, the boys, were now peacefully relaxing around a full can of elderflower fizz in the kitchen, all chatting at the same time, boastful and impatient.

He stopped in the doorway, pop-eyed. The warrior girl grinned at him, exposing the gap between teeth and gums, and wiped her lower lip with the pointed tip of her tongue. She continued to manipulate the scissors, plunging them into the paper without seeming to mind the newcomer, while he, instead of leaving, remained still, watching her and wishing he could find inside himself the courage to stop her, to snatch the torture tools from her hands and to expose her, shame her, humiliate her.

He came closer and stopped right next to her, stepping on the precious scraps of paper that lay on the floor. He heard neither protests nor sighs. Like a little robot, she had returned to her snipping, and he stood still for a long time, waiting for her to reach for the pages beneath his feet, looking forward to her asking him to set her loot free.

When she touched the tips of his toes, she looked up, languorously and all feline; he saw her imaginary tail twirling and coiling up his ankles like poison ivy, her eyes beseeching without a word. But he didn't yield. He knew her – he had seen her wandering around the neighbourhood – and he had also heard various boys making passes at her; he had heard of their escapades and the cheerful hormones that made their eyes bulge. They had gone soft and tearful, and they had exiled him from the centre of the group to the margin; they had shown him what real loneliness meant, how different it was from the imaginary kind he hypocritically liked to cultivate.

He had found himself watching her moves and waiting, in horror, to find her one day at the centre of the gang, a merciless ruler. He expected her to execute him in a trice, ignoring him and thus teaching the others a lesson: they needn't stand gaping at his stories, listening to him piously and even believing him, for they could do perfectly well without him – they could even feel freer and happier, for they would discover by themselves what he once gave them for nothing, enslaving them by his omniscience.

And now, as he stealthily entered the room, sniffing her scent from the doorway (for her skin had the stench of hell and of terrible banishment), he was facing the end and had decided to confront it with woe and helplessness. This was an unexpected decision that had thrust its claw in his head and now held him as a light bulb, strenuously screwing him into a smaller and smaller socket as it increased its urgency: to conquer her, as he had done with the rest of the gang, to subdue her and then to annihilate her with their boyish weapons.

'Do you need any help?'

She put on a wry smile; pushing out her lower lip slightly and making it tremble. He was enjoying the moment and would have died to be able to capture it, to stick her dumbfounded face on a poster and to put it at the head of his bed next to the hairy rock stars – to remember, a long time from now, that instant of ephemeral glory, and to show it to anyone who might doubt him and his leadership qualities.

He knelt and handed her the magazines; she took them, half cautious. She hesitated before opening them but, because his humble attitude could have tricked the most skilled double agent, she opened them and went on hacking. With her nose in the cloud of dust, she uttered a stifled 'Thanks!'

Sal rose to his feet and sat down on the couch, right in front of her. The slender body and the sharp shoulders supported a round head on which a round mouth, two round eyes and a small nose with a pinkish tip were drawn. The black hair, cropped short, made her look like a tomboy. Only the thick, long and beautifully curved eyelashes gave her away for what she was: a girl infiltrating the sterile and safe environment of the trouser-wearers. His daydream was interrupted by a grumble that sounded more like a noise in the beginning.

'I beg your pardon?'

'Are you angry at me?' she asked in a loud, authoritative voice that suggested the answer.

Sam was sure now that she had done it on purpose. 'No,' he answered idly.

'I have the impression that you are enraged... because of me.'

'Nonsense. I don't even know you!'

She raised her eyebrows. 'That's strange. I know you. I know you well. I have seen you several times on my street.'

'On *your* street?' he exclaimed, emphasising the words. 'A friend of *mine* happens to live on your street. Maybe that's why you saw me, if you *did* see me.'

An ardent smile had bloomed on Emi's face. She had no need to say anything else; he could say it himself, he could blurt it out before she opened her mouth to mumble who knows what nasty thing.

'So,' she drawled, slowly and clearly, 'you know where I live, which proves that you also know me, just as I supposed and said before.'

The only noise remaining was the drill of the scissors advancing, this time through his flesh. He wanted to leave, but the very thought of the effort it would take to rise from the couch and to walk all the way to the door, across the carpet of paper scraps, followed by her eyes, exhausted him. There was no way for him to win her over now, because the girl had bared her teeth and, in an ambiguous yet significant way, had declared war, making him understand that she was not willing to leave the battlefield very soon – at any rate, not before a few drops of blood had fallen on the carpet.

He was hurt by the unspectacular defeat. Of course, it was a matter of time to allow for the intruder's thin-skinned image to wear out, but was he really powerful enough to last that long under the soft, fluffy slippers that burned the crown of his head?

In the midst of this thought, he felt the couch slip from underneath him and, before managing to come back to his senses, he realised that the girl, having turned around like a whirligig, had already seized his calves with her arms and was now pulling him, with an unbelievable strength, off the couch and down beside her. He fell on his hands with all his weight.

He let himself down on his behind, shaking his head a few times uncomprehendingly. It was only after seeing the tiny beads of blood flowering through the pores on the soft skin of his hand, as if through blotting paper, that he started to feel the smarting pain. And over the pain, burning like acid on flesh, lay the shame.

Emi was frozen in a funny position, in full assault, but seeing that Sal was struggling not to whimper or release the whines that would have eased his pain and calmed his scare, she started to laugh doltishly. Then she settled down and looked him up and down with eyes in which he could see the mad sparkle of victory.

'It hurts; say that it hurts! A chicken would be braver than you!' she concluded, turning her back on him and muttering away in her sleeve. She grabbed the scissors and bent over the magazines, as if, in the same instant, she had already forgotten he was there.

He was angry, but at the same time he realised that much of their encounter – and of his defeat in their confrontation – was his fault, the outcome of carelessness and weakness and of the confidence with which he had entered the room, underestimating his opponent. His tailbone and his palms hurt and, while standing up, he felt the ground slipping under his feet. He staggered a bit, so slightly that it was as though the room seemed to have staggered and then fallen upside down, and then the ceiling fell over him like a blanket full of glass wool: heavy like glass and light as wool, or like a cloud with the appearance of candy floss, only it was neither glassy nor sweet or sticky but dense and fluffy.

The girl hurried to lift his head off the floor. She had made a net around him, had spread her legs sideways and was all over him, suffocating rather than saving him. He pretended to be sick for a few minutes – he surrendered, benumbed in her arms, and secretly, through his eyelashes, watched her fidget and make wry faces, full of regret and grief. He was gaining ground just watching her change, but her image – the struggle between crying for help and her suspicion that his illness might be feigned – gave him confidence and made him feel sorry that he hadn't really fallen sick so that he could squeeze out all her pity and compassion, all her guilt and promises for the future. Because that's what usually happened on occasions like these, and a man of honour knows what it means to do someone wrong and to pay for one's mistakes.

'Get up, please do get up, please be okay, will you? Can you hear me? Will you tell me if you're okay? You're okay, aren't you? Please forgive me, come on! Speak to me! Are you sick? Please, speak to me! Don't be sick! Wake up! Open your eyes!'

And to the tune of her words, Sal released within, through his whole inside-out body, a moan of pleasure. She had said it, and all that was missing now was a recording tape to capture, clearly, her whimpering voice. If only someone could have fetched him a tape recorder at that moment, so that he could play it again and again to the boys, let it unwind, flowing through huge loudspeakers. He would let it haunt them as the ghost of their feeble consciences, throughout the neighbourhood, as if his eyes were watching over the whole neighbourhood and they were that whimpering voice, pining and begging for forgiveness. He got himself together and jumped up, before her spiteful eyes.

'You faked it!'

'Yeah, I wanted to see your reaction. You're putting on too many airs. You know it's not right, don't you?'

'I have no idea what you mean,' she replied, offended, straightening her back.

'I mean cutting up Johnny's magazines – the ones he bought under the counter, the ones he paid for, went to great lengths for. I mean sneaking into Harry's room, snapping at me. Do you think you can take my place?'

With her small, scattered teeth sparkling in the light, Emi threw her head back and started to giggle, waving the scissors and sawing the air.

'Ha-ha! Is that what you think? I couldn't care less.'

She turned her back on him, sniffing a few times in contempt.

He let her scissor on and left the room, closing the door slowly as if he feared he might wake her.

In the kitchen, the boys chatted heartily. Max's voice covered all the others, trying to command the noise. Max was famous for the lies he intricately constructed, like a professional storyteller; but because his stories were flamboyant, with countless ambitiously and thoroughly rendered details, he forgot them in a few days and started to mix them up, to alter them to the extent that a girl he had met at a certain moment on the street, and with whom he allegedly engaged in conversation, soon became a grown-up woman around thirty whom he had noticed in his mother's consulting room when waiting for an opportunity to snitch a couple of medical leave of absence forms to use at school. They all made things up: they all had an imaginary girlfriend, kept in a drawer, well hidden, who popped out swaying her hips like an odalisque at convenient times.

The only one Sal was really tempted to believe was Harry. He was, in their small gang, the conqueror. He also seemed to have a secret life, helped by the fact that Mrs Demetrescu, his cheerful and masculine mother, who had been single since forever, was away most of the time. She would climb inside her white Dacia, which was always splattered with mud; she would manipulate it, jerk it, turn it around, spinning the wheel like a truck driver, and she would shout that she was leaving him to rule over the house and to remember always that he was the only man she could count on, as she slammed the door and exited like a hurricane.

Of course, Harry wasn't exactly the only one, but he definitely was the one in sight. For Mrs Demetrescu, despite her lack of femininity and coquetry, constantly had suitors buzzing round her, but she had chosen to protect Harry and she preferred to carry on her romances, be they few or many, out of his sight. Ever since Mr Demetrescu had gone overseas (to a place seemingly at the other end of the world: somewhere, according to Mrs Demetrescu, in South America), forsaking them to the extent that for several years they hadn't even received *Season's Greetings* in embossed golden print with a signature scribbled underneath,

Harry had become the gravitational centre of their three-bedroom apartment and the embodied idea of force and manhood behind the golden plate on which a name was carved, in luxurious type: *Fam. Engineer Paul Demetrescu, Ph.D.*

Nobody seemed to miss Mr Demetrescu, except for the neighbours who pitied the woman left behind, alone, to manage her good-for-nothing boy. But all this seemed exaggerated because Mrs Demetrescu didn't seem to worry about her son's blunders, nor did Harry, 'good-for-nothing' as they called him, allow any glimpse inside his secret life. There were only assumptions and hunches, encouraged by his perpetual wry smile, by the skinny jeans he wore emphatically and by the chewing-gum he champed noisily and ostentatiously, bursting from time to time huge green, pink or yellow bubbles. But Sal liked him like that, boastful and unreliable, perhaps because, due to his boastfulness and undependability, Harry was the only one Sal could trust. He was absentminded and, though inquisitive, Sal was only really interested in his stories about girls: beautiful or ugly girls, toothless or big-eyed, tall or stubby, swarthy or rosy, naïve or clever, long-lashed or thick-lipped, flat-chested or clad in puffed shirts – they only had to be girls to emanate that smell that threw them all into cruellest torment and burned their nostrils, sharpening them.

And in Harry's puffed-skirt pursuits, he had also hunted Emi, positive that shortly after the boys gathered in his kitchen finished recounting their fantasies and clumsily emptying their sacks full of erotic dreams, he would return to the room and the girl, lost among the pages of the magazines, would allow him to fondle her breasts, moistening her deer eyes when he made her lean her head back and surrender with a moan. Maybe not even he, skilled as he may have been, knew exactly what the surrendering of a girl was like, but from the bottom of his muddy heart, he was hoping to find out.

'Hold on!' yelled Max in a hoarse voice. 'Hold on, you haven't heard the best part yet! After my mother left the consulting room, the bird started to undress.'

'No kidding!'

'Yes, man, why are you so surprised? She took her blouse off, slowly, one button at a time, while she was swinging to the beat of the song...'

'What song, man? Didn't you say you were in the consulting room?'

'Yes, I was, you dick, but my mom keeps a radio on so she can hear the news.'

'And tell me, who was singing? Marina Voica?'

'No, Harry, it was that one with *The House on the Hill*...'

'Look who's talking,' Max snapped. 'Tommy, maybe you want some spanking!'

'Come on, settle down!'

Sal had spoken from the doorway, and they all turned around to face him. He had felt the need to intervene and break in abruptly on the conversation in order to make the boys forget about his absence and, especially, to take up Toma's cause. Actually, Toma had nothing to be afraid of because they all liked him, even though they called him 'chicken' and sometimes made fun of him, for in the end they were all touched by the mousy face and the small lively eyes moving behind the thick lenses. He seemed helpless, but they knew it was very likely that he was the smartest of them all, which is why all the exercise books for algebra and geometry homework succeeded each other on his desk and he filled them with fractions, root signs, integrals and exponents, tangents, bisectors, theorems and axioms. But if you asked Toma himself, the one he got on best with was Sal, because when they were alone Sal was the only one who listened to him talking about the gigantic computers that controlled space missions on the moon and on Mars and about the triangular-headed and mucilaginous-bodied mammals on other planets.

'Bam! What did I say?'

Max, annoyed, had taken a step back. He was always cautious; he would rarely upset his parents and seldom disobeyed them, definitely not before holidays or vacations, and to his friends he would nourish some sort of perpetual promise: the promise of procuring medical leave of absence forms or of bringing them magazines, full of naked women, or cigarettes and chocolate, or office supplies from his doctor mother's safe full of goodies. But he would leave lingering behind him the message of certain obligations that, when the time came, his indebted friends would have to fulfil for him. He hadn't asked them anything yet, but Sal was watching him and was expecting to hear him utter the magic words any day now.

'You didn't say anything, man; it's just that you yelled at him like...'

'Like what?'

'You know perfectly well like what. Leave him alone – he didn't want anything.'

Max headed for the door, disappointed. 'Very well, then! You're the ones who are going to be sorry. I won't tell you another word!'

The boys began to beg him to continue, mimicking disappointment in false voices: 'Come on, Maxoooooooo, pleaaaaaaase, tell us!'

But Max went out, shaking his head and slamming the door behind him. Everybody was relieved; it was hard to withstand his chattering. They had to constantly mimic listening to him, feigning interest, while in fact each of them was waiting for the appropriate moment to recite their own stories and compare their delusions in order to check their authenticity and the likelihood of ever manifesting themselves in the real world. Silence fell and Sal noticed Harry's impatience. It was the first time he felt his knees give way under him. He knew what Harry was waiting for: he wanted to see all of them gone as soon as possible and to be left alone, at last, with the girl who kept on scissoring a room away.

'Why on earth did you call that one?'

'Who?' Harry asked, pretending not to understand.

'You know, *that* one,' Sal said, pointing his chin toward the back room.

'Oh.' Harry played on. 'Well, never mind – I gave her some magazines so that she wouldn't bother us.'

'Well, it seems that she has been bothering us already!'

'How come?'

'Well, Max left because he was ashamed of her, that's why; you know him too well. Otherwise he wouldn't have left before telling us all. He wouldn't have given up so easily.'

Johnny nodded in consent, convinced on the spot by Sal's theory. Toma had been convinced before, while Harry remained gaping at him, unable to express eloquently and quickly enough his astonishment and his indignation.

'Next time you better tell me who I should invite over to my house,' he answered slowly, enraged.

Sal spread his arms akimbo and a generous, conciliatory smile bloomed on his face, suggesting *Isn't it a pity for us to fight over a girl?*

'Next time bring Clitt or Iss!'

Each time the boys laughed their hearts out. It was their favourite dirty joke; even Toma laughed when hearing it, although they suspected he had no clue what it meant whatsoever. But the laughter was infectious, and even when angry they couldn't resist the joke. 'Clitt or Iss' had become the character haunting their dreams, wetting their sheets, tickling their senses and rousing their laughter; she was their dearest imaginary friend and, in secret, they all thought about her when happily awakening from sleep at night. And it was her, again, who conciliated them now, when they were close to butting each other with their thin and clumsy horns. 'Clitt-or-Iss'... Sal smiled just hearing her name ring in his mind.

Behind them, however, standing stiff in the doorway with angry blazing eyes, was Emi. The boys had fallen silent; he was the only one still laughing, trying to keep the good spirits going. But the girl had already overheard part of their conversation and, probably bored with so much scissoring; she had left Harry's room full of scattered papers and was getting ready to scuttle away.

Later, when he had returned home, Sal would never cease to wonder what on earth had made him so obstinate about helping her get away and why he hadn't just left her to the ogre in that empty apartment that invited debauchery and neglect. He left right after her and found her in front of the apartment building waiting for him. They stood there a long while just staring at each other, not daring to talk. After a while, she suggested she should walk him home and, even though he knew it should have been the other way round, he allowed her to walk him home. When she stopped him and pushed his back against the fence – while around them mulberries were falling, staining their T-shirts with cherry-coloured traces – he stuck to the rough planks and felt her small palm resting on his bony shoulder for only a moment, while inside his eyelids, images flickered before her lips touched his hot cheeks.

'Why be enemies when we can be friends?'

Who could have resisted such an honest question, whispered closely on the edge of the road; who would have given an ambiguous answer? When they reached his building, Sal suggested that, to honour their new friendship, he should walk her home too, and so they went one way and then the other several times forgetting which way they were headed, for in the meantime darkness had come and they had to hide from their friends who were out to play in the evening shift. Harry, Toma, Johnny, Max the karate kids of year seven, the garrulous girls living in the horseshoe-shaped building, the tramps living next to the brewery: they all roamed the streets and had to be avoided by sneaking into buildings and unlocked gardens or behind the thick trunks of the trees in the small circular park in the middle of their neighbourhood.

In the end, remembering that they were expected at home, they said goodbye in front of Emi's gate and promised each other that they would speak very soon. Only when they were both in their rooms did they realise, and the discovery shocked them alike, that they hadn't exchanged phone numbers, so Sal called directory enquiries and recited the address. The harsh voice on the other end of the line asked if he was noting it down and then recited the digits, which he scribbled in a hurry on the off-white cover of *The Castle in the Carpathians*. And since then, for three years, at four o'clock sharp, Emi answered his phone call no matter what.

Now, on his way to see Emi, Sal went past Toma's house and looked up, just to make sure the two lenses weren't visible behind the windows. Sometimes, Toma stood for minutes languidly watching Sal speak at random. Emi insisted, with raised eyebrows suggesting certainty, that Toma was in love with Sal and that he himself knew it quite well. Whenever Emi trumpeted her theories, Sal would blush angrily and fall silent, while Emi would laugh sharply and then encircle her arms around his neck, embracing him tightly.

While walking away from Toma's house and thinking about all that, walking on the margin of the kerb as on an imaginary beam, Sal spotted a big, black cockroach on the pavement that had just emerged through the sewer grate and was now crawling idly along-side him. He squatted and got closer to better study the insect, slowly lowering his finger above the black shell that was sparkling in the sun.

Sal was fascinated by bugs. At home, in the living room, he had framed an insect collection in which all sort of specimens, from cockroaches to *Mantis religiosa*, lay pinned and which he had aligned like soldiers, scribbling below them the date when each had been captured. 'Funeral stones,' Sal explained to those staring in disgust at the still life hanging on the white wall of the room.

He thought a while and then lightly touched the cockroach's hump with his nail. It stopped, curled up and slowly moved its legs, seemingly begging to be left alive. Sal lifted his finger and sat down on the kerb next to the cockroach. On his knee he had a freshly cicatrised wound he had received after falling off his bike. He lowered his nail onto the thick, brown crust that covered the old wound and started to scratch it. As he poked at the crust on his knee, a thin thread of blood began to trickle under his index nail. He moaned. A piece of the crust was coming off, revealing raw flesh. *Raw flesh*, as if, he thought, the flesh were raw only under this thin cover, so pleasant to the touch, called skin. While it was under the cover, the flesh lived independently.

The cockroach was gone. Birds were fluttering noisily above, and clouds had covered the sky. He could smell the rain; the air around him was electrified and he could almost hear it buzz, prompting him to get up and walk farther. Before long, raindrops started to whip his cheeks and arms. Suddenly, the rain started to patter: *a summer whim,* as his grandmother used to say while bustling him inside, sheltering him as well she could from the short, rich gusts with all her body, with her large, soft breasts and with her armpits. He instinctively lifted his arms up, pulling his T-shirt over his head, and looked around at the slender trees and the plastic roof supported by four posts before deciding to seek refuge in the lobby of Harry's apartment building to wait there for the rain to calm down.

Once inside, he shook the water off like a dog and then remained still, listening for noises in the building. Although he heard murmurs and squeaks, short cracks followed by a slow friction, a rugged rustle coming from the elevator shaft and brief trampling, the silence was still overwhelming. All these noises meant nothing compared to the absence of people and of the sounds made by them.

He breathed in several times, filling his lungs with air. A stench, at first faint as a breeze, then increasing as his sense of smell got accustomed to the interior, remained clinging to his nostrils like icicles in winter. It became stronger, stinging his nose and reminding him of the nail polish remover that diffused throughout the bathroom after his mother wiped the polish off her nails and left the soaked and reddened cotton swabs on the sink. He looked up through the tunnel made by the staircase handrail, making sure there was no one there. The flow of air made the smell grow stronger and then fade in waves. From upstairs he could hear a window banging rhythmically against the wall. After slamming like that for several minutes, while Sal pricked up his ears to hear the other noises inside, the noise of its shattered glass falling on the floor followed.

Sal expected someone would come out in the hallway to see what had happened, but nobody did. He decided to go upstairs despite the nausea already filling his chest and forcing up all his lunch: chicken soup with noodles, roast meat with boiled potatoes and tomato salad, followed by a jam and meringue cake topped with grated chocolate especially sent by Grandmother in a greased, paper-lined suitcase. Upon reaching each new floor, he leant with his hands upon his knees and tried to take a deep breath to push the food back down, but the inhaled air only managed to disturb his bowels more and bend him under the weight of his rebelling body.

On the second floor, from behind a massive wooden door with a carved golden handle, he could hear a recurrent rustle. Putting his ear to the varnished surface, Sal tried to make out what was on the other side. The rustle was pretty close, but its regularity betrayed a spring-loaded device.

He drew back and climbed to the next floor. There, overwhelmed by the heavy air, by the decomposed mixture of sweet and sour smells, he stepped on the floor covered with shattered glass, lifted his body with a powerful push by grasping the window sill and, with all his weight resting upon his thin wrists, leaned on the edge, then bent out and let the drops of rain fall on his face.

The feeling of relief only lasted for a few seconds, because as soon as he trickled back in, careful not to make any sounds, the nausea reappeared. He bent his head between his legs, curled up at his joints and threw up until only a thread of saliva trickled from between his red and swollen lips, trembling lightly like a murmur echoing the spasms of the flesh. He remained bent with his eyes covered by the fog of effort and nausea, his mind empty and his temples beating like a heart. With a last struggle, he straightened his back and limped up the remaining stairs to Harry's apartment in what looked more like a crawl.

Outside, the heavy rain kept falling, while the smell made it harder and harder for him to stay inside. Thinking about the moment he would breathe in, filling his lungs with the stuffy air in his friend's rarely aired house, hidden from light behind the thick, velvet, tasselled curtains, he dashed up the stairs to the last floor, moaning and cursing. Once there, he pushed his finger into the bulging electric bell and made it ring in a short spurt;

when he saw that no one was coming to open the door, he rang a second time, this time for longer.

In front of the closed door, he began to ponder. It wasn't the best idea to enter Harry's house, for Harry would insist that he stay and, if he showed eagerness to leave once the rain had stopped, Harry would certainly sound him out, curious as he was. He crouched, rummaged through his pocket and took out a piece of chocolate wrapped in tinfoil. It had melted and its shape had changed, but Sal used his nail to remove the wrapping that was stuck to the brownish mass.

He had felt a softness in his legs, some kind of tremor hidden in the flesh, and had lost contact for a moment. However tempted he may have felt to lie down on the doormat and allow himself to be carried by his thoughts, he still thought that somewhere above him drifted Emi's tousled and impatient head, with a well-defined wrinkle already visible between her eyebrows and a sparkle in her eyes that could have ignited the whole neighbourhood. Perhaps he could wait until Mrs Demetrescu found him and, in terrible alarm, lifted him and carried him under her arm as if he were a bundle of woodchips, bringing him inside the house and calling his already-worried parents in a firm voice with little trace of excitement. Sal heaved a long sigh and leaned against the doorjamb, calmly munching the piece of chocolate. He thought he heard, on the other side of the door, a stifled noise followed by a thud, and he stopped and listened.

'Harry...' he whispered, concentrating. 'Harry, is that you, man?'

No answer. He knocked softly, carefully. It was only his breath in the hall, no other noise; his breath that had frosted the wood varnish on the door.

'Harry, say something if you're there.'

He drew back, looking up at the dark eye in the peephole. Rising on his toes, he thought he noticed motion behind the concave lens.

'You must be very stupid not to open the door, Harry. Just stay there and giggle,' he said, and from inside he could hear clearly now, as if it were very close, a stifled giggle.

He went downstairs two steps at a time, trying to breathe as little as possible. As he got closer to the ground floor and the smell became stronger, diversifying its nuances and penetrating his clothes and his skin, it inebriated him to such an extent that he nearly fainted. This was a building without pets and old people. He knew almost all of them, for together with the boys in his gang, he had harassed them all in various ways. It was not from the cleaned and scrubbed apartments that the smell came, nor from the stairs that were swept daily and then washed with a rag curled around a wooden stick.

By the time he reached the ground floor, he had figured out where the smell was coming from. Outside, the rain would have hidden the putrid smell, annihilating it. There was only one place left that he would have to inspect, although he wasn't looking forward to doing so and had little courage left: the basement. On the ground floor, there were two apartments and the door that led to the basement, where the storage rooms were located. It wasn't a very pleasant place to visit, especially when alone. But it was still raining outside, ceaselessly; it was raining cats and dogs, as Grandmother used to say while looking absentmindedly out the window, and Emi would undoubtedly have to wait. He opened the last door, while at the same moment a horrid stench hit him so violently he staggered and moved a step backward.

'I'll be damned...'

An infinite disgust impressed itself upon Sal's face. He slammed the door wildly, as if someone were rushing at him from beyond the threshold, and remained with his hand on the door handle, seemingly trying to figure out what was to be done. A few long seconds passed.

'I'll be damned,' Sal repeated in a stifled voice. 'What the hell is this smell?'

He stood with his arms akimbo like a bewildered old man, assessing the danger. Opening the door again, he looked inside to the darkness that lay at his feet. He tried his best to be brave, but the pitch-black inferno of the building had opened its huge mouth and was preparing to swallow him, the way children swallowed pickled autumn tomatoes brought from basement storage rooms by the housewifely mothers who had been careful enough to store supplies for winter.

Sal's fingers had gone white and he could no longer feel his limbs, but he didn't understand very clearly if this was because of his sickness or because of the cold that had caught him unaware. The door was open, and the dark was already licking the tips of his shoes. Sal felt dizzy with nausea; his body was numb and his head kept spinning.

He took a step inside. There, with the dark swallowing half of his body, the air no longer seemed so unbearable. He took another step. The dark clung to his face. He should go on, he thought, emboldening himself; he should take another step. So he took another. Suddenly, he rolled down the stairs without feeling any pain. His body seemed wrapped in a sponge and, through the soft fabric, thousands of eyes had popped out. For the first time, he saw everything as if in a huge glass panorama. The horizon lay both in front of him and behind him, bewildering him.

He landed on the cement at the bottom of the stairs. Shaking the dust out of his clothes and checking himself for sore spots, he could feel absolutely no pain. He felt neither the nausea that had strangled him upstairs nor the dizziness; he could breathe at will. For a split second, he thought he was dreaming. He stayed still, trying to come back to his senses.

A small, narrow corridor lay ahead of him, with doors to the storage rooms aligned on each side. Sal stood up and, leaning against the wall, advanced one step at a time. With the tips of his fingers, he felt some kind of strange dampness that caused him to draw back his hand hastily. He rubbed his index finger against his thumb, remaining still. A faint, barely perceptible hum floated now in the darkness.

After a few seconds, Sal's eyes got used to the lack of light, and he began to discern the space around him. The foul smell was gone, and now he began to smell the odour of plants in the air.

'Oh, God!' he said to himself. 'I think I've gone crazy.' Emi was waiting for him in her cheerful room, clad in her transparent dress through which you could see her thighs and her underpants and, sometimes, when you looked closer, even her nipples, but only when it was cold and Emi was all in a shiver. What on earth was he doing here? Why wasn't he resting in peace, his head in her lap? Maybe he could even have taken a little nap before seeing the boys.

He came to a door that was ajar, pulled away the broken padlock that hung from two metal loops and pushed the door to the wall. The darkness inside was even thicker than it had been in the corridor, and Sal groped slowly along the wall, searching for a light switch, but couldn't find one. He stepped into the room cautiously, following the slow, deafening rhythm of his heartbeat, and had the strange feeling that everything had frozen still – no heartbeat, no hum in the air, no muffled sounds from outside, nothing at all. And then the stench rushed upon him in even greater intensity, with a hint of jasmine and anise.

'Is there anyone here?' Sal whispered, overcome with excitement.

He took another two steps, and time began to rush. He began repeating in his mind, mechanically: 'Emi, Emi, Emi.' Then, when he had somewhat recovered from his fear, when he had measured the distance in the dark with his eyes, when his hands had stopped trembling, only then did he think that everything was a big pile of nonsense. How could a smell scare him?

The voice within him gave a high-pitched shriek, like a hysterical woman. Sal advanced blindly through the room, trying to grab onto something. The smell would come and go as if a draught crossed the room, somehow eluding him. Suddenly, there was the metallic edge of something hip-high. Sal cheered up and measured the cold expanse with the tips of his fingers: it was something that seemed to be a table. He closed his eyes and continued to feel the edges with more caution, advancing along a surface that had changed in consistency now; his fingers slid on an unpolished surface less electrifying than the metal on the sides. And then, suddenly, the terrible softness set off the putrid smell again.

Sal! he heard Emi call with a broken voice. *Sal!* his mother shrieked at the top of her lungs. *Sal!* the seemingly friendly basement echoed, bathed in a grey light. He turned his head, a scream stuck in his throat. He made a move to go, to run as far from that terrible place as he could, but the buzz clogged his eardrums and the machinery inside him had lost its will to move. He stood there, with his fingers prodding the soft surface, trying to understand what was under the thin membrane of his terror-rippled skin. But because his eyes couldn't help him see and his nose couldn't smell a thing, he pinched the softness under his fingers and felt clearly now that under the skin on his fingers lay another skin.

He cringed in terror. He knew quite well what was on that table. It was someone. A human being, a body, a creature. Maybe Harry himself, wanting to scare him. That would have changed things.

'Harry,' he whispered, his voice strangled with excitement. 'Harry, answer, you son of a bitch...'

He waited for a sign. It wasn't only his imagination; the tips of his fingers still bore that unexpected touch. He was shaken by a strong shiver. Then he made a decision: to touch again, to see what it was and, if it proved to be Harry, to make that bugger sweat for it. So, with a sudden jerk, he jumped forward as if playing rugby and landed upon the heap of flesh. He flew across the dark room, accompanied by the voices of his mother and Emi as if by two nagging angels; his hands were the first to touch the pane of the table, then his skinny body, his bare knees bruised on the football field, his red and calloused elbows and, with his heart pounding in his flat chest, he ended his flight and landed on a stone-still body. He made a last attempt, gasping in pain and fright: 'Harry, you fucking wanker, if you don't answer I'll beat the shit out of you... fuck...'

No answer; no motion. Sal was shaking all over. He braced himself, and without climbing down, clenching his teeth, he started again to grope, this time consistently: here was something resembling a shoulder, higher up something that felt like a neck, there was an Adam's apple, the chin, the face... As he proceeded,

Sal began to recompose, blindly, the human being – there was no doubt now – beneath him.

He jumped off the table, but didn't move away. Drawing a deep breath, only then did he feel the heavy plant smell wafting around his nostrils again. This time it was faint, as if a draught moved the air from one side of the building to the other. It was strange, because he could swear it was from down here that the smells had risen.

Sal was more concerned with that presence now, with the body lying still on the table – he imagined it as a dissection table in order to better envisage the dark reality he was just probing. He was dying to find out what was there. It couldn't have been Harry or another one of the boys. It was in fact, he finally admitted to himself, a woman, and that was the only thing he could say about the body he had plunged upon. He had felt, through his sweaty T-shirt, her breasts; he had clearly sensed their shape, he had anticipated them even before having touched them. He lifted a hand slowly, fumbled in the dark and then lowered it gently. Again, the skin with a silken feeling to it, a bit damp, like Emi's skin was after she had run a whole afternoon on the streets in their neighbourhood and she fell in his arms, dead tired.

It was then that Sal managed to touch her at his ease, to grip her flesh without the fear of being questioned, without revealing the pleasure that made him tingle all over. But the body of the woman lying on the table was supposed to resist, was supposed to move, to struggle; the woman perched upon the dissection table was supposed to protest and to scold him...

The finger had come to a bend. It was heading upward now, in a slow, almost dreamlike ascension, to the peak, the nipple – he tensed, for he discovered an iceberg on top: the breast was cold, frozen, stiffly jabbing the boy's palm as it explored larger and larger surfaces. A hand migrated to the abdomen; the other was on its way to the other iceberg. But the encounter with the left breast was even worse. The coldness, the skin wrinkled over the flesh, made him shiver. And time stopped still again, as if the coldness of the body he was groping had overflowed into the surrounding world, freezing it.

Sal blinked mindfully. He lowered his hand and felt her belly – it was a little swollen but soft enough for him to sink his fingers into the elastic surface, pleasant to the touch. He carried on until he encountered a smaller, bony bulge, covered in wiry hair. When he gave Emi a hug or when he touched her, accidentally, on her flat chest or her bare thighs when she wore shorts, he would feel her tense and that gave him immense pleasure – a pleasure that would follow him into the night and into his sleep. But with women it was a different story.

His cheek had many times been buried between the huge breasts of his grandmother's friends, who admired him and who would always spit three times to guard him from the evil eye. 'There you go, beauty. Come to Mummy; let me give you a hug.' And he would abandon himself in their arms, uncomplainingly indulging in their adoration. His nose sunken deep between the two mountains, he was surrounded by the whiff of aged skin and of the perfumes the ladies would dab behind their ears, on their necks and inside their cleavage. It must be that women couldn't feel boys' touches; they were but ethereal beings that passed unnoticed through the world of curvy women, and neither their filthy thoughts nor their immodest desires could be read. If it were so – if Sal could at least make sure that the lady lying here on the table couldn't feel him, if he knew he had the freedom to explore her body while she slept, to inspect every hidden corner, to examine every pore – how he would look down at Harry then, what stories he would have to tell the boys!

He decided to look for something he could light the room with. He drew back slowly and, groping around in the same manner he had got there, he crept back out. The dark hallway had awakened and was moving; the walls were quivering, and along them one could vaguely discern the aligned doors to the storage rooms. Sal got scared and took a step back, trying to calm his own heartbeat now blasting all over the basement: 'There's nothing to be scared of, there's nothing to be scared of.'

Repeating this chorus in his mind, Sal decided to cross the dark hallway that seemed, nonetheless, much friendlier than the den he had just emerged from. Near the door, he stumbled upon something that made the basement resonate with the loud chime of the stuff scattered on the floor. Had he disturbed the sacred order of the stinking vault – had he awoken the haunting ghosts, overcome by boredom and with their ears buzzing from so much loneliness? Now he was filled with regret; he wished he could take his steps back so that the box with its belongings remained in its place undisturbed.

Sal bent down and groped along the ground. His hands bumped against all sorts of objects, and carefully, but still trembling with excitement, he searched among them. He felt an oblong shape like a flute; the material the object was made of, however, felt strange. He put it down and continued his probing, down on his knees. A metal box. He took it in his hands, fumbled for its rims with his nails and tried to open it. The box slipped from his hands and the corridor vibrated in a long, shrill shriek.

Sal stopped dead. Emi's cheerful image and her luminous face flashed in his mind, and he felt his heart ache while his eyes began to glow. She was looking at him and waving her hand with her fingers unfurled, bidding him 'Farewell!' in her childish manner. He was suffering abstractly for the first time, and stopped in his tracks. When the girl's image had disappeared, he found himself in a panic attack: doubled up in agony, standing on all fours and rummaging indiscriminately through the objects on the floor hoping that, if he made as much noise as possible, either he would be heard by someone who would come down to save him or the ghosts, deafened, would take flight in their shady gullies. He came across the sharp, cold blade of a knife that briefly nicked his skin. Sal released a sigh, this time relieved upon encountering a shape he finally recognised. He took the knife, stood up and headed to the storage room, groping in the dark.

It was chillier still. His head was heavy and his heartbeat was muffled, as if coming from a jar of molasses. He was afraid and, if he had had the guts to let the tears run, he knew the fear would have subsided a bit – or at least it wouldn't have mattered so much. After a few steps, he stopped and decided to turn back.

He fell on his knees again and started scrabbling in the dark for the metal box he had dropped a few minutes before. The floor was slimy and touching it turned his stomach, but he continued to search and finally returned to his feet holding a box of matches with the tips of his fingers; from inside it he could hear the friendly sound made by the matches in their cardboard shell. Sal carefully opened the box and took out a match; he struck it once, twice, three times, but the cardboard was damp and the match broke in two with a short crackle.

He took another one out, and this time the match caught fire, throwing out a mellow light. But it wasn't exactly what he wished to see. All along the corridor the moving air carried a cohort of dust specks. With his eyes wide open, he tried to make an imprint in his mind of all the details – the cobwebs hanging in corners like brocades, the black doors, the shiny floor reflecting the dark ceiling – and then he closed them. Two big beads of water trickled down his cheek like two tears. The flame of the match slowly singed his skin, and he let go of it and lit another. He squatted, looked for the metal box, found it, clasped it in his hand and let the cool metal ease some of the pain the burn had caused. A whiff of air put out his flame, but now he was more serene. He had a good supply of light in the matchbox, a penknife and a metal box – the latter he had taken as a souvenir. He returned, fumbling in the dark, to the door that led to the storage room; he opened it with his foot and, after entering, he stopped.

His eyelids felt heavy, as if someone had poured wax on them. Blinking was such an effort that it made him dizzy. The smell was gone and so was the fear; all that was left was a deep exhaustion. 'That's because I didn't sleep enough!' thought Sal. But instead of lighting the match, Sal groped his way again to the table with the metal pane. His thighs hit the edge and he stopped. Shaking the matches mechanically, as if to make sure they were still there, he opened the box, took out a match and then clenched it with the tips of his fingers for an instant, motionlessly. When he struck it, the light of the match gave out a matte, smoky light.

In front of him lay a woman. Just as he had perceived, the

woman was naked, stone-still, with her eyes closed, seemingly sleeping. Sal brought the match's flame next to her motionless face: a white face, with beautiful, smooth skin, an angular nose and a rather small mouth. There was nothing special about the immobile face and, probably, if he had closed his eyes again now, it would have been impossible to recompose her countenance in his mind.

He looked around. In a corner, there was a pile of floor tiles, some wooden slats and, immediately next to them, a few cardboard boxes and a small chest with broken doors. Sal lit another match and headed to the chest. A petroleum lamp rested on top of the kind his parents had at home and which his father would use whenever there was a power failure. He lifted the part made of glass and lit the snuff; the light grew stronger and the room was enlivened by his shadow on the wall.

He turned his head to look at the table. The woman lying there had long, black hair, carefully combed over her shoulders in a sensible way that contrasted with her cold breasts and her uncovered genitals. He approached her again, put the lamp on the table and took a step back. It was only now that he noticed the walls were gleaming, as if covered by a curtain of water. He wanted to really get a feel of the skin that shimmered unobtrusively in the smoky light of the lamp – to wake up the sleeping woman and ask her what she was doing – but not before sniffing once again the fine, damp skin, not before caressing the stiff breasts that prodded the air.

'Miss...' he whispered in a hoarse voice.

She remained silent, unmoving.

Sal lowered his hand to her shoulder, covered in the black hair. 'Miss!'

A bead of sweat stood hanging on the tips of his eyelashes, distorting his view of the woman into asymmetric shapes.

'Are you feeling OK? Do you want me to call an ambulance?'

He placed his small, young hand upon her white, smooth-skinned, fine-fingered hand, with red-painted fingernails grown slightly to reveal a pinkish semicircle. Its touch gave Sal the creeps.

The woman in front of him either couldn't feel him or didn't feel like answering or even opening her eyes. He leaned above her and put his ear to her tightly closed mouth. She wasn't breathing; everything about her was still. He noticed on a finger of her right hand, hidden behind her body, a black stone, crossed by golden streaks that glittered in the lamp's light. He lifted her hand and looked at the stone: it was a simple setting, in silver. The ring made him think of Emi – how boyish and hasty she was sometimes and how warm and full of love at other times. Girls lived in a different world altogether. And the lady on the table, with her ring, with her breasts prodding in the air, with her red, overgrown fingernails and the beautifully combed tresses on her shoulders, was, as likely as not, dead – or as dead as a woman as beautiful as she could be.

A cold draught crossed the room, as if all the windows had been opened at once. Sal let go of the woman's hand and turned toward the door. Then he looked at the lamp, but the flame stood upright in the dark, still throwing its dim light into the room. His whole body was overrun by a wave of heat, accompanied by a pain that gripped his chest. He looked at her again and almost without realising it, he lay down on the table alongside her, draped his arms over her soft flesh, over her damp skin, placed his cheek on her shoulder covered by black tresses – the hair had a herbal smell as well – and the fear, the pain and the cold went away. Never before in his life had he seen such a beautiful woman, such a tantalising nakedness. He hardly felt time pass, but when he sat up the room looked different. He climbed down from the table and rummaged through his pocket to retrieve the penknife and the metal box.

The flame undulated slightly, moving its shadows around. Sal tried the sharpness of the blade, placing its tip against his finger; then, with an unmoving face as if in preparation for an execution, he took hold of her right hand and gripped her ring finger, on which the black stone rested, between his forefinger and thumb. Contemplating the finger, he adjusted it and then started to cut it scrupulously, without even a flinch when the bone gave way.

Finally, the finger was severed from the body. Sal put it in the metal box, closed it, and watched the motionless body again.

'I love you...'

He had started to sober up. He plugged his ears. The summer heat had poured into the basement. From outside he could hear the sound of a racing engine. He took the box, put it into his pocket and dashed out the door, his heart pounding in his chest.

'I love you...'

The basement smelled bad again, and when he was outside, out of breath, Sal stopped a little and fell to his knees on the burning asphalt. The heat had dried out all traces of rain. And in Sal's ears, the two words that had been so funny before, giving him butterflies in his stomach, still echoed: 'I love you...'

II

'FAREWELL!'

In the summer afternoons, when it is very hot, the neighbourhood seems to be asleep. Yet it is actually all an illusion, because real life runs its course inside the houses, away from the heat, in the shady corners where people stay still for hours on end or move very slowly to preserve their body temperatures. During those afternoons, in which the heat pervaded all living spaces, Emi was bored to death and would have given the world to run about at leisure on the empty streets, alone but for her thoughts. Her body, throbbing in all its joints, didn't seem to be inconvenienced in any way by the heat but with things as they were, she had to stay inside, pretending to sleep and waiting for the call from Sal that would announce four o'clock. Emi hated to sleep, and that was partly because she had no patience. She felt she was losing precious time which she could have used for thinking or for doing lots of other things. For instance, she could have crept to the attic and from there onto the roof, from where she could have spied any movement up to two blocks away. She could have stayed indefinitely like that, watching people swarming by and passing one another blindly. Up on the plate roof soaked in sunshine, she felt that nobody could know she was there, the small god of the neighbourhood.

She pricked up her ears. Fully dressed, she was sitting up in bed, with her knees drawn to her chin and her toes outstretched. Her forehead rested on her kneecaps, and she scrutinised the streaks in the bed's upholstery, inside the grooves of the fabric where the threads blended in a secret mesh. She heard the same noise again. Jumping out of bed and rushing to the window, she caught sight of Sal, staring up at her from the pavement below. When he saw Emi, he waved his hand and signalled to her to come down. She opened her window.

'Why are you so late?'

Sal threw her an outraged look – what did she mean by '*so* late'? It was raining, that's why.

'Come down, will you?'

He was late because strange things had been happening to him, things he could talk about with no one but her.

'In a minute!'

Emi slammed the window shut and dashed to the door. Behind her, a woman's voice squeaked angrily: 'Emilia, where are you off to?'

Emi darted through the front door and rushed into the street, bumping against Sal, who was just about to enter. They stopped and gazed at one another for a moment until Sal, happy to see her at last and still excited, put his hands on her face and brought his lips to her mouth. It seemed to Emi that she completely abandoned herself to the kiss, staring straight into his eyes while he was kissing her. There was a sweetish, slightly off-putting that somewhat turned her stomach but at the same time gave her tingles up her spine: that dampness that met hers, the slippery tongue that groped around and clumsily cuddled itself around hers. Then Sal let go of her, taking a step back. Emi remained with her eyes riveted upon him, visibly thrilled.

'What was that?' she babbled.

Sal broke out in laughter. 'Are you afraid?'

His question was mistimed and turned a key in the girl's interior mechanism. Emi's expression suddenly changed and she cast a nasty glance toward him, ready to fight, then rushed upon him and thrust him away, 'Oh, dear. You love to show off, don't you?'

Sal made a wry face. Then he swung around and started off down the street, heading back to the apartment building. Emi stared for a few seconds in his direction, astonished.

'Sal... Sal, where are you going?'

The air was full of little floating fluff balls, chasing each other on the pavement. Across the street, an old lady was carrying two overflowing shopping bags. She would take two or three steps, then stop, put the bags down, heave a noisy sigh and start again. When she lifted the weight, her face muscles strained in a funny grimace. Although she had started halfheartedly on Sal's trail, Emi shuffled her feet and had time to study the old woman from a distance, watching her as she crossed the street in front of Emi. The woman had just put the bags down again and was adjusting the silk-spotted coloured scarf on her crown.

'Do you need any help?'

The old woman gave Emi a long stare. The girl repeated the question, shouting in a high-pitched voice: 'Missus, do you want me to help you?'

Sal had already reached the corner, but was halted by Emi's voice chiming in the air. She had stopped across the street from the hag, pointing to her bags. Then, after the hag seemed to have answered, Emi started again, coming his way. When she got near, she put on a dismissive face.

'Who was that?'

'I don't know; how would I know?'

'Well, I saw you speaking to her...'

'I speak to a lot of people!'

Emi started ahead, with Sal following her like a good dog.

'Are you upset?'

Sal's voice trickled toward her ears, surrounding her, and Emi felt the need to get revenge.

'Look, if you don't feel like it, we don't have to see each other every day. Only don't have me wait, okay? I hate it!'

He threw her a distressful look. He thought she was unfair, and all of a sudden all the expectation and pleasure of seeing her was gone. He noticed that her features had become sharper and felt that nothing was the same: he could no longer tell her what he had found in Harry's basement. He knew that the woman in the cellar had to remain his secret, and this made him extremely sad. Yet immediately he started to search his mind for an excuse to leave as soon as possible. Emi the girl was extinguished inside him like a flame over which a very weak draught had blown.

With the tip of her shoe, Emi was now prodding a fluff ball

37

that had gathered at the corner of the street. It looked like candy floss without the stick, and this thought cheered her up.

'Listen, Sal, doesn't this fluff look like candy floss? If we stuck a stick inside, we could give it to Toma to eat. Wouldn't that be cool?'

Sal became even more distraught. 'That seems to me like the stupidest idea I ever heard.'

Emi giggled; she took his anger as spite. 'Why? I would like to know why, exactly, you find it stupid.'

'Because Toma would never eat fluff instead of candy floss. Because Toma doesn't even like candy floss! And because Toma,' Sal added, almost shouting, 'is not a moron!'

No sooner had he finished uttering his last word than he swung around and started walking back home – although actually he wasn't walking toward home. It just so happened that Emi had given him a good idea as to whom he could confide in about the woman in the basement. Even if he decided not to tell him everything, then at least he could intimate, through a parable, that the woman existed and that he had discovered her on that torrid and rainy afternoon. He was ready to share his discovery with a trustworthy person, with someone who deserved it.

He could still feel Emi behind him, thrusting daggers straight into the back of his head, but now that he had escaped, he didn't mind much. He could bleed at leisure, with the arrows still in his back, until he reached Toma and could forget about her in the rush of conversation. Toma was a true friend, the most honest of all; he was like a boy version of Emi, without her airs and her whims. Sal was relieved. Now that he knew which way to go, the day had recovered its meaning.

A soft breeze had started to move the hot air around a bit. He didn't want to look back, because he feared he might change his mind and turn around. Yet as he advanced, the thought of Emi, stranded in the middle of the road with tear-filled eyes weakened his determination and slowed his steps. After a few seconds, Sal stopped and looked straight ahead at the street that joined the boulevard. He could hear the faint sound of the joggling trams, dragging in the heat. Suddenly, he didn't feel like braving their thundering noise, or facing the dust and the squalor; he didn't feel like waiting for almost three minutes for the traffic light to turn green; he didn't feel like going to Toma's anymore. He realised that Toma would insist to be shown the corpse, would want to see it. Toma wouldn't be satisfied with his simple account of the story; he would go on his own exploratory survey, even if Sal refused to go with him. And maybe, in the end, Toma would discover something absolutely dreadful: that the woman wasn't even dead, or that she didn't even really exist because, apart from having seen her and touched her, what other evidence did he have – how could he prove to anyone that it wasn't just another fancy of his?

Sal turned his head. The street was empty. A few fluff clouds still drifted to and fro.

'Hey!'

He gave a start. From behind him, Harry had popped up out of nowhere, dressed in shorts and wearing a yellow T-shirt resembling that of the national football team. He had the number 10 printed on his back as a tribute to the great player and, as always when he was wearing this T-shirt, Harry had an overconfident attitude and strutted like a turkey cock.

'What are you doing here, man?'

Sal looked him up and down.

'Nothing. Where are you going?'

'To the playing field, for the game.'

Sal brooded a bit. 'I've been looking for you.'

'Really? When?'

'Half an hour ago, or so.'

Harry sniffed. 'Impossible.'

'How is that?'

'If you had looked for me half an hour ago, you would have found me. I was at home all day.'

'Hm. I lingered for a while in your building – it had started to rain. I thought you were at home.'

'Well, I was, man, didn't I just say so? But I'll be damned if I heard you!'

Sal gazed at him. He could have sworn that Harry was telling a pack of lies just because of his uncharacteristically transfixed face and his thoughtful look.

'Who else is going be there?'

'What?'

'For the *game*, man, who else is going be there for the game?'

'Oh! Well, who do you think? Those two from 112, the Stoicovici brothers, Maxone, Toma...'

'Is Toma coming, too?'

'Yeah, he's coming to gawk. Are you coming?'

Sal looked over Harry's shoulder toward the boulevard. 'That depends...'

'Come on, are you coming or not?'

Sal nodded and set off beside Harry toward the school's football ground. When they crossed Emi's street, Sal looked along its distance, hoping to see her sulking on the street kerb waiting for him, but Emi was nowhere to be seen. He wished he had stayed with her; he really didn't feel trashing it out on the field with the others. He was bored and tired. Shoving his hands in his pockets, his fingers sought the creases of fabric, trying to find their place, when something stopped him dead. In his trouser pocket he had encountered the regular shape of the metal box in which he had put the severed finger.

'You know, man, I don't know what to say, but I'd rather not go...'

Sal stopped and apprehensively dropped this line to Harry, hoping that he wouldn't hear it and wouldn't even notice his absence; that he would keep walking to the football field on his own. But Harry pulled a long face. 'What's with you, man, have you gone crazy? Why would you rather not come?'

Sal shrunk. 'I don't have my gear...'

Harry burst into laughter. 'Big deal! Like it's Champions League!'

He hurried off and Sal followed him. Harry had started talking again about the last game, the one Sal had missed, during which they – the guys from school 122 – had scored ten goals. As he struggled ahead with the hot air pressing upon his skin, he heard Harry's words as from a dream.

The two crossed the road and turned left. At the end of the street, they could see the school, a white building with grates over the windows and casements painted bright blue. Harry continued to talk, kicking every now and then at any stone he would encounter on the road. Two silhouettes slowly started to move toward them, the only people they had met on the street in the last half hour.

Sal took the hand he had been keeping on the metal box out of his pocket. His palm was sweaty, so he wiped it against his T-shirt. The approaching figures could now be seen to be a man and a woman. The woman, wearing big sunglasses, was dressed in a sheer green skirt, through which one could discern the shape of her legs, and a white linen blouse. She was gesturing in an exaggerated manner and, from a distance, Sal thought she looked angry. The man was walking beside her, his hands behind his back and his head slightly lowered in a reverential attitude, paying close attention to her. After a few steps, Sal overheard pieces of what the woman was saying. Here and there, her voice acquired acute inflections and she would lose her temper. They were quite close to each other, and this slow approach made Sal feel drowsy. He turned to Harry, who kept talking: 'Shut up a little!'

Harry cast him a puzzled glance. The man and the woman had stopped. She was still talking, but just as they passed by the man looked up from the ground and straight into her eyes, saying, 'You know, for me nothing has changed; everything is just the same...'

Sal felt like turning around to look again at the dark-haired woman with shoulder-length curly hair and the tall, blue-eyed man with a youthful face. No sooner had they taken a few steps away than their voices faded away as if they had vanished into thin air; still he looked back spitefully. The two were moving slowly away, the man still holding his hands behind his back and the woman brooding beside him with her arms hanging limply alongside her body. Sal kept walking beside Harry, who was now engrossed in a stubborn silence.

They reached the lattice fence surrounding the school's football field. A few boys were already on the field warming up, shaking their legs, running on the spot or doing squats. Seeing them, Harry started to shout at the top of his voice, followed by the other boys who shouted in return. He turned to Sal, reiterating, 'Are you a fool, man? Would you have missed *this*?'

Sal appeared to be about to answer, but then he changed his mind. When he stepped onto the hot concrete amidst the cheers welcoming Harry, a breeze touched his cheeks, and when he reached the middle of the field, a wave of heat hit him right in the face, rising like a curtain between him and the girls perched on the dilapidated benches who were watching the boys get ready for the game. And from that moment on, Sal forgot all that had happened to him. He jumped in place together with the others, he swung his hands in the air, he bent down and leaned sideways while the blended voices of the boys and the stifled giggles of the girls roared in his ears. And when they started to play, he let his feet carry him over the field in a continuous dash, with an almost indiscernible flight over the concrete.

His mind was empty and his eyes brushed only intermittently against the faces of the girls who giggled and bashfully tried to cheer them on; his feet barely touched the uneven surface that covered the endless distance between the two goalposts. The boys were shouting, swearing, tugging his T-shirt, but without stopping for even a second, Sal kept running after the ball that rolled on tirelessly. At a certain moment he thought he saw Harry gesturing something, but he didn't bother to find out what it was. He was chasing the ball, and then he was touching it with the tip of his shoe – bouncing it off his toes straight between the goalposts. It was then that he heard a choir of voices covering his own, after which came the arms and bodies of the boys swooping upon him in an upsurge of joy. A wave of sticky sweat trickled down his whole body. The other bodies touching his own made him shiver with bliss, and soon he was driven, just like the other boys, by the desire to win.

He felt Harry hug him and shout in his ear how good they were, what a sucker he had been, what he had almost missed, how the chicks were staring at them now and so on and so on.

'Sal...'

Harry's voice seemed to emerge from somewhere deep inside his mind, hot-blooded with success and heat. He managed to escape the boys' embraces and, just as unexpectedly as before, he bolted and started for the exit. Outraged cries followed him, and Harry started jumping around in a desperate attempt to stop him.

'Where the hell are you going, man? We haven't finished the game – don't be an asshole!'

But Sal had peeled off. He was running as fast as he could; he was running back, on the tree-shaded street, stirring the yellow dust behind him. When he slowed his pace, he was already halfway there. Carefully, he studied the houses that languished like old ladies with their hands crossed in their laps and their chins cast down. The heat had been eased, and the leaves rustled above his head. From one of the houses came the noise of a coffee grinder, and he stopped and sat down on the pavement. He felt short twinges of pain in his tired legs, the still-tense muscles twitching from time to time. He watched the skin's surface contract slightly and wince, as if animalcule colonies were swarming underneath. The coffee grinder's noise suddenly stopped and a female voice cried from the bottom of the yard: 'Would anyone like coffee?'

Each morning at his grandmother's after breakfast, the coffee steam would reach out to him and lure him out on the veranda. Next to his grandmother's cup and that of one of her friends stood a small cup with a drowsy layer of cream floating on top. She was the only one who had offered him, as far back as a year ago, that token of maturity, his passport to the grown-up world. And despite the fact that the place smelled of lavender and mothballs, and mole-crickets would show up now and again from under the old furniture, his grandmother remained the only woman in the family with whom he got on well and who didn't pester the life out of him. She was the one who listened to his long soliloquies when he woke up dripping wet, scared and eager for anything but sleep, after one of the nightmares in which a huge butterfly chased him through a thick-walled house.

The loneliness felt in dreams was tremendous, more dreadful than all he had been through in Harry's basement, uglier than the mole-crickets crawling undisturbed in his grandmother's house, more shocking than Emi's long silences she hoped to impress him with. That loneliness contained something overwhelming that would crush him, as if the mere effort of the mind produced an earthquake that crumbled down the whole stone-made edifice of his enforced and self-inflicted enclosure. He couldn't tell Emi about his dreams, but in those moments when his grandmother sipped the hot coffee with her puckered lips, Sal would take heart and start to spin the yarn of his dreams. Grandmother Meri, after heaving a deep sigh with every sip, would nail her fat-lidded brown eyes upon him and appear thoughtful. She would neither reprehend him nor make fun of him the way his parents did at home. In those summer mornings, his grandmother would concentrate on his mouth as it uttered a rapid-fire stream of words like balls hurtling down a bowling lane.

Sal would have loved to tell Emi about everything that crossed his mind, but especially about his dreams and his fear of death, about the colonies of insects that swarmed under his skin every time he made a great physical effort. Right now, he especially wanted to talk to her interminably, to describe in great detail – if he had had enough words to do so – the woman in the basement whom he had just discovered and to whom he could talk to nobody about.

The back gate opened and a woman his mother's age, dressed in a homely dress with pink and blue flowers, looked up and down the street. Sal, with his head turned in her direction, felt the urge to say hello, slightly bowing his head as his mother had taught him to. The woman looked him up and down, then shouted something behind her, but Sal couldn't understand what she had said. He stood up hesitantly and hit the road again. If he had had the choice, he would have gone to his grandmother's to take a nap in her living room, with its windows shaded by trees.

With his grandma in mind, he retraced the whole street and crossed Emi's street as well. When he came to himself, he was on the boulevard at the traffic light, unwilling to do anything. The metal box was bumping against his leg, through the fabric of his shorts, as he walked. The cars were zooming on one side and then on the other, and the red traffic light flickered its countdown. The people gathered on the other side were gazing straight ahead, waiting for the green light.

'Sal!'

He looked right and then left. Someone was tugging his shirt from behind. When he turned around, he spotted Emi, who was panting with her hands on her knees. 'Sal, where the hell have you been?'

He looked at her delightedly. Emi straightened her back and started to talk, waving her thin arms in the air. Sal was watching her and, listening to her discontented talk, full of indignation at the unreliable people who left girls standing in the middle of the street and went God-knows-where, Sal decided that now was the best moment for him to share his finding with her. He grabbed her wrist and pulled her for a few steps.

'Emi, I have to show you something, I really have to!'

Emi stared at him in disbelief. He grabbed her other hand as well, the one that was hanging close to her body. 'Actually, I want to give you something!'

Emi seemed to cool down a bit. 'Well, give it to me!'

'No, no, not here. Let's go to your place!'

'You know perfectly well that, if we go to my place, my mother will stuff us with food and get in our hair and not allow us to talk.'

Sal was silent.

'See?' Emi went on. 'We'd better go up to the roof of my building.'

They remained still for a while, pondering. It was the first time she had told anyone about her secret place. Something in his tone and in all the events of the day had made her mention it, and now she regretted doing so. It was the place from which she could watch over all, including Sal, and now that place was about to disappear, open to all the eyes in the neighbourhood. It was exactly as her mother had told her: boys couldn't keep a secret, and only girls had the inner strength to love others and keep secrets for themselves.

'On the roof at your place?' Sal marvelled.

Emi had pursed her lips, but now it was difficult to back off. 'Let's go, Sal, and make sure you hold your tongue and don't tell anyone!'

They started to walk slowly back to Emi's building. The heat had abated and a soft breeze had started to blow. Sal put his hand into his shorts pocket and rested it on the metal box. Coming across Emi had changed his state of mind: she hadn't abandoned him, she had looked for him, and now the fact that she was disclosing her secret place proved that she had been thinking about him.

'Where were you?' Her voice had a squeaky sound. 'I've been looking for you everywhere. I went to your place and your mother told me you were out to buy ice-cream... Jesus, Sal, is that what you tell your mother when you come to see me - that you go out for ice-cream?' Emi laughed, flinging her head back. When she laughed, her black, round eyes had a mischievous look. But they also had a bright shimmer that simultaneously subdued Sal and amused him.

'I say all sorts of things... today it was ice-cream, tomorrow it will be something else. Tomorrow I'll tell her I'm going to a table-lifting séance.'

Emi stopped, laughing even harder. 'I see your point!'

She dropped down with all her weight, then jerked him forward, running and forcing him to run behind her. Sal complained, telling her that he was tired, but the girl had rushed ahead stubbornly, pretending not to hear. Sal's temples were twitching, and he could feel how the small insects under his skin had started to rebel against the tyrant who was bothering their sleep. But despite his somnolence, his legs were rolling forward, obeying the girl who had suddenly become his bright spot. Eventually they reached her building and Emi, panting and her face gleaming with sweat, pressed both her palms onto his chest.

'Not before you swear that you won't say a word!'

Sal hurried to swear: 'I swear!'

But Emi shook her head in distress. 'Not like that; that's rubbish!'

Sal stood perplexed. 'Come on, say what you want me to do!'

The girl's round, black irises disappeared behind her eyelids. Emi kept her eyes closed for several seconds, and when she lifted her eyelids again, fluttering her long eyelashes, she had once more that exhilarated look that somewhat scared Sal.

'Look, it's no big deal, but you need to have guts! Can you do it?'

'You bet I can!' Sal rushed to answer.

'So this is what we'll do: we'll snick our fingers, drip a little blood on a shard of glass left over from my father...'

'On a glass slide...'

'Right, and then we'll spit and mix it well together. You'll smudge my forehead and I'll smudge yours, and then we'll swear to keep the secret.'

Emi's face was beaming with delight, but Sal just watched her with amusement.

'So what? Do you think that will prevent us from talking? Spit and blood?'

Emi put on a long face – not because Sal was deeming risible the importance of the oath, but especially because he could never participate in her games, or in any games for that matter. He did the same with the boys. That's where his funny lies and pretences also came from, because it was beneath his dignity to take part in their nonsense. Sometimes she had the impression that Sal would rather have stayed alone all day, lolling about or meditating on the things he thought he saw, because Sal had this gift, which many thought was just a fancy, to see things that were invisible to everyone else. But she believed him, because she could read on his face the uneasiness bestirred by the beauty or the horridness of his findings – like now, when he showed reluctance in swearing to keep her secret.

They stood by the gate looking at one another, sweaty and panting.

'All right, Sal, we'll do as you wish!' Emi started to climb the stairs, two at a time, while he followed her at a slower pace. They went up all four floors, and on the last one, Emi squatted while she waited for Sal to catch up.

'You know,' Sal told her out of breath, 'my word should be enough. I would never betray you!'

Emi lifted her head, gazing at him. Then she braced herself, took off and jumped to catch the hanging metal ladder that led to the roof. She lifted the hatch and put her head out, scrutinising her territory with her legs still hanging inside and half her torso outside. After a few seconds she disappeared, thumping on the hot roofing sheets. Sal heard her voice trilling from above, urging him to climb faster. Her secret was safe, he thought. When he had said that he would never betray her, the words had bound him more than an oath. While saying them, a thrill had crossed his body. He was stirred by a commitment that opened a long road ahead of them. He had butterflies in his stomach and felt a choking happiness.

Emi was holding on to a television aerial and leaning over the gutter, inspecting the space below them. Sal advanced falteringly. When he reached her, he sat down on his bottom. The roof was still hot, burning and diffusing the heat stored at noontime and in the early afternoon, but as the seconds passed the unpleasant feeling started to wear off.

'Look!' Emi pointed somewhere in the distance. 'I can see the roof of your house. In the afternoon, when I can creep out of my room, I climb here and stay on watch. I imagine what you could be doing under the roof. I imagine you living in a rum *baba*, Sal...'

Emi turned to him and burst into laughter. Sal was delighted by the comparison of his house to a cake.

'I remove the top and watch you sleeping on piles of cream...'

The sun was melting into the horizon and, although the air was still sultry, the heat had somewhat abated. Sal invited her in a subdued voice to sit beside him. He groped again for the shape in his shorts pocket, just to check: it was still there, sitting quietly. He realised he didn't exactly know what he was looking for with that strange gift on the roof, with Emi who was already staring at him with her round eyes wide open, waiting for the secret he was offering in exchange. Because that's what Emi was waiting for, actually: an honest exchange, so she could set her heart at ease and keep on spying on her friends perched up here.

'I have something very important to tell you. But you have to promise, like you had me promise, that you'll keep your mouth shut and that you'll take my word for it. What do you say?' Sal smiled at her, but Emi remained still. She didn't seem to hear his jokes; she was eager for the swap.

'Okay.'

He put his hand in his pocket and took out the metal box. There were a few beads of sweat on its lid. Sal wiped it clean with the back of his palm and handed it to Emi. His hand remained, hanging aimlessly in the air, for several long seconds. Emi was still watching him, uninterested. 'What's that?'

Sal held the box forth again, but Emi continued to stay in the same position, refusing to look at it. 'Is this your secret, Sal?'

He nodded. Emi extended her fingers for the metal box and grabbed it with disappointment. She opened it hastily and a slanting light splashed her face. The hacked finger, with the black-stoned ring sitting stately upon it, smiled to her from inside. Sal was beaming with joy. His sweaty face had ecstasy written all over it, and his eyelids were closing with excitement. Emi touched the stone with the tip of her index finger, stroking it gently. Dumbstruck with amazement, she looked at Sal with tears in her eyes and exhaled in a slow sigh. 'Oh, my, Sal, what a beautiful ring!'

Then she cautiously touched the red-lacquered fingernail. 'How beautiful!' she went on wondering, and then lay down on her back, satisfied.

Sal lay down beside her. He thought about the things he had done during the day, about his walks, home from school and then out to Harry's, about the goal he had scored and about the cheering girls and about the flower vases that smiled on the windowsill of the dentist's office.

'Did you buy yourself an ice-cream after all?'

'No...'

'Maybe we'll go down later and buy some waffles at the corner.'

They could hear a siren wailing from below. Emi sighed. 'Do you realise, right now, at this very moment, someone is passing by – someone who is sick, maybe even dying, someone who is going to die tonight...' Her eyes narrowed. 'Do you realise, Sal?'

At least twice a month, Emi had fits of melancholia that sometimes led to a sorrow that lasted a whole day. He liked to listen to her thinking out loud, because that was when she dared to reveal her tiny anxieties, speak honestly about herself and admit that behind her naughty face and her inquisitive glance, her girlish fears lay hidden.

'Look at the sky in that direction! I think it's going to rain again.'

Emi looked where Sal's finger was pointing. In the distance, the sky had turned purple. The colour of their skin had changed, too.

'It hasn't been raining today,' she sighed, wiping her forehead dry with the back of her hand. 'Where did you get this finger from?'

'Harry's building...'

'You found it there? On the ground?'

Sal put his arms under his head. 'No, I actually cut it off.'

Emi opened her eyes wide, screwing up her lips in a surprised *O*. 'No kidding!'

She seemed to ponder. Sal's disclosure weighed more than his secret. She had to consider whether to sound him out further or not. What secret could she have offered in exchange? She rummaged in all the corners of her mind. No, she had none left... Emi's trunk was empty; there was only some small change left at the bottom, which she was wondering now if she should lay on the table. But curiosity was gnawing her inside. And the finger was luring her with its black stone.

'How do you mean you cut it? You cut it off someone's hand? Is that what you mean?'

'Well, yes...'

Emi stood up, looking blank. 'I don't understand. How could

you do something like that? Whose hand did you cut it off?'

Sal suddenly felt sleepy. He was dying to close his eyes that very instant and sleep with no dreams. But he knew that Emi was going to use her weapons and, eventually, force all the details out of him.

'Tell me, Sal, what have you done?'

And, as always, words started to pour out of Sal's mouth like so many beads. As he told his story, time itself seemed to have stopped, because the light had frozen still and was bathing them now in its dead colours.

'I want to see her myself!'

He had known perfectly well that this would happen and that, if he was against it, Emi would have gone anyway to Harry's basement to poke about. And he didn't find it in his heart to let her grope in the dark by herself. They climbed down from the roof and then dashed to Harry's building. Sal was silent while Emi ceaselessly chattered about her dream from the previous night, about the ladybird collection she kept in a box, hidden in the bathroom cabinet, about spying from the roof and about the chilled elderflower juice waiting for her in the fridge when she returned home. But when they were about to enter the building, they ran into Harry. Sal sighed with relief.

'Where did you go, you bastard?' Harry exclaimed. Then he cast a murderous look at Emi. 'It's because of you that we lost the game, you know?' He turned to Sal again with a mistrustful look and started to sound him out: 'What were you doing here?'

Sal sized up the circumstances. They were looking for the body of a woman that he – Sal – had discovered in Harry's basement, that afternoon when he had been the only one to take shelter from an imaginary rain. It was the answer he should have given, serenely, assuming a countenance that would suggest he wasn't willing to go on with further explanations. It was the answer he felt floating in the air around Emi, who was piqued about the charges that had just been made against her. That's why he made a step back and mumbled a lie. It was already dark outside, so nobody noticed him blushing. Only Emi, when grabbing his hand, felt his sweaty palm and gave out a muffled giggle because she knew that Sal was an awful liar.

They parted in front of Harry's building, each heading in a different direction. Emi was mad about the encounter that had broken the spell between herself and Sal, and because she hadn't been able to see for herself what he had seen so that she could give him the hottest secret in exchange. She wanted to tell him what she had found out pretty late herself, almost half a year before, when Sal had been sick in bed and gone for a week, giving no sign whatsoever.

Back then, Emi had shifted rapidly from feelings of spite and hate to despair, regret and vengefulness. Sal's disappearance meant a lack of concern for her, carelessness and, ultimately, abandonment. Her mind was filled with a rapidly fading image of Sal, with the memory of his voice and the amazing stories he told when he felt like it, with the places they had roamed together. She understood gradually that these things had become important and were smouldering now inside her, like cake dough on the stove. And, albeit reluctantly, she had begun to register the indescribable feeling that haunted her, and to be scared by it.

When she found out, after three tormenting days of uncertainty, that Sal was sick in bed, febrile and delirious, a happy smile emerged on Emi's face. Then a shadow covered her face again and she refused to leave her house. She locked herself inside her room, lowered her blinds and took it into her head not to eat anything anymore. She would say she was sleeping and now, looking back, sleep was all she remembered. One day not long before this episode with Sal, her mother had told her – matter-of-factly, while knitting her a pair of leg warmers – that love was a rare thing that you'd better not let someone in on unless you were sure it really existed in your soul. Actually, her mother added after a break, you'd better not ever let anyone in on it, because people are inclined to take advantage of any weakness. It is only in movies and in books that people say 'I love you' to one another at every turn.

But love is feebleness of the body, like some kind of disease that takes a long time to heal. And Emi, in all those days in which she had been waiting for Sal, felt her whole body weakened, with a feeling of emptiness inside and a vague pain radiating to the very depths of her being. She had made a vow, in those three days of self-imprisonment, not to breathe a word to anyone about what she had discovered. On the third day she decided to go and see him as if nothing had happened, as if she hadn't even noticed his disappearance.

She found him lying in bed: pale as a ghost, bathed in a dense sweat, like a pellicle that blurred the features her eyes were used to. The Sal she knew had vanished under that pasty layer and was shouting out voicelessly, begging with his eyes to be released. Emi sat down on the side of the bed and took his hand, gripping it. First she gripped it gently, then harder and harder, with all her strength, but he remained still and his hand didn't twitch for a split second in her grip. His eyes were open, and he was just staring ahead in a dreamy state. Emi stuck out her tongue, made all sorts of funny faces, but he remained stuck in idle reverie. Finally, convinced that Sal was absent from this world, at least for the moment, she lay down over him and took him in her arms. A few clear tears dropped from her round eyes, through which Sal saw her, magnified. After less than five minutes, Emi fell asleep. She woke up soon afterward and remembered then – which she would later completely forget – that she had dreamt something terrible.

She was fumbling down the dark corridors of a hotel. The hotel was shabby. The walls were covered in textured red silk and the doors, made of black painted wood, looked like embedded coffins. Emi was looking for a man in one of the rooms. She could already visualise him lying flat on his stomach, naked, across the crumpled sheet. With all her senses sharpened, she was advancing slowly on the red corridor, holding on with the tips of her fingers to the silk yarn on the wall to keep contact with reality. She stopped a little, pricking up her ears. From the other end of the corridor she could hear voices and a commotion. And then, out of the blue, she saw a bunch of people rushing toward her. She fumbled anxiously and pressed the first door handle, which opened right away. She entered an empty room, illuminated by two reading lamps; It was perfectly tidy. The noise on the corridor had died out while Emi inspected the room, but the voices burst out again outside the door. Emi opened the closet and hid inside it. It smelled like jasmine. Someone entered the room. She hunkered down with her mouth pressed against her knees, trying to hold her breath. The jasmine smell choked her to the point of suffocation. The person in the room stopped in front of the closet door and leaned against it. Emi squeezed her eyes tight, waiting for the door to open and for her location to be disclosed. And suddenly, outside the closet, she heard the faltering, tearful voice of a woman.

'Please, tell me, before someone walks in!'

And from somewhere very close, as if he were speaking to her – to Emi – came the husky, tired voice of the man.

'What do you want me to say?'

After a break, the woman resumed, seeming to struggle: 'I have the feeling that things have deteriorated between us – that it's over.'

Emi heard a long sigh followed by loud crying. She wished she could see the woman in the room, but that meant she would have to come out of her hiding place. The voice outside died away in sobs. The woman was panting for breath and in Emi's mind the desire to see her took shape, stronger than her instinct to stay hidden, stronger than her fear of being disclosed. She wished she could step into their argument and reconcile them. Her soul felt hollow and she suddenly started to miss Sal, to miss him so ardently that she started to cry, too; first silently, then louder and louder, indifferent to whether she would give herself away or not. And the jasmine smell choked her so badly that she darted out and found herself in the middle of an empty room, exactly as she had left it before hiding in the closet. She woke up with her face bathed in tears and saw the boy gawking at her from behind the pellicle of sweat. She tried to fall asleep again and resume her dream, but Sal's mother had entered the room and her face showed surprise of having found the two children cuddled together in bed.

That's when Emi had found out what love was, in the strange dream whose story she had immediately forgotten, retaining instead the feeling of fear and apprehension she had experienced upon awakening and seeing the face of the sick boy begging her to stay with him, just like the woman in her dream. So that's what it was supposed to be: a long suffering, an unceasing array of anxieties, followed by a slow death. Her parents had broken up a year before, but instead of suffering, Emi had been relieved. The coldness in the house had been replaced by some sort of tranquillity and by the freedom to do what she pleased.

She had discovered the roof a long time before, but it was only a year since the pleasure of sitting perched up there and spying on people's moves had become absolute. And it was there that she retreated again, after saying goodbye to Sal and to Harry, to reflect on what had happened that day. She didn't have patience to wait until the next day, but she also lacked the courage to go see for herself what was in Harry's basement. She was experiencing the same curiosity as in that dream of long ago which she barely remembered. She opened the box from Sal and fingered the darkness inside it. The living finger and the dead one met. The living one grabbed the dead one and took off its ring. She put it on her ring finger, but the ring was wide: if she had lowered her hand, it would have slid off, rolling over the gutter and into the air. She lay on her back, put her head down and, a few minutes later, she fell asleep.

III

EMI IS DREAMING

He woke up with a heavy head and feeling nauseous. There was a commotion in the house, and he remembered that it was Sunday and that his parents were at home. The thought made him sad, because he would have to lie again that he was going out to play with the boys. For unknown reasons, his mother didn't like Emi at all, and to avoid wry faces when he mentioned her, Sal preferred to mumble a lie. He heard a few knocks on the door, and then he heard his father's voice urging him to wake up. It was nine o'clock sharp. He lay back down and closed his eyes. Outside he could hear the automated buzz of a drill press; its long, even noise had invaded his room and had now settled in his mind. In a way, it was pleasant not to think about anything, to let the wish to concentrate on anything in the exterior world beside the noise outside fade away and die. He propped his mind against it and abandoned himself to the feeling that he was floating above the bed, supported by the ceaseless sound. But the noise stopped and Sal jumped upright. His headache was now duller, its bolts seemingly digging into his skull with a squeak. The hustle and bustle outside his room got louder, and he could hear his mother's shrill voice, chatting with the woman who was helping in the kitchen.

In less than an hour, Sal was back romping on the streets of the neighbourhood. First he had to stop at Toma's to exchange games. He had no idea where he got them from, but at Toma's he could always find Monopoly, Snakes and Ladders, Treasure Hunt, Spintop, Mikado... and now Tomo had allured him with a new and pompous game Sal had already heard an earful about called The Sphinx. Sal wasn't much of a game freak, but he found playing in itself mind-expanding and it helped him to better orientate himself. It shed light on his friends and on the way in which he could approach them in tense situations. Actually, for some time, he had been regarding his friends and the streets they lived and walked on as a huge game with several strategic points, whose stakes were survival in isolation, keeping secrets and, last but not least, seducing the girls. Wasn't that what he longed for all day long? Wasn't that his carefully pursued aim? What would Harry have thought of him if he confessed one day that he'd rather chat with Emi instead of playing ball with them on the school field? How long would it have taken Harry to tell all the boys what he had found? An hour, perhaps, but Sal didn't care; he wasn't interested in what they said but in the fact that, once his friends abandoned him, the game wouldn't matter any more. Once there would be no one left to hide from, his secret would disappear as well, vanishing with the ones that threatened it. And maybe, he assumed, the pleasure of getting together with Emi would disappear too, the pleasure of hearing her squeaking voice answer his phone calls at four o'clock in the afternoon, pretending not to know who was on the other end of the line as if it made no difference to her whatsoever who it might have been. The freedom of going to her place would have impaired their relationship. And the fact that they were hiding was steering them, one step at a time, to a more complex level, which he had trouble defining precisely but which he felt drew them together in an inexplicable and beautiful way.

Toma had the wealthiest family among them all. He lived in a proper house, with a ground floor and a first floor, with a terrace on which in summer the ping-pong table sat in state. The boys held championships, and they were always treated with iced Coke and all sorts of cakes laid out on a table brought especially for the purpose and set in a corner of the terrace. The championships made Sal especially happy because, when they gathered there, Toma was considerate enough to also invite the girls in the neighbourhood to liven up the atmosphere, and since the day Harry had decided it was so, Emi was one of those girls. Among the boys, warmed up by the exercise and competition, Sal and Emi felt as if they were in a cocoon. They would dart furtive glances at one another: their eyes speaking thousands of words, secretly making fun of their friends and flirting as if they had just met.

One day, Emi had dragged him through the labyrinth of what seemed to be Toma's enormous house. The rooms were arranged in a circle; with doors that opened onto other rooms. You could start at any spot, then cross several rooms stuffed with paintings in thick frames – some simple wooden ones, others adorned and gilded, but now all crammed into each other – along the walls, You would bump against several old armchairs with silk upholstery arranged in symmetrical order and finally come full circle to where you had started. Sal loved to hang around that house and always discovered beautiful objects that he would touch hypnotically; he would have lingered for hours in contemplation if the boys hadn't almost always called him back to play.

That day, Emi had sneaked in from the terrace and beckoned him to follow her. They crossed two rooms to get to a third, which was usually locked and where he discovered a cabinet full of old weapons in one of the dark corners they hadn't managed to explore so far. Getting closer and pressing his nose to the window, Sal saw a few pistols with inwrought wooden butts placed next to two rifles, a harquebus and a musket and, in the middle, three swords aligned next to their scabbards with inlaid oriental decoration. The swords seemed to be the oldest items.

Sal touched the wooden edges of the cabinet with his fingers. He wished he could open it a little and hold in his hand the marvels gleaming beneath the window, but the weapons were locked away.

'What are you doing here?'

Emi was glancing at him, amused. He showed her the cabinet. 'Look!'

Emi drew near and looked over his shoulder. The weapons didn't seem to make such an impression on her. She shrugged her shoulders and grabbed his hand. 'Come on! I'll show you something else!'

But Sal stubbornly refused to move. 'Just stay a little while!'

Emi pursed her lips and plonked herself in a bergère, as Toma's mother would bombastically call it. She lifted her knees to her chin and propped her yellow sandals on the pink silk. 'What are you up to?'

Sal tried again to see if he could open the glass that separated him from the weapons.

'Do you want me to tell you a story?'

She raised an eyebrow. 'Uh-huh,' she said, screwing up her face and huddling in the armchair.

'It's the story of two people, a man and a woman, who loved each other wondrously but, for reasons yet unknown, didn't manage to stay together, and their story had a sad end...'

Emi winced, shivering all over. Sal propped his elbows against the cabinet's window, took a deep breath and started.

'First, I have to tell you about the boy. Ever since birth, Tristan – for that was his name – had an unfortunate destiny. He didn't get to know his father, who had died on the battlefield, or his mother, who had died while giving birth to him. That's where, I believe, his name came from: Tristan, from *triste*... The boy is adopted by his uncle, a powerful king, and raised at his court. But as you can foresee, Tristan is no ordinary child. He is brave and smart and has a magic lamp, but he also has a special capacity; that of seeing things that others don't see. Moreover, he has warrior blood flowing through his veins. So, hearing that his Uncle Mark's kingdom is haunted by a child-eating ogre, he sets out to challenge the monster and kills it. During the fight, however, Tristan is poisoned by an arrow. Resigned to the idea of death, he sets out to meet his end like a true hero: at sea.'

Emi sat flabbergasted in the armchair open-mouthed in wonder.

'Well, and since love has its own way, Tristan was soon brought to the shore of the kingdom whose princess was called Isolde. And she is the one who saves him from death. But Tristan is so blind that he doesn't notice the beautiful girl with black curly hair cascading down over her shoulders and goes back to battle instead. And he keeps fighting until, one day, he is summoned by his uncle and ordered to find the girl whose arms are snow-white and whose hair is black and curly, covering her shoulders, so that she can become his wife and his queen.'

'Isolde,' Emi whispered.

'Tristan set out to search for the woman described by Uncle Mark, not realising that it was Isolde he was seeking. And, as love has its own way, once again Tristan reached the shore of the kingdom whose princess was called Isolde. And there he finds the royal stronghold besieged by the barefaced man whom he had been warned against. Sure enough, as any barefaced man is wont to do, this one tries to deceive him, but Tristan figures it out in time and manages to kill him. However, as he is hurt again in the battle, Isolde nurses him for the second time and saves him from death. Taking a better look at her, Tristan understands that she is the chosen one his uncle has ordered him to find, and so he sails away back home with her.'

'What about her? What does she say?'

'Well, I suppose she says nothing; she wants to be a queen.'

Emi seemed to brood for a while, making a disappointed face.

'Wait. So on their way back, Isolde's handmaid, a redoubtable witch, accidentally makes both of them drink a magic potion meant to make people fall in love for life. And the poor things drink it, and that's when all the madness begins. Tristan falls in love with Isolde, and Isolde with Tristan. Love pushes them into each other's arms, and all through their voyage they live as husband and wife, you know... but sometimes love is not enough. So at the end of the voyage, Isolde decides that she was destined to be queen. You might wonder how come love wasn't enough... so did I, but I haven't found an answer. The fact is that Isolde rushed into the uncle's arms, secretly shedding a tear for Tristan. But rumour had already reached the king that his white queen, Isolde, had lost her innocence during her journey at sea with his nephew. And the anger caused by jealousy knows no limits. With extra - ordinary courage, perhaps even bordering on recklessness and pretence, Isolde volunteers to pass a test. She is ready to dip her hand in a molten tar cauldron under the oath that she had only been in the arms of two men, Mark and the monk who had helped her jump ashore from the boat. Isolde dunks her hand in the molten tar cauldron and, to the surprise of everyone present, she takes it out white as snow. But who do you think had been hiding under the robe of the monk who had helped her jump ashore?'

'Tristan,' Emi whispered, her face beaming with admiration and joy.

'Yes. Do you realise? What a liar!'

'Yes, Sal, she lied because she loved him. It doesn't count.'

Sal, taken aback, was now gawping at Emi. How could she say something like that? A lie was a lie, and Isolde, aside from cheating on her husband, had also lied to him unblinkingly. And love – he pondered for a while – love can't justify such things. Not to mention the fact that Isolde wasn't really in love with Tristan; it was the potion that had poisoned their blood and was now talking through her mouth. He rattled off his theory to Emi, but she made a wry face and answered:

'You say that because you have never been in love!'

The light had stopped shining, the wind had stopped blowing, the sounds had stopped vibrating and Sal's heart had stopped beating. Everything had stopped dead. He didn't dare ask her a thing, but unyieldingly carried on his story as if nothing had been said.

'Then Isolde married King Mark and became what she had always wished to be: a queen.'

But the spell between them had been broken. Sal rooted for the brave knight, Emi for the deceitful adventuress. Emi could feel the grudge, the resentment and the misapprehension in Sal's voice. The only thing that prevented her from leaving was the curiosity of seeing what would follow.

'But the couple's love affair on the ship had been witnessed by other people, who started to talk, and the talk eventually reached the king. Doubt-stricken, Mark chased Tristan away, hoping he would rid himself of his nephew. But Tristan, like a true hero, held his ground. His love for Isolde was stronger than any threat.'

Emi was fidgeting on her chair impatiently. 'Well, I'd rather you told me how it ends. Do they stay together?'

'Yes and no... Actually, they die in each other's arms. So they stay together, but it kind of doesn't matter anymore.'

Emi seemed to miss the point at first; then she jumped right up from the armchair. 'You are mistaken. If they die together, as you say, then thereafter they are still together! Love has conquered all!'

Sal looked again at the locked weapon cabinet. 'One evening, after they run away from King Mark's court, Tristan and Isolde wander through a dark forest and becoming very tired, they lie down under a tree. In the morning, the king's men find them sleeping side by side, with Tristan's sword lying between them. They say it was a symbol of innocence, but I think it's just a sign that their love was doomed.'

Sal took a break to behold the reflection of his pale face in the window, furrowed by the gleaming blade.

'There is no hereafter; this world here is all there is. If I took this sword and ran it into my stomach, I would abide with you for a while: I would probably see you screaming and crying, and then, in my eyes, you would disappear and there would be nothing left. The only things that would exist after that would be the room, the weapon cabinet, the furniture, you and my gradually cooling and decomposing body.'

He remained gazing straight ahead for a few moments. Images of the story unrolled before his eyes like a slide show. He was trying to visualise the two lovers, but what he saw instead were a few familiar neighbourhood streets and himself stopping in front of a house that seemed very familiar: a house with a ground floor and a first floor. There, at the upper storey, the window was open and a piece of the white curtain was flapping outside like a flag of surrender.

They found him collapsed on the floor, his left hand full of blood, lying among the glass shards of the weapon cabinet from which pieces of glass were still hanging. Sal only came back to his senses when they reached the hospital, but even then he couldn't manage to explain where he had got the urge to run his small fist through the shiny, transparent surface.

That's when his warrior image had sprung into the minds of the boys. They had only seen something like that in action films

– although Sal thought he resembled Clark Kent, lying breathless on the floor, more than Superman. On the white sheet, on one of the six beds in the desolate ward of the emergency hospital, Sal contemplated the gauze bandage under which his warm hand pulsated. For the first time, he encountered that dull pain, getting sharp now and again, that suddenly separated his body from his mind. A new body was being born on his inside, growing under his skin, different from all he had felt so far. It felt different from the bike spills and from the blows received from the gang of bullies on Toma's street, the fifteen- or sixteen-year-old tough guys who had put their bikes away in the attic long before and were now shamelessly touching and poking girls.

The pain had seeped into his blood and was now forcefully pushed through his arteries, making his blood cells rush chaotically through all his organs – this unprecedented pain that had thrown him into the seclusion of the white hospital ward, made him stay with his eyes riveted to the ceiling for several hours in which not a thought, not even the most trifling and insignificant of thoughts, crossed his mind. His senses were petrified in a barren dream; his mind was stuck on his own inverted image into which, little by little, he descended.

If you wish, you can do anything. You can jump with the soles of your feet right on the ceiling; you can hop around the neon lamps placed in the middle of the room like cracks in the walls of an open box through which sunshine seeps in. You can brush away the cobwebs in the corner and you can write your name in the dust. You can stay there, hanging unseen. But at the slightest relaxation of the mind, the image would turn back over, and the dizziness would make Sal close his eyes and jump off the bed with his feet on the floor. And, one Sunday before lunch, while he was heading to Toma's to get a new game, the truth suddenly hit him, with the force of a boomerang returning to the present after a circuit of his personal history and jolting him out of his dream.

That evening on the ward – with his ears whizzing, feeling dizzy from the iodine smell after an unsuccessful attempt to sleep – he felt an obscure urge to climb down from his bed and leave his room. Now that he was alone, he wanted to take a few aimless steps on the neon-lit hall of the hospital. He advanced on the circular aisle without encountering anybody, without hearing any sound apart from the jerky whoosh of a machine that was pumping air. When he thought he had gone all the way round and was about to return to his room, he opened the door of ward number 23 and saw before him a woman with black, curly shoulder-length hair held in place by a plastic hair band. She must have been around thirty, with a very pale complexion and round eyes like two black buttons. She was sitting on the edge of her bed, dressed in a T-shirt that only just covered her briefs. Sal drew back a step, but the woman reached an arm toward him.

'Wait!'

He stood still with his hand on the doorknob, daring neither to enter nor to cut and run out the door. He realised now that he had felt like leaving the room and running away from that pale and long-suffering lady. But she beckoned him to come in. And, as Sal advanced, her eyes became increasingly vivid and bright, as if two gems had grown inside them and taken the shape of the cheap buttons on his mother's two-piece suit.

'What's your name?'

'Mary Jane,' a smooth voice murmured in his ear, and he almost felt Emi's lips tickling his nape. The woman reached her arms out to him, and Sal advanced until he found his hands grasped by the woman's translucent hands, which had bluish veins protruding through the skin.

'Are you lost?'

Sal relaxed. Instead of chilling him, the cold touch gave him a feeling of comfort and bliss. The gems had become eyes, the wiry hair had become silky and the skin on her cheekbones was glowing with colour.

'I'm looking for my ward.'

'What's the matter with you?'

'I cut my wrists and I lost a lot of blood.'

The woman touched the tips of his fingers sticking out from

under the bandage. 'If you need anything, just tell me. What did you say your name was?'

'Sal.'

She smiled at him. 'Sal... we are both so lucky... Probably that's why we are sitting here together, in the hospital, all by ourselves, because we are both fools.'

Sal withdrew his hands slowly and spotted her thin, bare legs, hanging limply.

'Are you sick?'

The woman burst into loud laughter, as if in that instant Sal had pressed a button and a tape machine inside her had released the hysterical screams. An inexplicable feeling of guilt snuggled within him and made him shiver. He didn't know what to do – whether to hold her in his arms or to set off running as he had intended to do in the first place.

'I would have been delighted to have such a handsome boy like you, to be able to snuggle up to him and to feel his smooth skin and his fresh smell.'

'Do you have any children?'

She sighed. It had been a stupid question. The woman had just told him that she had none, but her proximity, the way she touched his arms – somewhat motherly, but with a certain sweetness and a scarcely restrained repentance – made him lose the thread of his thoughts.

'I wished for it dearly. It's not too late yet, but I don't really know... When you're confined in a hospital, alone, you kind of lose hope, don't you?'

Sal nodded, without a clue as to where the conversation was heading.

'Do you have any brothers or sisters?'

'No.'

'I'm an only child, too. Some say it's not okay, but I enjoyed it. They just let me be and I minded my own business.'

She paused, visualising something in her past. 'How come you ended up here?'

'Oh, nothing. I told you, it was an accident.'

She took hold of his hands and inspected his bandages. Then her brows knitted.

'One hell of an accident. What happened?'

'Well, that's the whole point – I have no idea. When I came to my senses, my wrists were cut. I was at a friend of mine's, we were playing table tennis, and I went to the bathroom...'

He took a break, considering whether to go on with the story or to stop there. But the woman seemed to be interested.

'That's about all. What about you, missus?'

The word that was so hard to utter and that put such a precise distance between people, between grown-ups and kids, between those who don't and probably won't ever know each other, had come roughly out of his mouth.

'What about me?'

'What happened to you? Why are you here?'

She took him in her arms. At first, Sal resisted, but the woman was much stronger than him and, moreover, he was afraid of seeming rude, so he let himself be hugged. After a few moments of embarrassment, he clung to her soft shapes. And in acknowledgement of that, she whispered into his ear:

'I tried to kill myself.'

They sat motionless.

'Do you know what that means?'

Sal nodded his head. Of course he knew. Maybe Johnny and Max didn't know, and he wasn't sure about Harry. Toma had a hunch, but perhaps it wasn't clear to him either. And he couldn't say a thing about Emi. His heart was pounding madly in his chest. He was so happy she hadn't succeeded that he was ready to fall onto his knees and ask her, beg her, to stay alive. What could have been so terrible?

She stroked his cheeks with her moist hands.

'It was a foolish thing to do, and I'm sorry now.'

She pushed him back and looked into his eyes.

'Sal, will you come to visit me tomorrow? And tell me what you dreamt of tonight? Will you?'

Sal consented with a nod. He wanted to ask her permission

and to lie next to her, to sleep side by side, embracing as they just had; he wanted to sniff her hair, to watch her eyelids lowered over the two black eyes that twitched in her sleep, below the noise of details. But the woman gestured for him to leave, pushing him away with her thin hands and showing him the door. Sal went out and found himself back on the aisle lit by the neon lamps with their ear-splitting buzz. He could smell her perfumed skin on his hands, and it aroused him. But she wasn't simply his first living phantasm, which he could touch and which would keep him awake all night; she was also his oldest friend whom he had only fallen in love with later, at about six in the morning, when he managed to close his eyes and finally fall asleep. That was right before falling into a dream during which he realised that friendship was nothing without love and that tremendous discovery your body makes upon meeting the other's body. He was spellbound. He stopped in the middle of the street, with his arms hanging down by his linen trousers.

The next day the large-hipped nurse appeared in the ward, dressed in a very tight white coat with the first two lower buttons open, revealing her plump legs through the slit when she walked. She was followed by his parents; all with bright faces, they were animated by a state of unconditional joy they felt compelled to induce in him as well. It was then that he understood more precisely the meaning of the reassurance their happy faces carried and of the recommendations the doctor, arriving shortly after his parents, made in a warm, professional voice. Was he happy at home? How were his grades at school? How did he get along with his teachers? What about his classmates? What kind of friends did he have? What kind of magazines did he read? How did he like to play? What kind of games? The lady doctor put it all down in a notebook. Then she turned to his parents, whose faces had lost part of their brightness in the meantime, and let them know in an authoritative tone that she wished to continue the conversation with them outside and that she wished to see Sal twice a week at the polyclinic. After she dictated its address, which the parents sullenly and obediently repeated aloud, the lady doctor was gone in a storm, saying goodbye over her shoulder. It was then that his parents threw him a ferocious gaze, in which Sal could clearly read: 'So long, friends, magazines, games and everything else!'

He crept past his parents, who were now dutifully listening to the nurse repeating all that the woman with the stethoscope stylishly hanging round her neck had said before, and slithered along the candy-pink walls, heading for his friend's room. He put his ear to the slightly open door, through which he could hear a man's voice. Through the slit, his eyes managed to carve out part of the white coat covering a figure leaning over the bed and half of the woman's face. She looked even more beautiful by day than she had in the feeble neon light the night before, but also very familiar. She was sitting the same way, with her head slightly leaning back, but this time her eyes were full of tears and she looked as if she were struggling to understand what the man dressed in a white visitor's coat was saying to her. Sal pricked up his ears and managed to hear him:

'You disappointed me. I thought there was no need for explanations between us, but I see that I was mistaken... actually, I don't know what you want from me. Do you want me to solve it all this instant...?'

The woman burst into tears with violent wails and babbled something unintelligible. The man in the white coat leaned over her and pressed her head to his chest. But with inexplicable force, the woman pushed him away, crying:

'I hate you! I hate you! I never want to see you again!'

The man lost his balance and, although he tried to take a step back, he didn't manage to find any footing and slipped in the air, landing two feet from the door. Sal ran into a big, bony, asymmetric face. The mouth was cut into the thin beard. When the man opened his eyes, Sal gasped and dashed away, frightened, back down the aisle that was now full of white coats and slippers shuffling on the linoleum.

* * *

There was no point anymore in going to Toma's. He had to retrace yesterday's steps, to take Emi with him and to start looking for the two grown-ups together with her. He stopped. Sunday, before lunch: not a living creature was to be seen on the streets, only the odd group of pensioners chattering on their way back from church. From the houses wafted the odour of stew, steak and meat pies. Sal sniffed, feeling hungry. Maybe it wasn't a bad idea to return home and grab a bite before starting his quest, or to go to Emi's and be stuffed by her mother, who had started to effuse waves of excessive affection over any male, child or grown-up, who set foot in her house ever since the departure of the one she had loved and whose name, after he had disappeared from her house, she had never mentioned again. Whatever delicacy Sal wished for, he could find it there; he only needed to utter its name, or just to hint at it, and it would materialise. Why not go there? Why not rest afterward, with a full belly and a drowsy mind, in his beloved Emi's slender lap, with his torpid legs resting upon the ancient phonograph that was still warming their afternoons with music from vinyl records as old as grandmother Meri?

Summer is a bothersome season. To be unhappy, you need concentration. And in summer unhappiness is disrupted, especially when all the birds are chirping at your window, in your mind, in your garden until dusk, and until night creeps in with its warmth, kicking you out of bed. Impossible when, the following day, the sun beats down on you with limitless enthusiasm, stripping off your clothes, and when light engulfs everyone and everything like a pest of eagerness to live. Impossible when people dress merrily and girls pluck up their courage and wear sheer dresses beneath which their legs, calves to thighs, quiver with pleasure; when lust blooms and spare time calls for idling and wantonness. How could you possibly be unhappy? How could anything rub you, of all people, the wrong way?

The background of your life is stronger than your true self; sickness is improper, and the sick have to be immediately banished from the small, cheerful sense of self that is threatened by sadness and commiseration. If one dies in summer, they're all gone.

Tears and sorrow fade away more easily and are promptly appeased with cold drinks out of the fridge and homemade ice-cream. Delights lay scattered everywhere: in the sweet shop windows, in the markets full of coloured fruit and vegetables, in the fridges packed with oily beer bottles, in the promise of holidays. Sal smiled, imagining that the woman in Harry's basement had been abandoned because it was summer. Just another month and all the pickles and relishes would be gone, so there was no time for mourning.

No sooner had he finished his thought than he found himself in front of Emi's building. How he had arrived there so quickly he had no idea. He had walked at a slow pace, even allowing himself a few reflections on life and death and stopping once to tie his laces, and there he was, in front of the street lined by fluffy poplars. It usually took him ten minutes to walk the distance, timed on his digital watch, the screen of which he could light by pressing a minuscule button on the right: the watch his father had given him as a gift for his birthday a month before.

Sal was born on the fifteenth of June, on the exact day school ended, so the exhilaration of the holidays was always lost among presents and special treats. Moreover, his father liked to organise surprise parties, which unfailingly turned out to be fancy-dress events, year after year. Due to the repeated formula, these parties had lost both their surprise and their originality and now weighed him down like the blade of a hatchet shining merrily in the sun. At the parties held to celebrate their son's birth, his father and mother would only invite neighbourhood children they thought worthy of crossing their threshold. Emi had never been invited, especially because of his mother, who disapproved of her brilliant son's association with a girl from a broken family with a somewhat dubious history. Her father's much-questioned disappearance and the bitterness and mistrust of a mother left alone, as well as the girl's wildness, were not the best recommendations. That was why, for the past two years, Sal had disappeared after the first hour of fun – taking with him the cake from the fridge, neatly wrapped in cellophane – and would only return home late in the evening, looking happy and without giving any explanation to his parents who were left standing in the middle of the living room. This year he had done the same, and when he returned and found them hollow-eyed, his mother with obvious traces of tears on her face and his father shaking a belt in his hand like a hangman disappointed that his victim shed no tears before the execution, he calmly asked them:

'Anything left to eat?'

The belt fell noisily, flapping in the air, and his mother sighed just once. Then it was quiet, and since then no one in their house had ever mentioned parties or clowns again – aside from when his mother, three days later, asked him casually to bring back the cake tray as she had no platters left in the house. Sal put on his wrist the watch he had found that evening on his bedside table, wrapped in coloured paper with a blue ribbon in the middle. Now Emi would never again need to complain about his being late.

'Emi, stop yielding to doubt and jump into the torrential river that carries you to your lover... Don't comb your hair with your fingers, just blink those shady eyelashes and look at the sky, Emi, have you ever seen a sun so red, red as my lover's lips, sha-la-la...' Sal climbed the steps two at a time and pressed his finger to the round bell. 'Emi, fly next to me, let us seek love together, my love, if you pay attention, love has just walked by you, it looks like a beautiful woman with her silky dress flowing, Emi, my beloved, when I think of you I get dizzy–' and so on, till he entered her room and saw her leaning over her varnished wooden desk, looking at a stamp in an album full of valuable items.

Emi hit the ceiling. 'Why are you showing up now? Do you know what time it is?'

Sal threw himself on the narrow bed, placed in a corner of the room. He sniffed, trying to trace the smell of her sleepy body.

'Did you have another fight with your folks?'

Sal shook his head.

'Come here...' said Sal, beckoning her to sit on the bed next to him.

It was the only pleasant thing in the world to sit together like that, idling their time away.

'Listen, do you feel like going out? I need to look for somebody – I'll tell you what it's about – and I don't want to go alone.'

'Where? Who do you need to look for?'

Just like all the other times, Emi was sounding him out. And Sal, more often than not, pretended not to hear. Then again, what could he have answered? Where were they actually going? Who were they looking for? Wasn't it, after all, the ghosts in his mind that were groping around in the blinding light of the summer sun, searching for a dark recess under which to shelter until the heat subsided?

'Do you want us to go back *there*?'

'Sal, *if you want to be a hero, follow me...*'

But Sal wanted to stay there, lying on the bed, to hear the leaves rustling outside and Emi breathing next to him. He drew her to him and made her rest her head on his chest as he had seen in films. But this time reality seemed better, because his body, too, ached to draw near the girl's body. He could smell all her juices and secretions; he could smell the fever of their heated organs and their thin blood through which tiny goldfish were swimming. She had resisted in the beginning, but now she lay tamely over him, with the hot crown of her head resting against his chin. Sal's nose could detect a hint of nettle shampoo and something else very subtle, a whiff of summer sweat that stirred him. Emi was excited: he could feel her body tremble like jelly freshly removed from the mould. Her strength was located exactly in that superior coldness of a girl who knew her body so well, down to the remotest corners. That was the limit drawn between them in red marker, which only she – the girl – had crossed now and then, while he had this inner voice singing to him that he should stay away from the forbidden things, stay within the lines, keep his partner upon a pedestal and behold her in her dizzying height.

But now his inner voice had started to hum its warning too late. Now Emi lay limp on him and, instead of the usual thoughts, Sal heard a mermaid song alluring him to ransack corners, to trickle under the transparent clothes, to put his head between the straight, thin thighs on which the flesh stood pink and proud. His body had changed its controls as well, and at that moment it was driving toward what had been locked and unknown for so long, wanting to smell, to glide across Emi. Sal took the girl's sweaty hand and, although she resisted, forced it inside his linen pants. At the same time he discovered, with the same satisfied wonder as always, the outgrowth throbbing with blood. He called her name, so that she understood that on the road they had now both taken – both, Sal emphasised – they were past the point of no return, and they had to soar together, blush together, and hide under the blanket at the end together. Upon hearing the name, the inert hand suddenly found its will and gently grasped the flesh undulating between its fingers.

Emi sighed. A few drops fell from her eyes, wetting Sal's T-shirt. But he didn't notice. With his other hand, he was stroking the crown of her head, her silken black hair, which he barely saw shining through his half-open eyes. What a dream! The girl in his arms wasn't the same girl he had played with for the last three years. The blooming breasts of the girl in his arms bulged through the linen dress, and everything about her was enticing him to discover more. There they were: round, with hardened nipples that prodded the tips of his fingers, almost wet with pleasure, almost speaking, although it was her mouth that uttered sounds, glued to his T-shirt like a suction valve. With her head buried in the soft cotton, Emi had no face anymore; the boy was left with nothing but a name he mechanically repeated and, the more it rang in his ears, the more aroused he felt and the greater his furious desire to turn her inside out... Not only did she no longer have a face, but the little girl had also grown curly hair hanging down to her shoulders and the pores of her skin had gaped and deepened, so now she was a giant embracing him and kissing his cheeks.

He pushed her away and struggled to take off her dress with a jerk that ripped it up the middle and left it in shreds on the floor. Emi was left in her white underpants, with a red print of cherries in a bunch. She was sitting in front of him with her round eyes gazing ahead, huddled up as if with cold though around them the air was burning. Her name reverberated mechanically another couple of times in the neatly ordered room her mother had taught her to keep clean and tidy. The hand was completely inside now, and in its palm laid the boy's penis, swollen and pulsating like a heart just removed from the chest: a vivid, outlandish piece of flesh. He grabbed her hand that was now stuck inertly to the fine skin and, with his own hand, guided it downward in a circular motion while releasing muffled sounds from his throat. His eyes were closed and his whole body had become an accordion.

Emi abandoned herself, curling around that unidentified sexual object that had seized all her boyfriend's power. It was growing huge and pulsating, and the girl's hand was led by the other hand that was in turn led by a will coming from another planet, from planet Radias! The hand was moving with so much strength now, nourished by the boy's sighs, that now the joints sent out a sharp pain to the torpid brain. She had to stop. Sal let out such a terrible grunt this time that it made even the lifeless things shake.

What was she doing? She wasn't allowed to stop now. With his free hand, he stroked her bare back on which the fuzz stood up rebelliously. Emi's wet hair had stuck to her temples; she looked at the disheartened boy. Before closing his eyes again he caught a glimpse of the bunch of red cherries, shining in the summer sun. Neither of them uttered a word, not even a sound, as his moans echoed in both their heads and her reluctance stood crushed between her will to break off and the the courage that had seized them to try it all at once, to go all the way with their exploration.

Sal put his penis between her legs and waited. He could hear her breathing heavily; she clung to him and gently rubbed her pelvis against him. He knew they were very close but, after a quarter of an hour, nothing else happened although they stayed in the same position.

Sal rolled over to one side and pulled on his shorts. He remained doubled up on the bed with his knees to his mouth. Emi was sitting on the floor, naked, with her tiny breasts breathing for her. It seemed to her that she was seeing the room for the first time, the room in which she had been living since she was born. The tidiness and the harmony surprised her: the books with *Ageless Stories* arranged soldierly on the shelf, the dolls sorted according to size and hair colour, the clock on the wall with its deafening ticking. But it was the linen dress, in the end, that made her come to her senses. She picked it up in a hurry and stuffed it in the wardrobe. Then she pulled her panties on and grabbed a Smurf T-shirt and a cotton skirt.

'What are you doing?'

'Getting dressed. What if my mother comes in and finds us like this?'

Sal stood up, hesitating. She wasn't looking at him anymore, and her coarse voice sounded scared. She didn't dare look at him again for fear that she would see, in his place, the shiny, pinkish penis prodding the air. Her body was struggling to recover its previous motions, its ease and its confidence.

Within seconds after they managed to get dressed, her mother's head, prim and fresh as for a festal occasion, peeked inquiringly through the half-open door. Why hurry away when they could first eat, drink lemonade, taste the apple cake in the fridge and only afterward plunge into the heat outside? The kids consented compliantly, and the mother left satisfied with her small victory, heading for the kitchen to set the table. Soon they could hear the clatter of dishes and the mother's voice, talking to the spices and dictating orders like an officer. Emi and Sal finally looked at each other, and Emi started to chatter serenely about insignificant things around them and make plans for the day ahead.

Sal stopped her before leaving the room. 'Nothing has changed between us, right?'

'Well, no, nothing really has. Nothing has changed at all, Sal – you are the same for me. And I hope this goes for you as well.'

Emi had one hand on the door handle and the other akimbo.

'What do you mean by *the same*? Does that mean we are still friends?'

'Exactly.'

75

'As in, we'll still tell each other our secrets? You'll come with me to Harry's basement and I'll show you what I found, and you'll call me up to the roof to spy next to you from now on? We'll laugh at the same jokes, and we'll keep hanging around in the afternoons starting at four? Is that what you mean by the same, Emi?'

'Exactly!'

'We will keep our habits and our places?'

Emi was frowning and looking away, chewing at her thoughts. 'What is that, *our places*? It sounds so metaphorical and pretentious. If someone overheard us, they would think we weren't speaking like children do. Especially you, Sal – you always speak like a grown-up. And you make me do the same. Listen to you! *Our places...*'

'Yes, the places we hide in, where everything is possible.'

His voice was trembling. He slid toward her like a snake, toward the girl leaning against the door who was careworn and petulant.

'And if you wish strongly enough for things to happen, despite all the hazards – actually, along with all the hazards in the world, with all the lies and deceptions – they will happen without you feeling any regret, although what they move in your world shall irretrievably ruin the equilibrium. Because your world is...'

Sal stared at her, touched by the way Emi was yielding to him and by the self-abnegation she showed in following him. Her mind was now troubled by doubt, by desire and by newly experienced sensations. She seemed to have stooped, trying to conceal the breasts showing through her T-shirt, to hide her boyish hips and straight, curveless legs beneath the inadequate clothes. Sex still fluttered its wings around them, and the boy's proximity made her retreat to her tiniest inner chamber, step by step, locking her padlocks.

'Your world is blind, just like love, and it's unaware,' he murmured with poetic intonation.

'And you are just the same,' she chimed in. 'I just warn you, Sal, do not change. That's all I'm going to say. Don't change and don't put on airs, for I will leave and you will never see me again.'

Sal burst into laughter. 'And you tell *me* I'm absurd! You're not going anywhere, because you love me and, even if you don't realise it, you will realise it very soon anyway.'

But he frowned the instant he spoke the words. A wave of coldness had risen ahead of him, freezing his very thoughts. Emi started to gesture and commanded him to get lost with a frosty voice that was incongruous with the situation. All of a sudden he threw himself at her feet, hugging them tight and imploring her not to send him away.

'Forgive me, forgive me, please. Actually, I should have told you that I love you and that I can't live without you. You are my Isolde.'

Emi relaxed. 'My God, Sal, the things you can make up! You spoil everything with a word and then say a lot of nonsense to fix what you've spoiled.'

They huddled, tired as after a very long day – although it was actually only beginning. Outside the door, the table had been laid with delicacies, and the caring woman who would watch them with wide eyes was waiting.

Before leaving the room, Sal cast a last nostalgic and regretful look at the small, hard bed, upon which he had lain with the singular thought of having a rest before setting out to search for the two strangers who seemed so unhappy. He beheld the room as an ultimate lost haven, the freshness and security of which he could never regain, for he would always be burdened by that memory that had nestled in their heads, and would remain there for so long.

'Do you think I don't know? We will change the moment we walk out this door,' Emi said, dragging Sal out of the room by the hand.

And the air inside rarefied.

IV

THE LONELY PLACE

The food slipped down their throats in tiny, hurried waves: the hors d'oeuvres on plastic, trident-shaped spears, the dumpling soup, the second course – an avalanche of mashed potatoes and pork steak pieces stuffed with thin wedges of bacon – and, finally, the apple cake, wrapped in caramelised sugar. They all sat in layers inside their stomachs, fuelling the thought factory. In the end, Emi sat up in her chair and decreed that if she took another bite, she would throw up. Her mother signalled discretely that she should mind her language in the presence of her guest. The wind had started blowing outside, after a voice with impeccable diction had announced high temperatures toward the end of the radio newscast.

'If the weather is nice, we can go to the outdoor cinema and watch a film,' Sal said, using the tip of his tongue to remove a piece of sponge cake from the corner of his mouth.

'You are so smart! And if Mum will give us some change, we can get two ice-creams,' Emi said lightly.

'When I was your age, I would play hopscotch,' her mother sighed, voicing a sensible yet bitter thought, for she knew too well that time worked in favour of the hidden desires she wasn't really willing to speak about, when the soul had just begun to ripen and the body was listening to other voices.

Emi was drumming her fingers against the doorjamb, calling Sal to part with his second piece of cake and hit the road. Sal, as in all the afternoons over the last three years, grabbed Emi's skirt and let himself be dragged slowly among junipers, among huge poppies bordering gardens enclosed by amber fences, by the roots of marigolds with plucked wings that grew back fluffier and more colourful. Sal was deeply inhaling the smell of dead plants and, page by page, leafing through the herbarium of the days they had been separated. Why would she, of all people, appear there, outstretched, like a raped odalisque, sprawled for contemplation?

'Do you think love is meant to be pure? I know that's what you believe.'

He thought more than that: love had to be concealed, never confessed, just lived. The aspiration for love was the only thing that really kept you at the surface – not even the aspiration for fulfilment, but the kind that is unaware of itself, like smelling out prey in the air. How could he have said that to her without irritating her and estranging her forever? Would she have understood that, by telling her those thoughts, he would unveil his most ardent wish: of staying together until their last gasp?

'Sal, where is your mind wandering?'

He dreamt of being able to snuggle on the bedcovers with her and of being forgotten, for a week or so of eating yoghurt and peanuts, telling stories, never visited by sleep. Since he had seen her lying on that table, pale and silent, he couldn't let go of her image and, even when they were together, he felt that longing grabbing his stomach like a claw.

'What are you thinking about?'

'You.'

Emi stuck the tip of her tongue out through her moist lips. 'I am not a *what*.'

The luminous trees, in the sunlight, were soldiers marking the way. It was a long time since they'd seen such splendour, for it lay enfolded in that boredom which was deaf and blind to all surroundings. The park gates opened in front of them.

'And how do you think when you think of me?' She was sitting on the kerb, stubbornly refusing to step inside the gardens until she got her answer.

'I think with fear.'

'Are you afraid of me?' Emi marvelled.

'No, I'm afraid something might happen to you.'

'Oh, Sal!' she burst out. 'You sure are a coward! You love to avoid difficult answers! Never mind.'

And she set out serenely, swirling the leaves around her. She hopped on the pied back of a butterfly, and they rose about thirty feet in the air above the giant grass. Emi combed the hair out of her eyes from time to time; Sal grabbed her waist and buried his face in her beautifully curved nape, on which the transparent fluff stood unravelled in expectation. On the ground, flowers clapped their petals upon seeing the two travellers. If only they could stay as they were now, embracing easefully, loitering and flying. Sal suddenly found himself philosophising again out loud,

'If you knew how many times I have been thinking about you, how many times I have seen you lying naked on the starched white sheets, sleeping after I had examined you and satisfied all my cravings and navigated, like a submarine... Why should I be lying to you?'

Emi leaned her head back. 'I have been thinking of you, too, but differently. I love you, but in another way...'

Children were playing on the lawn, shrieking with sharp voices that prodded the air from all directions. They looked happy and free, at any rate untended, for there was no eye concealed by thick lenses to admonish them. But their faces had a dull air, as if temporary freedom meant nothing, as if it were forever. One of them, a nine-year-old blond, a chubby and angelic imp, rushed to another and knocked him down in one motion, squeezing him under the white pads of his tender flesh. The fallen child tossed under the angel's weight, moaning and coughing, which brought happiness and delirium to the others' faces. One by one, they all jumped on top, making a tower of bodies. They laughed and thrashed about, as if swimming in a sea full of lather and ducklings and mothers whose extended arms were reaching out to catch them. The child at the bottom was lost under the cries of the riotous crowd. Emi was staring agape at the swarming construction.

'What are they doing to him?'

'Nothing, Emi, let's move on. Let's get out of the commotion.'

She followed Sal, who advanced along the park alleys like a rattlesnake. She could almost hear his hissing next to her ears.

'If your friends had jumped like that over me, crushing me under their weight, would you have saved me? Would you have taken me out of there? I think you would have let me suffocate.'

Sal started to tell her that she was wrong, but he stopped. Above their heads, trees were whispering with entwined branches. The alleys were empty, and from the balconies of the houses adjacent to the park they could even hear voices, music and Sunday noises. Sal sniffed the air like a hound. In front of them, a fat beetle was crawling slowly on the concrete, heading for a bench. Upon reaching it, it stopped, wagged its legs a couple of times, then disappeared in the thick greenery stretching up to the lake.

'I will never leave you. Why can't you understand that?' Sal's voice had come out faintly. 'You force me to make these phony-sounding statements. Do you really feel nothing of what's going on?'

Emi turned to him without answering. She measured him with her round, full gaze that could sometimes look so naïve. But Sal knew it wasn't naïveté. It was something else, undefined, a thought of hers that she never voiced; the same thought or different versions of it, blacker or more detached. She felt nothing of what was happening to them, just as he didn't manage to comprehend either, for things were terribly intricate. On a green-painted bench, he saw two bodies that were moving slowly, their faces melted together. From a distance, they looked like shadows thrown by the trees on the wooden beams. Sal took a few steps toward the two, but Emi remained still, admiring the lake.

'Isn't it beautiful? How about getting a boat and going for a ride?'

Sal turned around and threw her an impatient gaze. 'It's sunny. If we get a boat, the sun will beat us senseless.'

Emi smiled. 'You have started to hate me already! And it's been so little time compared to what lies ahead.'

Sal lunged forward and knocked her down in the grass. The girl tossed under his weight and her laughter mingled with the gurgles of the kids on the nearby lawn. He was touched; he felt he was melting above her with love. The boats were passing peacefully on the lake, and the grass rustled under the short gusts of wind that reached them from time to time. From far away they could hear the cries of a bird signalling to its sisters. While Sal's mouth was pacing the girl's neck, her body lay limp, periodically shaken by a shiver of pleasure.

'You won't change, will you? Promise me.'

And to carry on with his exploration down her neck, he promised.

'I won't change. And even if I were to change, I will only do it for you. Because you will ask me to. I will be altruistic and careful to guard against the things that could harm you. Is that all right?'

'What does altruistic mean?'

'Altruism is when you would die for someone and stand by them no matter what.'

'Huh. I thought it was something else.'

'No, that's what it is,' he lied, and nestled his face in the scoop between her neck and her collarbone. There was such a great smell there, a mix of fresh sweat and deodorant traces. He was pressing her with all his body; he had grabbed her hands and they were now swimming in the grass with generous motions, preparing to take wing. Soon, very soon, they would again see the park unfolding beneath them like an old map, animated by minuscule creatures.

'It's strange, but you should know, Emi, that all your worries are unnecessary.'

'Do you think so?' she piped.

'I'm sure.'

'Why do you think your parents don't like me?'

Sal blinked a couple of times, tickling her cheek with the tips of his eyelashes. 'It's not that they don't like you. I believe they just don't understand what's going on. That's what I think is the matter.' After a pause, he continued in a dark voice: 'They don't see the point of such a friendship. They'd rather see me spend more time with the boys, having more fun. They probably wish I made the same mischief as Max, for instance. As for you, they just can't figure you out.'

Emi sat up, letting Sal slide slowly into the grass. 'You sound as if something bad is going to happen.'

'It will. Not now, right away, but after some time.'

'What?' Emi sighed with a gloomy face.

Sal rolled on the grass until he was close to the border of the lake. He stretched his hands to the shiny surface and placed the tip of his index finger on the black mirror. The beetle was now advancing on the cement ledge, stopping from time to time and kicking his hind legs. Sal remained still, his face in the grass.

'Can you see those two people sitting on the bench to the right?'

Emi turned around and looked the way Sal had indicated. On the bench, the two figures sat estranged, with a small distance between them.

'I've seen them before. Yesterday. Actually, not only yesterday.'

'What do you mean?'

'Today, when I came to your place, I wanted to tell you about it. I've been bumping into them lately. I seem to know her from before, though it may only be a resemblance. They seem to be fighting, although they are always silent as they are now.'

Emi remained staring at the two. 'Do you think they are lovers?'

Sal rolled face-up. 'Why do you say that?'

'I don't know, the way they act. They seem to be afraid, like people who love each other, but they can't show it. Don't you think so?'

'You are so smart, Emi! You are right. And you put it very nicely. The fact is, I keep bumping into them. Actually, after I come across them, I get so sad the whole day.'

Emi got to her knees. Her body was swinging slowly from left to right. 'Let's follow them to see if I'm right.'

Sal closed his eyes, shaking his head. He no longer felt like following them; he felt great just lying on the spiny grass, with his ears tickled by the pleasant sound of the water rippling near his head and the breeze carrying the girl's smell to his nose from time to time. 'Wouldn't you rather stay here a little longer?'

But Emi was already on her feet far from him, mesmerised, like a butterfly noisily flapping its wings and spreading a coloured powder around him.

'Emi, come back,' Sal whispered and then fell.

But Emi was already lying in wait.

The man took her hand into his. He was relaxed and didn't appear to be thinking about what he was doing. He had made the gesture like a robot would, and now he was sitting with the inert hand in his lap, playing with the fingers that were falling, one by one, on invisible keys. She would look at him from time to time, scrutinising his face.

'What are you thinking about?'

He shivered. 'Nothing. Actually, it's something stupid. From our kitchen, you can see the kitchen of a woman living right across the street. We've been living there for six years, but I still haven't got the slightest clue as to what this woman even looks like. Her windowsill is full of flowers: cacti, geraniums, Zanzibar violas. Recently, she's also bought a *Monstera deliciosa* baby. I watch every day as its aerial roots grow more chaotically. She waters it incorrectly, more often than she should. But the baby plant is stronger. If it had been mature, it would have rotted right away, but young as it is, it sucks the water and laughs in the sun.'

She pulled her hand from his, and chillness set between them.

'What now? What have I said?'

'You didn't say anything. It's just that talking about your neighbor – about the kitchen from which you can see her flowers – seems very cruel to me. Have you thought that, although I try my best not to care, I don't like to hear things like that? About your house and about your neighbour?'

'I didn't mean to upset you!'

The man stood up and took a few theatrical steps. Her face had coarsened; it had become edgy, and her cheeks had hollowed in an unhappy grimace.

'If I were to judge by appearances, I would say that you're very unhappy with me.'

'How come?'

He noticed her uncommonly striking contours.

'What do you mean?'

'We both knew from the beginning how it would be.'

The woman released a sound, something between a sigh and

a cry, stirring the leaves around her. She doubled up and pressed her head between her arms, burying it in her lap.

'Will you please look at me when we talk?'

She shook her head. She didn't want to. *Monstera deliciosa*: that's what he had said a while before, serenely and detachedly, throwing his aerial tentacles toward her. She wanted to snuggle in the past and freeze time at a certain moment.

'You've changed a lot – I can barely recognise you! You have your own life; you haven't stalled, you have moved on, you have someone to work for, someone to earn and save money for, someone to make future plans for. While I... And you promised... I was stupid enough to believe you!'

He appeared to ponder her words. He stood in front of her with his arms hanging limply alongside his body, slouching in a helpless pose. He wished he could run off, disappear in a second and be spared having to confront her, with all her fury and her incriminations that he had no answer for. They had both known it from the start. Unlike her, he also knew that this moment would come, when all the words they had ever said to each other would turn against them.

She stood up and approached him, her eyes welling with tears. She grabbed the tips of his fingers, but they slipped away and she threw herself in his arms like a tragedienne. They were standing in the middle of the alley in a ridiculous and clumsy embrace. From behind them a beggar popped up, scrounging for some change; they parted uneasily and the man rummaged in his pockets for coins. She got herself together and fixed her clothes. Things were back to normal. She smiled at him half-heartedly. She didn't like scenes, but she couldn't help it. These were her last attempts, because she felt she was melting into thin air and he could not see her anymore. He was no longer willing to accept her and, even worse, he had developed some kind of defense against her foreign body.

'Forgive me, please...'

She tried to embrace him again, but he kept his distance.

'Please...'

'I can't keep defending myself all the time. If you are so unhappy, maybe we should break up.'

'No!'

How could he say words like these so easily? 'I don't want us to break up.'

'I think you haven't got the slightest idea what you want.'

He walked away, and she went after him, crying. All eyes were riveted upon them; everybody was watching them, some with an all-knowing grin, others feigning concern so as to feed themselves remorselessly on that amusing agony. She grabbed his elbow and clung to him in haste, imploring him to stay first in a low voice, then louder and louder, regardless of anything else.

'I'm not unhappy. That's nonsense. I swear I'm very happy.'

He looked at her as you would watch the grass from above, harbouring an abstract compassion for all the insects hiding below that you know nothing about. Love has a rough side that tramples on sophistication and shame.

In her haste, she lost a shoe and tripped. She made a few tiny steps forward in an attempt to keep her balance but eventually lost it and fell flat on the ground, then remained lying on the alley as if she had suddenly died. He walked along, leaving her behind. To see her like that was beyond anything that had happened between them so far. It was more important to understand how she was going to withstand the lonely nights, pondering and unwinding the film that would alter her common sense little by little. If he had looked, even for a split second, he would have seen a *Monstera deliciosa* drowned in too much water. But he wasn't cruel enough to leave her there, so he stopped and turned back, then helped her up by her arms, struggling to repress his urge to slap her smooth face, covered in pearly pink makeup that was glittering in the light. With his sweaty hands, he whisked the dust off her clothes as if she were a child and arranged her hair behind her ear before they continued to walk slowly along the alley. He was holding her elbow as if he wanted to make sure she wouldn't escape. They walked like that for a long time – drawing circles around the park, girdling it with magic rings – in silence, for the mere sound of words would have disturbed the already precarious equilibrium of those afternoon hours.

'Do you remember the lemon tree in my garden? The one we planted together?' she finally asked him in a coarse voice.

He shook his head.

'That's impossible. We sang incantations one night so that it would grow. Don't you remember?'

'No. Maybe you planted it after I left.'

'No, no, you left a year after the lemon tree died. I'm quite sure of that. You forgot. Anyway, a few days ago I bought one from the market.'

'Why?'

'I don't know. I guess I just wanted to feel that sour-green smell in the house.'

He stopped. Her face looked tired and all her features drooped, flowing downward and making her look older.

'When are you supposed to be back home?'

'I don't know. In an hour. Why?'

He didn't answer, because he had no idea why he had asked. He wished she would have said she had to go now. The questions in his mind reached hers in a strange way and then nestled there, tormenting her. There were different suspicions every day, and they would take shape and grow according to various signals she received from him or from around them. Every minute reality changed and, the more minutes passed, the more she expected to find an ogre at the other end who would gobble her lungs, pierce her chest and tear out her guts, wrap them around her neck and choke her with them, all the while watching her suffer and comforting her in his real voice with the same pompous words they used to speak long ago when no suspicion troubled them.

They had met again after more than twenty years. They were both standing, back to back, in a crowd of sweaty and impatient people by the counter of a downtown post office. Each of them was immersed in their own thoughts about what they were going to do that day. He was thinking especially about his daughters who were going to start school in autumn, although they already knew, at six, how to add and subtract, and occasionally they could also multiply if their father gave them simple numbers. They would read *The Little Prince* by themselves in the evenings, in two voices, and they wouldn't ask how children were made. He was charmed by his taciturn girls; he felt them threatened by the premature discoveries they would make on their own, and sometimes he was tempted to sound them out, to rummage through their minds, to find out how it worked. In the warm and humming post office, like an animal in whose belly they had all found refuge, he thought about his girls, who were more silly than brilliant.

It made him drowsy to lean on the backrest of the huge armchair, nicely dressed and wearing yellow shoes whose rubber soles, upon which you could still discern traces of a label with the number 33, squeaked at every move. He wanted to get out but, while he pushed his way through the crowd, he bumped into her face: almost paralysed with excitement and staring at him in disbelief, seeking assurance. They embraced and exchanged telephone numbers. Before long, she called him to confess how happy she was at their reunion. He added that his only regret was they had lost so many years without knowing a thing about one another. Yes, she said, carried away, especially as all this time she had often been thinking about him.

The hardest part was getting over the self-consciousness in the beginning. But once they went beyond it, the embarrassment of the reunion worked like an aphrodisiac, inebriating them. Not for a second was there any feeling of guilt toward their partners. They had found out from the first sentences that they were both married, and he had proudly added that he had two daughters. They laughed, congratulated each other with hypocrisy and immediately chased from their minds the details of their lives so far. They had to re-establish an order in the universe and, little by little, the order really started to be re-established. They weren't essentially taking anything that hadn't already been theirs before; that they hadn't been robbed of long ago. And now they were mending the abandoned machine and tying together the broken links.

Yet the pure relationship, overcast by vague purple clouds, had changed into an ordeal, a small-scale apocalypse, an *amor mundi*. 'It's all about the look you cast around you,' someone had said to them once, and someone else had sententiously proclaimed: 'Break-ups harden souls.' Now he would have told the first one that they were right and the second one that they were mistaken. 'Breaking up cannot nourish what we no longer have,' they both said to themselves and continued to see each other serenely, without the slightest shade of guilt.

She waited for his answer and, as it was slow in coming, she continued, 'But it's not mandatory. I mean, I can delay it. I can say that I had work to do in the office, which is true.'

He threw her an angry gaze. She said things like that with such serenity, as if she didn't realise. She complained that they were living like outlaws and that their lives were interlaced with lies, and a few minutes later she volunteered to make up stories only to stay together a bit longer. And this ceaseless swinging between two equally unreasonable extremes – between the reproach of not having had the life they deserved and the guilt of having to find subterfuges that humiliated them and made them feel cruel – exhausted him. He foresaw nothing good in the future. Where to search for happiness when it had ceased to exist for you?

'But then again, if I lied for so little, it would only do us harm. I would always think I did it for you and would later come to hold it against you.'

Sometimes he fancied he could hear her thoughts, as if she stood nestled in his mind and answered him with that air of superficial innocence. He wasn't sure she had really thought about him while they didn't see each other, but he had been thinking about her. The memory had grown, inflated from within like a bubble about to explode, and she had become different: many-faced, many-featured, with many personalities, all loved, adored and, in the end, loathed and punished. The game had repeated indefinitely, in the marital sheets, in the official postures, in respite, in their sleep and in their dreams. If he were to feel guilty, the guilt would be found there and not here, where solutions were simple and so familiar to them. He had even made up a defense speech in his mind. It was one of the overwhelming arguments prepared for Matilda: that betrayal had taken place long before it had been consumed and that the absurdity of it all resided right in these indisputable yet delusive and belated facts.

Today these facts no longer meant anything: that they were fucking like horny dogs in parks, afraid they would be found out, in cheap hotels neighbouring the railway station or on the outskirts of the city; at work or in the greenhouse where he grew his plants and took his daughters every week. Nothing of what they hadn't already accepted as inevitable could be disclosed. It was weird to acknowledge that their perceptions, albeit naïve, extended to all the other people around them. They were sure that witnesses lived with the notion that they were tied by the cause-and-effect chain, and that it wasn't out of the ordinary for them to be seen together, to touch one another in public or to behave more intimately with each other than normal, since their previous friendship seemed to condone this. They passed unnoticed; sometimes eliciting sympathy and other times envy for the fact that a friendship could be resumed after so long. The world around existed as a setting, an imitation of an abstract reality, a surrogate in which it was easy to leave the secret life exposed. This excessive and newly experienced freedom discouraged them at first. And later they had used it, in all its details that supplied them with alibis and covers.

'Last night I dreamt that I was home alone, lying down on the couch. There was a purple light in the room, and I just stayed anesthetised, overcome by fatigue. Suddenly, an image appeared on the TV screen, fuzzy at first. But after a few seconds I realised that it was actually me. I was speaking about us. I was very tense. I had on garish makeup; my lips were extremely red. I was recounting to the man in front of me, a dark-skinned midget of a man, how unhappy we had been together. I was amazed by the fact that he seemed interested in the story. I threatened to describe our relationship in the smallest details: I was telling him how you had left me although you promised not to; how, when we broke up, I had threatened to kill myself. Then I burst out crying. The midget tried to comfort me, but he kept this awkward smile on his face and, every now and again, he would turn and wink to the camera. I wished I could turn off the TV, but that deplorable image of my abandoned self kept me awake. In front of me, I could see a cunning and self-assured woman bearing my features and my name, collapsed with her head on a desk in a demonstration of agony. And although I loathed her, with her cheap clothes and her grotesque countenance, I somehow commiserated with her and wished to see her avenged. '

'So, it wasn't really us.'

'Yes, it was us, unfortunately. Our names and our bodies.'

'I find it strange.'

He stopped. The city unfolded before them. Only a few steps away, the greenery and the light disappeared. 'I find it strange that you chose to tell me about this dream now, of all moments. I understand it otherwise: you feel you are living promiscuously and you would do anything to escape.'

The woman grabbed the bottom of her dress. They had both calmed down; the argument had worn off and only its remains lingered now, scattered across the path of the park.

'Stop talking to me like that. You have no idea what's in my mind. I'm very tired now and I feel totally worn out. I think I have been too accommodating and that I'll soon hate you, because everything that I did today was entirely for you in order to protect your pride.'

On the balcony of a two-storey house with large arcades stood a man, his elbows leaning on the railing, absently contemplating the view. He was a famous actor and they both flinched when recognising him.

'Isn't it that actor...?'

'Yes, it's him. Although it looks as if it's just someone who resembles him. He looks better on TV.'

They waved to him, and he waved kind-heartedly in response. He acted as if he were on a steamboat, waving good-bye to relatives standing on the pier flapping their tear-soaked handkerchiefs, while they felt like travellers just having discovered a compatriot in a totally foreign country. They cheered up, as everything else around them had cheered up. The voices of the children remained behind them in the park, echoing over the vegetation, beyond the fences.

'If we had met that man on the street, you wouldn't have dared show you recognised him, would you?'

He laughed. She wasn't very brave herself, but her hidden glance, like that of an introverted girl, made her seem self-assured and contemptuous. 'If we had met, *he* would have looked at *you*, not me at him.'

'Nobody looks at me. Sometimes, when I walk on the street, I feel invisible. Most people look at me as if they didn't see me. I realise why they say that beauty comes from within.'

'What do you know? You are a fool. You are the most beautiful woman I have ever seen. And you have no idea.'

That was where the park ended. They had stepped beyond the safe zone. Cars buzzed by in smooth motion, slaloming around the marks that seemed like gigantic hopscotch courses made for adults. The playground was full; the cars came in all colours and shapes so that grownups didn't want for anything. They came with different horns, with leather interiors from which lifeless dummies breathed in the clean air ventilated from the outside in, while music filtered note after note out the exhaust pipes. The music rose up to the sky, but not very far, because halfway up it would evaporate into small particles that pricked the noses and eardrums of passersby. Confined in their beautifully smelling bubbles, the dummies would weigh their gestures, pull away and stop correctly, at statutory distances. The slightest deviation would have created chaos. But there was no deviation. Strung out on the road, nicely aligned, the coloured bubbles flowed before their eyes, making their way to mysterious destinations.

'I should take a bus from here.'

'I'll see you off.'

She threw him a distressed gaze. He only said it to be polite, because he knew that he couldn't see her off properly and that, even if he did see her off, he would only have extended that wearisomely endless day.

'No, no. You don't have to.'

She imagined how it would have been if, instead of parting at the bus stop, they had both climbed on the bus and rode together toward the same destination, had got off the bus in the same place, had headed the same way, on the same street, to the same house number, and at the door they had discovered that they had identical keys. Life together was rather what they shared now, she told herself, getting on the bus and watching the man left behind, looking at the vehicle that droned away with coloured array. She had an unsettling feeling of satisfaction, and she had no idea where it had come from. The secret, borne with such style, seemed less terrible. Buried among the people in the bus – some sweaty and fussing with their clothes, others clinging limply to the metal bars waiting for the next stop – it lost its power and became an ordinary secret. All the passengers of that bus had at least one similar secret.

At home, waiting for her husband, who always came on time or always called when he was late, their affair resumed its dramatic dimensions and had to be buried appropriately. She also had to prepare herself to endure the serene and carefree man from the moment he walked through the door, always cheerful before dinner and drowsy afterward, to the moment he left again the following morning. She heard the telephone ringing in the other room, but she didn't feel like getting out of bed. If there was a chance she would wake up and still be alone, then she preferred to find out later.

The telephone gave out another long buzz. Its sound was infinitely amplified by the overwhelming drowsiness that had seized her. Eventually, she woke up and struggled to her feet, groping for the receiver, guided by the tune.

'Did you get home safely?'

He almost never called her at home, so his voice gave her a start.

'I've been thinking that today has been a strange day for us. For me, at least, it has been a hard day.'

Now she wished she had stayed in bed and not answered the telephone. How could you choose? What time could you set your alarm clock for your life to take a good turn?

'I don't think we should talk about this anymore.'

There was silence at the other end of the line. Sometimes they would stay on the phone for minutes on end without talking. The first time she had felt tempted to fill the gaps with chit-chat, but in time she realised that it was enough to just breathe.

'Where are you calling from?'

'I've just arrived home myself.'

He couldn't have got there so quickly. He had to cross half the city and, even by taxi, it still would have taken him at least three quarters of an hour. And the fact that she had to imagine he was somewhere else, lying to her only to comfort her, drove her out of her mind. He did so only to make a full stop, to invoke her well-being, while in fact she would then have to chew it over, turn the events inside out and find explanations, and then accept the fact that he was somewhere else. For that, he deserved it if she hung up on him and didn't answer his calls for another week. She could already see him lurking round her building, watching the entrance, spying on her movements at the apartment's windows, shivering at night and sweating during the day.

'Next week, we're leaving for the seaside,' she said. 'I wanted you to know.'

'It's good you told me. We'll probably leave, too, but I don't know where and when yet. You should tell me the dates you'll be gone. But we'll talk again.'

'What do you mean, we'll talk again?'

'We might go at the same time as you or we might leave exactly when you're coming back, which would mean that we'll talk later.'

'And when will you find out?'

'I haven't got the slightest idea. It might be just a couple of days before, but that wouldn't help us. Maybe we should let things take their own course and see after that.'

'You drive me crazy. See *what*?'

'You make it sound as if I knew!'

'But then how can you say, 'Let things take their own course'? It seems cynical, to say the least, unless you want by all means to hurt me worse than you already did today.'

She felt him writhe and become shrewd at the other end of the line, where only he knew the truth. If she had hung up on him then, he would have continued to call, and that stupid tune – a piece by Bach, chosen by Matei – would have tingled in her ear, wearing her out. In the end, they would have been in the same situation they were in now.

When they had started seeing each other again, she made him promise solemnly that they would be honest. He had laughed and said that the last thing two people in love wanted was honesty. But she was careful to emphasise that what disgusted her most was that metamorphosis in people's behaviour when they suddenly became too intimate, because they knew each other so well to the finest creases of their bodies. It seemed to give them immeasurable freedom that could lead them to destroy the human before them, whom they had previously loved despite the distance. She didn't like love; she found it aggressive and incomprehensible, and it was because it was incomprehensible that people started to behave ignorantly, wishing to survive it. She assuredly watched him promise that everything between them would stay the same. And in that instant, when the words had flown off their lips, a straight and bewildering road opened before them: a road that seemed endless, even if endlessness was simply their wishes' fulfilment.

On that street they had roamed together a thousand times, from one end to the other, love seemed friendly and sincere – and so did the promises. She believed him especially because, ever since she had known him, all he said became true. His words really shaped reality; he was a wizard hidden inside a lonely and moping child. How could she not believe him? After such a long time, after years of searching for his face in crowds of people, after the lush dreams and the lonely nights, after regretting all that she hadn't said at a certain moment or all that she had hidden deeply, he had appeared out of the blue, just as she had given up hope.

'I would feel more comfortable if you told me when you leave and how long you're going to stay,' he insisted. 'You can ask. It seems a natural question to me.'

'It would be a natural question if it didn't come from you. I never requested that you ask anything on my behalf. You told me exactly what you thought appropriate, and I did my best to understand. It didn't kill me to not know what you did at the weekends or in the evenings or during the day when we didn't talk and didn't see each other. You'll have to deal with the same.'

'You're amplifying it. It won't help us to hide.'

'Well, it seems to me that it helped us so far. If it doesn't suit you, then I suggest that we let it all out! Let's tell the others the truth!'

'Oh, dear,' he sighed. 'When did we start bringing the others into our conversations? Actually, the more I think about it, the more I realise it was impossible for this to turn out differently.'

Now was the moment for them to say all that they hadn't managed to tell each other throughout the day. It seemed that one of them wanted to receive what the other couldn't possibly offer. And there also was that constant feeling of dissatisfaction, of a promise that was fading day by day, worn out from their playing with it.

'As far as I'm concerned, you can call me and ask me where I am or what I am doing anytime. You are free to tell me whatever crosses your mind. You are the only one to constantly remind me that we need to behave. Come on, drop it – didn't we argue enough today?'

Nothing could be heard any more from beyond the receiver, not even breath.

'Are you still there?'

The answer came from a choking voice that struggled to repress its trembling. 'Tomorrow at four, as usual. All right?'

She could have said no. She had the feeling that, if they had chosen a different hour, they both would have ended up groping in the dark and everything would have come easily apart, as if they had woken from a dream.

'Yes, it's all right.'

'Are you going to bed now?'

'I don't know. Maybe I'll read something before I do. I had fallen asleep when the phone rang. I have no idea what time it is.'

'It's nine. We separated four hours ago.'

'Four hours. Then I must have slept. I had the feeling I had barely closed my eyes...'

'Good night.'

A bluish fog floated into the house. There was a single table lamp on in the living room, its light filtering through the slits. She cautiously opened the door and looked around the room. The TV set was turned off, its remote control neatly placed on the coffee table in front of the couch. All objects waited inertly for the return of their owners. She went on with her inspection: in the kitchen, in the remaining rooms, in the pantry, in the bathroom. She was still alone.

She could have sworn that she had only fallen asleep for a few minutes. This meant that it was sheer luck that she hadn't been found out and, deep inside, she was angry that things had not taken another turn. No sooner had she finished her thought than she heard the key turn a couple of times in the front door lock, with that monotone noisy snap. The smell of cologne rushed in, invading her nostrils. A big man entered the room, rattling a big bunch of keys in his hand.

'I've been calling over and over, but the line was busy.'

He drew near and squeezed her in his arms. She relaxed. Her weariness showed, but she smiled like a saleswoman trained to sell her goods. She watched herself from the outside and loathed it.

'I don't know what to say. I've been sleeping.'

Matei left the living room and she followed him, thinking of what she had just said. Her words had echoed as if in a bottomless cave. When they had moved into the house, ten years before, everything seemed to invite happiness. They had arranged it all according to her taste, according to her extreme attention to detail.

Each corner of the bright rooms, painted in different colours, had been imaginatively enhanced. It had taken her half a year to decorate the whole house, during which they migrated from one room to another, as they were finished. His patience and her passion had pleasantly enlivened the place so that, when all of the work was finished, they had both sighed in relief and lounged on the uncomfortable couches in the living room, thinking that, from that moment on, *at home* had acquired a new meaning for them. 'At home' was a cabinet with lots of precious and useless shiny objects on display, a meeting place in which movements needed to be adjusted so that they didn't disturb the objects.

When you are poor, you dream of wealth is like this simple sandwich that beckons to you from beyond the TV screen, and when you are unhappy, happiness is this suckling pig stuffed with delicacies from which you eat continuously and never satiate yourself. And when poverty is replaced by wealth, you get the idea that you are a step away from being wealthy *and* happy too. Their home was the sandwich she had eaten without any appetite. She had been chewing on it for ten years. Now, as time went by, that dream of endlessness was becoming a tiny, personal nightmare, about which there was no one to complain to. The rooms had worn out in time, the order had been disturbed and the initial neatness had faded. The furniture was scratched, the sofas had lint on the edges, the fibre of the carpets had thinned, and objects had chipped or broken or been lost. Eventually, she came to think that nothing lasts forever and that, once objects wore out and even disappeared, your habits, and even the life you lived would disappear as well. You start a regression back to the time before the reality you built. But it hadn't happened exactly like that.

All that was left of the sulky girl was a discontented woman. Over ten years, she had built herself an elaborate history made up of conflicting parts. Her mother represented a part, her father the other. Her father was more visible and more spectacular, while her mother withered day after day, the exact opposite of what happened in real life. The stories came and went like the tide, and she would dress up and embellish some of them so that the whole picture didn't look gaudy. Matei would sit and listen, and the image of the woman standing before him achieved more sophisticated shades, the light falling at different angles that she frugally left exposed to view. Habit insinuated itself between them, one way or another, along with the stories: the TV set glowed upon their faces every evening, providing them with new conversation topics, and they would have fed it nectar and ambrosia, as if it were a god, only to keep it on. Spending weekends away and planning holidays twice a year took up an important space, preceded by intentions and followed by solutions and ideas – the weekly shopping, the small presents he bought her, the bills – which provided continuity and bore witness to their united life.

You can't even tell when a face becomes that familiar, overlapping with your own. In ten years, their faces had come to look subtly alike, borrowing from one another's countenances, reflecting the lines. Yet the more striking the reflection was, the bigger the differences were as well. As years went by, they would count them like butterfly collectors, happy to complete their panoply with another exhibit pinned in the collection. During her childhood, she had owned a herbarium in which she pressed all sorts of flowers she had picked in parks, the Botanical Gardens, on trips to the mountains with her parents or just from neighbours' flowerpots. She had arranged them in alphabetical order according to their scientific names, accumulated tirelessly after befriending a caretaker in the greenhouse in Liberty Park. The caretaker looked like the hunchback of Notre Dame, just as the greenhouse itself looked more like a cathedral in which the religiously grown plants – kept at optimal temperatures, preserved, well nurtured and taken care of – seemed to be more a mummification of the former creatures through which sap used to flow and which now were but relics for freaks to come and pray by.

Beside the fact that, in summer, it was pleasant to sit there and admire the exhibits with exotic names she had learnt by heart – *Ranunculus acris, Anemone nemorosa, Helleborus purpurascens, Pulsatilla montana, Levisticum officinale, Papaver somniferum, Lunaria rediviva, Syringa vulgaris, Atropa belladonna, Centaurea cyanus, Lilium cadidum* – the mornings she spent in the greenhouse were surrounded by the mist of sacredly kept secrets. For her, it had been like training for later life when the secrets would diversify, become more serious and more important. By then, the herbarium with pressed flowers would have already rotted in the basement of her parents' house. She had no reason to complain, because in the ten years that had passed, her thoughts hadn't been spoiled, maybe only benumbed, while the people she had met, the roads she had travelled, the places she had been were enshrined in her mind like a holiday photo album.

How long does it take for a plant to die when its light is cut off and nobody waters it or speaks to it any longer? The hunchback had told her, and she had checked for herself on the border of the brackish water of the lake in Liberty Park, that if you know how to speak to them, plants have their methods of answering and of showing you their love. Since that moment, she had begun to murmur all her secrets to their stalks, all the experiences of her day, whether great or small. At the greenhouse, she had even started a diary divided according to subject, days of the week and times of the day. She kept talking to them like that until one day when she decided to stop talking to them completely. She suddenly deserted them because she had nothing left to tell them. She deserted them out of sheer selfishness and the plants withered away – though not as fast as she had thought, but much slower, over time, tormenting her and haunting her nights.

When they ran into one another again, in the crowded post office in which sweaty, over familiar people were jostling against each other, she had locked those ten years in a greenhouse com - partment. Now she was afraid to go there and find that they were dead.

'When do you want us to leave on vacation?'

The words had flown solitarily across the room. Matei was seated at the table eating greedily, moving his jaws and the whole bone structure of his face in a reassuring, albeit mechanical, sign of life. It took him several minutes to answer.

'I don't know. I was thinking that, if we want to go both to the seaside and to the mountains, we should leave for the seaside next week, maybe go to a more secluded place, and then we can plan ahead at leisure. At the moment, the seaside is the problem; the rest will work out easily.'

She had listened to the answer without thinking. She found it incredible that she had asked. She was trying to trace within her the broken stitches the words had escaped through, but it was impossible for her to examine herself now. She could feel the tears rushing in her throat, but she swallowed a few times and managed to hold them back.

'So, next week it shall be.'

It was a statement, but it had sounded like a question.

'Yes, that's what I say. Did you want something else?'

She shook her head. Suddenly, an unforeseen feeling of relief took hold of her; the thought of their leaving made her inexplicably happy. She almost felt like hugging him. The cologne smell in the room had faded. She took a deep breath and leaned back. The dim evening light had mellowed her as well. She watched her husband eating composedly, his head bent over the plate. His face, carved in that slanting position upon which light fell partially disfiguring him, was the face of a monster. The park was rustling behind him and the trees had entwined their branches, whispering up above. She startled. What if he could hear them, too? What if he heard what they were saying?

'Emi, let's leave.'

Emi turned to Sal, whose face was drowsy. She let out a stifled chuckle and scuttled away on the alley that wound among the green hedges.

V

SUN ALLEY

Sorin Alexandru Lemnaru, or Sal as his friends called him, was born at two o'clock in the afternoon. His mother was in the labour room for a week. The doctors looked sceptically at her from behind their white masks, shaking their heads. At the end of the seven days, an overweight, cyanotic and very silent baby emerged. Some find it utterly inappropriate to talk about things like that, but for Sal entering the world was painfully connected to a lot of noise and a very long wait. They say that after so much time, salty water becomes bittersweet and life turns into death. But any generalisation may be hazardous when it comes to extracting the known from the unknown, all the more so because the way back has proved equally dangerous. After another seven days, Sal came home to the house on Sun Alley carried by two sturdy arms and, from that moment on, the world was immersed in dreams and mystery.

Strange, amber-faced creatures crept into the dark universe. Gilded tadpoles, with the innards of their translucent bodies illuminated. You would only need to grab their split tails to wander through the darkness in which the occasional figure would appear from time to time, although the darkness was more like a steam, diffusing in the compact matter; a humid heat would whip you, alternating with a chilliness that clung to your body like cellophane. Glowing, hot circles, chained to one another, flew on both sides, fading into a lilac-coloured horizon. The smell of rain and wet hair pervaded everything, although the dry atmosphere paralysed the breath and arrested any movement, throwing you into an inanimate agony which touched not the inside, but the surfaces.

The touch itself prompted hundreds of thousands of millions of other touches, and their sharpness penetrated the epidermis, piercing every millimetre with painful sensations. From a certain moment, which could not be recorded, the circles became very slightly deformed, breaking the harmony. Although they remained in their places for a while, regenerating and multiplying apparently endlessly, they finally betrayed their exhaustion. Soon, that tender abandon would become an expanse occupied to its fluid borders; an interior territory collapsed over reality or over what would later generate a reality consisting of ticking, sleep and wakefulness, sweat, pilosity, panic and fear. It would be followed by groping in the dark and by the transition into another state, similar to bliss, but disturbed by falls and leaps and smells running through the whole body, by weird outgrowths protruding through the skin like knives prodding the sour air, and then by boulders tumbling down, pushed by a fleshy mass from an abstract point and set in motion by noises. The possibility of leaving a spot, moving in a straight line, and returning to the same place. To see the other end exactly as it is, but to nonetheless cross through full of hope.

The sounds were burning. And sometimes, there was a bizarre regression in the darkness he had come from; translucent waves, through which immobilised limbs struggled to advance, threatened the slippery being that took refuge inside, screaming in terror. During the perfumed sieges that spread the fear of the end around them, you would hear strange cries; the faces would trickle through the liquid, through the wet transparency that was either cold or too hot, while beyond them the starry darkness smiled through a silent disco and the coloured sequins twinkled within, blinking in solitude and revealing the flesh that quivered in shame, touched by the luminous petals of the rainbow.

'Ssssssssssal! Ssssssssssal! Ssssssssssal!'

A monochrome thread crept peacefully among the kaleidoscopic pieces and the bubbles gurgling on the illusory surface, breathing through the lung-body; it made the darkness open up and start pulsating, made it sonorous and fluid.

'Ssssssssssal!'

The sound goes round, haloing the skull, while the mist dissipates further, pervading the two caves and then going full circle, knotting its ends.

'Ssssssssssal!'

After the whirlpool drags you for an angstrom or so, you remain nailed because the attraction of the fractions is so strong. Each growing part, in ceaseless expansion, hangs down with the weight of death. You go back in your mind to see your point of departure, but once the image has vanished, its memory disappears as well. You are suspended between spaces, and time flows disproportionately.

'Ssssssssssal!'

Then, every now and again, passages would open. But you could hardly see anything because the luminous spots became blinding, their brightness preventing you from distinguishing beyond their own outlines. The light, dividing the fractals and the quarks, released a callous and lazy smell. It was followed by a furnace-like heat and incandescent vicinities. They would splutter and smoke and cry out for the giant tubes reaching for the water strip suspended in the void. The stifled, thick sounds would tumble down again from over the huge blanket of oily liquid, kneading it and blending the small being into a dense layer that rendered it immobile. And then the raucous sounds would change into hoarseness, into gnashing, and the epidermis would stretch like plastic film, buzzing over the whole atmosphere and rarefying it.

And all the while the breath would weaken, because the silence around acquired a pasty consistency and the motions made gruelling sounds, like spoilt musical instruments with snapped strings and broken parts. It was the music of the inside, and the creatures populating it were identical, continuous and translucent, as no being can ever be in reality. But that breath pounding in your eardrums was the blind and empty outline, and while the sounds projected naïve drawings on the bed of cumulus gathered in the yawning globes, the feeling of closeness would attract celestial shapes. Mimosas gaping in astonishment, their mouths rounded in perfect, incandescent Os, would throw out flames as if heaven's gates had opened and it was through them that the diurnal wonders would spill out.

The voice trickled along the ears, like dry molasses, and

penetrated the words that were nothing more than the cry of the lonesome rhymester.

'Ssssssssssa!'

He was turning on the tips of his toes and the motion hurt, ringing out in the atmosphere and shattering the density. But, as it had been foreseen, the turn had shifted the balance and the painful outgrowths were now protruding from their ethereal picture. It wasn't easy to cover the distances in such a short time, all the more so as praise would have awaited you at their far end. But the love of life that brings together all creatures changes obstacles into anthills and disgust into tolerance, all because the parts stay in love forever. The surroundings acquire a mottled colour and, thus, the uproar becomes tired.

One at a time, the pieces come together, calmly, repetitively, reiterating the same swaying motion. The void regenerates as it flows out and the particles gather back together. The distances contract and life becomes even in time. You can measure it in your mind, however unbearable that might be. Measuring has an endless appeal. And the sounds become light steam, utterly vanishing. You yield to this boredom which you call infinite, although the name is just the frivolity of a myope, articulated in order to tame the beast repeating, 'Why? Why? Why?' like a blunt child.

It would draw near and move away, like a cold snake, like a series of numbers in endless arrays, always different. Scary and hard to grasp. Although what appeared was only the memory of the bygone fear, the astonishing avalanche was now breathtaking. It was fracturing time, cutting it in two. What-had-been in the mirror of what-was-no-more, generating its missing image and its memories of itself, that would be lost later when everything fell into regular shapes. The sounds had mellowed and lost part of their weight. They were delayed in reaching the huge ear that covered the body like a funnel. The ear had become larger than the universe and stood stiff and alert, shaped like a carnivorous flower ready to swallow the small insect on its gaudy petal. The size and the shadow of the funnel prevented the rest from growing, from releasing the sounds that would have saved it from solitude.

The perpetual noise nurtured the animal giving birth to the endless arrays of numbers in the huge cave. It looked like it would never end. It would sever the chain with its shiny blade reflecting the monstrosities and then they increased and decreased at will, with the tenacity of termites. At the end of a long waiting, a bud opened, and from it rose the sun with its rosy petals. Spiralled and demure, fluttering their volatile wings, they quickly spread their smell around. He followed that strong, deafening smell and let himself slide on that slime-covered chute, heading toward the shapes that had now started to connect.

He had almost fallen asleep – with his eyelids welded shut and his eyelashes entwined, the tears inside had formed a lake on the border of which he now stood dreamily, watching the vines move slowly, bubbling – when the first creature appeared on the horizon. It was something he could recognise, although he saw it now for the first time: an arched, continuous and motionless line, a shape that attracted him more than all the previous illusions. The siege of the shape, squeezing him now like an enormous whorl, left him breathless. As he struggled to inflate the hollow pillows in his chest with oxygen, he could see it better: it resembled him and was suffocated by his presence, but it just hadn't managed to hold on. It had dropped from his yet unformed hands all the infinite rows of numbers and now it lay, lifelessly, at his feet.

VI

THE CITY OF PERENNIAL PLANTS

Harry's building rose menacingly in front of the two children, who were beaming with excitement. Above them, the clouds had formed a wreath of filthy cotton wool covered in fine dust. The wind was blowing around their feet, knotting their footsteps. They stayed in place, their eyes riveted upon the iron door with latticework that resembled the patterning on Linzer cookies. From behind the door came muffled noises, as if all the things hidden in that building, ideas both said and unsaid, had gathered together and were waiting to be unfettered. Their eyes twinkled in the darkness that had now pushed the day away, and in the surrounding fog one could still spot traces of withered sunbeams. Emi took the first step toward the door and turned around to face Sal. Her round face gleamed faintly in the grey, rarefied air.

'What do we do now?'

She had asked the question as if it depended on him whether they would go inside Harry's building or not.

'Do you have the ring with you?'

Emi took a step back. She looked at him for a split second, trying to read the right answer on his face. The truth was that she didn't have it.

'I left it at home. It's too large; it falls off my finger. Did you want it back?'

Sal grabbed her hand and dragged her along. He opened the iron door and squeezed into the lobby. The smell inside had changed: it was pungent now, making his eyes sting. Emi had the sullen air of a child that had just been woken. She watched him, expecting him to show her something spectacular worth the suspense. Still holding her hand, Sal could feel her shaking. They arrived like that at the door that led to the basement. Stifled noises came from the staircase, differing in sonority and intensity: some from the inside, others clearer and with an echo, coming from outside. All seemed meant to maintain the unbending illusion of reality.

After opening the door, Sal relaxed a little. He no longer felt his heart pounding in his chest, nor his eardrums throbbing, nor his blood pulsating in his arteries ready to make them explode. He relaxed from the cool air coming from below, or maybe from the damp hand of the girl who had gone silent behind him, or maybe because he was no longer alone.

They stopped at the top of the stairs. They were blinking frequently, trying to gradually get used to the dark. Then they began to descend. He was glad that Emi had left the ring at home, although he didn't understand where that relief came from. He wasn't superstitious: he didn't take three steps backward whenever a black cat crossed his way, he didn't believe that fulfilment of wishes came from eyelashes fallen on the cheek and he didn't knock on wood or make crosses with his tongue on the roof of his mouth. He wasn't even terrified of seeing the woman lying on the table again. He was only worried about how Emi might react upon seeing her: he even imagined her running away, disappearing helter-skelter and refusing to see him ever again for being a freak who busied himself with digging out corpses. He stopped.

'Are you sure you want to see her?'

White as a sheet, Emi's face beamed in the dark. He felt pity for her. She was squeezing his hand with so much strength that she was about to crush his bones.

'Yes, I am.'

He had watched her mouth, but didn't perceive any movement of her lips; no waft of air, however small, had blown his way. Emi's pale, round face glowed like a motionless and silent full moon. Nonetheless, he had clearly heard the determined, unflinching, almost inhuman voice. She was in front of him but, with all the fear inside her, she seemed half asleep.

Downstairs, they could hear nothing but their own breath. They advanced with caution. This time, Sal counted the doors in his mind. The last door was still attached to the broken padlock, a little ajar. He stopped outside it, staring through the slit, but couldn't see anything through it. He felt scared for Emi again. She was quiet; he hadn't even noticed when she had pulled her hand out of his. They entered the room and stopped in the semidarkness.

'Sal.'

He turned round and grabbed her fingers again. She was reserved now and self-controlled. Her touch contained something vigorous; the moment they had stepped over the threshold of the room, the girl behind him had changed into a monstrous and authoritative creature. Her face was sparkling.

'Is that all?'

He pricked up his ears. Down by his feet, a cold draught wriggled around their ankles. He wanted to ask Emi if she could feel it too, but he stopped himself short. Although he couldn't distinguish clearly around him yet, he had a growing certitude that if he had closed his eyes for a second, he would have discovered that the dissection table and the room were empty and that nothing, of all he had seen, existed anymore. His heartbeats accelerated and he felt a claw at his throat, choking him.

Rummaging through his pocket, he found the small flashlight he had meticulously taken with him upon leaving home. He turned it on mechanically, trying to shake the fear off, then turned around and accidentally pointed the thin beam of light at Emi's face so it trickled down to her like a trail of smoke. She was smiling, serene and relaxed. The shadows furrowing her cheek on one side made her look older; her curly, cropped hair made her look like a thistle in the artificial light. *Centaurea calcitrapa.*

Sal burst into laughter. His roars hit the empty walls, making a grim sound. He ran the flashlight around the room, furrowing the walls with the beam and revealing small areas. Sal's hand was shaking impatiently, and he handled the flashlight as in a sort of dance, as gymnasts would handle the ribbons. Then, when the performer had settled down a bit, the fragments came together and the first shapes emerged from the darkness almost unaided: the corners of the table, the metal pane reflecting the surrounding light, the boxes piled up in a corner of the room, the perches in another corner, buckets of dry paint with glued mason's brushes inside, three plastic chairs stacked one on top of the other. He turned again to the table and, just to be sure, he swept the light over it one more time. Only a few seconds before, the absence of the corpse, however troubling, had made him recover his peace, but now a tiny midget had grown out of the cold and empty surface and lay crucified on the table. He was dumbfounded. He turned off the flashlight to be able to think, unseen.

'Emi,' he said, in a choking voice.

He heard rustling and a stifled giggle. He turned the flashlight on again and saw Emi, perched upon the table, amused.

'So, is that all?'

He could feel the blood throbbing in his temples. This time, he had only been afraid on her behalf. The fact that something could happen to Emi froze his heart and made him lose his temper.

'This is so not funny!'

'Did I scare you?'

Sal leaned back against the wall and pointed the torch at her face. He didn't have the heart to leave her there alone, although she deserved it. He tried to get a grip on himself, to gather his strength and find his words. He was going to tell her something, something important for both of them; he was going to make a pretty difficult announcement. He had been thinking a lot about the best moment to do so, had pondered upon the introduction and upon how he was going to continue once astonishment and pain had started to mingle on her face. He also had a solution, but he planned to let her in on it later after watching her reaction and feeding on her emotions for a while.

Emi put a hand before her eyes, signalling that the light was disturbing her. 'Please could you turn that shit off?'

Sal put the flashlight on the table. 'Come. Climb here next to me.'

Emi enjoyed bossing people around. Yet Sal felt no trace of humiliation or surrender when he humoured her, just as he did now, by going over and climbing half-heartedly on the cold pane next to her. He felt that her wishes mysteriously matched his yet unspoken desires. Maybe it was just their strong connection that explained everything, making him feel that they actually had identical wishes. It was hard to say. He could feel her next to him now, reclining on the table with the same voluptuousness with which she would lie on a blanket in the sun. She was a loafer with fits of authority, and he knew how crazy it was to listen to her unquestioningly. But he would still lend his charmed ear, as he was doing now.

'Maybe you will say that I'm crazy, but although there is nobody here, I *know* that there was someone. I mean, I believe you when you say you saw someone.'

Sal listened to her carefully, then heard her burst into laughter.

'What the hell?'

'So you don't believe me...'

'I'd like to, but I can't because of the wound on my calf.'

'Your what?'

She ran wild like a hurricane, disappointed that she hadn't seen what she expected to see: what she had been promised she would see, what she privately started to feel belonged to her. She sharpened her thin beak at once to peck at the flesh around his eyes and his mouth, making him bleed in silence next to her.

'Look, I have the feeling that I'm boring you.'

Sal didn't answer right away. He suspected it was another game, but he felt her tense.

'I think,' Emi went on, 'that since those things happened between us, you've drifted away from me.'

'What things?'

But as soon as he asked the question, Sal realised what she meant. 'Those things' were the issue. And all that he was going to say would only confirm to Emi her theory: that he had found a solution to get away.

'There is something I need to tell you,' his voice croaked.

He didn't mean to start like that, but the words had just come out. He was bothered by the sepulchral silence around them; he wished he could hear at least the sounds of the building, some sign of life that would make his story more humane and less dramatic. She gaped at him, the shadows making her look like an aged child. She wondered if he would love her as much if she were wrinkled, with dark circles under her eyes and a puffy face. Fat worms would probably creep into her skin some day, sucking out her youth, her freshness and her poise.

Poise was a word his grandmother would use. When referring to a woman she admired, the synonym for beauty was *poise* – which probably meant a lot of things apart from physical features, since upon uttering it, his grandmother would straighten her back, sway her hips, push her chest out and simultaneously bring together all five shrivelled fingers on her right hand. It was as if she wanted to say that although she spoke a simple word, she actually had in mind five ingredients, five magic potions whose formula was known by no one but her. When she would see Emi withered, she would open her fingers and let all her secrets fall through them.

'I have been thinking about the best way for me to tell you this. If I start with the beginning, you will link my words to what you said to me earlier. And it would be wrong. We would fight, and then I probably wouldn't get to tell you the end of the story. So I will start with the end.'

He took a break and moistened his dry lips.

'Long story short, we must run away.'

He took her hand again, but he felt some resistance, so he squeezed it tighter.

'We must run.'

Once he was under the impression that he had things under control, he started to tell her that his father had recently informed him that they would be leaving the neighbourhood and moving to another place, that his mother was going to have another baby, a brother or sister for him, and that consequently they would need another room. Furthermore, his father had been happy: this meant Sal would be able to make new friends, diversify his activities and find new conversation topics, because now he was excessively silent, had no visitors at home and hung around with girls – and when his father said 'girls', he had a look on his face that implied that they both knew to whom he was referring. He had advised Sal to begin saying goodbye, little by little, to all his acquaintances in the following month. 'That's the appropriate way,' his father had added. From that, Sal inferred that their new house was too far away for him to keep seeing his friends or for them to spend time together.

He had been thinking for a week about what to do, and finally he had an idea. He couldn't understand how he hadn't thought about it from the very start. It was simple and doable. To run away together. Their good behaviour so far, the silence his father complained about, the conformity and the sacredly respected curfews would be their cover. Nobody would suspect anything beforehand because they would do it all according to their daily schedule. Money was not an issue: he was going to snatch all the money his father had in his wallet that day, and they would go from there. The plan was to get on the first tram that came to their stop and get off one stop before the terminal, then take a bus in a totally different direction from where they had come and get off, again, one stop before the terminal.

'And where will we end up?'

Sal shrugged. He had no idea, and it was all for the better. He couldn't have said where they were heading, even if someone had tortured him. He could only have said that they were heading for freedom, that their flight was the tunnel that would lead them out of the cell where they were held captive, and that the only alternative was life in hell. After showing their concern about the fact that he was seeing Emi too often, his parents had told him compassionately that love would come much later and that for now he should enjoy childhood and the company of his friends. They had a condescension that enveloped them like armour and prevented them, at the same time, from seeing and acknowledging reality. The look on their faces told him: 'Shut up! We know better than you do what love is. This relationship is a piece of kids' nonsense – your minds have become infested with things you can no longer handle. We know better what love is about. Can't you see? Look at us!'

He had been unhappy and morose all day long. For the first time, it had crossed his mind that maybe it would be better if he were one day to wake up to an empty house and hear his voice hit the walls of the rooms with an echo. Then he would grab the telephone and call Emi over. They would lock themselves inside and then live happily ever after. Now he understood perfectly that something like that was no longer possible. It was out of the question for him to wait for a miracle. The moment they had informed him that they would move house, it had been clear that it was all up to him and that, if he didn't make a decision soon, everything would be gone.

Emi asked him once again: 'And where will we end up?'

The truth is that she couldn't decide whether to trust Sal or not. Her mother had taught her that you should never believe what boys told you, because every one of them wanted a certain thing, and that, if you could afford to have relationships, the secret of their success was to be cool and indifferent. Now she was forced to make a decision that would upend her beliefs.

It crossed her mind that it might be cheap histrionics through which Sal was making her open up her soul, so that he could laugh at her afterward. But when had he done something like that before? Never. He had never given her reasons to doubt not only his friendship, but also the love that floated around their every meeting. Why, then, was he forcing her to do crazy things, things that would cost them the freedom of seeing each other and hanging around together? She wished she could consent and then grab his hand and pull him down to lie beside her. They could fall together into that reassuring darkness. Compared to the words that had been uttered, the darkness had become friendly and safe. She wished they could stay on a little, to settle down and to keep the silence untouched.

'Emi, you do want to go away with me, don't you?'

At that moment, they heard a rustle outside the door to the basement as if someone stood there listening to their conversation. It was the first time they felt the proximity of a living presence and, however unpleasant the presumption that their words had been heard, it was better than the certainty that they would remain there alone and estranged. He held her tight. He wished he could drip the will to leave into her pores, induce all his energy and the clarity with which he saw the situation they were in. He also wanted her to understand that, although he didn't like to say it to her all the time and use too many words, he loved her in his own way; he felt like squeezing her palm into his and feeling her sweat moistening his skin.

'You have to tell me now: do you want to come with me, or are you staying here?'

This time, they heard a more distinct sound from the corridor. It was the sound of somebody's footsteps, groping along outside as they had done. A door opened, very close to their door. They were surrounded by life, and the silence around them had broken. They had to go.

Sal climbed down from the table. He fondled its surface, still hot from their bodies, and then took a couple of steps back. He was waiting for her to answer, although he knew that the world frightened her and that her uncertainty, so cleverly disguised in fits of rebellion, usually overturned her heroic decisions. And so he would have happily delayed the moment. Love was not enough. He knew that, if Emi had had to endure the disapproving looks of adults and friends, she would have locked herself inside her room, would have suffered for a few days and would have come out tamed and helpless.

He put his ear to the door. The noises had died out, which meant that they could come out from the room. He turned to Emi. There was nothing left of her but a thin shadow, sweeping the walls as it moved. She approached him insubstantially, as if swallowed by air, until she clung to him. He could smell her breath, like the odour of rotten apples. He wanted to hold her in his arms, but his fingers stopped in midair and remained sprawled, as in a pantomime. She was before him, and yet she was immaterial. It was an optical illusion: Emi was still up on the dissection table, while the shapes brought to life in the room were the projections of an incandescent globe.

'If you think that's what we should do...'

Her voice had a faraway sound, coming from behind the palms that covered her face.

'And, if it were so, I would at least want to know where we're going, where we're going to stay. It might be easy for you to say, but one day you might want to return home, while I, for one, can't do the same. It's more difficult for me.'

She breathed, and Sal was touched by the warm waft of air. He rushed and took her in his arms, but Emi was struggling angrily to get free. She forcefully pushed him away with her fists.

'There's no need for you to convince me – I'll come!'

And that's all there was to it: he had his answer. It wasn't how he had imagined it. He had thought it would take more time, that he would need to invest more energy into it and that, in the end, they would both accept the idea. But Emi seemed to have resigned herself as if she knew it was just another whim of his. He had imagined that the petrified woman on the table would help: that the shock of seeing her would be so strong that, compared to her tragedy, nothing could scare them anymore. They were together, and that was what was important. But now *together* meant nothing anymore. He remained next to her, not knowing if it was wise for him to say anything else and disturb her thoughts. Pushing the door ajar, he saw a thread of light crossing the corridor. Emi was in the same position in which he had left her when climbing down from the table. For an instant, he feared it had all been a dream.

'So, do we have a deal? Are we leaving?'

Emi climbed down and came to him; she was calm. She consented and crept out the door. When they were upstairs in the lobby, they looked at one another.

'Tomorrow morning, I'll come and pick you up. I'll go upstairs to Harry's now. Actually, I'll go in a couple of minutes, to give you time to leave so he doesn't see us together. If they have to piece together my disappearance with yours, it's better that they do it later. It'll give us more time. I'll promise to meet him tomorrow. And you go home and act as if nothing has happened.'

Emi listened to him and then headed for the door. She cried to him again: 'We have a deal!'

He could see her walking, with her ample, boyish, cocky gait. He smiled at the idea that everything had worked out so easily, but his train of thought was broken by an ugly forewarning that disturbed his calmness. It was growing inside him like a wave of heat and panic; it emblazed his cheeks and inflamed his stomach so that he rushed to the stairs and ran up all four floors, hoping that the physical exercise would make him forget.

He rang Harry's doorbell and, in a few seconds, Mrs Demetrescu opened the door with a large smile. She looked like a clown, with her cheeks cut by the risen corners of her mouth and crossed by two parentheses. Mrs Demetrescu had a few friends over, and when he passed by the living room door, Sal greeted them respectfully and caught them all in a glimpse: talkative and in a hurry to take the words out of each other's mouths, they fell silent when the boy showed himself. They greeted him back, all in one voice. While he crossed the corridor that led to Harry, the choir of voices grew back behind him. Harry was laying on his belly on the rug, bobbing his head with headphones over his ears, while Toma was sitting at the desk as usual, his face almost glued to the pieces of a dismantled portable radio.

'Here comes the prodigal son!'

Sal started. He stared at Harry, knitting his brows. 'What's that?'

'I'm saying that you vanished without a trace. I waited for you with Tommy, to go to Union Square together. We went alone in the end – if we had waited for you we wouldn't have done shit.'

Sal backed away. 'And? Did you get anything?'

Toma mumbled. They hadn't bought anything. Anyway, they had discovered that they didn't have enough money; moreover, Harry's mum, who had driven them there, had been in a hurry to get back to work.

'Guys, listen. Forget the shopping centre. I have something important to say.'

'Shoot,' Harry mimicked him.

'I'm going to leave...'

Neither of the boys seemed too impressed. He repeated: 'I'm leaving.'

'Come on, you just arrived. Stick around a bit more.'

Sal found it difficult to lie. But he had to deliver an official lecture, as his father had asked him to, so he didn't arouse suspicion. He had entered the room with a feeling of superiority, but the truth was that, seeing them both there, so absorbed by their world and carefree, he envied them and wished he weren't forced to run away with Emi.

'We're moving because my mum is going to have a baby.'

'What?'

Harry was staring at him, pop-eyed.

'A baby.'

'Yeah, I got that! What the fuck? You run off the field and leave us in the lurch, then you make an appointment and snooker us and now you come over with this stuff about your mother being knocked up. What fucking shit is that?'

'Man, I don't understand why you're so mad.'

He sat down on his bottom with his feet beneath him. The boys he idled his time away with when Emi wasn't around were like a charmed forest around him.

Once, on a dark spring afternoon, the whole pack had been heading to the basketball field of a professional high school nearby. Toma and Johnny were leading, talking about musical gear and videotapes and heavy metal bands; Harry was on his left, and Max, blowing chewing-gum bubbles and mumbling like an echo, was behind him, when they were caught in a heavy rain and took refuge in an abandoned garage.

They had all sat down to wait until the rain thinned out, but from the darkness behind them four strapping lads popped up, with T-shirts tightly fitted on their weightlifter bodies and stonewashed blue jeans clinging to their thighs, ready to burst at the slightest movement and denuding their stone-hard buttocks. They were all flabbergasted. It had started as a quiet afternoon. That day they had abandoned their jackets and remained in their T-shirts. It was the first sign that warm weather was approaching, and then the summer holidays. Moreover, it was a Saturday, when everyone, starting with parents and ending with bums, stayed in their houses or in some kind of shelter and took their afternoon naps or just slept to appease their hunger. At this time, the neighbourhood was deserted and stayed like that for an hour or so, after which it slowly started to become repopulated. At first you would see a few scattered people and then their number would grow imperceptibly, as if they were glassy shards of metal fallen off a file and gathered around a big magnet. That's why they liked to wander then – without fear of consequences, since by the time the streets started to get crowded again they were already back in their own neighbourhood, over which they ruled.

The boys that had popped up from behind them didn't have friendly faces and didn't seem willing to tolerate them under the roof of the garage. The question that they all asked themselves in those moments was whether they stood any chance of retreating peacefully; knowing they had trespassed upon the older boys' territory, they could no longer just leave. Judging by their villainous expressions, ready to draw their guns, the friends realised that the solution of running away was no longer a serious one. And they didn't have too much time to think.

The moment they realised they were not alone, the boys had jumped to their feet and stopped dead, their backs to the street and their faces to the dark. The only thought was the humour of the situation they now found themselves in, shifting so quickly from pleasant languor to excitement and fear. It overwhelmed each and every one of them until their whole file, aligned as in the army, started to shiver. One of the giants approached Toma and grabbed him by the chin until the boy, standing on the tips of his toes, started to swim in the air, waving his hands about. A voice shook the shelter then, causing their teeth to chatter.

'Say something now! You were the talky one!' barked the guy.

Toma closed his eyes, shrinking behind his glasses.

'Say something, motherfucker, or I'll stick a knife in you and cut you like a pig.'

Nobody was breathing any more. Outside, the rain had stopped and Sal, bursting into laughter, realised that they could now leave. The brute put Toma down and turned to him.

'Look at this guy! You think it's funny, huh?'

He grabbed Sal by the arms and lifted him up now, squeezing him as in a vice. But Sal remained stone-still, his eyes riveted upon the eyes of the flesh-and-muscle heap, which shot fire back at him.

'Ho, little prick! What, are you playing macho? You want to save the tiny one's ass?'

'You are three times bigger than my friend. And three times bigger than me. We would be out of our minds if we imagined that we could measure our strength against yours. Can't you see? We are peaceable!'

The giant was dumbfounded. The others were laughing under their breath, while the boys had all closed their eyes so they wouldn't have to witness what was about to happen.

'What are you, motherfuckers?' he answered, turning back to his own gang. 'And what the fuck are you laughing at? Do you have any idea what it means? Yo, wanker, tell me, what did the little prick here mean?'

'Wanker' shrugged his shoulders, revealing his wide, milky-white teeth, split by a gap through which the wind was whistling. They had suddenly become interested. But to everyone's amazement, when the situation just seemed to have unwound a bit and the aggressor was about to let go of his prey, Toma dashed headfirst and hit the bundle of muscle, proceeding to pummel him repeatedly with his feet and fists. He looked like an insect squirming on the brim of a glass full of alcohol, inebriated by the fumes: swinging between life and death without knowing it.

The one who had been about to speak up fell silent then, watching the boy with a touch of pity. The gang had remained stone-still. Toma was writhing, his face distorted in a grimace of bitterness and pain. His blows seemed to act like a boomerang, bouncing back from the bundle of steel muscle to the bag of bones with spectacles that barely stayed on the tip of his nose, hanging by a hair like the destiny of the lad who was brainlessly braving against the odds.

Sal was dumbstruck with admiration and horror as he saw Toma flying in slow motion toward the back of the garage, hitting the stacked sheets of corrugated iron that made a glorious noise. He landed at the feet of the four others, who had regrouped now, in assault position, in a semicircle. But none of them managed to take another step ahead.

Three of the intruders had placed themselves forming a human wall, while the fourth turned Toma into a sack of blood and bones. The sounds he still managed to make sounded more and more like gurgles mingled with hiccups and snorts. It only lasted for a few minutes, but to them it seemed like an eternity.

The boy's body was swinging like the hand of a clock, cleaving the air. In the end, it landed on the ground, its temples resting in the dust that had swelled in the atmosphere after all the uproar. After the correction had been administered, the wall fell apart and the boys could see Toma lying on his belly, full of blood and defeated but with a touch of pride in the way he drew his shoulders back, as if saying that he may have received a sound beating, but he still had something to gain from this incident: a victory over him that would change him in the future. They remained on the spot even after the bullies scattered one by one, throwing threats about 'next time' as they left.

What could they have done? They took Toma in their arms and carried him home like that. The blood dripped behind them, drop by drop, out of the boy's feeble body, forming a chain of red beads on the pavement. They had such a long way to go back to their neighbourhood that it seemed you could have filled a jar with all the drops. Sal's mind was split between the image of his brave friend and the deal he had later formed with the others when danger had appeared. They had left him alone, as you would leave a piece of clothing on the line before a storm.

Toma was rolling his eyes and mumbling meaningless words from time to time, but neither of them felt like solving word puzzles any more. Half humiliated and half terrified, they were carrying the body of their friend with spite, as if they had been carrying a corpse. If someone had encouraged them, they would have immediately abandoned that body, reminding them as it did of the failure of their newly sprouted manhood and of the kindness they had all been brought up to foster. Once they reached the threshold of Toma's house, without even conferring with each other and exhausted from the mental and physical turmoil, they lay him down on the door mat, which bore an inscription in black handwriting on a brown background bidding them 'Welcome!'

They left him there and moved away. Only one of them returned in a haste to press the doorbell. That was the sign that it was time for them to scuttle away, each to his own house, and forget all that had happened. But Sal just stood there flabbergasted, waiting for the door to open and for Toma's severe and obtuse parents to come out; he wanted to watch their sour expressions change before his eyes upon seeing their mutilated child, to see their wry faces struggling to hold back their tears. He imagined that pain would defeat them, drowned in helplessness and unknowingly contaminated by the germ of failure and regret, of irreparable guilt that floated in the air. The door opened at last, and the Cerberuses swallowed him inside in one mouthful.

Nobody was reprimanded, neither on that day nor on the following days. The days that followed were really some of the worst days in Sal's life: they were the days in which he tried to figure out who he actually was. The boys had all vanished. After a period of silence, he summoned them to the little park at the intersection of the streets where they lived. He arrived a few minutes late and watched them gather one by one, penitently heading for the meeting place with long faces and their screwed-up eyes cast down. He knew what would follow: he knew perfectly well that the feeling of guilt that he himself had been fighting against during that interval would bring forth violent outbursts and release heavy words.

He watched them like that and deliberately lingered for another half an hour. He wanted to see whether the waiting would loosen up the stiffness between them and would untie their tongues.

Then they would forget what had kept them captive inside their houses; they would leave it all behind, returning to their previous lives and their little problems. He wanted to catch them unawares in that certain moment, in which they would be relaxed and would have definitively forgotten that one of them was missing.

The boys remained silent for a couple of minutes. They mumbled a greeting, their gazes flying over the burgeoning trees, all seemingly brooding. They were thinking, Sal said to himself, how it would be if their guilt disappeared and they became the carefree children they had been before. They sat scattered on the benches aligned on the park alleys and began to wait. Johnny was holding a book in his hand and leafing through it mechanically. Harry sat sprawled on the bench, a hand resting between his legs in a cowboy attitude, and contemplated the horizon with empty, expressionless eyes. Meanwhile, Max, with his usual superior air, sat with his eternally worn cap pulled down to the bridge of his nose and his bizzare disco clothes, from which only the music and the glittering globes reflecting phosphorescent colours were missing. These boys were all his friends and, at the same time, they were Toma's only friends.

Every single day of this long repentance, Sal had phoned Toma's house, and each time someone had picked up the receiver, he had hung up. He had been playing like that for hours on end, listening to curses and threats, sometimes to the occupied tone and sometimes to hysterical shrieks. Then he had extended these phone calls to his friends. Harry had even asked once, exasperated, in a conspiratorial whisper: 'Sal, is that you?'

He was stubbornly trying to understand how all these brave young men, whom he saw and heard daily, had behaved like the lowest of cowards.

The boys stood motionless without uttering a word. Sal himself was stone-still in his hiding place, but he was determined not to move an inch before he saw which of them would break the silence. The one who would break the silence was the traitor. But the thought of it made him laugh. This worked for detective novels, not for them – because in their case, each and every one of them was the traitor and they all knew it. And he also knew that, had they been together, Toma himself would have laughed at this nonsense. He would utter the strangest words in the most inadequate situations, as if he wanted to release the moment's overload of pressure.

An hour had passed and nobody had made any move. Sal was overcome by boredom and despair; he was impatient and over-excited. Time passed, and with each elapsed second their resources for finding something to say to each other diminished. Actually, he wished at least one of them had started; he wished the bravest of them had broken the ice, for then he would have climbed down from his hiding place and would have been able to disappear into their clamour. He had hidden behind a tree growing next to the brewery's fence and had nestled there, squeezing his shoulders and crossing his fists under his chin.

After the long wait, he saw Harry make a couple of steps backward. The boys all looked down, pretending not to notice his movements. From a distance, they looked like performers in a ballet show. At first Sal thought that Harry wanted to stretch his legs a bit but, after a few seconds of hesitation, Harry turned his back and left without a word. Then, one by one, they all scattered back to their own houses. As far as Sal could tell, they left much more relaxed. They considered that, after making the effort to come there, after waiting in vain for so many minutes, they had atoned for their sin.

Now, at Harry's house, Toma was pottering about over the scattered parts of what had been a portable radio, his eyeglasses fastened at the back with a coloured elastic band from which all sort of brass crucifixes, pendants, paper clips and safety pins were hanging. He looked like a tamed savage. Only his meek face betrayed him.

'Do you remember when you got beaten up by those guys?'

Harry frowned and looked up at him. 'What's wrong with you, man? Have you blown a fuse?'

But Sal didn't give in. 'Do you remember when they beat up this guy here, and we carried him to the door and then abandoned him on the doormat? Do you remember, man?'

Toma's fingers, which had been moving up until then, had stopped in midair. He was still looking at the scattered parts on the table. Harry gestured to Sal, but then lowered his hand as if with fatigue.

'Say what you want to say. It sucks, anyway.'

Sal settled down on the rug and, after a moment of silence, he went on. 'I keep remembering, ever since I found out that I was leaving. What, you mean to say that you never thought about it, even if none of us ever mentioned it?'

He was talking to Harry as if Toma had vanished from the room, but Harry didn't seem to hear him. He calmly replaced the headphones that had been hanging around his neck and started to hum something out of tune, his eyes staring at an imaginary spot.

'And when are you leaving?' Toma had woken up and was watching him from behind his lenses, half turned toward him.

'In a month...'

Sal felt sorry that he had to lie to him.

'Apparently, I should be leaving in a month.'

But he changed his mind. Any weakness could turn against them.

'That's if everything goes as my parents planned. But I wouldn't worry – you know how they are. They never miss a thing.'

'I will miss you.'

And, after saying the words, Toma mechanically turned back to the machinery with its exposed innards.

'I didn't mean to annoy you earlier. I only wanted to let you know that I'm sorry for that incident.'

'It's okay; never mind. After all, it wasn't your fault, was it?'

Were they talking about the same thing? Harry had put his headphones back on, while Toma was fiddling on, dull and confused. Maybe Toma had done it on purpose – maybe he was just testing him – but to Sal it was all the same. He had a hard day ahead of him tomorrow, and the boys, as far as he could see, had already silently agreed to speak no more of the old incident.

'And now we're even,' Toma added.

Sal waited. They were certainly talking about the same thing. But he wasn't as sure now that Toma had let go of the past. He was starting to foresee now that Toma wasn't going to let him get away so easily and that, if he found out about Sal's plans, he would be the first to give him away.

'What do you mean?'

Toma smiled and shook his head, making the trinkets hanging on his eyeglasses' elastic band tinkle.

'Well, just like that...' He stopped, seeming to concentrate upon the wires he was trying to knot together. Then he frowned, as if the revelation had confused him. 'Do you remember when you cut your wrists in my father's weapon cabinet? And they only found you half an hour later, fainted on the floor in a pool of blood?'

'Yes...' Sal pondered for a while. 'But it wasn't for half an hour, it was only for a few minutes. Emi ran for help immediately. If it had been half an hour, I would have died.'

Toma flashed a superior smile. He was staring at Sal, his look suggesting that he knew better what the truth was but was waiting for a question to say it.

'You wouldn't have died, Sal. You didn't die, as you can see. And Emi had left long before. I mean, she left right after you rushed into the window with your fists like a jackass.'

'How would you know?'

'Because...'

'Because what?'

The trinkets tinkled again, dimly. Toma was speaking with his eyes closed.

'Because I was there, watching you.'

Sal grabbed his head with his hands. 'Man, I really don't get what you're saying. You couldn't have been watching us, because I would have seen you. We were alone in the room and Emi ran for help right away.'

'Emi had left!'

Toma had cried out so loudly that his voice had sharpened. Then it had drowned in his chest.

'All right, all right. What does this have to do with what we were talking about? What's come over you?'

'I always thought you were my best friend.'

Sal nodded.

'I'm telling you this because I don't want you to be upset. But I noticed that you wanted to speak about what happened, that you were sorry, and I would like you to leave with your heart at peace, without thinking about this anymore.'

'But I *am* leaving with my heart at peace. And I don't know why you insist on acting this way, now of all times. Seriously...'

Sal went silent and waited for Toma to go on. Even if he had a conciliatory voice, he wanted to show him that, against all appearances, he was capable of the same cruelty.

'Emi was angry at you, so she left. She was angry because I think that she expected you to make a declaration. I think that she had listened to the story you told as if it had been about the two of you, and the fact that you deluded her in the end made her mad. That's why she ran away and left you there.'

He took a break, watching Harry, who was lying on his back with his eyes closed. Only the tips of his toes, in their plush socks, were moving periodically to the rhythm of the tune playing enigmatically in his headphones.

'Actually, she was right. A declaration was supposed to follow – otherwise why would you have told her what you did? You called her there to impress her. If you had told her what she wanted to hear, nothing would have happened anymore, right?'

Toma wasn't expecting an answer: that much Sal was sure of. And even if he would have had to answer, he doubted he could have uttered a word. The sounds were stuck in his throat while his mind was looking for a way out. He felt obliged to find at least one clever, funny thing to say in order to defuse the atmosphere in the room. He could have dashed toward Harry and snatched the headphones off his head. But Toma seemed vigilant and his attention was sharp. He was following Sal's every gesture and reaction. Besides – and maybe that was the most important part – he had brought Emi into their discussion, and he kept hinting at her, insinuating that she had left Sal there, to die, in revenge. And it would have been the worst idea to spring to her defence now: that was exactly what Toma was waiting for, and all the boys would have found out about their relationship after that. It was bad enough that there was one of them who suspected something. At least he found solace in the thought that the secret would be kept, even though the number of those who knew about it had grown.

'I bet you're anxious to find out where I know all the details from.' Toma revealed his sparse set of teeth, thrust into his gums like squares of plastic. 'And you're perfectly right. If it hadn't been for that unfortunate incident, I probably would have never found out. But I saw that you left after her. You've done this many times, and every time it amused me that you two were exchanging glances and imagining that nobody noticed. I was watching you. But it was only on that afternoon that I followed you. I think a day or two after that I also read the story of Tristan...'

'And Isolde...'

Sal had said it in a whisper, barely able to hear himself, but Toma stopped. He was surprised because, although they had spoken simultaneously, Sal's voice sounded as if he had to do justice to the woman whose name had been left out.

'Yes, sure... Well, after I read it, I saw things more clearly. I was hidden in the other room waiting to see what was going to happen when I heard the sound of broken glass. She ran, and when I entered the room, I saw you lying on the floor. I was scared. I stayed like that a bit longer – I don't remember exactly how long, but I know that I waited, believing that you would come to your senses. No – actually first I thought that you were pretending, to impress her, but after that I said to myself that she had left and you weren't that stupid to put on that act and lie there for nothing. I was afraid you'd died.'

Sal was speechless. He was looking at Toma as if he were an apparition that had taken over his friend's body, smirking and making wry faces from behind his glasses. He understood now what Toma was referring to. Silence had fallen in the room.

Harry opened his eyes and rose up on his elbows. He took his headphones off one ear, looking at the other two as if he had just woken up.

'What?' He had asked Sal, but his eyes drifted to Toma. 'Did you say something?'

Sal shook his head. Harry lay on his back again, put his headphones over his ears and sank back into his music.

'After that, everybody said that you tried to kill yourself. Only I knew very well that it wasn't like that, but I was ashamed to tell them. Do you understand now?'

'I understand.'

'Are you angry?'

'No way!'

'When you didn't spring to my defence, you were in danger yourself. Those guys could have beaten you up as well. In my case, it's different.'

'You were scared.'

Toma sniffed. 'That I was scared is not important! But to follow you and to eavesdrop on what you were talking about...'

'Look, let's bury the hatchet.'

'Okay. But I didn't want you to leave without knowing.'

'Uh-huh.'

But upon seeing how he stayed staring, with his mouse-like face, Sal added, 'Let's never speak about this again.'

Toma was grateful. He nodded and turned to the radio on his desk. Sal gazed upon him with wisdom, but with a touch of sadness as well, just like one should regard anything in an uncertain situation.

'And to nobody,' Sal added, stressing his words. 'There is no point in involving Emi in this old story.'

'To nobody,' Toma confirmed, changing his tone afterward, in a theatrical manner, to mark the end of the subject. 'So you're leaving...'

Sal poked Harry, but the latter remained with his eyes closed, swinging his legs and wriggling his body. He bent over him and took the headphones off his ears. Harry winced as if he had been lashed, protecting this precious tool that none of the boys had ever managed to touch before. 'Hey!'

He jumped up suddenly and knocked his forehead against Sal's jaw. They watched each other for a couple of seconds, in dismay.

'What's up, man? What do you want?'

Sal got up, slowly rubbing his jawbone. Toma was working scrupulously, holding a pair of pincers between the tip of his index finger and his thumb, concentrated like a surgeon in the midst of an operation. Although Toma wasn't looking at him, he knew that Sal felt the need to extend the conversation. It would have helped him to clear his conscience and tickle his pride. But because Harry started to shriek with laughter, Sal laughed too: not about their accident, but about Toma. He laughed about him on the sly without watching him, seeing with the corner of his eye his satisfaction almost floating around the room, spreading like the smell of cooked food.

There was a knock on the door, followed by Mrs Demetrescu's smiling head.

'Everything fine, boys?'

They stopped with a grin imprinted on their faces.

'Harry!'

The voice drowned in the roars of laughter that started again upon Harry's mother's appearance and grew vigorously, imperatively.

'Hariton, come, please. The girls are leaving, and I want to see them to the bus stop. Lock the door behind me.'

'Oh, come on, mum! What the hell?'

'Please, I don't want someone walking in on you.'

'*Who* could walk in?'

'Look, I asked you nicely. Don't push me. Come on!'

Harry clumsily got to his feet, groaning and pressing his hand to his aching temple. From behind, he looked like a dwindling old man fighting against gravity. Sal got up too. His visit was over.

Harry disappeared out the door after Mrs Demetrescu.

'I'm leaving, too.'

He had said it on a natural tone, wanting to test Toma's attention as well; it seemed that from the moment they had put an end to their conversation, he had drawn a line, implicating that he wasn't interested in what else was happening. He retreated two steps toward the door. Toma turned his head. 'Are you leaving?'

'Well, yeah – my mother's waiting for me. And I promised Johnny that I would drop by.'

'I see.'

Toma thought for a while. 'When you leave, can I have the Metallica poster?'

'You don't like Metallica.'

'I never said I did. If you don't want to give it to me, it's okay.'

Sal bristled. 'I never said I didn't want to. You can have it. It's just that I was surprised, that's all.'

'Man, if you can't, forget it.'

'Oh, come on, man, don't be a pussy. I told you that I could. Anyway, I wanted to give them all away. Just tell me if you want anything else.'

'Okay. I mean no, nothing else. Just that one.'

'Okay. I'll bring it to you tomorrow.'

Toma smiled at him, comradely. Then he waved goodbye and resumed his work.

Watching from a distance without knowing them, one might have come to the conclusion that each of the three boys had something to hide, something that was a matter of life and death. In reality, just one of them bore a secret within him; another had wanted to get rid of his, while the last probably didn't even know it yet. The impact between Sal and Harry looked like the collision of two atoms: the crash had taken place in Mrs Demetrescu's fourth-floor apartment, but its effects would show in a different place altogether. To Sal it seemed that the meeting with the boys had been pointless, but nevertheless he somehow felt that he had disentangled certain things while complicating others. He regarded it as an investment in their future – his and Emi's – and smiled within, thinking that later, maybe after several years, he would be able to explain to his friends what had actually happened that afternoon.

VII

NAUTILUS

If you looked close, screwing up your eyes, you could see that a veil of salt had settled in the folds of her caramelised skin, as if a fine snow had fallen all over her body. It appeared to be a barren expanse of soil covered by sparse blades of grass left over from the autumn before, on which white frost had settled. That wasteland was the battlefield where he usually confronted his enemies. Uncertainty made him anticipate the potential foes. His gaze reached far away, scanning beyond the horizon, inferring and prefiguring situations. He was captain over an army consisting of one soldier, whom he nevertheless continuously suspected of treason.

He watched her lying on the linen sheet, one of her legs bent and shadowing a strip of her body, her hands outstretched, her eyes tightly closed, blinded by the strong light. Sitting like that, transformed by the burning sun, she seemed to be offering herself to the whole starving tribe. Whoever might have wanted her need only stretch their hand and tear off a piece. At first glance, she seemed to have a propensity for dissoluteness. But at the same time, she had stayed with him, had waited for him all that tormentingly slow-passing time. There was no way for him to put pressure on her or to enforce rules. Patience had been their watchword so far, but the truth was that neither of them knew what they were waiting for. They would secretly drag themselves along every morning amidst the sand dunes, their eyes hollowed from lack of sleep, slouching under the sun, isolated from the world. A couple of miles away, their drowsy families were lazing in between the sheets, without any shadow of doubt wafting above their eyelashes.

'How did we get here?' she asked him one day.

She was a conscienceless lizard.

She rolled over to him, pressing her calves together and covering her face with her left arm. The skin on the inside of her arm had remained white, almost translucent. It was fluffy and still young. The breasts had slanted and looked, in that position, like the breasts of an old matron, furrowed by fine vines, thin as the cracks on canvases displayed in the unfavourable conditions of full daylight. In the dense and heavy air, on the tiny strip of beach on which they hid themselves, a vague feeling of happiness floated, despite that fact that the reclusiveness they sought could never be truly reliable. The sand would heat beneath them as time passed; sometimes an hour, sometimes less, depending on the schedule of the ones back home, on their own apprehensions or how soon they yielded to the fear of being caught.

They had already been there three weeks and they were used to sneaking away, to dissimulating, to sniffing each other from a distance. They had gotten used to it all: to seeing one another only when the others didn't see them, to daily meetings, to daily approaches, in the conjugal rhythm they had created. Besides sadness, it gave them a strange feeling of possession that threatened to extend to the hours in which they weren't together. Sometimes it was a good feeling, because it subdued them and promised them false delights; it was a feeling of sweet casualness and abandon to the beautiful illusions crowning any lover's head. It gave them a feeling of safety never experienced in Bucharest, with their busy schedules and their responsibilities, and the city itself, with its lack of places to hide and its nosy people, its hotelkeepers with suspicious, sugary looks, its chatty taxi drivers, its prying bartenders and waiters. It wasn't a city that would protect or cover up the tracks of those who ventured to lead double lives.

She was watching him through the acute angle made by her arm, hidden, carefully examining him and trying to guess if he was thinking of leaving or was just lost in thought. If he had allowed her, she could have stayed like that for a long time: silent, motion - less, secretly watching him and imagining all sort of diabolical plans. Out of exasperation, he would ask her why she couldn't trust him, but she kept stubbornly reminding him that he had left her once, with no regrets, and that it could happen again anytime. No promise in the world could have comforted her. And, somehow, he agreed with her. He felt the need of reassurance himself, but he couldn't ask for it, because she was clever and would have summed things up right away: none of them had the right to ask the other for reassurance. Because, years before, despite all the promises and well-devised plans, one of them had still left the other, and that was enough to ruin their trust.

He knew her argument perfectly. As a matter of fact, when he thought of 'the two of them' he had a feeling of optimism as if, however bad the situation had been and even if it was more than likely that it wouldn't change for the better too soon, at least for the moment things looked nice, despite the millions of particles breaking on the inside, each with its direction and its will. These thoughts always led him to his grandmother, whom they had found lying on her bed with her black, varnished, ribbon-shaped buckle shoes on, dressed in yellow stockings and a red and green plaid skirt under which you could glimpse the lace at the bottom of the petticoat, with a frilled white puffed sleeve shirt under the black vest. Everyone thought that Grandmother had dressed up to go to the theatre, and her rather inappropriate clothes convinced them, for a couple of minutes, that she was alive and just asleep despite the sour smell in the air. When they finally wondered why Grandmother had togged up like that, they started to suspect that the stylish woman had prepared, in fact, for death.

Yet he often thought about the future and made plans: how he would slowly drift away from those back home, how he would manage, also little by little, to become more and more dispensable and invisible, until they got used to his absence; how he would take his clothes, one at a time, then a few of the books he loved – not many, but definitely *Robinson Crusoe* and a few botanical atlases; how he would stretch like a rubber cartoon character, first with his arms full of suitcases, then with half his body, bringing his left foot forward and then, with a last, graceful effort, pull his right one forward as well, without his toes touching the ground.

'Why are you laughing?'

He knew that, however nicely and amusingly he had recounted his fantasy, she would have sulked and wouldn't have spoken to him anymore. She would have told him reprovingly that this day he was dreaming about wouldn't come too soon and that, anyway, it could only come if he did something about it.

'Do you think we should leave?'

'No. Why?'

Childlike, he pushed her face onto the beach mat and said, with a stifled voice, 'Because you look restless. If you want to leave, just say so.'

Then he drew himself to her and mounted her, crushing her under his weight. It had been a deft move; he had jumped like a cat, leaving her no time to realise what was going on. She found herself under that monster, suffocated by his love. He had decided to make her realise that she was wrong. They would always waste their energy in conversations, implacably drifting toward the subject of their relationship, which she saw intricately, with adoration and disgust, and he with indulgence and fatality.

'What are you doing?' she asked him, out of breath, her face distorted with repugnance. But then she changed, looking as if she had accidentally pressed a button and the machinery inside her had started to work again. From a distance, they could see the growing upside-down silhouette of a boy with a ponytail, holding a surfboard under his arm. He had come out of the cornfield, from between the maize that had grown its silk to the sky, dragging his flip-flops and advancing with difficulty, seemingly tired already. She tried, with a dignified and disfigured smile, to pull herself out from beneath, but despite all her effort and her struggling, she only managed to free one foot.

'Please, get off. Everybody will see us.'

'So what? You said I wanted to leave. Look, I'll show you that I don't.'

'I know, you've shown me. Now let's go.'

'I can't.'

'Why?'

She screamed, and that made him stifle her voice by pressing her head into the hollow between his collarbone and his arm. He could feel the contour of her face on the inside, sunken in his flesh, and he could hear her feet rustling, like a breeze coming from the sea. He held her tight for a minute or so, but it seemed longer. Finally he let go and saw her flushed, irritated face with its lines deepened by anger. A second later, tears began to trickle down her cheeks in thin, winding streams, leaving an imaginary semicircle on her cheekbones and falling on the mat. He could have sworn that he could hear their sound.

The surfer passed them by with his head down, swinging his free hand alongside his body and seemingly oblivious to what was going on around him. On a sunny day like that, on a beach where you could see a single sheet with a couple of lovers lying on it, what could go wrong? He could have killed her right there and then, in the seconds in which the boy was leaving them behind, without raising any suspicion. He could have left her in the sun to decompose, so that no one would recognise her anymore. The surfer would have remembered there had been someone in that place, but it would have been difficult for him to say precisely who. The local police would have discovered her and connected this with the disappearance reported by her grief-stricken husband. He would have wept for her, failing to understand how something like that had happened to them, of all people, and then soon she would have been forgotten. At that moment, death seemed an easier solution, and the thought made him wonder.

They spent the rest of their time in silence until he saw her get up and start to gather her things. He did the same, glad that it hadn't been him mentioning that it was time to go. He didn't realise how angry his gesture had made her. It had been an unjustified, adolescent impulse, similar to that in which boys sometimes feel like hanging an arm around their partners' necks, signalling possession and arrogance at the same time.

When they separated, after dropping her off at the corner of the street, he lingered on for a while in his car, watching her move away. She had resumed her self-assured walk and was moving innocently, as if she were coming back from the morning's shopping. There was no need for them to set appointments; they were both on the beach at 8 o'clock every morning, never more than a couple of minutes late unless something unexpected came up.

He pressed his right foot to the acceleration pedal, slowly releasing the clutch with the other. Going to the seaside on holidays hadn't initially been in his plans. For the kids, the news came like an accidental meeting with Santa Claus. He had warned them ever since the beginning of the summer that he could only be away from work for a couple of weeks. He had, somewhat cruelly, made them decide between the seaside and the mountains. He wanted to make it seem that it was their decision. Up till then, he had heard his girls daydreaming countless times about the waves that would break against their feet. And then, on a Sunday visit, his brother-in-law, who had two girls himself, came up with the idea of going together to a guesthouse in the Western Carpathians. Although in the beginning he had tried to explain with a certain irritation that they had already made plans for the vacation, he had noticed with amazement that everybody – especially the girls – seemed more and more charmed by the idea of a mountain adventure, despite their reservations about the company of those loud and noisy little cousins.

Milk and honey flowed out of his brother-in-law's lips in his storytelling enthusiasm, and the mountains he depicted seemed like animated giants waiting for nothing but the arrival of the beautiful young ladies from the city, ready to carry them on their backs and lay rugs of wild strawberries, blackberries, honey mushrooms and golden chanterelles at their feet. The girls, lying on the floor with their elbows under their chins, were drinking in their uncle's words accompanied by ample, majestic gestures. Their eyes had already begun to rummage in the marvels: they had settled upon and now relished the copious dishes laid on the peasant tables, turned inside out the pantries full of preserves, jams, sherbets and fruit jellies, sniffed the hay barns and overturned stag beetles with a simple touch. They even screwed up their noses from the cold air, taking deep breaths to clean their lungs of the dust gathered over the year while the wind wafted through their hair and a round sun like a cantaloupe smiled above their heads.

Although up until then they had whined and begged and made him swear that they would roast in the ultra-violets – which for them were some kind of flowers similar to those their father worked with – in less than a second all previous plans had been scattered. The mountain peaks already flashed in the distance, unfolding at their feet a magic carpet on which they all climbed and closed their eyes, taking flight and moving away. Although their father had beckoned to them a couple of times, knitting his brows, the girls had no eyes for him and only looked into the distance, imagining themselves sprawled on a meadow, purring by the blades of grass and cooing with pleasure. When they returned back home, the decision had been made without him, and for the whole night that followed he thought only about how he would tell her and how they would have to make arrangements so the separation would be as short as possible.

He stopped in front of the house and took the car out of gear, lingering for a while and waiting amidst the dull sound of the purring engine. He wanted more accurately to remember the moment when he realised, upon returning from his vacation in the mountains, that he couldn't bear to wait for her another month. His thoughts had jumbled up in his head and he had started to devise fanciful means of bringing her back. At the end of several days which he had spent roaming the streets, gesturing and talking to himself, he had decided to go after her, realising that the answer had been there from the very start and that the effort of finding another solution had been sheer hypocrisy. Now he felt ashamed for dragging the kids into all this madness, for tempting them to be, again, the ones who make a choice in his place. In the hours before their departure to the seaside, when the rest of the house was all agog – feverishly packing, throwing clothes into suitcases almost at random – he had locked himself in the kitchen and contemplated from there the withered plants of his neighbour in the garret across the street, which were once the woman's pride and joy but had now been neglected.

He looked along the road ahead. It was very early, and he suddenly realised that he could have stayed another half an hour on the beach. It also crossed his mind that, if he had managed to kill her, as the surfer could have reported later to the police, he probably wouldn't have stopped the engine but instead driven on like in an American film, swallowing miles and raising black clouds behind him. Maybe he would have become a fugitive, but he would have calmed down with the knowledge that he would only have to think of her as a memory.

He had returned from the mountains and found a white envelope, without any sender address, in the letterbox. He seized it at the same time as Matilda, and they exchanged looks. She was the one to let go of it first, so he managed to read her fine lines, handwritten with fear, announcing that despite their agreement to return at once, she had decided to stay at the seaside with her husband for the whole summer. 'We need this!' she had written, and it took him two days of soliloquies to decide which of them she meant: the one she had left with, or the one who was waiting for her. In the end, he was sure that she had meant him, and he had drawn the conclusion that she was wrong.

That was why he announced to his family that he was offering them a holiday extension. There was no point in his calling his office because, at the end of his tether, he wouldn't have known what other lies to concoct. By that point, he was indifferent to any punishments they might give out upon his return. He wouldn't have changed his mind even if they had humiliated him, frowning and pointing to the rows of dead plants, to their dark, blood-red stems, as if pointing to horrors brought about by his cowardly departure. He knew that it was all part of a pretty vile plan, but he stubbornly insisted on persevering in it, on immersing himself in the all-encompassing plot whose victims they had all become. So he had left without looking back, as if complying with the wishes of the females who were all chirping in the old second-hand car. He didn't have the slightest trace of remorse or regret; he wasn't afraid of the fact that he would probably have to explain many things upon their return.

Once they had arrived at the seaside village, he stopped at the beach tavern. He had gone alone, on the pretext of inquiring about a house to rent, and the first thing he asked the bartender, leaning over the dusty counter, was if anyone could tell him where a couple of friends he was looking for were staying: a tall woman with curly black hair and her husband, a tall, red-haired, freckled man. After a moment's thought, the bartender seemed to recognise whom he was speaking about, saying that he had seem them and that, as far as he could tell, they had rented the house on the seafront close to the village end and told him that they would remain there all summer. He returned to the car with a triumphant smile on his face. He hadn't found anything, he told Matilda, but he was confident that after a good meal, the house would practically come their way.

He took off his shoes at the door and entered slowly, walking on tiptoe. But besides the hot, stuffy air that hit him, clogging his nose like two cotton balls, something else troubled him: a faint noise, like a hissed breath, coming from the living room. He carefully put his flip-flops on the floor, put down his backpack and advanced warily. When he entered the room, he saw Matilda sitting on the couch, kneading a towel in her hands. Her eyes were riveted upon the door, greeting him. She seemed more worried than angry, so he managed to compose himself in a split second.

'What happened?' he whispered from the threshold.

Matilda answered, full of tears, with a stifled voice that obscured her words. He drew nearer and repeated the question. He reached for her hand, but grabbed the towel and felt that it was wet.

'Mari is sick. She had something like a loss of calcium, I don't know what. I found her shivering all over. First I thought it was a touch of sunstroke, but it couldn't have been that. We didn't stay long on the beach yesterday. After that, I saw that her teeth were clenched and that she was white as a sheet. She kept pointing to her chest.'

She stopped and placed her own hand under her breast, drawing in a deep breath with a sigh. 'Her heart was pounding like crazy! And she had such a scared little face!'

Listening to her, he was terrified but he felt calmer and increasingly relieved. He had lived the terror of having been found out, or at least suspected. Suspicion was much worse, because they would have had to be twice as cautious. And now he had unwound and was happy – happy it had only been about Mari. Stroking her hand mechanically, he remained silent; if he had spoken, his voice would have come out in a high pitch, as if it could hardly contain its happiness and was ready to trumpet it.

'She's asleep now.'

He shook his head and kept on stroking her hand.

'We should go back home...'

'No! By no means!'

She came back to her senses and looked at him, knitting her faded eyebrows. In that mood, her face had acquired a maternal personality. He thought that if he would ever have to remember her, most probably that's how she would remain imprinted in his memory: with that wrinkle like an apostrophe throwing two black shadows, like two dark reflections, upon her pale, freckled face. He was determined to hold his ground. He had decreed that nothing bad enough could happen to the six-year-old girls to necessitate their return. He grabbed her wrist and squeezed it tightly; he had reckoned that the pain would put her off and distract her.

'I'll take her to a hospital in Constanţa to be seen by a doctor. As soon as she wakes up, we get her in the car and go together. Is that all right?'

She was watching him with moist eyes. He presumed that the tears came rather from the pain of his grip than from her concern about the girl. Nothing bad can happen to a six-year-old girl. He repeated it in his mind a couple of times, not because he wanted to infuse some life into his conscience, which would have been useless, but because that gave him inner strength to make her believe as well.

'Yes, we're going to the hospital... nothing is wrong...'

Then, without blinking, she broke loose from his grip and looked at him with milky eyes, buried inside the fluffy, swollen, pillow-like eyelids.

'Where have *you* been?'

'Jogging on the beach.'

'You went jogging?' she repeated mechanically, leaving the impression that she hadn't even heard her own question.

'I've been jogging every morning for ten days. What do you find so amazing? When I woke up, she was fine. I went to check on them. They were sleeping peacefully. And now, in the morning, the same.'

'I see. You didn't tell me.'

'Yes, I did. But, anyway, it makes no difference now. It's not what this is all about.'

He saw her absorbed in her own thoughts, drifting away. She was probably thinking more about his early departures and less about the girl lying in bed. At her first reproach, he would have flung in her face that she was selfish and saw only disaster around her. But they didn't utter a word.

The day slowly elapsed in between Mari's bed and the living room, where the three of them, huddled together, kept vigil over the child. Dori had nestled in Matilda's lap, grasping her toes. She played with them mechanically, spreading them in her palm and then stroking them as if they were a small tamed animal she was just befriending. It was already dark outside, and the only signs of life came from the beach. They could hear the belligerent, sexual cries of teenage girls warmed by the sun and over-excitedly calling to boys to reunite in the pack. Those sounds pierced the air like poisoned arrows and sank between his shoulder blades. The girls had huddled up together and moaned in unison, although it was clear that it was Mari who struck the key note while the others' grumbles followed like an echo; groggy from their sister's agony, they reverberated like empty barrels whose volume multiplied indefinitely. Eventually, he pulled Matilda out of the room by her sleeve.

'You should go to sleep and allow her to sleep as well. I'll stay.'

Matilda's eyes sparkled in the dark. She clenched her jaws so tightly that he could hear her gnashing her teeth. She was unmerciful when it came to her nest. He hadn't taken that into account; if she sensed anything, her meanness would have pushed her to acts of significant cruelty.

'Come on, please, go! And take Dori with you. There's no point in keeping her up all night. Everything will be fine by morning, you'll see.'

His voice was sugary and silky; he behaved cajolingly in perfect contrast to her sharpness and her harshness, to the intransigence with which she had related to the situation for the last several hours. And suddenly she collapsed into his arms, grabbing his T-shirt with her claws and swinging from one side to another in a lamentation that would have squeezed tears out of stones, let alone a man she called her husband, in whose hands she had entrusted her whole life. He saw her to the bedroom door and gently pushed her inside. She was still crying with occasional noisy sobs, like a doll that squealed pathetically every time their girls pressed their fingers on its tummy.

'You promise to wake me up if anything happens?'

'Sure. I promise. But nothing will happen, you'll see.'

He helped her into bed and pulled the sheet over her. He departed in a hurry and, before closing the door, threw her another look from the threshold. She had remained still, wrapped as in a shroud, and he had the distinct impression that he had seen her before, or was going to see her like that again. She had the repulsive look of a corpse that, although it hasn't yet started to diffuse the sweet stenches of death, makes you anticipate them and shiver beforehand with disgust and fear. He took Dori to bed in the living room and returned to Mari's sickbed. He remained there until the next day's dawn when, overcome by fatigue and tricked by the sunlight, he fell asleep.

When he woke up, he was lying on the girl's bed. There was no one else in the room, and the light coming through the window had formed a huge orange fire in the middle of the room. He sat up in bed and pricked up his ears to check if there were any noises in the house, like the times he used to spy on his parents when he was a kid. His first thought was neither about the sick girl in whose bed he had awoken, nor about her potentially worrying absence, but about the woman who had waited the whole morning at the beach on her mat, petrified with grief and astonishment with every minute that passed, trying to understand what she had done or said wrong the day before. With a vacant look, he remained thinking about her. That thought, the image of her alone, helplessly worrying, making assumptions, swallowing her reproaches, dumbfounded him but also sent a thrill of sick excitation all along his body.

He got out of bed and left the room on tiptoe. The house was empty. Only a few things – the girls' swimsuits and other freshly washed clothes – animated the stale air of the living room. He opened the windows and only then saw the swing in the garden, rocking slowly back and forth, and three pairs of tamely hanging legs, two smaller pairs on the sides and a bigger one in the middle. At first it crossed his mind to leave the house like a thief, to run to the car and drive away in a rush, heading for the beach with the reckless hope that he could still find her waiting for him. Only the futility of the thought kept him in his place, in blind, objectless contemplation. And so several days passed just like this. Actually, he couldn't have said exactly how many, because he spent them in a state of anaesthesia and oblivion. Each morning, he would shave away with an imaginary blade any trace of her nearby presence.

Mari had recovered: she was back in bloom and excessively lively, as if the sickness that had confined her in her bed had infused her with miraculous powers and she had now revived in the form of a pesky elf that pestered everybody and consumed their energy. The day would pass very quickly because of her and the fights she constantly provoked. But the shrieks ringing in the house were better than the silence to which he had awoken on that afternoon. And the rain that followed was better than the sunny days in which people went to sunbathe.

Somewhere, in a corner of his mind, she was still on the mat that was now soiled with a mixture of wet sand and seaweed; water was streaming through her black hair that had curled even more and shone under a black sun. While it rained, they stayed in the house and invented games. The girls seemed to enjoy the weather change most, and hence they had taken hold of things and people. As parents, they were both paralysed by guilt. Neither of them showed their wish to go out of the house anymore. They ate all the supplies in the fridge and then ordered food to be delivered to them at home. They opened the huge Monopoly board and played all their money, buying and selling. More often than not at the end of the game, when the stinking rich girls, falling about with laughter after having defeated their parents, begged for another round, he would lift them both under his arms as if they were two twigs and spin them around the house. And, in that pleasant vertigo, he saw her multiplied, hundredfold, thousandfold: her image would magically recompose from tiny sparkling pieces of light and shadow, from coloured fragments, and explode into the room in smaller images, all merry, all optimistic. But one day, he fell to the ground with the girls. Dori and Mari pulled away crawling, awoken from their splendour, while Matilda released a terrible yell. She rushed at them and picked them up, gathering them in her arms and crying: 'What are you doing? Do you want to kill them?'

He looked at her dumbstruck. And, thus, the period of peace ended. That afternoon, the first sunrays appeared as well and, together with them, the girls' desire to get out of the house broke out. Although they had both had a serious fright and come away with a couple of bruises from the fall, they weren't angry with their father at all. After a few minutes, their faces had resumed their bright and inquisitive expressions.

'We want ice-cream!' Dori decreed, stamping her foot on the ground like a soldier.

They went out, heading for the centre of the resort where people had gathered, humming and delighted by the return of the good weather. They had been in the house for four days. He had the feeling that his skin had darkened and that, under the brown hair, he had started to grow scales like a set of armour, permanently keeping him in the shade in an unpleasant coolness, foreboding death.

'Daddyyy! Daddyyy! Tell us another flower tale!'

The girls had started a travel journal, assigning a flower to each day that had passed. Under the flower, stuck with sellotape in the centre of the page, they wrote its Latin name and a story, told by their father, following their imperative requests. Mari had come up with the idea and Dori had enthusiastically clapped her hands right away. Each would then put down the version of the story they remembered so that, upon reading them, the two notebooks were in fact totally different, although to neophytes they might have seemed identical.

'Be patient until we get back home. I tell you stories every day.'

They put on long faces, disappointed. Two pairs of wide-open eyes stared at him in disbelief.

'But do you promise, when we get home?'

'Sure.'

'Do we have your word?'

Matilda stormed at them, 'He promised once!'

The girls rushed to the first open-air restaurant terrace they laid eyes upon. Their mother tried in vain to persuade them that they would find something better only a few more steps away. He watched them silently argue. As touching as the image of the two tiny kids who had formed an impenetrable wall against the adult slightly bent above them may have been, as touching as their resolute whispering was, their negotiations always seemed to him like those between the fishiest of mobsters. Matilda had often upbraided him for not being more involved in the girls' education, for turning them into tomboys, on account of his silence and his long absences. But one day he had made an effort. He wanted to scrape, from under the sediment of his memories, those fragments of his life long ago on top of which a layer of mineral cotton seemed to have settled. And he remembered perfectly well that grown-up people's words couldn't stop the minds of children from running about and devising means of escape. He decided that he would allow them to do everything they wished, accept the consequences and change according to the suffering they would put themselves through. They had to become what they were dreaming of. They had to become their own dreams. Just as he had become, just as she herself had...

The twins stopped, looking at one another as if looking in a mirror. They had pulled silly faces upon hearing the voice still mumbling behind them. They seemed to wonder whether to answer or not. If they had turned back, they would have had to take into consideration the reproaches made against them. Because of that, or maybe just instinctively, the girls chose to walk ahead, maintaining their empty and meaningless gaze. They sat on the wrought-iron chairs, rubbing their buttocks contentedly against the fluffy, sponge-filled pillows like brooding hens. Their elbows were propped against the table and they waited for their slave-parents to fulfill their wishes. He drew near them and sat down obediently, waiting for everybody to decide what they wanted. He knew that Matilda, after being angry for a few minutes, always resumed her good spirits. She hated it when the girls disobeyed her, but because they did it more often than not, and she couldn't accept taking second place in their preferences, she would change her state of mind toward them in no time. They had formed a semicircle in front of him, consulting about what each of them would order: the girls wanted ice-cream, but as the photos on the menu showed dozens of goodies, they were now following with their fingers what their mother was reading to them and oscillating between combinations of berries, pistachio, chocolate, mocha, peanuts and caramel.

They were surrounded by a crowd of people who were drinking refreshing beverages, waiting or chatting about how clear the sea had been up till then and how it would be after the storm, about places to eat well and places you should stay away from, about clothes stores and sunscreens with high protection factors, about hotel rooms and houses to rent, about friends and acquaintances and then, again, about food. Actually, food seemed to be the favourite subject in an immensity of pleasures, boredom and wellbeing. The waiter took his position next to their table, with a notebook in his hand and a pen resting against the white sheet of paper. Matilda ordered for the three of them, although the girls were still grumbling, obviously unhappy with the final choice.

'We ordered three different sorts of ice-cream, so we can taste them all,' she announced to him, as if he hadn't been there. 'And lemonades. What would you like?'

He mused for a few seconds. 'I'll have a beer.'

Matilda repeated the final order to the waiter, then turned to the girls and whispered something to them. They all burst into laughter, looking at their father who had put on a poetic and dreamy air. But the cheerfulness was slowly starting to vanish into a cotton-wool silence. He was struggling to distinguish the voices, to tell the close sounds apart from the distant ones. They had all become equal, blending into a single long, constant noise similar to a stifled hum. He let himself be driven by a primal instinct, like an animal sniffing its pray from miles away. And in that balancing of heads that were bending, swaying up and down over spoons of sweet delights, a horizon opened to him that made him shiver with happiness and terror at the same time. Three tables away, right in front, he picked out Emilia's silhouette. She was stiff, in an unlikely position, stone-still like a statue. Not even her eyes moved in her head; her shoulders were thrown back like a soldier, her back was bent, her arms hanging along her body. The man in front of her was serenely leafing through a newspaper.

He looked around, making sure nobody saw him, but the girls were busy giggling, Matilda had overturned her bag, rummaging for God knows what, and everybody around had fallen silent. He could hear her husband rustle the newspaper pages, he could even hear the words enunciated in his mind, he could hear his thoughts and then he suddenly relaxed, realising that they were both above any suspicion. After that short revelation, he decided to get up from the table, unnoticed, to make his way to them and to stop, placidly, by the silent couple who had been lingering for almost two whole hours in the noisy garden. He lowered his hand upon the copper-coloured arm, which quivered as if an ice cube had trickled drops of clear, cold water upon the chocolate, scorched, fuzzy surface. The lights were out and all the spotlights had turned now upon the three protagonists. The woman had raised her eyes and lowered them back down in a split second. The man hadn't noticed him yet and was turning page after page. In the sepulchral silence, a stifled voice sounded close to them:

'Emilia, don't you recognise me?'

They both looked up at the same time. The man who was standing showed too much boldness for such a hot summer day. Nobody around would have dared introduce themselves with such an attitude, with such a firm, inflexible voice, with such a tomcat gaze. They were all astounded, but in different ways: one was afraid and had been rendered speechless, one found it hard to believe that he had had the guts to make such a gesture and, finally, the third one was expectant. Not more than a few seconds passed and not more than a few glances were exchanged. If someone had known or had been willing to recognise the signs, they would have shown in all their comical nakedness, in their fresh, albeit outmoded, frankness. But, as happens most of the time, nobody paid attention to the two people who sat, distraught after a day at the beach and waiting for a refreshing drink – nobody, not even Matilda, busy regrouping the twins who had started to fidget again.

'Do you recognise me? I'm Sorin...'

The silence had made his lungs airtight, his ears were tingling and the earth was spinning like a windmill.

'Sorin, from Sun Alley...'

They had been in danger of being found out many times. Of course, they had never planned ahead; they hadn't built strategies, they had no escape solutions handy, but it went without saying that they had to be prepared for such situations. It only took a careless mistake from one of them, and that would be enough to cause everybody to come to harm. But seeing her had been so unexpected, and the time elapsed since they had last seen each other had passed so painfully, that the luck of bumping into one another in such a dull place was so priceless and he got carried away by emotions. He had been pulled to her by a thin string, invisible to the inattentive eye. He watched her struggle to regain her composure. She left him standing with his hand outstretched for several seconds. She was transfigured, theatrical, out of key, as if she had no clue who the man in front of her was but suspected he must be some kind of acquaintance. He took a deep breath, steeling his heart, and, laughing, turned to the bearded man who had put the newspaper down and was following the scene half curious, half amused.

'She doesn't recognise me. We used to be friends, as children...'

He paused shortly as if to think things over, but then decided to rudely raise the stakes as if in a poker game.

'Women have a tendency to erase the past. Emilia was my first girlfriend. We haven't seen each other for at least twenty years.'

The man stood up ceremonially. His face was subdued and he seemed excited. She stood up too, so as not to be the only one seated, and held her bag to her chest; she probably considered she would be able to control the situation better that way. The men shook hands, introducing themselves at once, so that their names, spoken in two voices, mingled. Emilia had remained with her arms crossed in front of her, her fingers clenched and her shoulders bent.

'Please, do sit down!'

The two of them sat down and looked at Emilia, who had remained in the same uptight position, though now a little less hunched.

'Emilia, let's sit down.'

He spoke to her as you would speak to a sick person, or as he used to talk to the girls when they were visiting someone and he noticed that they were fidgeting. Then, after they sat down and she released a long sigh, things started to fall into place. After another few awkward moments, the conversation centred on the nonsense through which those who haven't seen each other for a while usually try to retrieve lost time, and through which those who have just got to know each other try to get acquainted. During this time, Emilia only uttered a couple of words. She feared she would give herself away, and at the same time she was amazed how good he was at playing his part: how natural he was when talking to her husband, showing not the slightest trace of remorse, not the tiniest feeling of guilt. He was perfectly composed and only his funny start could have betrayed him. And then a thin hand appeared on his shoulder, its fingers clutching the soft fabric of his T-shirt and tugging it firmly. From behind him, a little girl popped up. Her pale face appeared angry and she looked at him reproachfully.

'Daddy, you left us in the lurch.'

The father was momentarily struck dumb in front of the elf standing bold upright with her legs apart, her eyes flashing fire at him, but he regained himself in a few seconds and laughed.

'It's my little girl,' he explained the obvious.

'Mummy said that you left us in the lurch,' she repeated, unrelentingly.

'I see. Please, go back. I'll join you right away.'

The bland-faced man winked at Dori. 'Well, I'd rather you all joined us at our table.'

He had turned to Emilia, addressing the question with a certain affected pompousness. Sal shook his head, trying to slip away, but she was inconvenienced and he had seen her transform before his eyes: the shadows on her face betrayed her feelings so much, showing that she would have done anything to run away from there, to avoid having to play that simulacrum of astonishment, delight and joy, to be friendly with his girls, whom she envied, or with the woman who slept on the other half of his bed. It was when he considered all this that he realised that he felt the need to hurt her and to see her further transformed, disfigured under that appearance of decency and earnestness. It crossed his mind that this humiliation would tame her and persuade her to accept the situation as it was – ugly, demanding, corrupted, unendurable – and to stop seeing it idyllically.

In no time, the two families were at the same table teeming with sweets, lemonades and scoops of ice-cream, all crammed together like the people surrounding them. The conversation was conducted by Emilia's husband, who had introduced himself to the members of the whole clan, one by one:

'Matei.'

Sorin had only heard his name once before, when he and Emilia had met in the post office and they briefly recounted their lives, but he thought that he had forgotten it. He mentioned Matilda whenever it was necessary, but she hadn't mentioned 'Matei' ever since. Amidst the sound of teaspoons touching the glass bowls, digging into the already melting ice-cream scoops that were sliding and mingling their colours and composition, Matilda marvelled, delighted that she had the opportunity at last to meet one of her husband's childhood friends.

'Even though the friend is a girl,' she joked. 'I hope you weren't lovers!'

Matei stepped in. 'I think that we can all use the others' first names. After all, it's as if we've known each other for a long time.'

Matilda was the only one to laugh and admit that pleasantries were unnecessary. Matei had visibly recovered his good spirits in the presence of the new acquaintances.

'Tell me, and I hope you won't think I'm too inquisitive, are you Emilia's age?'

Sorin cleared his throat and said yes. The man talking to him was a character. Sorin was oscillating between feeling the impulse to jump at his throat and admiration for the moderation and the sometimes ridiculous maturity he showed. He was neither too improper nor too handsome; neither too smart nor careless. He had a way of placing himself on a par with everyone, even the twins, to whom he would cast a comic glance from time to time.

'I asked you because that's what I had presumed. I'm three years older, and many times you can feel this difference between me and Emilia, even though it seems so small. Well, some are separated by ten, even twenty years. I'm not talking about this kind of anomaly. But even in our case, you can feel it. Maybe it's the distance between professions as well – Emilia with her French, while I'm a mathematician. We have totally different taste. She's more emotional.'

'She always was like that.'

'Really?'

Matei laughed again, revealing his white, shiny teeth. 'Well, I would have guessed so. Is it the same with you? With the profession difference, I mean.'

Matilda suddenly joined in, with a long and serious face. 'And how! When I met Sorin, I knew that plants mattered to him more than people: if you water them every two days, it means that you love them.'

'I'm sorry, but I don't understand. What does this have to do with plants?'

'Sorin is a botanist.'

'A botanist, is it?' Matei marvelled. 'A profession as difficult as mine, if not more so. Where do you work?'

'At the Botanical Gardens.'

'At least it's a quiet place. You must be able to take the girls there.'

'The girls are crazy about the place,' Matilda confirmed.

'We should go, too – pay him a visit when we return to Bucharest. To be honest, I haven't been to the Botanical Gardens since childhood. In school we had to make these herbariums...'

Matilda became animated. 'We used to make herbariums as well. And those notebooks we'd pass around full of quizzes everyone would have to answer – we called them oracles. Remember those! I know the questions were silly, but we would read the answers with such excitement... God! I'll never forget that. Children can be so narcissistic!'

'Why do you say that?' Sorin asked her.

'Because we actually wanted to see what we looked like to the others – if they loved us and if we had managed to charm them. Aren't all children seducers? Don't they all actually want to win over their opponents?'

Matei shook with laughter and turned to the girls. 'Listen to that. What do you have to say?'

The girls made no gesture. They had started to drill deeper inside the ice-cream sauce, which had an eggnog consistency and from which only two hillocks stood up, shining in the sunlight.

'This gentleman asked you a question!'

'Oh, don't 'gentleman' me! They can call me Matei; I want us to be friends. All right?'

The girls looked up, their faces half smudged with ice-cream, and nodded. Dori stopped with her spoon suspended in mid-air and seemed to think for a while, then half-opened her mouth, looking at Matei. After a break, she asked: 'What's an oracle?' Then she dipped her nose back in her ice-cream.

The grown-ups laughed; only Emilia had a gloomy look. The white scarf tying her hair back had slipped toward the crown of her head, and the curly hair exploded from somewhere behind the white margin, over her shoulders, giving her a lunatic air. She didn't dare look at him and she had taken on an absent appearance, ignoring everything around her. She didn't have the courage to look at Matilda either, though she was busy with the girls anyway. Emilia rarely took part in the general cheerfulness, only putting on an artificial smile like a character in a melodrama.

He found it hard to recognise the woman he loved in that apparition, and it seemed equally difficult to exchange at least a few words with her: to tell her, for example, that he would be waiting for her at their spot the next morning, to apologise, to explain what had happened. He knitted his eyebrows and turned to the twins, who had just finished eating and were now gathering the traces of caramel off the plate.

'I hope you won't fall ill again!'

The man was the first to rise to the bait, as he had expected. 'What was wrong with them?'

As if complying with her husband's unrevealed and hastily brooded plan, Matilda started to chatter about Mari's mysterious illness and the moments spent by her sickbed in helplessness and despair. He had finally managed to draw Emilia's attention. She had pricked up her ears and was now following this account breathlessly. Close to the end of the story, he could have sworn that she had tears in her eyes and that the tips of her fingers were slowly trembling on the table, moistening the metallic surface.

She got up from the table, making an excuse and mumbling something to her husband. After that, Sorin heard only the low-heeled sandals clicking on the floor tiles until the noise was gone.

'Is something wrong? Where's she going?'

Matei waved his hand. 'I apologise.'

It had suddenly gotten dark, and in Emilia's wake a milky, creamy way had opened, with the traces of her steps still shining upon it. Graceful shapes were floating in the air, dancing around him, befuddling him with their hot skin, leaving behind them tiny, coloured beads of sweat, falling like drops of rain off the leaves of the green trees. He wished he could jump straight into that thick river and abandon himself in its flow, up to the spring, over which he could see the embossed effigy of her sphinx-like face. She had cheekbones made of stone and thick eyebrows made of rust-coloured, autumnal grass. Her juicy mouth gaped from raspberry bushes, and her eyes sparkled faintly from two hollows that made you believe you could step to the other side on the moist realm of hope. He heard Matei continue.

'Emilia believes that she is sick and stuffs herself with pills. Today it's her heart, tomorrow it's her swollen lymph nodes, or dizziness, or headaches – you name it. We have a doctor friend and I asked him to prescribe her some mild antidepressants, which give her these fits of somnolence.'

Matilda's face was mellow with compassion, but also aged and puffy from happiness and relief. Or that's how Sorin saw her from the other side of the table that stretched now so far it had become the other part of the world.

'I'd better go...'

'Where?' Matei asked, intrigued.

'Wouldn't it be better for someone to stay with her? To make sure she's all right?'

Matilda's face refreshed itself in a couple of seconds. Surprise and malice had had a lifting effect upon her features. But Matei wasn't blinking, as if the possibility of there existing a relationship between this old childhood friend and his wife – however feeble, however tiny and unimportant – was definitely out of the question. And this blindness, this absolute confidence, this unflinching ownership he discovered in small gestures and words, in the brutal revealing in his paternal tone of the hypochondria Emilia allegedly suffered from, slowly poisoned his mind. But Matilda raised her voice.

'Sorin, please. This is unnecessary.' And, in a lower voice, she added, 'It's not our business.' Then she courteously turned to the serene husband and made him the most amazing proposal. 'I would say, if you don't mind...'

'Of course I don't mind!'

'Sure – I meant, if you don't mind and if Emilia is fine with that, I'd like to invite you to come to our place tomorrow. We've rented a little house from a local; it has two bedrooms and we also have a small garden. It's very pleasant and cool in the evening. We can also have a barbecue if we like, can't we?'

He was hanging on her words and consenting dutifully, silently encouraging Matei, who seemed to hesitate in accepting the invitation.

'Only if you would really like to...' he added, trying to elicit an answer.

Without this certainty, the following days would have been continuous madness and suffering.

Matei got up slowly, a smile glued to his lips like a sticker. He was grinning politely at the happy family while rummaging in his pockets for change. After a few seconds that seemed like hours to Sorin, he drew out a couple of small bills, but his gesture brought about immediate protest.

'No, no, please, the pleasure is mine. I really didn't expect to meet Emilia here, after all these years. And I want you to give me now a firm promise that tomorrow evening, at seven, you will come to our place. Matilda, please, tell him how to get there. We have a deal!'

Sorin put his hand out and shook Matei's hand vigorously; not exaggeratedly, but firmly, as if they had just closed a deal. His gesture meant that, although they hadn't put it down in black and white, they had a gentlemen's agreement. Of course, Matei hadn't managed to say anything in agreement, but even his silence could have been taken as an approval. Silence meant lack of resistance, a discreet consent, an abdication.

He said goodbye as abruptly as Emilia had and moved away, saying to the girls, over his shoulder, that he was going to pay and that he would wait for them in the car. As he left behind the table full of leftovers from the feast, he felt invaded by a feeling of foolish bliss, en exaltation that disturbed his entrails.

When he reached the car, his head already felt heavy. He leaned against the wall surrounding the parking lot and threw up with tears in his eyes. Someone had put all the images that made up reality in a huge mixing bowl, so that all its elements – all the particles, fractions, impulses and stimuli – had lost their destinations and were now wandering round the world in aimless pieces, just as he was wandering in search of his old partner. If he had had some time, he would have returned to Bucharest and searched for his old playmates, would have gathered them all together, all except Harry, and would have presented her with them as a gift, so she would see all that they had lost and then recovered by miracle.

Under the soles of his feet ants were hysterically swarming, seeking refuge under a dying cockroach that was treading the air with its feet. Sometimes, feeling upon him the eyes of the stranger rising fatally above, it would stop for a couple of seconds, begging for mercy or hoping that maybe that way its agony would pass unnoticed. He grabbed it between his thumb and forefinger and lifted it off the ground. The insect waved its feelers another couple of times, then became as still as stone. He remained fascinated by the insect for several moments, noticing that it looked like an emissary of death, sitting with its mutinous horns and its long, thin, graceful legs supporting a shiny, smooth-backed, green-black body, radiating baroque shades of purple if he turned it to one side.

'Fabricius,' he said to himself, and the cockroach answered with a final spasm.

'Is that its name?'

The girls were standing behind him. Dori had been the one to ask the question, while Mari was looking at him with a face that had repulsion written all over it. 'Yuck, that's revolting!'

'Would you like to hold it yourself?' her father tempted her.

Mari broke into a run, heading for the car, where Matilda was already waiting. He offered it to the other girl. Dori caught it between her plump fingers as if between two claws. Her face was beaming, illuminated by an unusual fascination. She was staring at the little cockroach that, after passing from one host to another, had come back to its senses and started to move chaotically. She watched it, marvelling at how fragile and frightening it was at the same time. Its frail legs probably sensed the end, for they were scratching the air. Matilda began calling her, out of patience and hungry.

Sorin put a hand on Dori's shoulder. 'Come on, put it down. And make sure you don't show it to your mum, or she won't give us any food.'

Dori revealed her small, white teeth and pinkish gums. She opened her small palm and slowly put the cockroach there on its back. There was a whole set of machinery behind the shiny shell: a tangle of tiny tubes winding like tendrils, carrying liquids. She reached with the tip of her index finger, preparing to inspect the inside of the factory, but then she stopped. She looked at her father with moist, loving eyes and a fleeting feeling of pride furrowed her face. For an instant, the father felt the same, but the moment flew quickly away. The girl, like a prestidigitator, caught the cockroach in between the two claws of the same hand with which she had laid it to rest and crushed it, revealing two fingers down which an ochre-coloured, gluey liquid was trickling. Pride was still floating in the air between the petrified father and the triumphant daughter.

'Are you coming?'

She handed the cockroach to her father, gaping at him with her round eyes and enticing him to take the prey. Sorin drew back one step and the girl, seeing the disgust on his face, started to yell and laugh. She probably hadn't expected her father to be such a coward, or maybe that's what she had intended: to see his reaction, to test how brave he was and what he would have been able to do for them in exchange. She threw the crushed shell, from which the viscous, honey-like liquid seeped, to the ground and rushed to her mother, who was already seated in the car, with sunglasses perched on her nose in annoyed expectation. The day had acquired another dimension, the cockroach's unjust death having placed a giant lens over the past and the future. He had a dull light in his eyes, as if what he saw there through that giant lens had brought about amazement but also childish misapprehension.

They returned home in silence, and that was how they ended the day as well. Even the girls had become silent, while Dori, after secretly studying her father during dinner, finally seemed to have realised that the merciless elimination of the insect had ruined their friendship and temporarily estranged him from her. Only after Matilda washed the dishes and threw herself on the living room sofa did Sorin have the courage to ask her, in a voice vibrating with excitement: 'I wonder, will they change their minds or really come tomorrow evening?'

Matilda threw him a tired look, similar to that of his mother when she would come out of the kitchen and lie down on the bed in her room, rolling up the pillows under her head and dozing half upright as if on watch. 'Why would they change their minds? They accepted, didn't they?'

'Thank you for that. I know that you did it for me.'

'Oh, come on, I think it's cute to meet your childhood girlfriend. And to learn more about you, no? Besides, they seem very nice people, very decent.'

She loved him, he had no doubt about that, but her love was like leavening dough: although he knew that it would turn into a glorious cake, that raw smell of flour mixed with water turned his stomach.

'You haven't answered my question, though.'

He started. 'What question?'

'On the terrace of the restaurant... Was she your first love?'

Sorin wasn't good at lying, and he was used to taking everything seriously. A mere suspicion would have made his life miserable, which is why he made each reckoning extremely fast, with a rapidity he himself was often terrified of. He put his head in her lap and grabbed her waist, sinking his nose in the warm layer of fat on her belly. Matilda had retained a layer of lard, flesh and skin around her waist that was soft and good but stiff to the touch. He liked to sink inside it and not have to look at her, to bury his forehead into that softness and fall asleep. When she lamented and felt sorry for herself because, after two births, her beauty had suffered beyond repair, Sorin would always gently remind her that it had actually been a single birth and that the damage done by it didn't bother him a bit. He would instantly add, 'I love to sleep in your lap!' and Matilda would mellow, believing him, because then he actually spoke the truth.

'First we were friends, and then I fell in love with her. Actually, she liked me first. But we were very little. It doesn't count.'

He could feel the body starting to shrink with tension.

'And?'

'And... and you know how it is.'

'I don't know. What happened?'

Sorin burst into laughter. 'Oh, come on, I told you, we were very little! What the hell could have happened? My parents and I moved to another neighbourhood, and that's that!'

Matilda held him for another couple of minutes; then she got up, gently placing his head on the sofa pillows. 'I'm going to bed. I'm dead tired and tomorrow we'll have a busy day. Come on!'

That night, everybody in the house slept lightly. Sorin, however, set his inner alarm clock for six in the morning. He had to be up at six and off to the beach in the ten minutes that followed. They needed at least two hours to set the record straight for the meeting, to compare their stories, to make a single one from the two. He fell asleep with her and their story in mind; he had found the perfect version and planned to dream about it till dawn so he wouldn't forget it.

VIII

THE PARTY

He jumped bolt upright, frightened. A strong light struck through the translucent curtains from outside, falling in blood-red streaks over the bedclothes. Matilda was sleeping quietly with her back to him. She was nestled peacefully like a little girl, her hair unfolded on the pillow as if arranged by hand into a fan shape. He had thought it was later than it actually was, so he left the room in a hurry without washing his face, only stopping to pull on a pair of trousers and a T-shirt he found on the back of a chair in the living room.

When he stepped out, the unripe light of the day and the chilly air assured him that it couldn't have been later than six. He had decided not to take the car to avoid the noise it would have made. He didn't know for sure when he would be back, and the missing car would have indicated that he had gone farther away. Without it, he could lie that he had gone for a short walk on the road winding along the seafront, that he had stopped to gather some shells from the beach – he knew Matilda liked to collect coloured seashells, which she would put in a huge, transparent glass bowl she had back home together with the others she gathered every year from all the beaches they visited – and that he didn't realise how fast time had flown. She would take walks alone in the afternoon herself and was willing to accept that, during holidays, walks were a pleasure she could grant to anyone.

All the way there, he mulled over Emilia and the situation they were in. There were other thoughts as well, mingled together; irrelevant, stray memories popping up on the empty and colourless surface of his fear-stricken mind: the cockroach Dori had mercilessly crushed, the faint remembrance of the indications he had given to his neighbour, the watering schedule for his flowers, each on a certain day of the week. If his neighbour hadn't respected the schedule, he would have found, upon returning home, that his perpetually blooming plants had withered away. He advanced through the thought thicket, rolling his footsteps on the asphalt and, farther along, on the dirt road that led to the beach. The stones were flying from beneath his soles, noisily hitting the pavement. He was in a hurry because he feared that Emilia would leave. But actually, the only thought he had been obstinately avoiding – although it had been pestering him for some time – was that she might very well not have come at all, that the humiliation and the suffering he had thrown upon her had now turned against him, had made her ripe for retribution.

He approached the beach with big strides; another three hundred feet and the monotonous expanse, interrupted by a thin line that opened another scene of monotony, would show itself, revealing the truth. He was barrelling along; he would have bolted if he could, but he feared she would see him from a distance and that he would seem ridiculous. Beads of sweat were hanging from his chin, tickling him slightly, and the T-shirt had stuck to his chest and shoulder blades. Because of the sweat, his shoes had started to eat into his flesh: first as a faint burn, then penetrating to the interior layers, delicately excoriating them. At the end of the three hundred feet, he stopped. First, he checked his hurt heel; the edge of his shoe was coloured a bloody reddish-brown. Then he looked up and gazed toward the beach.

A woman wearing an exaggeratedly large-brimmed hat lay on a mat, propped on her elbows. Her skin had, in that position, a couple of folds. From his angle, she seemed old, but her face was hidden under the brim's shade and he couldn't precisely tell her age. He stopped and sat down, then remained hunched, watching the sea. He had known ever since leaving home that he wouldn't find her, but he had secretly hoped, nonetheless, that their meeting again and his daughter's illness had softened her. However, it was not the fact that she hadn't come now that alarmed him, but the thought that she might not ever want to see him again. Was it possible that this wasn't just a momentary impulse, a wish to teach him a lesson, but that maybe love had died for her the morning she had waited for him in vain, just as they had so often spoken about? It happens. He knew that people ended up like that sometimes.

The woman stretched her feet and pulled the hat upon her face, like a peasant lying on the grass after mowing it. He stretched, too, fanning his toes. That tiny, insignificant motion made him relax and see the situation with much more optimism. They would see each other in the evening, anyway, and they would have the opportunity to set things straight. As the air stroked his fanned toes, his plans gained momentum. He would tell her that he had decided to break up with Matilda and would summon her to do the same with Matei. Now, after seeing him, he was certain that she had nothing to do with that ape, who talked about her as if she were a schizophrenic, a hypochondriac, a lunatic. Who spoke much without saying anything, and gestured time and again and acted as if he knew it all – except what was happening right under his nose.

He had no idea when he had drowsed off and fallen asleep while watching the sea and the lady on the beach who was sitting graciously with a raised knee soaking in the sun. He only knew that he woke up a couple of hours later. The sun was shining high in the middle of the sky, in an angry blaze. His body was numb, wrapped in a corset of sweat and exhaustion. The awakening was painful and the lack of any will to open his eyes and come back to reality made him assume that the presence of death must be similar. But it was not death itself that scared him at that moment, but the way they would find him: the position of his body, the stench, the swelling and the burns the masters of embalming would have to conceal. He had resigned himself to the thought that, ultimately, there was no age for settling your accounts. When he was a child, his parents had always told him before going to bed that only old people had to worry and that he had nothing to be afraid of. He had always suspected they were lying or, better, that they had left out a pretty important detail: to mention when exactly old age began. Emilia complained that she was getting old, that she wouldn't have time to be happy. Matilda always told the girls that, from now on, the future was ahead of them while she and Sorin would only be left with the past. At work, they had asked him whether he considered, or already had, a private pension plan.

His heart was pounding in his chest like a brass band with drums and woodwinds. He had the feeling that the now-populated beach resonated from their shrill noise. He started to get up, but only managed to move his arms and find that his entire left side was stiff and painful. 'Maybe I've died!' he said to himself, and then was embarrassed by the unworthy thought. His wet clothes had penetrated his skin, turning into a set of armour on his inert body. Finally, after several attempts, he managed to get up and, barely standing, tried to find his way back.

As he advanced on the stony path toward the road, the feeling that he had forgotten something on the beach became stronger and stronger. He felt his trousers to see if he had the house keys, and the keys dutifully clinked in his pocket. Only when he reached the road did he realise that the pain radiating throughout his body was emphasised by the fact that he was barefoot, and that blood was trickling from the bare soles of his feet as they scratched against the thin, little stones, sharp as ground glass. But it would have been inconceivable for him to go all the way back. It wasn't really that important that his shoes were missing.

Suddenly, he felt happy and motivated. He remembered the feeling of exaltation he had fallen asleep with and tried to revive it, but he was too exhausted and all he actually wanted, upon closer consideration, was to get home and take a nap, to gather his strength before the evening. He started to walk slowly along the road toward their house. Thirty feet ahead of him, the road sign showed that the village ended there. A little over a mile and he could say he was home.

A red car coming from the opposite direction passed him by, honking, and then slowed down two dozen feet away. Sorin stepped away from the margin of the road and gestured to the driver with his middle finger. Then he walked on, wearily, but after a couple of steps, he stopped. He turned his head and saw that the car hadn't moved. He bent over, leaning his head against his knees, and all his blood rushed into his temples, making him dizzy. He remained like that for several minutes and, finally, he burst out crying in loud, angry sobs. All the absurd events of that day were jammed in his throat, bursting to get out. When he couldn't cry any longer, he started to howl in a shredded voice, regardless of the people around who had stopped to watch the show put on by the flushed, sweaty, madman.

After a while, he woke up at home. He had no idea how he had got there. He could hear Matilda working around the kitchen and the girls' stifled voices from somewhere farther away. He stretched out on the bed that was covered by a sticky, dusty synthetic bedspread and leaned his head against the headboard. He fell fast asleep in an instant and, in almost another instant, he woke up. The direction of the wind had changed and so had the light, whose brightness had faded. He realised that he had slept deeply and for a long time. Only now did he feel overcome by a feeling of guilt and pressure, since he would have to explain what he had done in the morning and how he had got home. Matilda walked in on tiptoe and inspected him.

'You woke up.'

He answered half-heartedly, with a groan. She came close to him, still standing.

'If you had slept a little longer, the guests would have arrived.'

'What time is it?'

'It's almost six.'

'You should have woken me.'

She threw him a reproachful look. 'Where the hell have you been?'

He sank into a gloomy silence. He didn't want to answer right away, because he lacked the power to say anything. He didn't feel like fighting with her and he wished he had been granted a respite to recompose his social mask, to be eloquent again. He wished he could have slept a little longer; he would have closed his eyes and, that way, Matilda would have gently disappeared, without him having anything to do with her elimination.

'Do you at least remember what happened? Have you been drinking?'

'In the morning?'

'I don't know, I was just asking. I see you don't want to say anything. Anyway...' She drew a few steps away and looked out the window. 'Now is really not the moment, with those people coming over, but I wasn't delighted at all when a stranger brought you to the door, carrying you in his arms. And I wonder what that woman must have said!'

'I wasn't drunk.'

'But you behaved as if you were.'

'I fell asleep on the beach.'

'But what were you doing, sleeping at the beach? I thought you said you were jogging! Is that jogging? Going to sleep on the beach and dreaming of running?' Her voice was rising, piercing the walls.

'What woman?'

'What do you mean?'

'You said that a woman brought me home.'

Matilda shrugged her shoulders. 'I didn't say that *a* woman brought you home. I told you that it was your ex-girlfriend, Emilia.'

'You must be joking. That's impossible!''Why?'

He looked carefully at her face, but Matilda was unchanged; no nerve was shaking, no sign betrayed her.

'Did her husband carry me home?'

'It wasn't her husband. And I really don't know what difference it makes who brought you, how they brought you... the question is what happened? If you're sick I think I should know, shouldn't I? You say that you haven't been drinking... what is wrong with you?'

Sorin got up, feeling all dizzy. 'I'm fine. I told you, I went for a walk, I wanted to pick some shells for you... I sat down for a bit because I had been sleepless all night, tossing and turning in my bed. I fell asleep on the beach, and probably I had a touch of sun - stroke. No sun shade, at over forty degrees. But I don't understand how it was Emilia who found me, of all people. It's unbelievable. I will apologise in the evening, when they come.'

He could feel her near him, mellowed, her resistance visibly melting; only the traces of worry were left, and he had managed by his voice's music to chase them magically away. And, still, he had almost told the truth.

'If they come.'

He looked at her intently. He still controlled his voice, but felt the need to sit down again.

'Why? Did they say they weren't coming anymore?'

'No, they didn't say. But with this incident today, maybe they changed their minds.'

'They didn't change their minds, for sure.'

Matilda headed for the door, conscious of the upper hand she held.

'I should thank the guy who brought me. Did he say what his name was? Is he a friend of theirs?'

Matilda shook her head without bothering to turn around. She went out, the question still floating gloomily around the room. Soon he would be able to sound her out about what had happened during the day, so he decided to stop questioning his wife.

But time seemed to flow much more slowly than he had expected. First there were the girls, who pestered him about telling them the promised flower stories. He had to give them his word that he would do it after the guests left, but as they knew perfectly well that the guests would leave much after their bedtime, they managed to wring a promise out of their father that the next day they would get two stories. Then there was the issue of getting dressed. Normally he couldn't care less about what clothes he would throw on, but now it was different. Colour could be meaningful. Seriousness or casualness could have an impact on the outcome of that evening. He spent an hour rummaging in the closet. The combinations of clothes slowly became characters, potential Sorins and possible solutions to the situation. For the most part, the solutions were dramatic and unsatisfactory, so the characters were discarded and a new labour would begin in search of a new character. In the end, he chose a pair of capris and a white T-shirt.

When Matilda showed up again, after the last preparations, to get dressed, she found him sitting on the edge of the bed, with the closet's contents turned upside down and clothes strewn on the floor. She stopped in the threshold, her mouth agape. 'What did you do here?'

But he was satisfied and content with the character he had pulled out of the box: a thirty-three-year-old dull, neutral man without too much imagination, who could have been at the same time a diehard family man or a womaniser.

Matilda got dressed in five minutes and, after another five, she had already settled in the living room, where on a table she had arranged four odd champagne goblets she had found in the kitchen cupboard. She was pleased and happy to have finished everything in time.

'Well,' she said, leaning back, 'now all we need is for the guests to arrive.' She laughed, opening her fleshy, red-painted mouth, like a jellyfish.

Sorin remained behind in the bedroom, putting his clothes back in order. He caught a fleeting glimpse of himself in the round mirror hanging on the wall opposite the bed. Although he had slept almost all day, he had a tired face; his skin was crumpled from sleeping, and you could see the wrinkles left on his face by the bedclothes. He could hear his ribs clattering in his chest and the blood gurgling in his arteries. He reached out his arm to put the hanger with the neatly arranged shirts back into the closet, but the gesture exhausted him so much that he had to set it down and take a deep breath. Then he repeated the motion and, after closing the wardrobe and lying back in bed, he started to think of the day that had just passed and of what lay ahead. The more he thought, the louder the movements inside rang.

He heard another muffled noise that made him jump out of bed and remain standing, horror-stricken, his sweaty palms stuck to his trousers. He heard Matilda's sandals shuffle; he heard the door handle go click-clack and, immediately after that, the voices: Matilda's, squeaking with enthusiasm, as it usually did when she wanted to be more convincing in expressing her emotions, and another one: a man's guttural voice that extended into a short echo he knew so well, a voice so familiar it seemed like his own. He tried to listen more carefully, but as all the sounds had grown louder and were mingling together, he got up and slid out the door on tiptoe, like a drowsy cat, to the living room, from where he managed to see the guests packed in the small hallway. The girls were holding onto Matilda's skirt behind her, gaping their round, cherry-shaped mouths at the tall lady all dressed in white, with a diva's air and strong perfume that had pervaded the house.

In a second, they had all rushed into the room. Matilda saw him and an expression of surprise mixed with irony spread on her face. He knew her so well, with that severe appearance of hers when she caught him lying or when something bothered her. She would always throw him that superior, reserved and contemptuous look, as if she had said: 'I know you too well! You act like a lizard, and that's why I have to constantly be on guard, always on the watch and vigilant!' Sometimes her look would say: 'I'm tired of being on the watch! I wish you'd disappear, at least for a couple of seconds!'

'See?' she smirked. 'You were afraid they wouldn't come!'

She seemed dreadful and terribly rude to him – she knew that he couldn't have contradicted her and that she had put him in an awkward position – but he clenched his teeth and grinned back with restrained enthusiasm. He advanced with steady, firm steps toward the two guests and extended his hand to Emilia, who squeezed it coldly, then to Matei, who looked downright handsome now after having washed and arranged himself; he had, as his mother used to say, a commanding presence, and that meant a lot in a man.

'I hope we arrived on time,' Matei said mindfully.

'You came at the perfect moment. Everything is ready; I just finished. And Sorin just woke up. He was tired after his adventure this morning.'

The two had an identical smile on their lips, sympathetic and absent at the same time as if, although they had heard and understood Matilda's words, they had missed something essential and stubbornly refused to find out what.

'I'm glad you made it. I had the feeling I hadn't explained clearly enough how to get here. Our house is a bit out of sight. It's easy to get here, if you know the way, but you can easily get lost as well. That's why...'

Matilda was silently pushing the two guests toward the door that opened onto the garden. As if caught in an invisible net, they moved with small steps toward the place where the cooler air was waiting, along with the plastic chairs and table, nicely set with a tablecloth and matching napkins. Outside, Sorin's lungs filled with a salty, choking breeze. He noticed the barbecue smoking unobtrusively, like an innuendo, to his right where the girls now played. So Matilda had really done everything: she had prepared the food, lit the fire, chilled the drinks, created a pleasant atmosphere. She always insisted that it was not just the taste of the food that was important, but also the place in which you ate it. Sorin found it a waste of time, but their friends seemed to appreciate Matilda's culinary displays, albeit only out of politeness. Passing around drinks from two baroque trays like an experienced circus performer, she reacted to each compliment with false modesty, acting as if she had suddenly found herself on the red carpet under the spotlights.

'Darling, can you play some music?'

He started. Yet music was definitely missing: some elevating and dramatic music to improve the taste of the savoury dishes. He hadn't looked at Emilia. Once in the open air, they had scattered around; Matei and Matilda remained grouped together and chatted in silence, so quietly that for a moment Sorin had the impression they were talking about him and the incident that afternoon. But he immediately realised it was very likely that Matei had no idea Emilia had brought him home, because he hadn't mentioned a thing upon seeing him.

He went inside the house, and while he was rummaging through the CDs they had brought from Bucharest, trying to pick one to Matilda's liking, he watched her. She sat out of the way, gazing at the girls with a certain nostalgia as if, seeing them, she was watching her past self. But as he watched her, he started to suspect that all her self-restraint was nothing but subterfuge. That lost air and her tragic, suffering look were only dissimulating another secret, one she kept not only from the cheated husband, but also from the credulous lover. He realised – and the revelation was so striking his knees gave way under him from pain and excitement – that all her kind behaviour, the waiting, the amorous game, were nothing but stratagems to divert his attention. He felt the urge to take Matei aside and reveal his wife's true character, to ask him if he knew who the man who had accompanied her that afternoon was. He had no doubt that he was infinitely more entitled to his fury at the unfaithful woman than her legitimate partner. He was infinitely more entitled *and* more legitimate.

He slipped a CD through the thin slit and turned up the volume. Rumbling sounds, like an explosion, burst from the house. The windows rattled menacingly and everybody in the garden remained astounded for several seconds, not knowing what had happened. Within the framework of the window, Sorin watched them contemplatively, with a vacant gaze. But Emilia moved only slightly.

All that evening, his only concern was to follow even her tiniest grimace. He hunted her everywhere, in all her gestures; he remained silent, on the watch, and in response, she did the same. The noise was provided by the girls, who had been granted the absolutely miraculous permission of not having to eat any more and jumping straight to dessert, and by Matei, who oscillated between paying compliments to Matilda and her unprecedented culinary gifts and making travel recommendations: 'You *must*' – he emphasised the word – 'go to Balcic as well. The place is incredible.' His mouth rounded affectedly. 'And the prices likewise. And you have to visit the castle. Well, 'castle' is an overstatement – it's more like a manor – but you can sense the good taste. That I guarantee.'

However, despite the harmony ruling over that night, something unforeseen happened. In the great euphoria that had overcome them, the girls, transformed into genuine whirlwinds, encircled the whole table at full speed in a tornado involving leaves, napkins, and the smoke of the barbecue sizzling on the coals. Then, one of them – no one could really tell which one precisely – caught the bowl in which the gravy delicately floated and upturned it right in Emilia's lap. The white linen skirt instantly absorbed the thick, orange liquid, and all other sounds died in the sauce now trickling from the edge of the table in a lazy river. Matilda rushed over at once with a napkin in her hand, blotting both Emilia's skirt and the edge of the table that had now turned into a gutter. The men remained in abeyance, looking at the two women, one agitated and the other one sullen. Matilda banished the girls to the house, threatening that they would stay in their room until the next day. It was then that Emilia finally spoke:

'Please, I beg you all, don't overreact! It could happen to anyone! Any one of us could have spilled it. I don't want you to punish the girls for such nonsense!'

But Matilda was ironbound. 'I told you two to calm down! I told them! This is totally unacceptable! Sorin, please, take them to their room at once! You will get two plates of food and dessert tomorrow! And that only if you behave!'

The girls were perplexed, totally unable to even try to exculpate themselves. Despite the objections of the guests, who seemed to take the punishment harder than the punished, they disappeared inside the house. Their withdrawal created a void among the adults, throwing them into a sullen silence for several minutes. The hosts fussed in between the garden and the house, where Sorin had disappeared with two plates of food full to the brim. The barbecue coloured the air with a cheerful smell, in sharp contrast with the tense atmosphere, as it was periodically fed pieces of blood-red meat that roasted in no time.

But when everyone was back, the first one to speak was Emilia. First she spoke about how much she loved children, and they all listened intently, not understanding what the point was, while her voice acquired dramatic modulations. Finally, she confessed that she had given up the joy of their having a child of their own, because she knew that the idea didn't really appeal to Matei and because

–here she made a longer pause and her voice started to tremble – she had always thought it wasn't the right time, but to hear the voices of children and to feel their rustle around her was her greatest comfort.

The silence around the table deepened. Sorin was the only one who was still paying attention and, although his eyes were riveted upon his plate, the sound of his fork scraping the white porcelain with a screech and his tense body showed that the words of his childhood friend hadn't left him unmoved. Fortunately, nobody noticed him.

'Your girls remind me of myself... when I was little.'

She became thoughtful, and for the first time that evening, he looked at her lovingly and wanted to tell her that his twins reminded him of her, too; that this was one of the reasons he loved them so and couldn't leave them. But he saw Matilda spying on him out of the corner of his eye, and he averted his gaze. She continued, 'It was the most beautiful time. I felt inexpressibly happy. And I had reasons to be.'

'What reasons could you have had at that age?' Matei interrupted her.

But Emilia went on, as if she hadn't heard him. 'I remember so clearly, is if it were yesterday. I can almost feel, on the tip of my tongue, the taste of the tea my mother used to make and of the homemade lemonade; I can smell her dishes in which she used to add lots of tomato sauce, I can hear her grumbling around the house in discontent; I can even hear my father, who left quite early on when I was only five, but still I can hear him even now; when I enter our house I can sense his cigarette smell... My father used to smoke two packs of cigarettes a day, and when you entered his room, the smoke was thick like fog. My mother would keep me away, saying I would fall sick if I sat there even a couple of minutes, and I believed her. That's why my father is such a ghostlike memory, because he used to shut himself up in his room and only come out for dinner. He would drink a shot of plum brandy beforehand and then spoon in the food without any appetite. Then he would wait for my mother to finish eating, for that was the rule: my mother had to set her fork down, and after she leaned back, we would both thank her and wait for her to get up, after which we were allowed to get up ourselves. When this happened, my father would bolt to his room, his already lit cigarette in the corner of his mouth, driving my mother crazy. Then she would keep grumbling while washing the dishes, hissing through her clenched teeth words I barely understood.'

Everybody was following her words. No one understood what she was getting at and where the thread of the confession had started. But she didn't seem to mind them, as if the past was the only thing around her. But Sorin's heart was pounding and a barely formed drop of sweat had appeared on his temple, ready to roll down his cheek. He couldn't even tell if it was the fear of hearing her give herself away or the excitement of listening to her. It was as if he was listening to music from his youth, which now brought to him not only the pleasurable sounds but also the memories of that old, long-ago atmosphere. But she had detached herself from the world.

'When my father left, I didn't really miss him. On the contrary, I can say I was delighted, because suddenly, what had been his smoking room – that I was supposed to carefully avoid for my mother's sake – became my room overnight. I took all my things there; I furnished it so you could no longer feel his presence. My mother stuffed the closets with lavender and put dry orange peels on top, so the smell was removed. We never mentioned him again, and I found a good place to hide from my mother's anger, when it broke out God knows from what.'

She sighed, then turned to Matilda. Her whole attention seemed concentrated upon the woman who listened with a politeness that barely masked the feeling of uneasiness on her face.

'When a parent has a problem, the child unconsciously tries to solve it. Even if the parent doesn't talk about these unpleasant situations, the child has some sort of radar, an inner eye that sees reality exactly as it is. That's how it was with my mother and I. She never told me anything about her misfortunes, but the way in which she was bothered by any little thing that wasn't in place, or by any deviation of mine from the common agenda, conveyed more tension than if she had honestly confessed what was burdening her. Well, now I know what was weighing her down, but it's too late; I can't help her anymore. But at that time, it made me withdraw into my own shell, and because I've never liked loneliness, I clung to my friends to lick my wounds.'

Sorin pricked up his ears. Her words were heading his way, although in the beginning they had seemed to have another direction. He found solace in the thought that the woman who was so serenely narrating, detached from them and from their plentiful table on which the grilled pieces of meat grew colder and colder, was no longer the woman he knew. But she wasn't finished.

'Some were funny and kept me in good spirits, and I sensed others liked me. Needless to say, it was the latter I tried more to draw near to. The smart ones were nice, but I needed confidence, support, and they were too busy then, discovering the world, investigating, having fun together. So I took refuge – let's say in the arms, though it wasn't quite like that – in the arms of a boy I had accidentally met in the neighbourhood when coming home from school.'

She looked at him, hypnotised.

'Sorin knows him. He was a charmer and we used to say we didn't like him, but I secretly found myself very attracted to his storytelling. And he always seemed to have time. Of course, everybody has time at that age, but some had to sleep in the afternoon, others had to read, to study or God knows what else. I could do what I wanted, and then there was this boy, who always answered the phone when I called. Not a single time did he refuse me when I called him.'

'And what did you used to do?'

Sorin's voice broke the rhythm of the story and the silence around it.

'At the beginning, we would talk...' Emilia seemed to speak more carefully and slowly.

'Well, memories...' Matei blandly intervened, trying to put

an end to the story. 'You're lucky to know each other since childhood.'

'It isn't exactly luck,' Emilia interrupted, obscured by a shadow. 'He wasn't the only one I was talking to, if that's what you mean. But at the beginning we just chatted. He was in the same situation family-wise, with a single mother who was away most of the time, and his house was almost always empty. Anyway, maybe we weren't even that close until something very bad happened to me, something that hurt me terribly.'

She stopped and swallowed hard as if she had struggled to stop her tears. But her eyes were dry, not mirroring a thing.

'Emilia, let's not monopolise the conversation,' her husband softly cut in.

'Oh, no, don't worry – I am truly interested!'

'So am I,' Matilda mumbled, although she couldn't have answered, had someone asked her, what exactly it was in Emilia's story that interested her most.

It was already dark outside, so they lit the candles that had been placed around – on the table, in the garden, around the barbecue. You could have said that the atmosphere was truly romantic if the warlike, quarrelsome spectre of uneasiness hadn't descended upon the small congregation. They could have avoided it or pretended not to notice it, but suddenly, the darkness had given each of them the feeling of self-control and self-assurance. In the girls' room the lights went dutifully out, while the candles flickered in the garden, their flames slowly wavering in the gentle breeze.

'You were at the point when you were terribly hurt...'

The voice had come out with a sarcastic tone, like in the old times.

'Yes,' she said, heaving a deep sigh. 'That's where I stopped. I apologise; there really is no point.'

'In what?'

'In my going on. The truth is that I have monopolised the conversation, you're right.' She leaned over to Matei and kissed his cheek.

'Well, I hope you don't mean that now you're going to keep

us guessing. You started to talk about your friend. Maybe I know him, too. I really found it interesting,' Sal prompted.

Emilia stubbornly shook her head. Matei jumped to her rescue, but the host's insistence didn't cease. He was determined to make her talk, because the unfinished story he had heard had revived inside him the terrible nausea he had felt in the afternoon. He knew he wouldn't be able to stay with them much longer; he saw them hazily and their images had started to fade, creating confusion: Matilda's face was standing now on Matei's athletic body, sporting on its chest Emilia's pair of round tits, with the twins' two pairs of curious eyes blinking where the nipples should have been.

'Come on, Emilia, don't drive me crazy, tell us who it was!' he cried, startling Matilda, who brought her hand to her chest and looked at her two guests with embarrassment. But he had already jumped to his feet threateningly, raging and flinging venom all around. 'Spit it out!'

'You know very well who it was!' she shouted in a sharp voice.

'I'm not talking about Harry! I'm talking about the one in the afternoon, the one who helped you bring me home!'

He looked at Matilda and at Matei and sat back down. His face fell back into place, as if the one who had come out and shouted like a madman had withdrawn inside, exhausted.

'Who?' Matei asked, as if awoken from a deep slumber.

It would have been wonderful to be able to erase that day and start it all over again. He was watching Emilia, who was confused and morose. Or maybe it would have been better if she admitted, forced by her husband, what she wouldn't ever have confessed to her old childhood friend and lover. He listened and thought he could even hear the crammed flutter of her lungs fussing inside her.

Emilia spoke to Matei. 'I dropped by with George today.'

'I see! Why? How come?'

'Who's George?' Sorin broke in, perplexed.

But Emilia completely ignored him and kept addressing the cuckolded husband with the same even voice she would use when calling him to breakfast in the morning. 'It's a long story. Maybe Sorin will tell it to you some other day.'

And so the conversation between them stopped as abruptly as it had begun. An unabated rage was growing within him. If the world had been built otherwise, he would have killed the reserved and decent husband. Instead, he directed his hate toward her, who had remained with her fat eyelids lowered like an immaculate saint, concealing her shame in a hypocritical attitude stolen from one of the paintings that used to send her into raptures. He knew her too well. If she imagined she could hoodwink him, of all people, she was wrong.

'Emilia, who the hell is George?'

'Why is that any of your business?' Matilda whispered to him, obviously bothered but struggling to keep up the appearance of respectability.

It was Matei who calmly answered Matilda. He told her that George was his brother, who had come, together with his family, for a couple of days and was staying in a nearby village, three miles away from the villa in which they were now. He was sorry for the conversation that had just taken place, but he had known neither the details of the meeting between Matilda and George, nor that they had dropped by their place. He understood from his wife, however, that it wasn't a story they were willing to continue and therefore suggested instead a toast in honour of the hosts. In no more than a couple of seconds, the glass sparkled above them in the light of the candles sizzling away, each in its own tiny box. Matilda monopolised the conversation, carefully leading it away from the flaming subject. Emilia had remained huddled up in her chair, her hands folded in her lap, partially covering the yellow stain on her skirt; she was following the conversation between the other two without seeming to understand a thing. She looked like a little girl – only it was a mean and false little girl, who dared believe that by wearing those white clothes, with her white face not betraying her hidden thoughts, she could trick them all and wrap them around her little finger.

'I see that you're wearing the ring!'

The two stopped. They looked at Sorin as if they had seen a corpse sitting up, ruining the joy of the wake.

'The ring...'

Matei looked at Emilia's hands, which had quickly disappeared in the folds of fabric. Amusedly, he took her hand, revealing a huge, black stone sitting in state on her long, lean finger. 'This one?' he asked.

Emilia drew back her hand, but Matei wouldn't let go. He kept holding it in the air, showing it to everyone. She forcefully jerked it loose; the first time unsuccessfully, the second time managing to pull Matei's hand down as well.

'It's very beautiful,' Matilda said. 'Is it special in any way?'

'It's a ring from her mother,' Matei laughed.

'It's not from any mother. I gave her that ring.'

'You? When?' Matilda studied it more carefully. 'When did you give it to her?'

'A long time ago. When we were kids.'

Matei looked at the stone again, then at Emilia, who had started to weep quietly. 'Look,' he said. 'I think we'd better leave. I don't know what's going on, but I think we'd better go home.'

He stood up ceremoniously and held out his hand to Emilia, who took it obediently. Matilda, trying with all her might to keep cool, followed them without insisting on their staying as a good host would have done. She was waiting for the same thing: to see the strangers who had broken her silence gone, to be over with the day that had started badly and threatened to end even worse. She wanted to turn back time and never to have made that uninspired invitation. Matilda and Sorin silently followed the couple, not caring anymore about mimicking the basic courtesy they would have been supposed to show to each other before saying goodbye. Everybody seemed to be waiting for the door to close and then, suddenly, in an unguarded moment, Sorin dashed upon Emilia, snatched her from her husband's iron hand and pulled her inside the house behind him, as if she were a sack of meat. He threw her to the ground with a strong blow and closed the door.

His first concern was to lock the kitchen door, which opened onto the back of the house. He could hear the other two whispering outside, but the noise of the wind and the sea prevented him from hearing what they said. Then it seemed to him that the voices were too high-pitched, and he suspected that it wasn't the adults outside, but the girls speaking in their room, only pretending to be asleep till then. Maybe they had witnessed the scene and were now thinking about how to get rid of their mad father. He looked at Emilia. She was clutching her waist where he had grabbed her. Her face had changed; it shed an evil light, and a feeling of victory floated above, revealing her appreciation that he had managed to overcome the fear and civility he had been fighting over the last years, even if pathetically and inadequately.

'You don't love me anymore!'

The voice that had sounded in the room was the voice of his childhood friend, but he was sure that it was she who had spoken. His head was swarming, and the thoughts inside were a tangle. He no longer knew for sure why he had pulled her inside and why he had locked himself in. He looked at her without even remembering what attracted him about the woman lying crouched on the floor, with her stained skirt, her bony legs covered here and there with tiny hairs visible in the light, with her white face and her ruffled hair, broken loose from the order in which it was usually kept. It was an ordinary woman, neither beautiful nor ugly, with no distinctive features, no bright ideas and no charm. It was a shapeless continuum that became repulsive when taken out of its bed. He leaned over her, full of pity. He had been sweating, and the smell spread in tiny streaks, making the air heavy. He wished he could open the doors and the windows at once, but he was trapped inside.

'Forgive me, please... I don't know what happened.'

She shook her head and all her hair came loose.

'It's my fault.'

He kissed her chest, her breastbone, then grabbed her breasts with both his hands and held them carefully, leaning against them. All this while he could feel her heart beat steadily, as if nothing out of the ordinary had happened, as if it had been a usual meeting, on the beach or in Bucharest, in one of their secret places.

'Emilia...' He stopped. He hadn't called her that for a long time, since they were little and he wanted to tease her. 'What did you say, at the table? What did you mean?'

After her breasts, her shoulders and then her cheeks followed. He touched her to make sure it was her, to find her familiar marks on the strange body that stood stiff and meaningless before him.

'I didn't say anything. It's all in your head.'

'Yes, yes,' he shouted, irritated, 'but what did you want to tell me? You started something... you wanted to say something!'

'I wanted to tell you that, if you hurt me, if you ever hurt me again as you did a long time ago, I will answer in kind.' She stopped and drew a deep breath. 'You kept me waiting. You are a filthy pig!'

'What have you done? Tell me, God damn it, forget the waiting. I kept you waiting, but now it doesn't matter anymore. Now we are together, aren't we? Didn't you want to see everything? Well, here it is! The girls, the wife, the vacation, everything! Now, go on saying what you started at the table!'

She took him in her arms, begging him to tell her that he loved her, and he repeated to her, syllable by syllable, that he wasn't going to say a thing before she finished her story.

Emilia cringed, making a wry face. He saw the folds in her cheek, her big pores, her pimples, the shiny skin, the fuzz above her upper lip, the dimple in her chin, similar to the dimple of a corny singer who used to be very popular in his childhood. He realised now what exactly he didn't like about her; what made her, on certain occasions, insufferable. It was that dimple, more prominent when she was angry, distorting her face. She had lost her roundness and her softness, and all that was left was the mark, reminding him of the songs listened to and played to exhaustion beside his parents in the gardens of Neptun and Olimp:

> Haaaaaryyyy, Haaaaryyyy, going on safari!
> Tooooooma, Tooooooma, scared of his aroma!
> Max-wax, on his tracks!
> Eeeeemi, cockamamie!
> Sal, Sal, be my pal!

She cried, and he kissed her and comforted her. He told her again that he loved her and that they would never part. They started to hear the noises from behind the door more clearly, and soon the knocking started: first reasonably, then louder, changing to full-blown, nervous, threatening bangs.

'Come on, say it! What did you want to tell me at the table?'

She took a deep breath. 'Do you remember that you used to call me every afternoon? At the beginning, you were like an alarm clock: every day, with absolute accuracy, at four o'clock sharp, the telephone rang and I heard my mother's voice calling me. But after a year, you started to be late. The first time I waited a quarter of an hour for your call, I thought it was all over. It seemed like forever, and I could have sworn that I would never hear you and never see you again. It was hard for me to say what that suffering was about, where it came from, but I just stayed like that, dumbfounded, in my bed.

'You finally called, but nothing was the same again. I would always wait out of breath. Sometimes you were punctual again, talking calmly and saying things that made me dizzy; other times you would arrive an hour late, bored to death already, and you would barely utter a couple of words. It seemed to me that you wanted to be elsewhere, with the boys maybe, I don't know. Then, there was this time when I waited until close to six for you to call. I called your place, but your father picked up the phone, so I hung up. I felt I was choking, but, more than anything, I wished I could know where you were and what you were doing. So I left home and went to the places where I knew you boys were playing. There was nobody there. And then I got to Harry's; I was in front of his building, and I found him there on a bench, talking to some neighbours. When he saw me, he seemed very happy; he took me in his arms, he kissed me on the cheek, he turned me around a couple of times, introduced me to the neighbours as his girlfriend and then he called me upstairs, to his house, to see a Corto Maltese cartoon.'

'He called you upstairs, in his house...' Sorin repeated in a low voice.

'Yes. We talked a lot, he also told me things about you... not much. Then we heard the doorbell. I don't know why, but I felt it was you; something inside me told me I had come to the right place. But Harry was in this mood, I don't really know how to explain: he wanted to see how you would react. He seemed to know perfectly well about us, although, as you remember, we hid ourselves as much as we could. Maybe he wanted to see what I would do. Anyway, we stayed behind the door and we could hear you speaking. I never felt worse in my life, just like a traitor. But Harry wouldn't open the door, and after a while I realised I didn't want you to see I was at his place either.'

'I knew it! I could have sworn that I heard him speaking!'

He put his hot head in her lap and breathed in deeply, inhaling her smells. It was a mixture: sometimes she smelt like lemongrass, other times like musky sex between her thighs or like skin washed and pampered with perfumed lotions – she was hard to bear and hard to sniff, and it was hard to think of something when she was around, with all the things she said.

'That's a lie!'

He had shouted like crazy, at the top of his lungs, shaking the house and rendering silent all the noises around. Even the bustle behind the door had stopped. He squeezed her arms and shook her, and when he felt her arms go limp, he grabbed her neck, fanned his fingers on her wrinkled skin and thrust them between the atlas and the axis. His fingers sunk in until the colour of her skin changed just for him to see. She was limp in his arms, releasing short groans, with the impression that she had given up the fight. When he let her go, she fell to the floor with a thud.

'That's a lie! You're a great liar! I've never seen something like that! You've tricked me, and I thought that I could see through you! I feel like laughing, but I can't, because I'm terribly sick!'

Emilia finally spoke in a strangled voice. 'Do you want me to go on?'

Sorin fell silent.

'I heard a thud and a rattle. I think that, for me, that was the end. I knew it was over. I even wondered how, all this time, up to now, despite the fact that I knew perfectly well there was nothing left, we met again and kept seeing each other. At first, Harry thought that you were pretending, but I started hitting him with my palms and fists and he finally opened the door. I found you collapsed on the floor. Actually, your eyes were open and you were babbling, uttering not words but sounds, like an incantation. You came back to your senses after a long time. You were lying on Harry's bed when I heard you from the living room, calling him. I had stayed to make sure that you were all right, but Harry kept saying that you were making fun of us. It crossed my mind, too, that you might have pretended, but I preferred to wait until you told me yourself. We went home, and in less than half an hour, I heard you calling me from downstairs. You were lucid; your eyes never betrayed for even an instant that you remembered anything. But then I knew it was over.'

He was still kneeling next to her. He had taken her hands in his again and was stroking them mechanically. The pounding on the door had grown stronger, and soon the barrier between them and the others would be gone.

He stood up and unbolted the door. Matilda and Matei appeared on the threshold with a bewildered air. They were each holding a candle, and if you squinted, you could imagine that they were ghosts who had come to haunt the two lovers.

Matei helped Emilia up from the floor and hugged her tightly. To Sorin, the image of the embracing spouses seemed bizarre, to say the least, and his lips curved into a smile – one that froze, however, upon encountering Matilda. She rushed past him fierily, like a storm, heading for the girls' room. In a few moments, she turned up again with them, holding their hands as if waving a white flag. He couldn't tell if she wanted to bury the hatchet with him or to levy war against the stranger who had dropped inside her home, but her tense body, ready to fight, and the position of her head betrayed her determination. She was the Earth Mother and Joan of Arc rolled into one; she had gathered inside her all the mythical women from schoolbooks and all the heroic literature; she was the ideal and its opposite at the same time, while the girls looked like old ladies roused from their sleep, scared to death, impassively awaiting their fate. Reality started again to drift away from him while, almost at the same time, the woman in Matei's arms became his lover again. Now he was wondering why they hadn't run back to Bucharest, where they knew their ways around and where the city could have offered them a place to hide. Nothing was clear here, and they had surrounded themselves with hostile people. It didn't matter anymore that she had lied to him; it didn't even matter if she had cheated on him these days. Her smell was imprinted upon his face, around his upper lip, and it drove him crazy.

'Don't you want us to leave now?'

He was surrounded by them, and she had remained in Matei's arms, tightly attached with millions of straps and bands. She didn't answer. The girls sat with their heads lowered, lacking the courage to participate in the tragedy in the living room, which had been their favourite playing spot till now. They weren't claiming it; all they wanted was to return to their beds where the sheets pleasantly rustled and where the mingled smells of lavender, rose and jasmine urged them to sleep.

'Matei,' he suddenly begged the husband. 'Can't you see that she no longer wants to be with you? Let her go, please!'

'Sorin, stop it!' Matilda turned to the other two. 'He wasn't well today; it must be from the sunstroke!'

She had uttered the words with a clear and metallic sound, like a judge passing a sentence. They weren't the last words said that evening, but she had spoken them as if they had been. Everybody remained respectfully silent, admitting that the host and mistress of the household should be the one to decide the outcome of that strange meeting. But, when all seemed to have lain down their arms, something like an unintelligible squeak came from Matei's arms, reaching Sorin only much later.

'I would like to go to the toilet,' Emilia repeated.

When nobody answered, she lightly broke loose from the embrace and started alone down the dark corridor. She was gone in a few moments, and a sigh of relief crisscrossed the room behind her.

They waited for Emilia's return for minutes on end. To some of them, those minutes seemed like years. They had all spread their wings, flapping them menacingly above, trying to win back their battleground. Matei had stopped looking at Sorin, and Sorin had stopped defying Matilda. Only the girls helplessly hung from their mother's hand, fidgeting impatiently. Finally, Dori said that she was tired and that she wanted to go to bed. As she received no answer, she started to whimper in order to get her parents attention, then tore herself away from Matilda's skirt. Mari, like an echo, imitated her sister, and little by little, the living room filled with a constant, droning lamentation. Amidst that noise, Sorin revisited the story Emilia had told him and asked himself, whether through an absurd twist or a memory trick, she could have been right; whether her story wasn't actually the real face of their history. But he laughed, and his laughter escalated when he saw them all waiting for the liar, with her arrogant air, to come out of the bathroom and leave arm in arm with her husband.

'Shouldn't you go and see if something is wrong?'

When he heard the question, he felt for the first time that Matilda had accepted the situation. Matilda... the mistress of their household. For a couple of years, life with her had seemed good and quiet. She would come every afternoon to pick him up by car from the greenhouses; she would make him breakfast in the morning and prepare his sandwiches for work. When the twins were born, there was a fire at the Gardens, so he had missed their arrival into the world. He hadn't been there, and fear had added to his guilt. The fact that the fire had occurred right at the time of his two daughters' arrival was a bad sign, while the idea that he would have to face two identical persons – two united bodies, two pairs of eyes that would look at him the same way, two minds working as one yet split apart and forever aspiring to reunite – made his hair stand on end. Actually, when he got to the Giuleşti maternity hospital, he found two elderly-looking, wrinkled and crumpled things. All the babies there looked alike, all were identical; if he had been given two other girls by mistake, he would have taken them calmly, as calm as he could have been at that time, and gone home with them without daring utter a word. It reminded him of when he was little and went to buy bread; he would take the change from the salesman's hand without counting it and always found at home that there was less money than there should have been.

Dori appeared in a haste and then stopped, grabbing hold of Matilda with all her might. She was instantly surrounded from all sides, asked what was wrong, comforted. The girl kept repeating over and over again: 'The lady is in the bathroom!', but no one understood why exactly she was crying and what had bothered her so much.

Mari still held on to Matilda, having taken over something of her mother's wise demeanour. Sorin asked her in a whisper if she knew what was wrong with her sister. She looked at him as if he were a stranger, but still answered, in another whisper, 'Dori is upset that the lady made a mess in the bathroom and soiled her beach towel.'

He crept into the hall, his heart pounding madly in his chest. He stepped with caution, careful not to knock over the buckets Matilda had just used to mop the floor and had placed next to the bathroom door. The door was ajar, but it was dark inside. First, he thought that Emilia had left: that she had jumped out the window, scuttling away, leaving them to sort things out by themselves; perhaps she had gone to her lover, the brother of her cuckolded husband, leaving them both, spectacularly and irrevocably.

He postponed the moment in which he would see the window open wide and the prints of her pointed shoes on the yellow tiles. He told himself that, if he were to lose her, he would rather find her lying dead on the floor in a pool of blood, her skirt and her blouse half soaked in the clammy, sweetish liquid. Better like that than to fall asleep knowing that she was with another man, crumpling bed sheets in crummy hotels. Better for her to be gone at once than for him to suffer because of her, to search for her, to haunt her, to secretly partake in a life that no longer included him. He had decided that it was better that way.

From behind the door, he heard a tiny voice, crooning:

'Haaaaaryyyy, Haaaaryyyy, going on safari!
Tooooooma, Tooooooma, scared of his aroma!
Max-wax, on his tracks!
Eeeeemi, cockamamie!
Sal, Sal, be my pal!'

IX

FIN'AMORS

She was lying in bed, a rumpled blanket at her toes and an extra-large white T-shirt half covering her thighs. Though her eyes were shut, there was a brief, quick motion behind her eyelids, a sort of unbroken back-and-forth movement that could have misled anyone who might have walked in and seen her stone-still. But there was no one in the room, and the chance that someone would come in was so slight that she hung limp, legs wide apart, already enjoying the delightful illusion of having risen up above the sheets, where she hovered happily. The day had worn on, as time goes by when nothing happens: you try to sleep on, but the eyes dry out beneath the eyelids and open fitfully, grasping at the faintest image, at the haziest noise. She was hastily approaching the night's sleep and yet was radiating an energy that could have moved all the hospital beds away. The neon lamps were whirring, the tables were whirring, the hallway chairs were whirring, the hallways were whirring at the blasting passage of the human-repair squad, the doors were whirring in tune with their long creaks. Her strained nerves themselves, seemingly animated with a life of their own, wearing her clothes and striving to survive on her behalf, were also whirring in vain abeyance, bathed in the dim, cold light.

She remembered Harry. In fact, it would be more accurate to say she had dreamt about Harry even before uttering his name at the party. He looked exactly like he did back then, in the room, when they had locked themselves in and he wouldn't open the door to Sal; he wore the same clothes – those short, ragged trousers reeking of soiled linen. Yet she had her present body, which made her look big and inadequate in the boy's Lilliputian room, striving to fit in. She sat on the edge of the bed and tucked up her white skirt, revealing her legs. Harry was laughing his head off, telling her how they would hide in Max's mother's medical office, peeking from behind the sofa at the ladies who undressed for the examination, and how they would masturbate, sitting back-to-back. She had felt disgusted and wanted to leave, but Harry had grabbed her ankle and knocked her down with unexpected vigour. Then he had climbed on her with all his weight, his legs astride and his buttocks on her chest.

She was choking and, as he forced the air out of her lungs, she could see him pulling faces and riding her, jumping above her in a way that, she realised just before collapsing, resembled the sexual jerks of a beginner. When she came back to her senses, Harry was sitting next to her, naked, his legs tucked underneath him and his palms resting on his knees. His pearlescent pink skin was immaculate, gleaming like a sheet of waxed paper; he was waiting for her with the face of an angel who ardently contemplated its host before getting inside them through their belly button and filling their bowels with feelings of guilt and terror. She tried to get up, but instantly realised she had been tied up with a string; it resembled one she would bind jam jars with after her mother had poured out the hot, pungent mixture from pots simmering on the stove.

Harry had grinned and bared a string of jagged teeth. She shut her eyes and told herself she was dreaming. And yet there was something very familiar, as if those intense sensations, meticulously curbing her urge to resist, were stirred not by the dream itself but by recollection. The boy had grabbed his penis between his white, thin fingers. It was a pinkish piece of flesh that, seen at close range, had a pasty texture. It was wagging about excitedly, bouncing and moving freely. He approached her, and this time he gently curled her legs round his thighs; before she could squeeze her eyes to try and wake up, she merely felt the piece of flesh sliding in through her labia, tickling her as it went. She giggled as if encouraging him to go on. As he kept fumbling around, failing to find the hole through which to enter, he made his way in with his fingers. They were extremely cold and tiny, particularly clumsy; they were scratching and furrowing the membrane, the internal walls and the soft, slippery flesh as they strove to get through. It only took a few seconds for the boy to lose his temper and start to bore as if digging the soil. His hands were sinking into her vagina, ripping out tiny red scraps of skin, while, sunken into a deathlike blackout, she could still see him moving further down, ruthlessly and cruelly, seemingly unaffected by the howls that, although not her own, were breaking down the walls.

Then she woke up, but Harry was still astride her, watching her with the familiar, mature gaze of somebody else. It was that feeling of intimacy that ultimately made her abandon herself, allowing the inexperienced boy to pluck up his courage. He inserted his small cock in her big vagina and started to wriggle until finally, exhausted and with dark circles under his eyes like a small animal, he picked up the motion. Harry was visibly growing above her, slowly turning into an adult who, lovingly and tenderly, was molesting her, almost with her consent.

When she truly woke up, she realised her dream was more like an echo of a recollection. She was at Harry's, just before she heard Sal collapsing outside the door, when he had taken her hand and placed it upon his dirty, soggy pants, straight over his bump, which had been stirring and responded to the touch. She wanted to scream, but he silenced her with his palm and kept her quiet for a long time; she imagined that would be the end, till Sal collapsed outside the door. For a long time, she thought he had known what was happening behind the door; that he had seen them, too, as he managed to see other things, and that the repulsion triggered by that image had not only made him pass out but also made him determined to show indifference later on. Only once did she want to make amends, or even thought of testing whether he actually knew about it or not. But Sal was unfathomable, and the Harry episode remained buried.

She opened her eyes, but the light in the room hadn't changed and the noises were the same as before. It may have been an hour or it may well have been only one second since her thoughts had wandered away, just as it could have been endless years since she had walked into the neon-lit room. By the number of spiky pills she had to take – twice daily at first, now solely in the morning – a whole lifetime might have elapsed since Sal's party, and she wouldn't have been surprised to see, instead of her own reflection in the mirror, the image of a brown-skinned, grizzle-haired lady, with bags under her eyes and swollen flesh on her bones. But she had only changed her T-shirt twice so far and, in their undefiled world, two T-shirts was too short a time for one to grow old. They only accounted for a couple of days of anguish and strain in order to forget what had happened.

She sat up and looked over her shoulder at the bedside table. There was a book, upon which her watch was laid, a plastic cup and a bottle of mineral water. It was a sign of Matei's having visited. She might have wished to see, instead of that bottle, a flowerpot with an exquisite plant from the greenhouses on Liberty Park's hill, or the slightest token meant for her. But the things resting neatly on the hospital bedside table conveyed no message at all.

The door opened with a slight creak. She sat up, but instantly lay back down and shut her eyes again. The entire room was drenched in formaldehyde, filled with that familiar fragrance which had been pervading her nose every bedtime.

Matei looked fresh and lively. When he showed up, he filled the room with joy; the spotlights turned on, sweeping the metal objects in the room with their fluorescent rays, making it come to life and move about. He was all smiles, and with the bunch of flowers fluttering above, he looked as if he had just returned triumphantly from the battlefield. He was glowing with an inexplicable exuberance that seemed to be hiding something; he had an ace up his sleeve that he was not yet prepared to wave in front of her, but which made him gloat in anticipation.

He dropped the bouquet on the nearby bed and leaned down to hug her. The scent of a healthy man, just in from the fresh air, made her snuggle into his arms.

'How is our patient feeling?'

His question was so inappropriate that even though she had been tempted to answer, she halted. She sat stone-still, watching him and waiting to see what was coming next.

'You look much better today! I'm so glad! That means we'll be going home in a short while.'

She resented the kind-hearted, haughty use of the plural and his obstinacy to deny any recollection of what had happened. Not a word was said; not a reproof showed through his exhilarating remarks. Before him was a dangerously sick person whom he had better not disturb or hassle with an unpleasant memory. Yet she knew that was not all. He appeared to have knowledge of something else, something she failed to grasp although it made her cringe within.

He sat on the edge of the bed, at her feet, and touched her ankle. They remained quiet for a few minutes.

'What do you want?'

She was the first to speak, since she somehow felt he would prefer it that way; she wanted to be through with it all as quickly as possible and to be left alone.

'I beg your pardon?'

'What do you want?!' She had raised her voice.

'I want you to get well and come back home.'

'Okay. And besides that?' She paused, cautiously. Eventually she decided to speak her mind without beating about the bush. 'First of all, I'm not sick.'

Matei laughed.

'I'm not. Or, if you like, I've been sick for quite a while, and since I managed to handle it this far, I'll manage to handle it from now on too.'

'Good.'

'Don't interrupt me!'

'I'm not.'

'I'd like to talk about what happened...'

'I don't want to!' he said, raising his voice.

'You promised not to interrupt.'

'Maybe I did, but you can't make me talk about something I don't want to. And besides, nothing really happened anyway.'

'Is that what you think?'

'What? That you have a wacky childhood pal? That you think

you're still in love with him? Or that he has the impression that if he keeps on squeezing you like this, we're going to break up? Is that what happened? In fact, you want us to break up, don't you? Well, it's not going to happen!'

Emilia closed her eyes and, as she used to do in her childhood, imagined she had disappeared. When she opened them again, she saw Matei staring at her, visibly irritated.

'Would you tell me one thing, if you please?' He didn't wait for her answer anyway. 'Has he come to see you? Has he been here?'

'Who?' she muttered.

'What do you mean, who? Has he or has he not?'

She shook her head.

'Speak up already!'

'I can't say exactly.'

'You're lying! See? If you told the truth, it would be easier for you.'

'I am not lying... what would you like me to say?'

'That he came by and you were extremely disappointed at his behaviour. That you were expecting something else. Maybe you were expecting him to kneel down at your feet and ask you to run away. Maybe you dreamt of his leaving his family, his wife and girls, utterly committing himself to your love, right? Wasn't it like that? Did he beat around the bush and suggest that you should be patient? Did he reprimand you for misbehaving at his place, in front of everybody? For driving him crazy? Did he ask you what you wanted from him? Have I summed it up clearly enough? Maybe deep down he was angry; maybe what he really wanted was to slap you and tell you it was over. But he didn't do it because of your condition.'

She buried her head in her arms and wailed. Matei stood up and moved away from the bed. He looked scared, but in fact he merely felt appeased for having spoken his mind even sooner than he had expected.

Emilia was still wailing jerkily, her face buried, as Matei opened the window and contemplated the view. The night had fallen and, from the seventh floor of the municipal hospital, you could see the Dambovita winding between deserted structures, wastelands and factories, heading toward the blocks of flats in the distance, where the swarming and the real life began. He had brought her in by helicopter, pulling every string he had, setting a throng of people into motion to make sure she got there safe and sound, after they had given her a stomach pump, sewn her up and bound her tight in Constanta. When they got there, the entire hospital appeared to be waiting on the rooftop, while Bucharest, dimly illuminated, was glimmering in expectation.

He didn't want to take her to the nuthouse, so he settled her in the best room of the neurology ward. His best friend, head of the unit, ensured him as he tapped his shoulder that such things occurred more often than he could imagine, adding that his sewn, washed and bound wife just needed rest. He had stood beside her for a day and a night, without closing an eye and hoping, despite the watchful care she received from the ceaselessly fussing nurses, that his wife wouldn't make it and would quietly pass away. She had made her decision, and now he wanted to comply with her wish. Had he seen her rattling and struggling between life and death, he would have let her alone, undeterred by the anguish and remorse that probably awaited him in an indefinite, misty future. He wouldn't have called for anybody. But she did nothing but sleep, dream and wince from time to time.

'I didn't ask you to come.'

'I know.'

'What do you want, then?'

'Nothing. Just to go back home and see what's next.'

'I can't...'

'You can't what?' He had grown threatening and turned gloomily away.

'I can't. How can you live with me after all this?'

'I didn't say I wanted to live with you, I only said we're going back home. Is that clear?'

Hearing his imperative and commanding voice and sensing his self-assured attitude, Emilia suspected that Matei knew a lot more.

'I want you to answer me!'

'We're going home.'

Matei headed for the door, but stopped short. He turned around on his heels and instantly hurled himself upon the numb body, shaking it, punching it and smacking it, venting his pent-up anger so carefully subdued until then. He was ridding himself at last of the overwhelming burden he had been carrying along. He was taking vengeance for his humiliation, while she didn't utter a word, trying to stay quiet so she wouldn't raise his pity, for she knew he would have killed her then and there. She was amazed to find out that, in spite of it all, she feared for her life and that she didn't want to die in the whirring room, in the rumpled T-shirt, with doubt hanging above the hospital bed like a cutting sword. He got up, exhausted, and mumbled a few words Emilia couldn't grasp. He smoothed out his clothes, arranged his hair and smiled before touching the door handle and walking out of that hell, as radiant as when he had come in.

The night went slowly by. She hardly closed her eyes and remained all ears, wincing at every noise. Once she thought she heard the door slam again, yet she couldn't turn around to see who it was. It might have been her fantasies or, if it had to be someone, she preferred to imagine it could have been Sal. Daybreak found her in the same position: crouched, her face turned to the window. She didn't even realise when night turned into day. The room felt more deserted now and even sadder.

After Matei's departure, a nurse had stopped by with a plate of soup and an apple pie on a tray. She had eaten them meekly, seated on the edge of the bed. The nurse had watched her closely while she was eating without speaking to her. She looked like a stern guardian, hired to watch over the lunatic confined to the tower. It was only after taking the empty dishes, while getting ready to leave, that she had sputtered over her shoulder: 'Your husband is coming to pick you up tomorrow morning at ten o'clock. Make sure you're ready!' By the way she had said it, Emilia felt her guardian knew exactly what the situation was and didn't refrain from showing her contempt.

At ten o'clock on the dot, Matei entered the room and found her dressed in the clean clothes he had left her. They walked out of the hospital in silence, accompanied by another nurse who, despite her apparent discretion, seemed eager to shake them off. Matei drove angrily on their way home, his mood significantly changed from the previous day. The vain sensation of victory over the woman who had stood beside him had been replaced by the stupefaction of having been cheated. He had grown accustomed to calling her his 'wife', someone he thought he knew everything about, whom he had never cast any doubt on and from whom he never anticipated any sort of surprise. Now that woman may have vanished, turning all of a sudden into his foe.

They didn't exchange a single word. Emilia was even controlling her breath, fearing it could disturb the silence reigning over the tiny space between them. From time to time, when Matei's hand came close to the gear lever, she got the impression he slightly, unnoticeably faltered toward her curved thigh and his hesitation made her wince on the inside. Eventually, she laid her hands over her knees, trying to cover everything up, to reveal only a few margins of herself. After an hour, they got home, cutting through Bucharest in a caravan of choked and heated vehicles lagging one behind another. Emilia entered the bedroom and Matei went to the kitchen, from which she soon heard pots clattering and glasses clinking. The noise lasted for a long time; so long that, wondering what he was doing there, Emilia dozed off.

When she woke up, it was already dark. No sound could be heard in the house. She had become very good at detecting a presence; she could even discern the movements in the apartments next door. She knew when the neighbours downstairs were fighting or returning home, when they were eating or sleeping. She would hear the main door in the entrance and, from the way it was closed, she could clearly tell whether it was Matei or somebody else. Then there were the steps on the hallway and the grating and rattling of the elevator door.

She got dressed stealthily and cautiously stepped out of the room. She paused, taking a deep breath, and then entered the living room. Matei was lying down on the sofa, his snoring like a growl. She watched him from the doorway. Sal's visit at the hospital had made her clearly see what was about to happen. He had neither given her hope nor told her anything decisive. 'Patience' had been the only word he uttered, and she had seen in it nothing more than a trite way of saying goodbye.

She stormed out and wandered the streets amongst the blocks of flats, till she fell down on the pavement far away from home. Then she looked for a taxi, got in and gave an address to the driver. She thought they had been driving for ages when she heard the man's voice telling her they had arrived. She changed her mind and asked him to take her back, and the man grumbled a little at her request, but she sunk in the back seat; her face vanished from the rearview mirror, and thus she was taken all the way back. Though it was late when she returned, she no longer felt sleepy. Getting upstairs, she found Matei in front of the door.

'Have you been to see him?'

She refused to answer, but he dogged her all around the house. 'Emilia! Answer me now!'

'Why do you want us to go on tormenting each other? Isn't everything that's happened enough for you? Can't you see how wretched I am myself?'

Matei took his head in his hands and doubled up, fluttering and teetering through the dim hallway like a beheaded hen; he wailed and sobbed noisily, he cursed the day they had met her lover's family at the sunny garden – he would have rather known nothing and carried on his life serenely. He knew he was being ludicrous, he wailed on, but so was life, and so were the ludicrous lovers. He was hoping that his wretchedness would move her. And Emilia, impressed, rushed to him and embraced him, swaying with emotion. He leaned on her chest and nestled there; then he clasped her waist and drew her to the living room sofa on which, a few hours earlier, he had slept a heavy and fitful sleep. At that time, he couldn't have imagined they would be sitting so close to each other and that he would be listening to that lying and deceitful woman again. Now, he suddenly thought it was but a dream and there was still hope for them. Their home, their family, their life as a couple – all these words that had momentarily lost their meaning in the meanwhile became real again.

He was inhaling her skin's fragrance, groping her with his fingers prodding in the synthetic blouse that was giving off a pleasant, sweaty odour; her whole body yielding slowly yet unrestrainedly in his clasp told him that the crisis had finally been quenched. They went to the bedroom, worn out. He undressed her the way he thought her lover did, brought her down on the bed and, as all he found beneath him was a lifeless body, he jolted her to exhaustion, as if relentlessly trying to soften a crumbling dough by pouring in water. He took off his pants and underwear, and even though the intense odour of his sex dominated, it was more the scent of fear that pervaded. He penetrated her feebly and wriggled above her helplessly as Harry had in her dream. But the more he tried, the more he went astray in that hole between her legs that seemed to be gaping and sucking him in. He sat back after a while and moaned.

A week went by and neither of them spoke about it. Matei would come back in the evening and she would listen to him from the bedroom, opening the refrigerator, uncorking a bottle of wine and then crashing on the sofa. They would seldom see each other, and they spoke mainly on the phone, as Matei called her punctually every day to ask how she felt, whether she had taken her pills and if anything had happened. She would answer curtly, and they would end their conversation within a minute or so. Then she would return to her room and wait for time to go by.

The following Saturday, Matei left in the morning and returned only late at night. He was tipsy, and the moment he came in, he gave off a sour smell. He called out to her in a hoarse voice, and she thought from his tone she'd better stay in the room. Yet she still went, advancing fearfully along the dim hallway, feeling that something evil lay ahead. Then she stopped and pricked up her ears. The silence in the house was so overwhelming that she gasped. She thought she wasn't dressed properly and wanted to go back and change, but she gave it up after a few steps. Tucking a strand of hair behind her ear, she stepped forward, her shoulders drawn back and her chin raised as if she were a queen walking to her execution. When she entered the room, Sal was sitting on the sofa, with his legs crossed and his nose pointing down to the floor, while Matei was leaning back against the wall with folded arms, his fingers drumming lightly in the air.

'Oh! There she is!'

He threw himself at her, grabbed her arms and dragged her into the middle of the room. Sal had already sprung to his feet.

'Here, I've brought him over, as you wished. Now I'm leaving the two of you alone.'

'You don't need to,' Sal muttered.

'Don't I? How come? Do you want to talk to your mistress in front of her husband? That would be odd. I'm kind of old-fashioned, you know; I think it's my duty and yours to keep up appearances. So I'll bow out now and return in an hour.'

While speaking, Matei was striding backward toward the door; he whirled away while uttering his last words, and before long, the entrance door slammed, shaking the entire house. They remained standing, face to face, looking at each other, each worried for their own reasons, as if waiting for something. Then they sat down in silence. Emilia was the first to sit and then he, next to her, keeping a certain distance that seemed appropriate in such circumstances.

'Are you upset that I came?'

She shook her head vehemently. Nothing could upset her any longer. She did not feel, like others may have, embarrassed by her state, nor by what she had tried to do. She thought her urge had been reasonable; only the timing may have been badly chosen. Her mind was shifting about swiftly; she could hardly focus and it was difficult to grasp what was happening to her. She saw Sal at her feet, his head leaning on her skinny knee, wailing about.

'Emi, we have both been so reckless! We need time to sort things out properly, don't you see?'

He was watching her keenly. 'Would you please tell me that you understand?'

Emi nodded meekly. He seemed to have shrugged a burden off himself and sat down next to her, released.

'I was sure you'd understand. Don't you think that all this time I've been striving to find a suitable way out of this mess? But, you know, there were my daughters and everything; but whenever I looked at them I would see you as a little girl. I couldn't do it out of love for you. I know it sounds awful, but I would think of you, your father, your misery. You say it was not like that, but it was obvious. I remember – when we came back, when they found us – my mother dramatically told me, speaking in charades as usual, that we'd better be careful, as a fatherless child would not be a complete person, particularly if the father was in prison. When I asked her why, she shrugged. I thought he had killed somebody, stolen something or had done something dreadful. And I thought it was so unfair because you were so beautiful, your soul was so pure and everything was perfect. Your father couldn't have been the one my mother hinted at. Only after many years did I realise what had really happened. And then I understood why your mother wouldn't talk about him, how terrible it must have been for all of you to keep low for fear of those bastards...'

'My father left home a year before they had him locked up. So it has nothing to do...'

'Yes, it has...'

'Listen, Sal,' she cut in harshly. 'Why have you come?'

He halted. He had grown excited and he wanted to expound his theory on the ex-convict who had been the victim of a giant conspiracy, but either her altered tone of voice or the fact that they were running out of time made him come to his senses.

'What would you like more than anything right now?'

Emi hesitated a little. She looked at him and her voice softened. 'I wish we weren't here, or at least, were I to be here, I would like to be alone.'

'Would you want us to run away together?'

'Where?'

'I don't know – just leave them and mind our own lives some-where else.'

'Where?'

'How should I know? There are places.'

'We couldn't afford to live more than a week.'

'That's not the problem.'

'Then what is?'

'Tell me, do you want to?'

'I don't know...' She made up her mind in a second, though. 'I don't think I'd like to.'

'Why?' Sal asked in a daze. 'I thought that's what you wanted!'

She hugged and squeezed him tight; she was squeezing him as if he were a child, pressing his head against her chest and kissing and stroking his hair.

'I wish we hadn't wound up here.'

'Yeah. But that's that now.'

'That's that,' she echoed.

He pulled away grievingly. The room had darkened, but since they knew each other so well, they didn't need to see each other to feel when one of them was miserable.

'Well, this is stupid. What's the point of all this? Just to make our lives miserable? You have to tell me what you really want so that I know what to do... and now you're telling me you want nothing. How come?'

'Because it should have been me! *I* was the one so horribly stripped of what was meant to be mine, and if it hadn't happened that way, *I* would have been the mother of your daughters and would had taken care of the flowerpots on your windowsill and the other plants, and I wouldn't have had to hide from anybody!'

'That's right. Though I can't just kick her out now and tell her it was a mistake. I can't tell Matilda she should simply leave. I couldn't make you happy by driving her away; surely you see that, don't you?'

'No...'

He felt his irritation well up and gave out something like a slight growl. 'I came to see you and ask you once again to wait a bit. Let's not go on with these charades any longer. Actually, it's not my fault that I have a family and two daughters. And it's not yours, either. I'm trying to make some changes in my own way, without hurting anyone too badly. I want us to end up together, because if it doesn't work out, then...' He stopped and covered his face with his palms. 'First of all, I came to ask you not to do that again. What was going on in your mind? What were you thinking of? Why did you do it?'

He looked ridiculous, gesticulating in the middle of the room in his red, short-sleeved shirt, ironed and starched, his watch chinking at his wrist; he was shaved and freshly scrubbed, with very few features left from his childhood self. She was struggling to remember what exactly she had recognised, despite the changes and the age, when she realised his mouth was wandering upon her face and neck. She felt his breath and the whiff of his skin, smelling like freshly-baked cake; she heard him gasping and panting in her ear, turned on, and realised there was actually nothing left of that little boy other than their routine of loving each other, of being bonded by thousands of words, memories, common pleasures and promises, and that, even if their love itself would one day vanish, all the connections between them would survive it for as long as they lived.

She lay down, letting him climb upon her and strip her of her clothes. It was neither the place nor the passing time that made him hurry up, but rather his desire to make her forget, to draw her attention away. Emi knew all his thoughts. But she found comfort in knowing beforehand what was about to happen, after all those days of uncertainty. And Sal could faultlessly pick out the spots where he should titillate her skin with his lips so as to hear her gasps of pleasure echoing in the room. They were seemingly two half-naked people, entwined, his head buried between her legs and hers between his; they were switching positions with the artistry of a synchronised swimming team performing their routine.

Time went by and the two lovers lay stretched like giant cats next to one another, their adjoined heads propped against the arm of the sofa. They rested in a pleasant silence, still secluded in the slick, mineral cocoon that concealed all but their watery, blank and glittering eyes. He leaned his head on her shoulder and closed his eyes. Snapshots flashed through his mind: the crowd from the post office where they ran into and recognised each other, when he had realised that the round-faced and brisk-voiced girl with whom he had shared so many memories had turned into a woman. Next came Matilda, who was telling him, one year after their marriage, that she was pregnant and was asking him, in the same drawling, amenable voice she would use when consulting him over what he wanted to eat for lunch, whether he wished her to keep the baby or not. She also slipped in that, should he refuse, he had to resolve it quickly, as the pregnancy was quite advanced and soon no one would want to operate. Since Matilda had been so honest and straightforward about the situation, he instantly consented to it, without even asking her whether she wanted it or not. But now, thinking back, he felt he had somehow been tricked.

This hunch that had been nagging his mind for quite a long time made him sit up. Emilia rested stone-still, the hand that had been stroking him frozen in midair. From the way she sat, through the hair framing her features, her round face, her eyes, her mouth and her nose had shown, and even her angular cheekbones had been rounded off and softened, calling the little Emi to his mind. He realised that even if he had turned her entirely inside out, he would have found her there, whole and intact; he would have removed her from the placenta and blood, dirty and scared as if she had been a newborn baby; would have washed her off, cleaned the slime out of her hair and the red streaks from her cheeks, and life would have resumed where they had left it. He suspected that she was to blame; if it had not been for her extravagant coquetry, her insatiable pleasure at being admired and loved, of enchanting everyone in the gang, of entering doubtful and equivocal friendships which implied that all the fondling and petting, the hide-and-seek, the hopscotch, the games of tag, signified so much more.

Sometimes he had felt that Emi would lie through her teeth, hide out and try to deceive him, availing herself with a grown-up woman's arsenal, silencing his suspicion while sealing off her secrets. If it had not been for all that, their life would have unfolded normally. He could clearly remember that, from a certain point on, he had become suspicious even of friends who seemed to have seen more than him despite all the time he spent with her. Even her confession at the party, for that matter, had not been unplanned. It had confirmed various doubts, giving rise to yet others. He was not the only one to whom she had belonged. She had belonged to all of them, and the thought of it burned his insides.

He fidgeted around, and when Emilia wanted to pull him back, he tore himself away smoothly yet resolutely and remained crouched, musing. His penis had receded and hung feebly upon his scrotum. From this position, she could see a lucid drop barely hanging from a crease of the wrinkled skin. He grabbed his member between his fingers and shook it a little. The drop fell into the velvet on the sofa cover and was soaked up instantly.

He had come only to ask her to wait a bit, but her anguish, her wan and drawn face, her eyes in which he could see death so clearly, had turned him on and stirred up his urge to get revenge. He would have liked to push her into the abyss with one hand and pull her back with the other. Even the thought of dying together had crossed his mind, and he would have done it if he had been certain that the whole truth would out. After they had met again at the post office and exchanged their phone numbers, he had waited for a few days, hesitating to call her, since he didn't want her to believe that, after such a long time, not only had he remembered her, but he was also still under her spell. But then she called him. She spoke in a studied, friendly tone, laughed a lot, and since he felt confident, he cracked a lot of jokes; in the end, he promised that one day soon he would invite her to the greenhouses, remembering her old passion for flowers and herbariums.

It was only after a month that he got up enough nerve to approach her. They threaded their way with words in the first place, each one revolving around that afternoon in their childhood when Emi had rummaged around in his pants and he had scrutinised the inside of her cherry-printed panties like a real scientist. They had never brought it up directly in their conversation, but the hints acted as aphrodisiacs.

Emilia disappeared for a week after that, and he fell sick during that time. He had had a flash of intuition – like an epiphany – that under no circumstances would he have ever accepted to lose her again. He lay in bed for three days, delirious with fever, striving to draw out from their conversation the slightest of details that could lead him to her. Although he felt dizzy and weak, he had eventually got up and, ballpoint pen in hand, written down everything they had told each other. Then he read it again and couldn't make any sense of it. At the end of this wearisome attempt, the telephone rang shrilly, and he heard her cheerful, friendly voice at the end of the line, now swept by a slight wave of emotion. He felt like shouting and reprimanding her, but he was still overruled by fear. A few days later, he had already rented a dim room with green-painted walls, a closet, a bed, two chairs and a lot of cockroaches chaotically swarming on the linoleum-covered floor.

Had someone asked him, Sal would have answered without hesitation that, apart from the childhood years when the future was glittering ahead, the time spent in that room had been the most blissful time of all. Emilia had walked in as if it had been their new home, and every day at four o'clock in the afternoon, they would arrive almost at the same time and flop down on the bed, from which they wouldn't get up until seven or eight o'clock in the evening. They would grab a bite and leave, each to their own places. They had given up the place the moment their landlady, a fat, wicked matron, knocked on their door and notified them – peering viciously under her glasses, particularly at Emi – that starting the following month, their rent would double, and since she had lots and lots of possible clients, they could take it or leave it. They left behind a green, glazed-tin coffeepot, two mugs bought from the Obor market and a heap of towels; since then, their makeshift family had been shattered, and they hadn't had the courage to put it back together. Thinking back, he thought it was their illusion of having a house of their own – sharing a kitchen, a bathroom, some towels and dishes, under the appearance of a life together – that had triggered the end.

He turned. Emilia had been watching him the whole time; even in his daydreaming he had felt her eyes staring at his back and scratching beyond the surface, trying to slip into his thoughts. He could clearly see that something had scared her as well, but he wasn't able to tell what.

'You don't love me anymore...'

So that's what it was. She would try him periodically with the same refrain-like words, in a sweet voice: 'You don't love me anymore...You don't love me anymore.' Sometimes he was tired and would mutter it from the tip of his lips; other times he would hug and kiss her theatrically, telling her all those mushy things she needed to hear.

'I mean it. I've been watching you for some time...'

'Please, Emilia, let's not go there again.'

But she was fidgeting behind him.

'I love you so much. There's no reason to doubt that.'

He turned again and pressed his lips against her smooth skin. Then he breathed a whiff of hot air, steaming her spotless skin. Emilia laughed excitedly. She cuddled in his arms and he could almost hear her purring. The alabaster-legged, round-faced Emilia...

'Listen... I've been meaning to ask you something.' He knew he would upset her, but her words had confused him. 'About what you said then, at the party.'

As if, by saying some words at random, they could reverse the past. As if he hadn't been so sure of what he had experienced and seen, especially when he had the irrefutable proof.

'About that thing at Harry's...'

She became tense and ultimately broke away from his grip as she was listening to him, drawing back in the corner of the sofa.

'Have I upset you?'

'No. But I was so sure!'

'Of what?'

'That this is what it was all about. I know you're not even aware of it, but in fact that's why you came here in the first place.'

'That's not true!'

'Yes, it is. I've been waiting for you to ask from the moment I began to tell the story. I've been watching you to see how long you could bear it. If it hadn't been for the whole mess, you would have rushed to question me.'

'To question you? Don't you see you're pushing it too far now?'

'Why did you ask me if I was upset?'

'Because I can feel it.'

'No! It was because you knew there was a reason for me to get upset. That's why. But relax; I'll answer any question you ask.'

'No! Not like that!' He had stood up and started to pace the room, naked and angry, shaking his head. 'I think you're looking for a reason to fight.'

'Why now? Just because we fucked, does it mean that we stilled all our suspicions? That you can turn someone into a slave? That you can toy with them as you will and squeeze out what you wish? You should have asked first, as soon as you came in, not now! If you ask me now, you only offend me!'

She had been yelling at him, flushed with anger. He was looking at her in bewilderment, feeling the ground slip from under his feet. He kept thinking that if he fell ill, the situation would have turned into something even nastier, and therefore he took a deep breath; but as the air was pumping in his lungs, a feeling of emptiness and despair pervaded his body along with the oxygen, poisoning him. He had become numb; his flesh was weighing down on his bones, and he was tingled by quick electric shocks. He sat again on the edge of the sofa and looked at her in exasperation.

'I think you're the one who doesn't love me anymore, although you keep asking me and make me spell it out. This has made you lose your zest for living. You've lost something, and you don't even know what it is. I'll tell you what it is. It's the love that faded away. And so it goes – don't you remember how I used to say that you just get up one morning and it's gone? You have a grudge against me, and until now I didn't understand why.'

'And now you do understand. That's why you made me tell you about Harry, right? You're a phony.'

'Maybe I am. It's not that I'm not interested... The Harry episode has troubled me deeply. But telling me that's why I came is a bit far-fetched. It's sheer exaggeration!'

Emilia had burst into tears. They streamed down her cheeks and trickled down her chest, giving her skin an intense glow.

'Please, stop crying.'

She stopped and wiped her eyes. 'Okay, I'm not crying, see? Ask me whatever you want.'

Suddenly calmed down, she waited. Her tears had dried out upon her nipples and her eyes were already dry.

'Well, I just wanted to know what happened then...'

'When?' she asked ruthlessly, folding her arms like a matron.

'You know... then, at Harry's...'

'It was exactly as I told you.'

'Tell me again.'

Emilia shot her mouth off, telling the whole story again. She added only that when they had opened the door, they found him on the doormat unconscious, although he seemed to be mumbling something as he was moving his lips – or that was what she had thought she had seen before she scuttled away.

'It sounds incredible. Do you remember that I came to your place?'

She nodded.

'I brought you something. You asked me where I had the ring from and I told you. You know perfectly well how it was. You were curious to see the corpse. Where do you think I took the ring from? Do you think I made it all up?'

'I don't know, and it doesn't matter anymore.'

'Then why have you brought it up?'

'Because I wanted to tell you that things aren't the way you say they are. When we were little, Max told me that one Saturday the two of you went out for a picnic with your parents, and while you were strolling around the Baneasa forest, you had shown him a two-headed monkey in a tree. He couldn't see a thing, but you had insisted so much that he eventually admitted for your sake that he saw it, too. But he didn't. He couldn't have.'

'Did he tell you all this?'

'Yeah. But there was nothing nasty about it. It was more like a remark, as we both admitted, as far as I remember, that you were the imaginative one.'

'But you still think I was lying.'

'No. It was more like a vision that welled up from your mind,' she said, laughing. 'But I was willing to believe back then that you could really see certain things, because I noticed you changing before my eyes.'

'And now you're not anymore...'

'I'm not what?'

'Sure about this.'

'No. I don't know what to say, but what I surely know right now is that you're a married man who is having an affair and doesn't know how to handle it. If you had magical powers, I'm sure you would make me disappear right away. Or her...'

'Well, it doesn't matter what you might think; I don't need magical powers for that.' He looked tired and disappointed, and he sort of wanted to sound her out a bit more, but at the same time he thought it worthless; it would only deepen her feeling that she had been cheated. He remembered he had to act cautiously and remained silent for a while.

'Are you angry at me?'

'No. Actually, I need to tell you that I just wanted to make a fool of Max that time. He was such a gullible sucker. He used to heed my words as if I were God. I could've told him to jump off the roof, and he surely would've. After a while, I really wanted to ask him a favour, to find out something for me... but it was too late. I had moved out, and he was already under Harry's thumb. Harry, the charmer...'

Emilia, listening to him, started to laugh. 'I can't believe you remember all this!'

'How could I forget them? I've been meaning to tell you for a long time, but if one of them hadn't ratted us out, we would be together now. I mean, really. If I had known, I would've killed them all and stashed their bodies away in cool basements.'

'How do you know they gave us away?'

'I just do.'

'I can't clearly remember what happened then anyway. I'm surprised you're still thinking about it.'

'I think about it very often. I think about it because our life would've been different, and because of a filthy wimp everything went crazy.'

Emilia had grown gloomy. 'We could've died.'

'Maybe. It doesn't matter anymore. Listen, I want to tell you one more thing before I go. Everything I told you was true. You had your proofs on several occasions. As for what happened at Harry's... I don't know, it's a mystery. I kind of believe that what you said might be true as well. That I passed out. But how can you explain, then, where I got the ring from? But you're right, it doesn't matter anymore. Anyway, what I saw there was nothing but a fantasy. I mean, if I were to believe it, then...'

'Then what?'

'Nothing. Once I did believe it, but it wasn't like that. Luckily.'

He picked up his jeans, pulled them on and started to look for his shirt. Emilia was watching him, coming back to her senses. 'What are you doing?'

'I have to go.'

'Please, don't leave.'

She leaned forward and hugged him, but he pulled back. 'I can't stay any longer. Your husband will arrive back soon, and Matilda might think I'm here.'

'And?'

She lay there, stark naked and gleaming, baring her teeth. He found it impossible to say what she liked to hear. She would have bit his throat if she could have, would have scratched him and pulled his eyes out slowly and painfully with her claws, sharpened by time and pain; she would have hung his skin on the balcony and his dripping blood would have watered his treasured plants. The sofa over which they had just rolled had reappeared in all its gaudiness, and he felt terribly miserable and helpless. He looked around, saw his shirt dumped on the back of a chair and seized it. Then he scuttled away down the dim hallway, jerked the entrance door open, rushed down the stairs and didn't stop until the corner of the street.

At home, he sank into his workroom, into which he had crammed a desk and a swivel chair. He stood hunched, full of remorse and regret, his ears pricking up at the slightest noise. Then, feeling stifled, he moved into the bedroom and lay upon the rough cover spread over the sheets. He heard Matilda walk into the apartment and the girls in the background, twittering cheerfully. Then silence fell and everyone hushed, as if at a sign.

He was wondering why he had run away. He had thought of going back, but he was afraid of the man he thought he had caught a glimpse of while running down the stairs toward the bus stop. He was wondering if, upon seeing his wife sprawled and bare-assed on the same sofa where he sat to watch his favourite TV shows, his anger had been so violent that he had beat the hell out of her or if he had simply knelt down, overwhelmed by shame and helplessness, begging her to stop this madness and to come back to him, repenting and reasonable. She was allowed to love someone else as long as she stayed home, obediently, without hurting him. This was what he would have done. Had it been his wife, he would have humiliated himself and asked her to stay.

Matilda walked into the room and stood still for a moment. She may have been watching him, or maybe she was afraid to break the silence around him. She might have thought that any noise could have altered his mood, but after holding his breath for a few minutes to study her movements, Sal took a deep breath and shifted onto his other side. Matilda got into bed and nestled next to him.

'Are you sleeping?' she asked him, but she got no answer.

He didn't necessarily want to make her believe he was sleeping; rather, he wished to remain motionless and wait aimlessly, to dive into his own thoughts, just like when he was a little boy and waited to fall asleep, curled down under the covers. While waiting, he slowly slipped into dreams, suddenly freed from the remorse of having brutally deserted her without any explanations whatsoever.

He was no longer tired, and a feeling of inexplicable happiness made his body soar. One last thought flashed through his mind before darkness fell: Emi might have betrayed him with Harry and the others, but she had loved no one but him. Should history by any chance trace their story, that would be the most important thing: their pure, unblemished love, travelling through the ages like thin mist and reaching people's ears even after they were long gone.

X

RUNNING AWAY

At daybreak, the neighbourhood looked different and strange. He didn't usually wake up at that hour, when the night was melting away and daylight hadn't set in yet, except for the times when he went on holidays or for a picnic with his parents on the outskirts of Bucharest. They would pack the car with the barbecue grill, the charcoal, old blankets and sheets, the barbecue meat and other food they gathered together along with the plates and cutlery. They would also take the badminton rackets and the camera, and during summer, his mother would never forget the Doina body lotion, which she would rub on every uncovered part of her body. Every time she got hold of Sal, she would smear some on the tip of his nose so that he wouldn't get sunburnt. He hated these weekend outings, and this was why it dawned on him that this particular morning he was stumbling upon a world that had been concealed up until now. The sun had not risen yet, even though a pale, wavering light was expanding behind the grey curtain.

He had slept with his clothes on and had stashed a backpack under his bed in which he had crammed some stuff: a jumper, some underwear, his toothbrush and a blanket. He had also thought about packing some sandwiches, but it might have looked suspicious, so the money saved in his piggy bank and whatever he had been pinching during the week from his father's pockets would have to be enough to provide for a week. After that, they would have to see what happened. Right now his chest was bursting with optimism, stifling him with joy and excitement. He took one last glance at the rumpled bed, the walls plastered in posters, the bookcase and the polished wooden desk, the white lacy curtains slowly waving in the air sifting through the slats of the pulled-down blinds, and resolved that he didn't feel the slightest regret. He wasn't even sorry for the pain and suffering he was going to cause his parents when they discovered he was missing, for what else was he to do? What feasible choices had they given him to fight the resolute decision of leaving this neighbourhood and moving away to God knows where?

He tiptoed outside the house, glided along the walls and caught a glimpse of a dwarfish, shivering silhouette at the corner of the street. He approached it; only on clearly hearing his footsteps on the pavement did the figure bare its head, so that Sal could now see Emi's sleepy eyes, her pale face and her mouth drawn into a single red dot that he could barely make out. He had been taken aback to see how quickly she had agreed to everything without questioning him. She had pulled a long face when Sal had told her about running away. He had said it as an order, and she obeyed as if confronted with an implacable fate. The day before, in the basement, he had assigned clear tasks to her: first of all, she should sleep well, because they couldn't know when and where they found shelter; she should eat everything she was given for dinner, as this would be the only food until the next meal, which could come any time in the next twenty-four hours or even longer. He had told her to cram her backpack with warm clothes, just as he was going to do, because they might get cold at night when sleeping outside and they wouldn't have money for new clothes any time soon. Above all, he warned her to act naturally, just as she always did; to neither behave nor misbehave, but try not to betray her feelings, to seal up her tongue and not let herself be seized with guilt or regret. Then, hugging and cuddling her up to his scrawny chest, he told her resolutely that the next morning he would definitely be waiting for her at the corner of his street, at a place where they wouldn't risk being spotted by anyone.

He motioned to her to get going, and she got up heavily, dragging her backpack, and followed him quietly. They didn't utter another word until they left the neighbourhood; once on the main road, they took one look behind them and breathed a sigh of relief.

They headed for the tram stop and got on the second carriage of the first tram. Sal gravely took out two tram tickets and punched them. They snuggled into each other somewhere at the back and he took her in his arms, holding her tight, for he knew she had been brave and proved her confidence in him, and that he couldn't have asked for more from any other girlfriend or from the first and only sweetheart he would ever have. After a few stops, the tram started to get crowded, and shortly afterward they found themselves squeezed amid a swarm of rowdy people, mostly women, who were elbowing their way through with bags and trolleys already crammed full of secret trifles. Sal was sizing up everyone from behind the two backpacks, which they had raised like a fortress wall. Emi had fallen asleep, her head resting on his shoulder, when he suddenly pulled on her hand.

She sprang up in her seat, startled. 'What is it? What's happening?'

'We have to get off!'

His voice had grown rougher and was as hoarse as an adult's. They got off the tram, jostling their way through the many pairs of breasts that had mushroomed in the empty space like sponges. Outside on the platform, they stood befuddled.

'Why did we have to get off?' Emi asked dozily, barely moving her jaw.

Sal didn't answer; he kept looking around, weighing up their options. It was out of the question to go back, and he didn't want to return to the chatty women who had penned them in, eyeing the two clean, well-groomed kids with backpacks that looked suspicious for their age and for the early hour. He beckoned her to cross the road, grabbed her hand and pulled her among the few cars that had stopped at the lights.

They were still on the main road, caught in a bustle that was growing by the minute. Sal quickly decided to get away from the crowded area, to leave this place where they still risked being spotted. They got on another tram, which was almost empty, and only when he stretched out his legs on the seat in front of him and squeezed Emi next to him did he finally give out a sigh of relief and let a smile cross his face. 'I think we're OK now. Are you hungry?'

She nodded and pressed her nose against the window, her breath shaping a tiny, steamy, coin-like imprint. He was worried about her, of course, wondering if he would be able to defend her from the perils they were going to run into and remembering the attack that had happened in which Toma was hurt. He had nicked his father's hunting pocketknife, the one with a wooden handle, a bottle opener on one side and a tin opener on the other. He took it out now, fixed his soft nail in the slit and strenuously pulled out the blade. It came out slowly, rusty and blunt, but the aggressors would have no way of knowing this; it was a pretty impressive pocketknife, with a blade that went the whole length of his palm. Holding it like this, with the tip pointing toward the enemy, he felt he was actually holding a sword. He folded it shut and cautiously put it back in the pocket of his backpack.

Through the window, they could see rows of houses in grey uniforms marching by like tiny soldiers: long houses with dusty windows, flanked by small, narrow yards with only enough space to let one person strain in through their rusty, wrought-iron gates. Looking out the window as the tram sped on, the houses might have been deserted but for those with open windows through which you could barely distinguish, just behind the dirty curtains, the crooked, famished silhouettes of the people living there.

Sal was surprised to see how variegated the city was and how little he knew it. Before deciding to leave, it had seemed to him that no matter how threatening their newly-conquered freedom might be, it was by far less threatening than the exile lying ahead. This exile was summed up by two words that had previously meant nothing to him: 'moving house'. It meant leaving the house where you had been born, where you had grown up, the house on whose walls your pen had scribbled important words discovered from the range of ever-growing books that you were reading faster and faster, words to be later hidden behind the pop-star and racing-car posters. Moving house meant leaving behind every nook and cranny, every corner and every secret, the entire building site that you had raked over stone by stone, every grain of sand, every person, every acquaintance; it meant having to start from scratch, toiling up the mountain of friendship again, climbing it under the spell of the same fear, repeating the same common mistakes over and over again. So what choice did he have but to search on his own for freedom, despite the obstacles that waited for him in the outside world?

And now the city was cutting its belly open with sharp, narrow slits, revealing its repulsive entrails to him. He had expected neither so much squalour and poverty, nor this sadness that had befogged the neighbourhood they were cutting across by tram. He had grown scared of getting off; the window seemed to be disintegrating, exposing him as easy prey to the passing people: men carrying their vinyl briefcases and women wearing calico skirts and shoddy blouses, home-knitted from linty wool. He squeezed the pocket holding the money he had pinched from his father's wallet and felt the knife once again through the waterproof pocket of his backpack. Leaning her entire weight on him, Emi was purring like a cat on its master's lap. She had become somebody else: a frightened girl trusting enough to embark upon a journey without knowing which way she was heading, escorted by a skinny, chatty boy who had lured her in with so many words, but who had carefully concealed the fear and insecurity that had governed him ever since he could remember.

The tram moved on with a jerk, passing over a railway switch; Emi's head swayed forward and rested on his chest in shaky balance. He kept taking deep, steady breaths, wincing at times. Two gypsy women had come on board and sat down a few seats away at the back of the tram, nibbling sunflower seeds. They were cracking the shells with their teeth, pulling out the kernels with the tip of their tongues and eventually spitting the scraps out on the floor. After a while, a black-and-white carpet lay at their feet, while the bulging pockets of the women's skirts were deflating by the minute. They were whispering to each other, the older one completely leaning over the younger and her knotty fingers pulling back the scarf that kept sliding on her forehead. As she continued whispering and spitting, from time to time her prying eyes searched the back of the tram. Suddenly, she sprang up from her seat, 'Yuck! Stop spitting on me, bitch!'

After shaking some pieces of shell off, a flood of words gushed out from her mouth, leaving Sal dumbfounded. She ruffled her skirts, giving off a rancid, oily stench. Then she gazed at the cowering boy holding the girl in his arms.

'What you looking at, *chavi*[1]? Hasn't you seen a cunt before? Say, do you wanna see one?'

She fanned out her skirts again, spreading them in front of his eyes as if at a bullfight, while Sal raised his hand, trying to protect himself against the invisible threat. The commotion woke up Emi, and she was now watching Sal in a daze as he defended himself against the two laughing women, baring their white teeth streaked with bits of sunflower shell.

'What's wrong?' she asked him softly.

The two gypsy women stopped laughing and fumbled through the pleats of their skirts. They took out two handfuls of seeds and offered them to her.

'Here, take this!'

Emi eyed them with suspicion, but the older one beckoned her once more to take them. She looked at the seeds, then stretched the edge of her T-shirt into a pouch and moved closer to the two women so they could pour them inside. She turned to him, beaming, and started cracking seeds, spitting the shells together with the kernel. The gypsy women got off at the next stop, leaving them alone.

'Why did you take them?' Sal boiled over.

'Why wouldn't I?'

'Because you're drawing attention to us, that's why!'

Sometimes he felt like killing her, especially at times like this, when she peeked at him through her eyelashes in overt mockery of his fears and his claims to be the superhero. He could hear her crunching and spitting, and he would have gladly scolded her, would have told her – perhaps loudly enough for other travellers to hear – that what she was doing was wrong; that she shouldn't have been spitting shells, that the tram belonged to the people, including them, and they should therefore take care of it. But he realised that Emi wouldn't have spoken to him for hours, maybe the whole day; rash and thoughtless as he knew her to be, it was likely she might even want to abandon him in a fit of rage or, even worse, to return home. So he braced himself and swore he would be deaf from then on.

But five minutes later his thoughts were already drifting away, and he was trying to figure out where they were and when was best to get off. Emi had stopped cracking seeds and emptied the rest into her backpack, explaining that he might appreciate the stash later when he got hungry enough.

'Mum says that gypsies roast the seeds in the same pots they pee in,' she added, laughing.

'That's so disgusting! Why did you eat them, then?'

'First of all, it's silly and it's not true. Secondly, I ate them because I was hungry. And finally, let's assume that what Mum says is true and that they really do roast them in the chamber pot – when you're hungry and you have no food, it hardly seems to matter, does it?'

He thought about it and agreed. The grey houses had vanished in the distance, and they were now crossing a tunnel made up of monolithic blocks of flats that loomed above their heads and only allowed them to glimpse bits and pieces of the sky. He envied all those who could melt away in that massive concrete anonymity envied the tiny balconies, the proximity, the well-planned and apparently cosy houses. He was drawn to the spiral staircases winding all the way up to the tenth floor, bringing together so many different people that you could hide among and pass unnoticed. Despite his parents' prejudice against such estates, he felt that, at this moment, finding a hideout in one of those buildings could have been their lucky escape. Trying to find them would have been like searching for two needles in a haystack, and he was sure that, after long, strenuous and fruitless searches, after shedding bucketfuls of tears and after countless sleepless nights, their parents would have eventually given up. But it would have been risky to get off now and start looking for such a place at random.

He thought of the conversations his parents sometimes had when they were driving through this kind of neighbourhood. He remembered them saying that in these kind of places people spied on each other, eavesdropping from behind closed doors, and that this would be the best place for a burglar to break into any flat: in spite of the vigilance and the cunning they displayed, the neighbours would never come out to save a victim. Of course, Sal knew very well that these were the exaggerations of people who had chosen to live in seclusion in a small neighbourhood cut off from the rest of the city, a place where the squalor, the ash scattered in the air and on the pavement, the gloom and the languor that here were so obvious, remained unseen, so they could go on with their lives ignoring them.

Lost in these thoughts, at first Sal didn't even hear the man in uniform, who had taken out his badge and asked to see their tickets. The brute in front of him, with a horseshoe moustache and oily, wavy hair gleaming in the late-morning sun, had to repeat his question, visibly annoyed and growing suspicious. Only then did Sal stare at him, thunderstruck, taking in his size for the first time and shivering deep down. Emi had shrivelled next to him and almost closed her eyes. He fumbled through his pockets, trying to stall him off, then went on to search intently inside his backpack, mumbling that he had the tickets somewhere, but he couldn't remember where he had put them.

Somewhere in the distance, he saw the passenger platform and the sign announcing the next stop. Another few more seconds, and – if he estimated properly the distance between the seats and the door and if Emi had been able to read his mind – they could give him the slip. Once out on the street, he knew they would have had chance to scuttle away and nobody would be able to catch them, neither the moustached brute nor his colleagues who were busy with other suspects at the front of the tram.

He counted silently, and when he heard the clank of the opening doors, he grabbed Emi's hand and jerked her, rushing down the stairs. But in the chase that followed, the brute seized the girl's clothes and stopped her short. Sal was already down in the street, balancing his full weight and pulling Emi's hand downward, while the inspector gripped her other hand. The girl started to cry and struggle, scolding him as her terrified eyes, bulging with fear, begged him not to leave her behind.

'Hit him in the balls! Emi, kick him in the balls!'

His cry was so loud that he could feel his lungs expand. At that very same moment, the doors snapped shut, leaving Emi's hand, still tight in his own, hanging through the rubber band between the doors. Immediately, he started to kick the tram's metal side; then, realising that the driver wouldn't hear him over the street racket, he flung himself against the door and with his free fist broke one of the narrow windows.

The sound of shattering glass startled even the inspector. The door opened again, and from the front of the tram they could hear someone swearing and hurried footsteps approaching. But Sal and Emi had managed to scuttle away on a street perpendicular to the main road; now they were running for their lives, leaving a trail of large drops of blood, gushing from the boy's hurt fist, and the bitter tears shed by the girl.

They kept on running until they sank into the concrete jungle. When the blocks of flats thinned out, they stumbled upon shabby houses where colourful yards full of tomatoes, herbs, sour cherry or apricot trees could be seen through the cracks of the wooden fences. They stopped in front of one of the gardens, and Sal poked his nose through two wooden planks to peer inside. The blood on his hand had dried up and become darker. Emi ran her fingers over the wounds and asked him in a whimper, 'Can you see anything?'

His face was pale. Two purple half-moons, streaked with small red veins, had appeared under his eyes. He hunkered down, leaning against the fence, and she huddled at his side.

'What now?'

'You stay here. I'll go in to see if I can find some shelter.'

'Isn't it dangerous?' she pouted. 'What would I do if something happened to you? I'd better come along.'

'Nothing's going to happen to me. Maybe a dog could bite

me, but we would've heard it bark by now. Stay here, and if somebody passes by, just pretend you're busy doing something, okay?'

She nodded.

'Say it! I want to hear you!'

'Okay, yes, sir, I got it!'

'There. It's very important not to raise any suspicion.'

She gave him a rueful look, trying to brace herself. Then she watched him slip through two crooked wooden planks in the fence; when the tips of his trainers vanished on the other side, she heaved a sigh, as if to herself, fearing the worst. He heard her, but he knew that it wasn't yet the time to soothe her. First, he should find a place where they could hide, and once they had managed to settle in, there would be time for soothing and belated moans.

On his right there was the one-storey house, with white, lace-curtained windows and some thick cushion rolls, probably homemade from ladies' stockings and old family socks, placed between the windowpanes against dust and the winter cold. On his left and in front of him: the vegetable garden, reaching out as far as his eyes could see. Beds of tomatoes, peppers, cucumbers, celery and parsnips lay at his feet; beyond them, he could see raspberry bushes separating the vegetables from what could have been an orchard. If you followed the path winding among the beds and the small fir trees guarding the grey walls like tiny soldiers, you would get to the front door. He crept stealthily along the path, passed by a water pump where a thick hose for watering the garden lay on the ground with a tiny stream trickling from it, dodged under some quince trees and arrived under the vine vault, where he could make out a glade and the front door, just on his right. There were a few steps, a wide-open door and, apart from the flies and bees buzzing around, dazed by the sickly sweet scents in the yard, there was not a soul in sight. He took another step, rustling the thick blades of grass that had grown between the paving slabs, and stopped short.

In front of him, a scrawny old man, wearing a pair of soiled boxer shorts and a greyish net vest, was resting on a deck chair. He had straggly white hair and a tanned face, wrinkled from sunlight and old age. His skin was sagging, and his lion-like head seemed heavier than his body. He was sprawled on the chair, legs apart, feet out of their plastic slippers, his arms hanging limp over the armrests, his eyes closed. Two flies were strolling on his face, but he didn't seem to mind them. At first, it flashed through Sal's mind that the man was dead, but he noticed his toes twitching regularly at short intervals, as if he had wanted to chase away the annoying buzzing of the insects whirling about him. Next to the house on the steps lay several unwashed dishes and some leftovers on a plate – bits of tomatoes and crumbs of bread. Above the old man, a vine vault, held up by a few iron pillars painted green, cast a cooling shade. Beyond him, there stretched a labyrinth of trees and grapevines and a dense orchard that one could sneak through and lose oneself inside, watching the motion around the house yet sheltered more safely than in a fortress.

Who would have thought of searching for two lost children amidst the weeds in an old, deaf man's yard? It didn't take him long to make up his mind. Before going back to fetch Emi, he only wanted to make sure there wasn't any other risk. He walked cautiously, passing by the old man and his muffled snores, tiptoed into the green labyrinth so as not to break the frail balance around him and kept on going, minding his step. Finally he reached the far end of the garden, closed in by a fence just as rickety as the one he had slipped through, yet revealing one final surprise: a woodshed. This shabby, ramshackle hut, wrapped in cobwebs at every corner and every hinge, was going to be their new home. All he had to do was help Emi across the fence and lead her quietly through the garden to this unexpected shelter, then settle there and see more clearly next morning what important decisions they would have to make.

The woodshed door was shut with a makeshift wooden latch, resting on a twisted, L-shaped nail. Opening it was easy enough, but he feared that the persistent squeak of the hinges would fill the entire yard. Popping his head in, he looked around: a few stacks of wood, some gardening tools, several piles of coal that covered the floor in a velvety tar carpet that looked cosy enough to offer rest to tired travellers – all this left enough room for two children. What could have brought the old man there in the summer? Except for the watering cans, the multicoloured hoses coiled and hanging over a pole, the rake, the hoe and some other iron tools he might have needed for working his land, there was nothing else he could have needed. They could find shelter in the darkest, remotest corner; they could perch on the stack of wood; they could build up some kind of fortress, just as he used to do when he was little, curling down under the puffed feather duvet where his mum would feign not to find him. Her image sprang to his mind as he was closing the woodshed door and pulling the latch; he was seized with a feeling of remorse, and a terrible homesickness flooded him unexpectedly.

He crammed his pockets with black mulberries, picked from the tree pouring its richness over the shingles on top of the ramshackle dwelling. Then he slowly started to wade his way back, throwing down a berry every few steps, while the rest of the juicy fruit started to seep through his trousers. He went crawling along like a true soldier on a mission through the rampant growth of weeds and the cool, scented vineyard corridor behind the deck chair. But the deck chair was empty. He stopped dead, awaiting the heavy fist that was bound to come down on him. He could already see its shadow growing over his skull; he could already feel a muffled pain behind his temples. His ears were hissing, amplifying the rustle of the leaves like a conch shell, and he could sniff an overbearing threat in the air around him. Closing his eyes, he dropped down and cringed completely, like sewage cockroaches shrinking in the face of danger. Then, as the blow seemed to tarry, he turned his head halfway.

There was no one around. All he heard was the clank of metal dishes behind the open kitchen window framing the white, wild mane of the old man. His legs were shaking and fever flooded his groin, pushing him onward. He crept on through the grass like a reptile all the way to the fence, still scattering the mulberries mechanically behind him. He eased himself through the same two planks and barged into the street.

The sun was beating down with such heat that even the planks in the fence were burning, scorching his fingers. Emi was no longer where he had left her. She was in the middle of the street playing hopscotch in the dust, hopping on one foot along the squares the local girls had drawn in coloured chalk, raising with each jump a whirl of tiny particles that shimmered in the strong daylight. She looked serene, seemingly on a break that her mother had granted in exchange for her promise to come home at the appointed time. She looked as if she had forgotten about the tiredness, the adventure they had embarked upon, the fact that he had disappeared through the shabby wooden fence, about their future fraught with uncertainty. She was alone in the world and carefree, as ten-year-old girls should be.

He approached her, tired and sweaty. When she saw him, her face overflowed with terror and astonishment. She froze on one foot in a shaky balance while sizing him up and down; then she burst forth and shook him. 'What's happened to you?'

She felt his tummy with her tiny, plump palms.

'Are you hurt?' she screamed, clutching him between her two little pincers.

Angrily, he took a step backward. He couldn't understand what all the fuss was about. He felt his sweat trickling down his forehead, his arms and legs. Emi leaned over him and wiped his calf, then stuck her palms in his face. 'What's this?!'

Her hands were red. He looked down and saw blood trickling from under his trousers. Then he became frightened and took a few more shaky steps backward.

'Are you sick?'

He shook his head. He only felt tired and hungry, but definitely not ill – not in the way he would have expected to feel after receiving a deathly stab. He could sense no pain that might have alarmed him; nevertheless, his heart was pounding wildly in his chest. Eventually, he mustered the courage to touch himself cautiously and discovered the mulberries left in his pocket. They both burst out laughing when they saw them, and Emi laughed even louder hearing that Sal had strewn them on the ground to make sure they found their way back.

'How are we even going to see them through the grass?'

'We will, don't worry.'

'You're such a character,' she interrupted abruptly. 'There's no way we're going to see them! So much effort for nothing!'

He mulled again over all those things he was dying to tell her: that this was no way to show gratitude to someone dear who had just risked his skin for you; that it was one thing to loiter around playing hopscotch, and quite another to shake with fear in a crazy old man's garden. He wanted to tell her to keep her eyes open against any attack; that once you set upon such an adventure, love and concern and solidarity for your companion are crucial unless you want your first mistake to give you away completely – and so on.

'Forget about that now and pay attention!' He pulled a sober face to make her listen to him. 'There's this old guy in the garden. I have no idea if he lives by himself, but at the moment there's no one else, so we must take this chance and go in. But you have to do exactly as I say: you will not stand up, no matter what; you will crawl along the whole way. You will follow me and do exactly as I do: if I stop, you stop; if I move on, you do the same. Right?'

Emi nodded idly. She didn't seem quite convinced by the drill, but she wanted to stop his nagging her, so she had agreed. Yet Sal knew deep down that at the slightest provocation, her head would rise above the weeds and her inquisitive eyes would explore her surroundings, lured by the strange voices of inanimate things, which she so often endowed with soul and will. He grabbed her hand and they slipped together into the garden, his eyes peering about carefully; he was no longer alone now, and being responsible for such a precious load, he wanted to make sure that the road ahead was safe and that they would reach their den with no dangers lurking along the way. He could hear her behind him, rustling softly, like a snake slithering through the beautifully grown vegetation; still wild, yet neatly planned at regular intervals by the old man's maniacal and tired hand as it tried to tame nature.

The deck chair was still empty and so was the kitchen; nothing could be seen through the open window but some charred pots hanging on the wall with flies buzzing all around them. The old man might have been asleep, or he might have been somewhere in the garden. He turned back to Emi to warn her and saw her half immersed in a raspberry bush, picking the dangling, sweet-and-sour fruit and biting them directly off the branches. At that point, he wanted to put everything behind, to get up and uncork the anger that was choking him, to rebuke her and reveal to her the real dangers that were rising and encircling them like walls. Was that what she wanted, to make all this tremendous effort worthless for a mere fistful of raspberries? But on seeing her like that, with raspberry juice smudged around her mouth and her keen attempts to shake the berries off the bush, he suddenly grasped the image of the terrible hunger that must have been gnawing her, obliterating any other detail unrelated to her craving for food. He had almost forgotten all about it; that mixture of strong anxiety and fear had put a lid over the hole gaping in his stomach and numbed his other instincts. But Emi, waiting and idly playing hopscotch, must have felt the first squirms and the claw tugging in her tummy; she had had plenty of time to think about the fridge back home, the comfortable table set in front of her, her granny's fine white cotton cloth embroidered with silk on the edges and laden with everything that could be picked from the sombre shelves of the grocer on the main street or from under the counter of the pot-bellied shopkeeper who always had blood and grease smudges on his white apron. He was the one who would plaster a sleazy smirk on his face as he saw the ladies out from his shop; as they bent over baskets hugged tightly to their chests, he kept his greasy hands pressed against their sweaty blouses and squeezed their arms meaningfully in a gesture that looked even more like abuse than if they had burst out naked and dishevelled from the back room where he sliced his meat and inventoried his stock.

Emi's hunger was storming down now like a hurricane, gathering heavy clouds above the garden where a moment before he had thought they could finally find peace. The trees were heavy with fruit, that much was true, but who could go on eating nothing but fruit forever? Fruit was meant to be eaten at the end of the meal, as dessert. 'To grow up healthily, you need protein, you need milk and meat and cheese and eggs; otherwise you will be small and puny, your brain won't develop and all the girls will laugh at you,' Sal's mum would preach in a thundering voice whenever she saw him squeamishly scattering his food with his fork, pushing aside bits of meat out of the tomato sauce in a string on the side of the plate. Then he would hear her grumbling around the house, voicing her discontent and complaining how hard it had been to get hold of the meat that she was forced to throw away because of him. How ungrateful he was, how careless of his parents' striving, working from dawn till dusk just to provide for their children! He understood that to still Emi's hunger, he should also set out on a quest for food, ingratiate himself with another shopkeeper, probably one that would be less repugnant than the one at their local grocer, and return with some slices of ham, some salami, a couple of sausages, a couple of yoghurt jars – supplies that would keep for a few days.

She finally noticed him. She picked a few more berries and pulled herself away from the bushes, her pouting face showing how regretful she was. They went back in silence, and only when they lifted the latch and opened the door to enter the woodshed, struck by a stifling wave of heat that choked both of them, did they give out a dull cry. The smell of wood and heated coal scorched the air and burnt their cheeks as if they had entered the bowels of hell. They put up their arms in defence, but to no avail. In vain did Sal try to take a few steps forward; inside, fiery mouths were spitting flames at them.

'Is this where you wanted us to hide?' he heard her say. He knew she was perfectly right, but this was the only place he could find.

At the very instant she spoke, they heard the plants rustle and stir outside, and the sound of muffled steps approached through the weeds. He only saw the wild mane of the old man at the very last moment, and all he could do was draw her inside, silencing her mouth with his palm despite her protests. The door had been left half open, and he held his breath. For about thirty minutes, he could clearly hear every movement nearby until, at the end, when they were almost unconscious from the heat and the terror, he saw the shed door close from the outside, locked with the wooden latch. They stood still, thunderstruck, and only dared to move long after the old man's footsteps dwindled away on the soft, grassy carpet. Even then, they moved cautiously and only to pull apart in order to breathe, to disentangle their bodies on which trickles of sweat were falling in large drops, streaking their young, fuzzy, golden skin.

Shortly afterward, Emi started to cry. She wasn't angry; she was crying more to herself, whining and bemoaning the moment they had decided to run away together. He could hear her thoughts buzzing in the air, and the hotter it got, the noisier the sound of her doubt was. The shabby walls of the shed were whirring, the cobwebs were strumming in the corners, and the twigs were rattling under their feet.

After ruminating on his annoyance and frustration all by himself, it struck him that he could stop her tears if he simulated – for he knew that he could only persuade her by pretending – an attempt to open the door. He squeezed his healthy hand through a slit between the doorframe and a wooden slat in the wall. But the opening was too narrow and, even though he slowly pushed it onward, gasping in pain, his hand was starting to give in. When he pulled it back out, besides the scratches that were already swollen and ready to release the blood collected inside, there were also splinters sunk deep under his skin. But not even this image of the self-flagellation to which her lover willingly submitted himself was enough to put an end to Emi's sobs. The sunbeams had started to seep in through the cracks in the walls, mellowing them in a haloed light.

'You do know there's no way we can get out of here?' he finally asked her, in a hoarse, worn voice. 'You're crying in vain. All you do is burn yourself out. Will you stop already?'

It sounded like a command, but he knew this was the only way to make her stop crying. Everything suddenly went quiet, and he could sense that, choking back her tears, she was waiting for an answer in return or at least for a heartfelt proof of his deepest remorse.

'There was no way for me to know he was going to lock us in. If we had stayed outside, we would've been caught, right? I know that deep down you think that it's all my fault, but I only did what I thought was right. When we left home, we were expecting things like this to happen, weren't we? I mean, it was clear that it wouldn't be all milk and honey. But we'll get through this; the important thing is to stick together. Let's not start fighting already. Listen...'

He halted, musing. Of course, he'd rather have had an honest fight, a sudden release of all the spite, but he had resolved that it was better to delay the moment.

'And what do you suggest we do, if I may ask?'

'Well, here's what we'll do. We'll look around and try to find some piece of wire to help me lift the latch.'

Emi stood listlessly on the woodpile, the tips of her sandals drawing trails on the dusty floor. He knew that was all he was going to get from her, so he started rummaging around alone. First he saw the bucksaws, hanging on several nails, then the pliers, the hacksaws, axes, hoes, reels of cable, rolls of tape and some scaly ropes. He rummaged through them with his uninjured hand, hoping he would come across the hook-shaped wire; he took them down one by one, then put them back in the same order so as not to arise the meticulous master's suspicion. But it was all in vain. He strangled a curse, like a worker who realises that his entire work has been ruined because of one nail. How could he have known that the cunning old man would lock them up in there? He grunted something before finally sinking hopelessly to the ground.

'Sal, we're going to die of suffocation in here,' Emi announced in a dull voice, like a long-distance call operator.

The more he fidgeted around, the more he felt the heat grow and his body shrink under the burden of guilt and the fruitlessness of the search. He took off his T-shirt, baring his shiny, jutting ribs and his outwardly curved sternum. The sudden relief filled him with optimism. He took off his shorts and remained with nothing on but his white cotton underpants. Emi was watching him with growing amazement.

'You should do it, too. It's so much better.'

It took more than a quarter of an hour for Emi to be persuaded. She climbed down the stack of wood and let her dress slip off. Then, to trump him, she took off her sandals as well and sat down by his side, wriggling her toes.

'It really is better,' she sighed contentedly.

Sticking out through their thin, fine skin, their bones looked like latticework. Sitting there, legs crossed, with their naked chests and their bristly chocolate buttons, they could pass for a couple of young boys about to face puberty: similarly narrow-hipped, with similarly frail bodies, thin, bare arms and bony shoulders, with the same bristly fuzz covering their nape, arms and legs; the same hairless, smooth, rosy-cheeked faces resembling two cherubs, and their tiny, bulging underpants barely covering their chromosome marks. At first glance, they could have passed for siblings. Close up, you could see that Emi's face was rounder, while Sal's was pointed and solemn. Besides this, however, they had the same long, thick eyelashes, the same straight nose, the same mouth with rising corners, the same slightly protruding ears, the same dark cowlick on top of their heads. He stroked her thigh, the flesh barely starting to thicken, and sensed her still-damp skin.

'I'm sorry things have turned out this way, Emi.'

'It doesn't matter. It's not your fault. But we can't stay here any longer. Let's say we'll make it tonight, but tomorrow we'll start over.'

Sal nodded and she went on.

'So, the way I see it, we have two possibilities. Either...'

She stopped short again.

'Either what?'

'Either we run for it the minute the old guy opens the door, or, when he does it, we belt him over the head with a shovel and we can stay here as long as we want.'

He stood dumb, following her train of thought. Of course; it was easy. The two possibilities were rising up against the shadows like a flawlessly devised scheme. But he was the one who had woven it; he had been the one who had brought her here, the one who had entered the garden, the very one who had dragged her to the back of the garden, where he had discovered the woodshed. He had been the one who had so intricately and ignorantly set the trap they had fallen into. He couldn't blame her for hatching survival plans, since his own had failed.

'What do you say?'

He held his head in his hands and waited. Dusk had fallen and the hysterical chirping of crickets could be heard from the yard.

'Think about it. We're going to have the whole house just for ourselves. Otherwise we'll have nothing but a woodshed to die in. And not even that.'

He didn't want to answer at once. He was racking his brain, wanting to find reasons, to identify the perfect excuse to extricate him from the words he had just heard. He knew that, had he confessed his concerns regarding her, Emi would have lashed out in an instant, accusing him of hypocrisy: 'You are a fake and a bragger! Here we are, locked in a shed, close to being suffocated or, if we don't suffocate, we're sure to die of starvation, and all you can think about is what's right and what's wrong. And you're so ready to judge me only because I dared to give a solution. What's more, I gave you a choice, Sal. You don't absolutely *need* to kill him. We can spare him. We can run and find ourselves another bigger and brighter shed.' She had not uttered them yet, but these were bound to be her words.

He avoided looking at her for a while, yet he unhappily found that he was still thinking about what she had said, that he was working her dreadful proposal over and over in his mind, because he had to admit it was the only solution at hand. Finally, he sized it up in the cold light of day. If they had left, where in Bucharest would they have found another empty house, with a garden full of fruit and vegetables on hand and a fence built up against the prying world, which could just as well have been at the end of the world? He could deny neither her skilfulness nor her pragmatism, but he still found it difficult to take that leap into the darkness from where her suggestion had risen. He'd rather have spelt it out himself; that way he wouldn't have to make a terrible decision while being, at the same time, burdened down by this horrible doubt about her humane side. He was still unsure about the proportions in which she could be trusted and in which she was still hazy and unpredictable – just as unpredictable as the prowling snow leopard or the splutter of a dormant volcano whose entrails were boiling.

The day had worn out, and as dusk had fallen, the scorching heat in the shed had turned into hot moisture. It would still be several hours, long after the night had truly fallen, before a faint breeze might stir the air. Emi was perched on the woodpile again and had withdrawn into the darkest corner; he could barely make her out.

'Let's say we do as you said.'

His voice sounded gloomily in the laden air. He heard no stir on the other side, not even the delighted rustling of someone gloating over their enemy's yielding words. As he got no answer, he felt bound to go on. And then the whole plan was pouring from his lips as if this twisted, crazy idea had been his own, as if not sheer words but the dreadful deeds themselves were leading them on a path of no return, fraught with regret and bitterness.

'Let's say we do it. Let's say that, at some point, the old guy is going to need something from the shed. He'll open the door and we'll be ready with the shovel. We'll take him by surprise and he won't even have time to fight back; then we smash his head in a second, with a shovel or an axe. Actually, an axe would be better, if we could find one around.'

The logs creaked under her weight, and finally he heard the

faint rustling he had been waiting for. Emi crawled down and he barely felt her when her breath touched his face. She had a will of iron. She would have probably stood the whole night out – and, who knows, maybe a few more – until she had heard him agree. That her ambition surpassed anything that might have bound them together till then made him sad. But he had to pretend he took no notice of her so that they would still be able to speak their minds. He was wondering, for instance, if it weren't better to spare the old man after all. Wouldn't it have been more reasonable to simply stun him with a blow to his skull, then tie him up, stuff a gag into his mouth, lock him up in the shed and come by once or twice a day with some food instead of letting him die of starvation? Wouldn't their consciences have been clearer and their sleep more peaceful? He shared these thoughts with Emi, but upon hearing him, she sprung to her feet; through the dark, he saw her put her hands on her hips.

'What are you saying? That we should stay with him forever?'

'No! We'll stay in the house and he'll be here, in the shed.'

'So this is your idea of a good night's sleep – to quiver with each squeak of wood, each crack, each step we might fancy taking in the yard? To be filled with dread every time we take a full plate to the back of the yard, wondering if he's still there – tied up, as you say – or if he's waiting for us behind the door, like we did, ready to smack us in the head? Should this happen, make no mistake, we wouldn't get out alive. We'd die, and that would be it. Why don't we end it now, if that's the plan anyway? Why suffer that much? Why stay here locked up, scorched and starved, if we're going to end up here anyway? What do you have to say to that?'

It was a question he couldn't answer. He knew, once again, that she was right, but the more indignant and persuasive she became, the clearer Sal could see her ruthlessness. Her cruel righteousness, devoid of any trace of humanity, would eventually bog them both down in an ancient and dusty dilemma. But having found solace in the idea that a solution would nonetheless come out soon, despite the blind alley they were in, he indulged himself in conversation.

'So we have no choice, do we?'

'I kind of think so. Of course, we could try to run, but I say that after he sees us, the old guy will surely alert everybody, including our parents, who'll find out at this point about your marvellous plan. It's going to be impossible for us to hide out any longer. We'll have our faces printed and plastered on every lamppost. People will point at us on the street –'

'Okay, I get it. No need to spell it out. It's the only way.'

'You're saying it as if I enjoyed doing such a thing.' Her voice was trembling, and shortly afterward, he could hear her crying nearby.

'That's not what I said!'

'No, but that's what you implied!'

'Emi, you're driving me nuts! What do you want now? Should I be thrilled that we've just decided to kill someone? When we left home, I had other plans. And it all changed because of sheer stupidity. I wasn't careful enough. I'm sorry, Emi. Now, will you please tell me what you're crying for?'

She stopped and snuggled into his arms. She nestled her face, streaming with tears and sweat, in the scoop between his neck and his shoulder and clung to him. It was her sign of surrender. She was letting him know, voicelessly, that there was no reason to go on fighting, because they were in a terrible mess anyway. He stroked her damp, boyish shoulder blades, held her by her armpits and then slid his hands down until they rested above her breasts, which were in truth nothing but tiny protuberances. Then he kissed her on her sternum and buried his head in her tummy, framed by the two iliac bones. He stood like that for a few minutes, resting his forehead on her panties, which still held the scent of fresh washing powder mixed with another, heavier odour given off by the sweat gathered inside the creases of her crotch. Emi blew against the back of his neck, her hands trying to separate his wet strands of hair in an attempt to cool him down; then she ruffled his hair fondly, running her thin fingers over the skin of his head.

'Don't you feel sorry at all for the old guy?'

'No.'

She had answered straightaway, with disarming honesty. He was no longer surprised. He somehow appreciated the honesty she displayed; it was like they were death row convicts sharing the same cell, counting down the seconds before the execution. But if it only had been so – if only the cruel, brave girl kneading his brain with her hands, blowing cold air against his nape, had been indeed the one who was talking and not her projection, the character she supposed she should pull out of her bag under such circumstances. A suspicion had insensibly started to sprout in his mind: that she didn't believe in this miraculous way out either, that she was scared to death and that, just like so many times before, she'd rather cloak herself in lies than tell the truth. And the truth was that they were trapped inside the woodshed and that the entire turmoil of the morning had been in vain; that they had no other choice but to wait for their parents to come and pick them up and that, perhaps, as a consequence of this reckless adventure, they would end up in reformatory school, just like Uwe, the son of the gypsies living round the corner.

'So we kill him?'

'We kill him! Straight off. Well, sure, we need to get ourselves prepared first, because even if there's two of us, he's bigger. Even though he looks so skinny and frail... you'd think you could break him in two with a single blow. If we're lucky, maybe that's all it takes.'

'What do you mean?'

'Well... maybe we won't do him in with the first shot. Maybe he's going to need a few more whacks. And it's unpleasant, because then we'll really have to see where we're hitting. And instead of the enemy, we'll just see a tiny old man cringing under our blows, covered in blood, his head cracked open...'

'All right, I get it, stop it! We'll be careful to take him down at once.'

'Great.'

She lay back in the black dust that was glimmering in the darkness, growing lighter and lighter as their eyes became accustomed to it. Sal leaned his head against the bony pubis that was prodding his ear, his hand tightly grasping her thighs. The weariness had finally seeped into his bones. He pulled himself higher, shut his eyes and thought he'd doze off for just a second or two, enough to help him get back on his feet again. He wanted to open his mouth and tell her that, should he fall asleep, she should wake him up. But his lips wouldn't obey him. His tongue slugged within, among the gritted teeth, like a scaly snake. He let himself loose for a few seconds with his body hovering, and this time his body yielded, abiding by every commandment of his mind; he had given up the struggle of every winter night when, lying naked on the sheets, windows wide open, he was trying in vain to stifle his chattering teeth, to tame the sensation of coldness that was ultimately sweeping over him.

Two years in a row he had trained himself to become an astronaut. He knew Rodion's lines in *Les Pionniers de l'Esperance* by heart and had read everything on Neil Armstrong. He had even heard that neither his white outfit with the American flag stamped on its sleeve, nor their stellar spiderlike spacecraft module, nor even the moon – none of these had been for real; it all was probably just mere stage sets, concocted in Hollywood's 'dream factory,' as one almanac had put it. But the more he dreamt of himself flying, the quicker he would fall ill, the sooner his body would fail him; it was the flu and the colds that had hindered him in the end from carrying on with his training. Yet now it was different. That he succeeded in staying wide awake even after his eyelids had shut was a marvel. He decided to count his minutes of rest and urged himself not to overrun a quarter of an hour. Emi had softened as well; her belly, on which he had laid his head, had slackened, and now his skull was sinking further down into her bowels as they strummed steadily, giving rise to a friendly background music.

He couldn't have told when he had lost the thread of his counting, but the thing was that all the time he had been gazing at the woodshed door while watching her sleeping and listening to the movements from within her. Even though it was already morning when he woke up and the heat had sifted through the window slats along with the sunlight, he could have sworn that only a second had elapsed. He sprang to his feet. Emi had stayed in the same posture, her mouth half open, and a trickle of saliva streaked her cheek, drying and turning into an off-white powder. He dashed to the door and tried the handle. It was still locked and no one seemed to have moved it. He pressed his ear against it and tried to hear beyond. It was difficult to pick something out from the daytime bustle: there was the garden rustle, the animal sounds, then another sound in the background of cars and people humming. Even the rattling of a train could be heard from a distance, though it was difficult for him to understand how such a thing was possible.

'Emi,' he called in a whisper. 'Emi, wake up!'

He hurled himself upon her and shook her. The girl mumbled sulkily and wanted to roll over, but he didn't give up and grabbed her arms, firmly lifting her up. 'You can't sleep any longer! Wake up!'

She opened her dozy eyes and looked at him lazily and indifferently. Then she smiled and stretched herself, moaning quietly the whole time, before sitting bolt upright.

'What's up?'

'Nothing. We didn't have time to plan something out, and the old guy could come any minute now.'

'Okay, so what?'

'What do you mean, what? Shouldn't we... you know what?'

'What?' she asked him, yawning without covering her mouth.

A brackish stench reached his nose and he thought that, had they been at home, it would have been time they brushed their teeth. They had their toothbrushes and the toothpaste in their backpacks. Now he thought how silly it was to have taken them; it showed how unprepared he was for such a flight. Was it possible that everything they had talked about yesterday might have been just a joke? Or maybe she pretended she didn't remember a thing so that he should be the one to shoulder the whole responsibility. He would have done it; it was the least he could do after having led her to a dead end, picked her up from her home, crossed the city with her, unwillingly thrown her in a cage, locked her away with no water, no food and no light – led her astray on their way to freedom when in fact they were dwelling in a living prison.

'I'm thirsty,' Emi whined, raking into his thoughts.

'Me too, but we have to wait.'

'I can't stop thinking about that water pump we passed by yesterday a few steps away, and I didn't even think of drinking heartily.'

'Emi...'

She didn't trouble to answer. She wiped her sweat off her forehead and did the same with her tummy. She had dark circles under her eyes, and her paleness was deepened by the light that was slanting into their tiny den. They were both wretched as the minutes dragged along. After an endless while, they finally heard the rustle of grass trampled underfoot.

They startled and clung together, quaking from head to heel. Sal, the first to come to his senses, dashed to the tools stacked up in the corner. He groped for a bigger one through the pile, tearing them down; the loud noises they made terrified him all the more. All he could find was a hammer. He lifted it up above his head and waited. Emi had backed herself into the opposite corner.

Sal stood still for over ten minutes. Then he grew weary; his arms started to shake in pain, and he was overcome by all the thirst and exhaustion he had felt in the past two hours. He put the hammer down, wiped his sweat off, and drew in a breath of hot, dusty air that staled his lungs and brain even more and tried to figure out when the moment would come for the emaciated, scrawny old man to slide through the door like a ghost. He wanted to take one last look at her, so as to be sure he was doing the right thing, but the place where Emi had withdrawn was dim and had cloaked her in a blurred outline. On the other side, the noise grew louder until they eventually heard the clanking of some metal sheets next to them, as if someone was right inside. The shadows danced before their eyes and the latch lifted slowly, letting the light spread through the whole woodshed and dazzling them. He stopped with the hammer hanging above his head, his eyelids idly blinking against the rays of light, sweeping away the specks of dust that drifted in the air. The door stood open, and when his eyes got used to the new light, he saw Emi cringing upon the stack of wood, clasping her knees, her head buried between her legs. Emi the brave hadn't had the guts to witness the murder that she had so cunningly devised. He had been waiting to thrust the iron straight into the bones and brain, but it wasn't like that.

Finally losing patience, he glided past the door and stuck his head outside. Two tin plates with some sort of scrambled eggs, half a loaf of white bread and a cloudy plastic bottle full of cold water had been laid on the threshold. He looked about, but there wasn't a soul in sight. The tin was still warm from the scrambled eggs, freshly poured from the pan; the bread was soft and fluffy. Emi dashed for the bottle of water first, took it to her mouth and didn't stop before emptying more than half of it. His fear was still there; he couldn't understand how she could go out in broad daylight without making sure there was no danger, completely oblivious of their ghastly plan. She gave him the bottle of water after wiping her mouth with the palm of her hand like a labourer.

'Have some!'

It was only then that Sal put down the hammer and bolted the water down. Then they hurled themselves upon the tin plates, tore off a hunk of bread and sunk their fingers in. When they finished licking the last bit of egg, they sat out on the grass and looked at each other: their faces were varnished as if they had been savages, both in their underwear, their scraggy chests all sweaty and blackened, their hair stuck to their heads.

'What do we do now?'

He brooded, but not for long. 'We're going to sleep here, outside. We lie on the grass and sleep, and when we get up we'll see about it.'

'You look terrible!' she laughed, her eyes shiny embers.

'You do, too.'

'Ouch! I want to wash myself! I want to wash myself!'

'We will, but let's wait a bit till afternoon. When we see that the yard's empty and the old guy's gone to bed, we'll go and wash ourselves at the water pump. You'll wash me and I'll wash you.'

They sprawled down; their tummies swollen and simmering.

'It feels so good!'

'It was terrible!'

They shut their eyes and a starry sky sparkled above. Their restless overnight sleep, the ghost of the old man they hadn't even had the chance to kill already, began to haunt them, creeping about and hissing like a snake through the overgrown grass. The remorse, the longing for things that could have turned out differently and that they would never know now, the image of their parents seized with pain and the effigies of Toma, Max, Johnny and Harry, along with those of their neighbours, flushed with anger and fury – all of these were dragged out. It was as if it had all happened for real and their lying in the grass, cooled off, full, with their souls at ease, soaring in the ether, seemed to be more like a dream. They fell asleep in an instant, not far from each other, under an autumnal sour cherry tree.

Time went by swiftly and night fell again. When they woke up once more, the heat was already steaming off the ground, and even if the daylight had waned and a breath of wind rustled the greenness all around, the late-afternoon blaze could still be felt. They rubbed their eyes and looked around. The charcoal, mixed with sebum, had started trickling down their faces and bodies, leaving white streaks. Emi rolled over in the grass a few times trying to rub herself clean, but her skin only turned greenish and purplish. In the daylight she looked like a gemstone. She was amused by what she'd done and finally gave up. They headed together to the water pump; this time they were more cautious, proving that the sleep had somewhat succeeded in clearing their thoughts.

'So the old guy surely knows we're here.'

'Maybe he overheard us talking.'

'If he'd heard, do you think he still would have treated us so nicely and let us go, left us food and drink by the door?'

'Yeah, maybe not. So he knows we're here.'

'What does that mean?'

'It means whatever we want it to mean.'

'Do you think he'll call the police?'

'If he wanted to, he would've called them by now. It's been a day and nothing's happened.'

'Should we leave?'

'No, I say we should stay. If we hear a sound, we run. We can run over the fence in the back and break free anyway.'

He thought she'd wanted to add something, but he didn't let her. They didn't run into any trouble up to the water pump, and after they splashed each other with cold water and rubbed their bodies, giggling and sloshing around, they made their way back, picking the fruit that hung overripe and lazy from the tree branches on their way.

Several days passed by; each morning they would find two tin plates full to the brim, a bottle of water, some elderflower juice or milk waiting for them on the threshold. They would empty it all on the spot, belching in contentment. At night they slept outside naked, and it was only in the morning that they retired to the woodshed without really knowing why they were so concerned. In the daytime the old man didn't set foot on their territory and stuck to his schedule unfailingly: tidying around in the morning, having his lunch no later than half past twelve, taking a nap, stretched out on the soiled deck chair, until four or five o'clock, when he withdrew inside and nobody saw him until the next morning. It was only once that they tailed him, one morning while he was watering his garden. He looked absorbed and picked at each tomato and aubergine seedling, examining the tree branches and pruning them. At that point, Sal sneaked into the house and Emi stood on the watch.

It was a shabby three-room dwelling, two of which were inhabited and the other left untouched like a sanctuary. Everywhere around there were framed pictures of a beautiful woman who looked like an actress Sal had seen in the *Cinema* almanacs. Her hair was dark, and her curls, wrought with a curling iron, were set around her face; she had a beautifully shaped nose, her nostrils slightly lifted, and dark, cheerful eyes. She was pictured in several different poses: dressed up in ball gowns, always surrounded by men in tail coats, on the street, wrapped up in fur coats, on thick heels, in a funny old car wearing a wide-brimmed hat or on the tennis court clad in a long, white skirt. There wasn't a spot on the wall left uncovered in solid wooden frames. The room was scented, and on each piece of old furniture, dusted and smelling of mould and lavender, a starched doily was set. It was obvious that nobody ever stepped into that room except to clean it. A yellow satin dress lay on a sofa covered in burgundy silk, and a pair of golden strappy sandals lay underneath. Sal felt the dress, smelled it, took a long, hard look at the sandals and rummaged through the closets. Colourful scarves were hanging among the neatly folded clothes in slips made out of plastic bags. He took a scarf with a big rose pattern that trailed along behind it the pungent smell of the past.

In the inhabited room, the rumpled bed with its shredded, dirty sheets gave off the same sharp smell. Except for the dim room, chunks of dried bread and mugs in which there were still traces of some liquid were scattered all around. He was about to leave when he heard the man in the garden, dragging the ladder and propping it up against one of the house walls. He thought it was strange that Emi hadn't warned him. Hiding under the kitchen table, he lingered there until the old man came closer, trudging his shabby shoes past Sal and entering the first room. He heard the wardrobe door creak, and only then did he scuttle away.

He found Emi basking in the grass at the back of the yard, eating sour cherries and spitting out their kernels. He handed her the scarf.

'Didn't you see him coming? Why didn't you warn me?'
'Didn't I see who?'
'Emi, you left me uncovered!'
'I didn't! If I'd called out it would have been worse.'
She hugged him and kissed him on the cheeks and mouth. He lay back and curled his arms around her neck. He loved her so

much that he would trust her no matter what. For the first time since they had run away, he felt elated, and looking around, all he could grasp was the sheer beauty of things: the coolness, the juicy fruits, the green, the ripening grapes, the blue sky, the silk dresses, the vegetables hanging on their stalks, the shadow cloaking them, the sun that brought colour to their cheeks, the fence standing between them and the outer world. And happiness – that was going to last forever.

XI

THE EXQUISITE CORPSE

It was not Emilia's physical disappearance that was hard to accept. Her death had been long foretold. He had been aware of it since he had discovered her body in the basement, years before. Since then it had been nestled in his mind, even if the only evidence of the exquisite corpse lying on the table in Harry's basement rested with her, on her long ring finger, that ended with an almond-shaped, perpetually lacquered fingernail. The evidence was futile, though, because everybody knew, even his childhood pals, that Sal could see things others couldn't, said things no child would say, did things few grown-ups would do. Even he had doubted the existence of the deceased woman after a while and questioned the true nature of his visions.

It was true that he was smarter than others, faster at counting, keener in memory, more accurate in his views; that, even though he shut himself off broodingly, he could understand better than others what was going on in the outer world; that he could instantly tell girls' desires, that he could read Matilda's complaints on the spot, that he would talk to his plants the way a woman would to the baby growing inside her womb. But none of that helped him unravel the mystery of the corpse or anticipate Emilia's death. He now had to face not only her disappearance, but also the loneliness he had to adjust to; even though he had known from the start how it all ended and had thought, for a long time, that any delay meant also sweeping the terrible vision away, he had only managed to make the closure even more cruel and dramatic, becoming witness to such a miserable outcome that even his betrayed wife would have pitied him.

He revisited the facts. After bolting out of Emilia's place and going home, he had shut himself off and refused to talk. In vain Matilda asked where he had been; in vain she snapped at him and warned him that, unless he stopped this nonsense, he would soon find himself with divorce papers in his hand. Sal knew just one thing: nothing he could have said would have soothed him any longer. He no longer trusted any word; he was incapable of the effort to articulate another sound. 'Silence is golden,' his grandma used to say, flicking her tongue across her lips. He did now what he had also done twenty years before, when his parents had popped up in a dark-coloured car at the gate of the old man who had so obligingly lodged them, after one month of frantic searching. They had trampled on the tomato seedlings and the flowers, ripped the clusters of unripe grapes, jerked open the door of the woodshed where he and Emi had been hiding; along with the baton spun above their heads by the man wearing a blue police uniform, angry words had also fluttered in the air, words hurled by his father, his face bristling with rage. Emi had fled from his side in a split second. She had been seized by some men dressed as shabbily as the man in uniform but whose cold looks showed they meant business. As soon as they had pulled her into a Dacia, with its tell-tale Securitate license plates, Emi had been erased from his mind forever.

Standing up under his parents' grilling, he had refused to speak, but not because he wanted to defy them. His parents had waned and scattered like dust among the blades of grass. He had refused to speak because he was struggling to call her features back from his memory: the shape of her mouth, the colour of her hair, the cut of her cheekbones, the slenderness of her wrists, the thickness of her ankles. All these had fled along with their owner, and Sal had sworn to himself that, until he could put Emi's faithful portrait back together, he would not breathe a word. His mother was holding her head in her hands, trembling regularly as if shaken with fever, and his father wouldn't stop snarling at him, fidgeting uselessly and excessively in the most bizarre manner. Shut up into himself, Sal found it all very amusing, weighing them up as if they had been two pieces of meat. He had severed all ties with both of them; had he been sure it would make a difference, he would have gladly finished them off right there, under the shade of the sour-cherry tree where he had slept so many nights with Emi by his side. But Emi had disappeared, their hideout had been disclosed and thus the adventure they had so confidently embarked upon had come to an end. His father wouldn't stop bawling at him, 'Sorin, what were you thinking?'

As the boy wouldn't say a word, his helpless father became even angrier. 'Sorin, if you don't answer me this minute, I'll smack you blind! Do you hear me, boy? Don't push it!'

But he didn't smack him after all, and when they got home and locked him up in his room, Sal discovered a shrine by his bed-side, his picture surrounded by lit candles and an oil candle barely flickering. His parents admitted aloud that perhaps it was better that the boy hadn't spoken, because had he done so, who knows what the policeman would have thought as he growled incessantly next to them and mumbled words like 'reformatory school,' 'police station' and 'court.' He stood awake for days on end; he had lost count. He kept his eyes wide open, staring at the wall, and a doctor who had come by pronounced a complicated word that had made his parents turn pale and walk out of the room as if they had seen him alive for the last time.

He didn't try to escape this new prison, because it would have been in vain anyway. Although he was less than a few hundred feet away from Emi, the distance that kept them apart was longer now and impossible to cover. In less than a week after their return home, his parents packed up the furniture and the clothes, wrapped the books in cardboard boxes, disposed of the few things they had decided in a family consultation they didn't need anymore and left behind the apartment in Sun Alley, where they had lived peacefully most of the time.

'Well,' Father sighed, 'in spite of everything, we did well here!'

'Yes,' Mother added in the same tone of voice, 'and let's hope we'll do just as well in the future.'

Huddled on the backseat, his hands resting quietly on his knees, Sal was also saying his farewells: not only to his room, his friends and the cherished places he had wandered countless times without thinking for one instant that they might disappear, but to Emi, too. He was lost even to that Sal from the past, the one who, deprived of her memory, would let her slip from his mind for good. He was saying goodbye, particularly, to himself. Little Sal had snuggled in the basement and was biding his time, waiting to come up, unscathed by the rage of the adults. Time went by, and settled in their new lodgings, eager to welcome the new member of the family, the grown-ups rubbed the little boy's blunder off their minds, blaming it on his age and his companions. Only once, having wasted a whole afternoon failing to adjust the roof antenna, his father had bristled at the taciturn kid who was staring blankly at the snow on the screen: 'Hey, Sorin, can't you at least tell me if there's any picture? Goddamn it, boy! Where's your mind? Are you doing it on purpose, or what?'

He hunched his shoulders and went on, his words striking like a clasp of thunder. 'I don't even want to think about it. If it hadn't been for your friend Harry, you would still be bumming about with that tramp of a girl, and who knows what would've become of you. Thank heavens he told us who you were wasting your time with and what was on your mind! Oh, my! It gives me the creeps!' He waved his hand in disgust.

Sal withdrew to his room, which looked exactly like his old one but for the Metallica poster he had given to Toma as promised. He sat down on the floor, legs crossed, and started dwelling on this new revelation. It wasn't easy to reach a conclusion, but, after deliberating in his mind, he resolved that everything was just a far-fetched story of his father's. How was he to believe that Emi had betrayed him – to imagine that, after leaving Harry's, she had snuck back to his friend despite his warnings and disclosed their running-away plan? It was mad to fancy Harry having nothing better to do than ratting him out to his parents – Harry, of all people, who in his unreliability seemed the most loyal of them all. Who could have believed such nonsense? Who could have cooked up such stories? From a distance, his friends now appeared heroic, almost supernatural. They had turned now into the mighty explorers of *l'Esperance*. The mere thought of them made him tremble with longing and excitement. They were brave, bold, compassionate to his misery and solitude, pure in heart and driven by noble feelings. And so he sunk himself in silence, staying that way for a long time, long enough for his parents to give up all hope and get used to the idea that their elder son had escaped from reality and shut himself off into a world of his own which they couldn't reach.

'Silence is golden.'

A few days after he visited her at her flat, Emilia dropped a note in his letterbox. It was Matilda who brought it to him, her face wan with irritation. She had opened the envelope and read the note; that's why Sal asked her, through his grinding teeth, what Emi had written.

'Aren't you ashamed to make me tell you what your mistress is writing? And isn't she ashamed? Shame on you both!'

She left the room, seeking refuge in the kitchen that was smothered in a dense fog given off by the steamer on the stove. But Sal dogged her, insisting she should tell him what Emi had scribbled in the note.

'Say it, Matilda! Is it something important? Does it concern you as well? Because probably that's what you had in mind when you opened the envelope. That she might have written to you as well!'

'So now I'm to blame for opening that filth! Not her, for trying to ruin our family, for being a slut that sleeps around with married men! That's really something!'

They kept at it, on and on, until Sal raised his hand above her heated head and kept it hanging in the air for a few seconds. He let his arm drop, and while stepping out of the room, he simply added, 'We're through!'

It wasn't the ideal breakup formula, but it seemed rather to the point, and as time was running short, he was glad that those few words could wrap up a decision he had been striving to make for years. He took nothing but what he had on: a grey vest with pockets, a black velour shirt, some shabby, ragged jeans he would wear at work and a pair of overused suede shoes. He also had a broken mobile phone with him, a fistful of ruffled banknotes, a Minolta camera, the car keys and a three-day-old beard. He had given up the books, objects and everything belonging to that house; he had left them all to Matilda, in exchange for his freedom.

In her note, Emilia had written that she would be waiting for him at the Banatul Hotel. A little while before, when Sal had been better off and could afford it, they had taken a room there for about a year. The hotelkeeper, a gaunt man with yellowish skin and bony, emaciated arms, would jot their names down in his tattered register, and after a while, seeing that they were good clients, had even given them a discount. Every afternoon, he would welcome them with his soapy smile, stooping and tilting his head a little in a subtle greeting and slipping the key to room 22 in Sal's hand. They would climb two floors; at the end of the corridor, the key slid into the lock, turned twice and, once the door banged open, their foster home lay ahead. It wasn't exactly like the green-walled room; they missed the impression of cosiness feigned by the few personal things scattered about here and there, but they knew that the sheets were freshly changed and cleaned, that the towels, despite their frayed appearance, smelled of soap and bleach, that they would find on the pillows two bars of chocolate instead of one. The water jug and glass tumblers glinted in the red light seeping through the red satin curtains that weighed down the windows.

Although their adjustment to their new condition of hotel lovers was difficult, although Emilia invariably had, in the first couple of days, dark circles under her eyes and the air of a sick person having lost all hopes of recovering, Sal knew he had to give her as much time as she needed to get used to it. In truth, it was far from being a delightful place: the dim corridors, covered in tattered silk that laid bare the seedy walls, the rugged wooden doors with massive door handles, the floor lamps with their glazed shades and dusty tassels darkened at the ends, the ashtrays in front of every door chock-full of stubs and giving off the smell of damp ashes, the replicas of unknown painters hung askew... all these things bore the stamp of a former brothel rather than that of a hotel. In fact, on their very first day there, Emilia had told him as much while sitting on the edge of the bed, peering around, her face screwed up in disgust: 'This place says a lot about us!'

Before taking the room, he had asked her if she agreed and she did. He had posed the question several times; as he was familiar with her anxieties and heard her whining about their living on the sly, with people looking down on her, he wouldn't have wanted to hurt her. She was fickle, though. She had not hesitated for a second to come to his place one cold winter day, when Matilda and the girls were visiting their grandparents. He had almost ripped her clothes off, rolling her over on the Persian rug that had been a gift from Matilda's parents. They had drunk their coffee later on from the same mugs that Dori and Mari drank their warm milk from every morning, and he had set her down on the same chair that was usually Matilda's. And she hadn't been troubled by any of this. She had her own moral scale, which she tuned according to whims and circumstances. What had seemed squalid in the beginning had become in time the place where they came not only to see each other and have sex, but also to rest, the way people do when they come back from work and stretch out on the living room couch in front of the TV, waiting to fall asleep.

He was nervous about going back there. He hadn't set foot in the hotel for a long time, and even though he wasn't surprised by Emilia's choice, he felt a threat floating in the air. He had been asking himself all the way there whether he should break the news of his splitting up with Matilda as soon as he went in, or if he should wait and see what she had to say first. At length, he decided he'd better confess right away. Emilia would be startled at first, clasping her hands together in prostration; then, while coming to her senses, she would instantly glimpse her future, bringing together all the missing pieces, the ones she hadn't even dared dream of. He was somewhat afraid of her enthusiasm, and deep down he was hoping she would be rather composed. After all, he had left behind two girls that would be unhappy for the rest of their lives and who, most likely egged on by Matilda, would never forgive him. He had cast off a big part of his painfully built, dull, ordinary life. He wished that in those moments she wouldn't leap into his arms, trumpeting her joy.

He felt like having a drink on the way. He stopped by a local pub shrouded in a haze of alcohol and smoke and asked for a Swedish bitter. When he was a student, bitter had been a fashionable drink. Hoards of boys would sip the bittersweet liquid, belt down glass after glass and, thus well-oiled, grope their schoolmates and strip them down in the stench of aromatic alcohol. Many marriages had been settled after those sleepless nights sprinkled with booze and shrouded in bluish clouds of cigarette smoke. They groped about in dorms and universities as if through a magic forest, and the first one to come their way was the chosen one. He had met Matilda after one of those nights. Now he drank the bitter and asked for one more. It was hard to tell how long he had stayed in the filthy pub, but when he walked out a thick whiff of tobacco was trailing him like chewing gum stuck to his clothes, hair and skin. Ever since he had met Emilia again, he had quit smoking on her request.

'Given the little time we spend together, it would be terrible if you got sick. I couldn't take it,' she had told him.

And he had obeyed her. One fine day, he had ditched his pack of cigarettes in the rubbish bin and Matilda had cheered. Then he had overheard her boasting to her friends over the phone: 'He loves the girls so much. I couldn't believe for the life of me that he would do something like that for them! You know he smoked like a chimney!'

Not even then, as so many times before, did he feel ashamed. He had let her believe whatever she wanted. Now, in the end, he craved to light one more cigarette, to puff it in her face, to tear down even this last image of a thoughtful father, to leave her at peace with the thought that shrugging him off was the best for her and the twins. Oddly enough, he felt freed from them, after all this time in which he couldn't even have conceived of leaving his home and forsaking his daughters, because it was his obligation to stand by them – at least physically, if not emotionally.

He headed to meet Emilia feeling rather elated: the alcohol

had liberated him, his feet barely touched the ground, and when he spotted the brick-coloured turrets holding the old hotel sign, with its fat and rusty letters, he chuckled. Now, since they needn't hide in such places any longer, he found it particularly amusing to meet her there. He told himself he'd ask Emilia to rent room 22 once in a while, so as to remember the way it had once been. What a strange twist of fate, he thought on fierily, to end up together again after such a long time. And when they would tell this story to their children – because, by all odds, they were going to have at least one child –they would leave them shocked, as such accounts were not to be heard every day. And their children would tell the story to their friends, who in their turn would tell other stories back, sewn in many golden threads, about their own parents. And the thought of being part of such a charming trade filled him with joy and assured him that life had been worth living after all.

The hotel lobby was empty. He waited for a few minutes at the reception desk in order to greet his old acquaintance. Despite his repeated knocking on the counter, he didn't get any answer, so he started up the stairs, climbing them hurriedly two at a time. Besides the familiar humming of the building, which he was amazed to notice he hadn't forgotten, not a soul seemed to be in sight. Down the corridor, the same dim light sweeping through the dusty tassels made the place feel even drearier.

Outside number 22, he knocked on the door. He did it softly at first, but as he couldn't hear a sound, he started knocking harder. He wanted to be courteous and see her laughing at his appearance, like a knight in shining armour, on her threshold. Finally, he tiptoed inside.

On the night table there was a lit lamp, its shade the same old silky fabric ending in linty tassels. Emilia was lying on the bed, dressed in her drab clothes, her hair spread across the pillow like a jellyfish. She was sleeping and dreaming as a wisp of a smile graced her face and her white, quiet skin reflected the light of the lamp back into the room. Her shoes were meekly set at the foot of the bed, tips aligned, and on the armchair next to the bed was her huge bag. Upon spotting it, he felt the urge to rummage inside; he could avail himself of her deep sleep to see what lay at the bottom of her trunk full of trifles. He had seen her taking out aspirins, lipsticks, keys, coloured pens, notebooks, planners, different sized boxes in which she kept pills, chewing gum or jewellery, wallets, key-rings, napkins – plain and perfumed, dry and wet – newspapers, hand and body lotions, balms and other things he wasn't even aware of. But, among so many things of no importance, a significant one might very well have been concealed, one that could tell him more about her than all the years spent together.

He stopped in the middle of the room. He shivered, nauseated, turned away and walked out again. Out in the corridor, he felt his weariness at last. The vapours of the bitter alcohol had gone to his head and made him dizzy. But despite the dull pain buzzing around his temples, he needed another glass to walk back into that room. He went down to the reception desk and found a skinny young guy with a shaved head and a round, crimson face. He flaunted his hotel uniform cockily, showing he hadn't been working there for long. Sal thought that he'd rather see his old acquaintance instead of this young guy. It would have been more convenient to ask the former guy what he asked this round-faced man instead, after greeting him in a soapy voice: 'Do you happen to serve drinks?'

The room clerk looked him up and down, and then blinked a few times as if to better comprehend his question. He answered after a few hesitating seconds that they didn't, but that, if he wanted, he could rush to a nearby kiosk, where his girlfriend was working, and bring him a bottle of homemade wine from her grandparents. Without waiting for confirmation, he asked him in a commanding voice, 'What kind of wine would you like, red or white?'

After a brief reflection, Sal mumbled that he wanted white, and the young man nodded, smiling as if he had made the right choice. 'Wait here, I'll be right back!'

He barely had time to sit down cross-legged on the broken springs of an armchair from the lobby when the young man popped back in, holding a plastic Coca-Cola bottle full of yellowish liquid.

He handed it to him, his face beaming with joy. 'The wine! You owe me a hundred.'

Sal gave him a long, hard look to see whether he was mocking him or he really meant it. But the young man kept his arm stretched out, and the cloudy bottle did give off a sourish smell of wine. He fished through his pockets and took out a hundred from the wad of notes. Their trade lasted only a second. Finding himself with the bottle in his hand, Sal realised he wasn't at all in the mood to drink alone. If he was going to get drunk on sour wine, he wanted some company at least.

'Would you join me for a glass?'

The young man faltered. 'It wouldn't be appropriate – I'm still on duty!'

'Oh, come on! One glass! My wife's sleeping upstairs and I've got no one to toast with.'

'Are you celebrating something?'

He mulled the question over. He would have liked to be honest, but he had already called Emilia his wife and that confused him.

'Yes. It's been twenty-five years that we've known each other.'

The young man stared at him, sizing him up. 'But how long have you really known each other?'

'We've known each other since we were kids. Since we were eight. We used to be childhood pals.'

'Wow! A lifetime!'

'Yeah.'

'And you've stayed together,' the room clerk mused. 'This really does call for a celebration!'

'Didn't I tell you?'

'I'll fetch some glasses and take a sip myself, so you don't drink alone.'

It was better this way. He hadn't told a lie, although it wasn't exactly the truth. The old trickster wouldn't have bought this story. He'd have had to tell him the truth: that he had run away from home and it was his mistress, sprawled in the sheets, waiting for him upstairs. Had he added that they'd known each other since forever, maybe he wouldn't have even believed Sal and would have thought him a liar. Not that he cared, but he felt safer like this. One more glass, and he'd be right back in the room where Emilia was sleeping sweetly; he'd hold her in his arms and lift her up high, until she touched the ragged tassels and signed her name on the dusty ceiling, scribbling their initials and putting the signs '= love' next to them. It was this single glass that stood between him and the love of his life. He felt intoxicated with joy even before taking a sip from the wine that the young receptionist smilingly handed to him.

'And what brings you to our hotel?'

'Oh! Well...'

The neon lights were droning like bumblebees, and the wine, once it was flowing down his tongue, tickled him pleasantly and warmed up his joints and thighs, adding to the faint sensation of arousal he felt, like a promise. He couldn't ask for more.

'We're just passing by.'

'But where are you from?'

'I beg your pardon?'

'What town are you from?'

'Oh, we live in Bucharest, but we thought it would be nice if we didn't stay at home on our anniversary.'

'I see. And your wife fell asleep.'

Behind the round crimson face, little wheels were spinning. Deep down, Sal was sure that the young man behind the counter was cut out for his job. For one second, he had doubted this and pitied him; he had imagined him to be the victim of sham customers. But the young man understood more than he let on.

'She was tired from work. She arrived before me. You know how it is nowadays; women work as much as we do.'

'Hee hee,' he laughed, the tip of his tongue showing between his teeth,' some of us don't work at all. Take my girlfriend, for example. She stays out all night at the kiosk selling stuff. It's dangerous – you never know what hot-headed guy might come up and put a gun to your face.'

'Well, not really a gun –'

'Why, but it is like that,' he interjected. 'It really is. Haven't you heard of that salesgirl that was shot right here, on the boulevard next to Inter? They might look normal to you, but you know, plenty of loonies roam out in the streets.'

Sal shook his head. He didn't know Bucharest like that. The city whose streets he walked was peaceful and calm, but he thought the very same city could be different at night.

'And where the hell do they get guns from? I mean, if I wanted to buy one tomorrow, where could I get it?'

'Well, because you're an honest man, you couldn't get one, but if you speak to the right person, you could get one in no time. Just like that!'

They stood silently for a while. The room clerk gazed at him, as if to read something on his face. 'So you really mean it?'

'What?'

The young man shook his head. 'Never mind.'

'The gun, you mean? If I wanted to buy one?'

'Yes.'

He resumed his look, and as Sal wanted to have some fun before going back to his room and was eager to continue the conversation, he felt encouraged.

'Well, if you want it, I think you could get one. But you have to tell me exactly what you want and we'll see what can be done. Discreetly and all.'

'I get it.'

Sal got up, stroking his beard.

'So?'

'I have to go up now. Thank you for your company.'

He left quickly, leaving the room clerk with the glass raised in his hand. He couldn't wait to tell Emilia the story and have a good laugh together. He had taken the plastic bottle with him, and all of a sudden, while looking at it, he thought this night had shown them a friendly face after all.

He crossed the corridor again, but this time, despite the lights that had unleashed fine and graceful shapes from the silky walls, he was looking around confidently. He found Emilia in the same position. At first, he thought it was only her smile that had faded away but there it was, still pinned there on her lips. He went to the bathroom and rinsed his face and hair. He couldn't wake up completely, and back in the room, he still felt that bliss for some time before it slowly started melting away into a grim slackness. He sat on the edge of the bed with a vacuous, glassy stare, and after a while, he stretched alongside Emilia and shut his eyes, lying in wait.

All their friends had gathered in room 22 of the Banatul Hotel. They filed into the room one at a time, slowly knocking on the door, the way he had done himself. They sat down cross-legged, encircling the bed in silence. In the beginning, Sal didn't dare to look at them; when he did, he peeked through his eyelashes at first. He couldn't recognise them. Just like him, they were grown-up people now; Harry, for example, had a moustache that gave him the rough air of an outlaw. Toma wore thin-framed eyeglasses and cut an athletic figure, which could have been a true impression judging by the way he was sizing everyone up with restrained wisdom. Max had some tight, flared jeans on and a sleeveless, clingy T-shirt. He looked funny, as he had the quaint air of someone who had come down straight from the set of a 1970s movie like *Charlie's Angels*. Johnny lingered somewhere in the shadows; Sal could barely make out his features. They were all acting like they had back then when he had summoned them in the park following Toma's beating. They were all confused, and Sal expected that any minute now one of them would ask why he had conjured them up. He wanted to wake Emi, too, but he couldn't find it in his heart. Sleeping made her skin radiate an intense glow that almost dazzled those who were lucky enough to be within its reach.

Sal clenched his fists and struggled to ignore the boys' presence. He was trying to get some rest, as the mix of alcohol had taken hold of him and he wanted to be clear-headed when he broke the big news to Emi. But after a few moments, he sensed a buzz and realised his childhood pals were talking to each other. Undoubtedly, the only thing they could have talked about was them: the two who seemed to be lying sound asleep on the bed, unaware. He wanted to sit up and beckon them to stop whispering, but his flesh was weighing him down and his dismembered body, having a mind of its own, wouldn't obey the commands of a single master. The voices rose and eventually came to sound like a choir, whispering and mumbling arcane words at random. Only the sound of their names came through distinctly, chanted in multiple voices. In the end, just their names alone could be heard and the voices melted into one.

He looked at her from his side of the bed. Her hands were down at her sides, and he noticed her ringed finger. She didn't look like the other one and that puzzled him. He would have expected to be taken over by the twin image, by her emerging in a waxen skin, with black-dyed hair and pale lips, with red-polished, slightly grown nails revealing a fine pink semicircle. But she looked just as before, with bristly curled hair and bony cheeks, dark-circled eyes and a rounded mouth. Her boyish body was unveiling itself more accurately as she lay motionless. The only similarity was the ring on her finger, but Sal understood it was not enough.

He stood up and started taking off her clothes, piece by piece. First he took off the grey collared blouse fastened with tiny, ivory buttons, then her starry-blue pleated skirt, her cotton bra and panties. He contemplated her as she lay naked, but he was still unsatisfied. He struggled to smoothen her hair, to groom it. He felt her breasts, but instead of coming across the tip of the iceberg, he found flaccid, lifeless flesh. He shivered and swung around to his friends to ask for help, but they had left. Most likely, they had had enough of the charade, were sick of all the pretence and lies. They couldn't stand the two of them anymore; they wanted a different couple of friends who would be honest and selfless, kind and gentle, with no secrets to hide behind. They didn't want to sniff the sickening, sweetish smell of decomposing female corpses or to breathe the same air in which they were preserved, or to be compelled to host their stiff bodies in the same lodgings in which they were now raising their children and spoiling their women. Abruptly, they had decided that nobody should ever talk about Sal and Emi or utter their names again. And thus they'd see them vanish.

istrosbooks

Sun Alley comes to you from **ISTROS BOOKS**,
a boutique publisher of quality literature in translation from
South East Europe. Our titles are now divided into two series

Best Balkan Books
and
Books from the Edge

Best Balkan Books 2013
Our series featuring the very best titles from the region

The Fairground Magician
Jelena Lengold
ISBN 978-1-908236-10-4
Winner of the European Prize for Literature
SEPTEMBER 2013

The Son
Andrej Nikolaidis
ISBN 978-1-908236-12-8
Winner of the European Prize for Literature
SEPTEMBER 2013

Ekaterini
Marija Knežević
ISBN 978-1-908236-13-5
'A story of human survival told through the female gaze.'
OCTOBER 2013